THE ANGEL OF ZIN

Also by Clifford Irving

NOVELS
On A Darkling Plain
The Losers
The Valley
The 38th Floor
Tom Mix and Pancho Villa
The Death Freak (with Herbert Burkholz)
The Sleeping Spy (with Herbert Burkholz)

NONFICTION
Spy
Fake!
The Battle of Jerusalem
The Hoax

UNPUBLISHED
The Autobiography of Howard Hughes

THE ANGEL OF ZIN

Clifford Irving

STEIN AND DAY /*Publishers*/New York

First published in the United States of America in 1984.
Copyright © 1984 by Clifford Irving
All rights reserved, Stein and Day, Incorporated
Designed by Louis A. Ditizio
Printed in the United States of America
STEIN AND DAY/*Publishers*
Scarborough House
Briarcliff Manor, N.Y. 10510

Library of Congress Cataloging in Publication Data

Irving, Clifford.
  The angel of Zin.

  1. World War, 1939-1945—Fiction. I. Title.
PS3559.R79A83   1984   813'.54   84-40251
ISBN 0-8128-2986-7

To
Maurice Nessen
true and dear friend
justum et tenacem propositi virum

Preface

Zinoswicz-Zdroj will not be found on any map of Poland. Its physical and administrative details are borrowed from Chelmno, Sobibor, and Treblinka. More successful revolts similar to the one described in fact occurred at Treblinka, Sobibor, Kolcyczewo, and other smaller work camps.

Writing in *The New York Times* of December 5, 1982, Michiko Kakutani warned that ". . . a kind of intellectual distancing has begun to occur in depictions of the Holocaust, which threatens to trivialize, even distort, the actual event."

It is a writer's obligation to make you see, feel, and ponder; the writer does not trivialize or distort historical events by shaping them into a design that is more visible, more deeply felt. It is not instructive to say, "Six million Jews were killed. Their Nazi murderers were beasts." Unless we are content to be victims of media simplism, it is necessary to know the names of some of those six million (even if those names are fictionalized), to see their faces, to empathize with their experience. It is also necessary to view the murderers not as beasts but as men and women who abdicated their humanity in favor of warped visions, brute economic need, and a dreadful conformity. Because, as Mordecai Lieberman is quoted as saying, "Perhaps this is just the beginning of man's possibilities."

My research has been extensive, but I owe a special debt to Jean-Francois Steiner's *Treblinka*, Erich Maria Remarque's *A Time to*

Love and a Time to Die, and Irving J. Rosenbaum's *Holocaust and Halakhah*. I also thank Evelyn Leavitt, Hede Richartz, and Valdi Sherwood for their confidences, Heinz Trökes for his hospitality in Wilmersdorf, Michael Hamilburg for his constancy, Dick Barkle and Pan Am for their friendly efficiency, and Renée Trökes for her passionate reconstruction of wartime Berlin.

C.I.
April 10, 1984

1

Berlin: April 1943

His alarm clock had been set to jangle at five o'clock in the morning, but Captain Paul Bach awoke some ten minutes before the hour. Yawning, he poked at the blackout curtain. The moon had set. No longer raven black, the sky above Berlin was still faintly powdered with stars.

A midnight raid had driven all the occupants of the apartment house down to the cellar for several hours. The captain's eyes felt grainy. He clicked off the alarm, used the toilet, then padded into the kitchen and struck a match for the stove. Dawn began to break over the River Spree, a dull silver light seeping through the parlor windows to reveal shapes of other apartment houses on Claudius-strasse and beyond. Most of them were whole; some were jagged in outline like sheets of gray cardboard carelessly torn. A church bell tolled mournfully in the chill April morning. Otherwise it was quiet, except for the distant wail of ambulance sirens.

He dressed silently in the black uniform of a detective-inspector of the Kripo, the Berlin Criminal Police: One sleeve of his jacket was tucked into a neat flap above the elbow. Paul Bach was just under six feet tall and slimly built—forty years of age, although he looked older—with corn-colored hair and distinct shadows under gray eyes. In his youth he had been handsome in the fashion of silent movie stars; he had once been asked to pose for a party poster, but had declined—it was incorrect, he stated, for a policeman to advertise himself.

His two children had not stirred. While the coffee perked, he entered each of their bedrooms and watched them sleeping. Erich's curls were matted with sweat. Ushi's blonde hair looked like corn silk. The captain bent to kiss each one's forehead in turn, a gesture they no longer permitted when awake. Then he reset the alarm clock for six-thirty so they would not be late for school.

He ate in the sitting room—chicory coffee, a slice of bread smeared thinly with margarine, ersatz grape jam. You could taste the chemicals. The room had a parquet floor, fine fruitwood furniture with ebony inlays, shelves of dark leather-bound books— Goethe and Hegel, Rousseau and Voltaire in French, Shakespeare translated into German. The apartment lacked a woman's touch. Sylvie, his wife, had been killed three years ago. After that his mother helped him care for the children. But she kept losing her keys and let pots boil over on the stove. When she suffered a stroke, Paul had been fighting in Russia. After he came back and was released from the hospital, a left arm still sinking into the snow at Demyansk, he visited her in the nursing home on Bismarckstrasse. She was paralyzed—couldn't speak, had to wear diapers.

"You have to understand, Captain," the doctor told him, "that she has the mentality of a very small child . . . at best. Most of the time she won't even know who you are."

"That's not the point," Paul said. He went anyway, three evenings a week for more than a year, until she died.

In the frail light he clumped down the brownstone steps, briefcase tucked under his arm. The façade of the house was decorated with stone cherubs; before the war there had been a concierge. The wheels of a child's roller skates rasped on the pavement. A man in a block warden's uniform stood at a window, yawning. In the west, as though the sun were setting at dawn, violet clouds of ash hovered like birds of prey above Charlottenburg.

At a lively pace, greatcoat flapping behind, Paul's long legs bore past the brick Lutheran church on the corner, then along the bank of the sluggishly flowing Spree, and then past a three-story dun-colored concrete bunker into the park of Tiergarten. He needed twenty minutes to reach his office on Werd'scher Markt. He passed green benches for Aryans, a few remaining yellow ones for Jews. Unless it was pouring rain he took this route every morning, relishing the pastoral illusion—birdsong, the early smells, the long shadows of willows and birches. He liked to feel the earth give beneath his boots, then quickly spring back. The winged golden spirit of the Victory Column on Grosser Stern Platz soared before him. After this war, he thought, they won't put up any statues. His old friends had been swallowed up by it, spat out—lifeless, limbless, their genitals shriveled like prunes. Or they were serving in Russia, awaiting their turn. Sylvie was dead, and his city was burning.

The sky began to clear. Above the Reichstag and the Brandenburg Tower the sun rose swiftly, a throbbing warm orange. It was unexpectedly beautiful. The captain took a deep breath.

That's it, he thought. The earth still spins. God doesn't care. No matter what we do, life goes on.

The SS Guards outside Number 5 Werd'scher Markt snapped to attention. Paul acknowledged them with a curt nod, filled his lungs once more with the cool morning air, then thrust a shoulder against the carved oak door. Inside, where steam heat already had set the pipes to clanking, the SS regimental sergeant-major threw him a smart salute.

As he crossed the vestibule, the heels of his boots cracked like hammer blows on the marble floor. Almost deserted at six o'clock in the morning, the main hall of the old police station was furnished with slightly stained German flags, portraits of Adolf Hitler and other dignitaries, platoons of filing cabinets and wooden benches. The benches and all the office chairs had been recently painted yellow—no longer tacky but still with that nasty sour smell. Someone in the Kripo's Quartermaster Division, Paul thought, had an odd sense of humor.

Dropping into a chair at his desk, he sniffed disinfectant and yesterday's cigarette smoke. Half of Berlin is freezing, he realized, but in here it's like an oven. He loosened the collar of his jacket with the twin silver lightning bolts of the SS patched to one wing, then stretched up to cross out yesterday's date on the 1943 wall calendar. The illustration for April showed young girls boating on the Wannsee. One of them looked a bit like Ushi, and the girls wore the same bright blue skirts and fake-velvet brown jackets of the League of German Maidens. Lilies floated by the bows of the rowboats . . . a pale yellow sun sparkled on the water.

He remembered how Sylvie had loved the Wannsee. On summer Sundays, with twenty thousand others, they had taken the S-bahn to picnic by its shores. No matter what the weather, Erich and Ushi clamored to ride the Star & Circle boat.

For a few moments his heartbeat staggered. Next week was Sylvie's birthday. Or would have been . . .

It had been the first British air raid, the one that Goering had promised could never happen. With her sister she had been rushing out of a theater on the Ku'Damm. The antiaircraft fire was tremendously impressive, the searchlights worried the clouds like dogs; but not a plane was brought down. "No significant damage," the radio crowed the next morning.

At the mortuary, after they had dug her out from the rubble of colonnades, the director had said to him, kindly, "Don't lift the sheet, Inspector. It will be better for you."

He had obeyed. The sheet had been drawn up to Sylvie's nostrils, so that he was unable to kiss her lips. He stared down at the smooth forehead buffed to an unnatural shine, as if a coat of flesh-colored paint and then lacquer had been applied. They had combed her curly brown hair in a style she rarely used; it made her look older. But now she'll never grow old, he thought.

He touched his mouth to her forehead. Not as cold as he had dreaded. Just dead. My wife . . . broken too badly for viewing. He whispered a speech to her that he could no longer remember. *Dulce et decorum est pro patria mori.* But not the women. Not you, Sylvie . . .

After that he was listless at work. There were not enough officers to command the galloping Wehrmacht across the steppes to Moscow. When he was posted to the Waffen-SS Death's-Head Division as a reserve captain, he took none of the normal evasive action. What for?

His eyes blurred a little. They always did when he thought about Sylvie. But he shook his narrow head decisively and picked up the first manila file that lay before him.

Then his desk telephone jingled. He was surprised—he had come in an hour earlier than usual to clear up some paperwork. He snatched the receiver and said crisply, "Captain Paul Bach here."

The instrument crackled in his ear. A voice murmured at him from what seemed like the other side of the world. The line cleared, the murmur sharpening into a cheerful bark.

"Heil Hitler. Paul, it's Willi!"

"Willi . . . ?"

"Willi Dietrich, for God's sake! I've been ringing you since five-thirty. Loafer! How are you?"

Paul's lined granite face slowly split into a smile of pleasure. Willi Dietrich was his oldest friend, the one survivor of the old gang that had become comrades at the police academy. He and Willi had played poker all Friday night, polo all Saturday at the fields reserved for the Prussian Civil Service . . . skied together at Kitz-bühel, drunk their way from bar to bar in Vienna, jumped hurdles on horseback for Weimar at the Paris Olympics. Young bucks serving in their hometown of Berlin, they shared money, an apartment, confidences, girls, the swift flash of youth. They were each godfather to the other's son. It was two years now since they had seen each other—just before Willi had been promoted to lieutenant colonel and posted to Gestapo HQ in Brussels.

"It's wonderful to hear your voice, Willi. . . ."

"But you didn't answer my question. Are you all right now?"

"Not too bad. April's a season of rebirth," Paul said, without conviction. "Do you remember your Rilke? '. . . many times between the leafless limbs/ a morning looks out, which already stands/ wholly in spring.' Are you still in Brussels?"

"No such luck. Warsaw! Can't you tell by the connection?"

"And how is life in Warsaw?"

"Troublesome. Let me simply and passionately say that I would rather be in Brussels. More important, how's your arm?"

"The one I left behind in Russia, I suppose, is fine. Probably just starting to thaw all over again." He glanced out the window at the gold rays of sunlight beating through the haze. "The one I've got here is getting damn tired of making out forms in triplicate."

"You are quite the same old grumbler," Willi said warmly. "The kids are well?"

"You wouldn't recognize Ushi. A blonde beauty. Erich's fifteen —he wants to join the SS, the Panzerkorps—anyone who'll have him. He's a believer. What more can I say?"

The static had jumped on the line again and Willi yelled, *"What?"*

"It wasn't important." Anyone could be listening in, he realized. The Gestapo, the SS, the SD, the Kripo, Military Intelligence—a mad jumble with no trust and a frighteningly high level of paranoia.

"... you're fading, Paul. Let's get to it. I need you to do a job for us. A little Gestapo and Kripo cooperation. Something rather unusual, but definitely for you. Homicide."

Paul tilted his head, pressing the receiver into the hollow of neck and shoulder. Immediately he became what he was meant to be during office hours: chief investigating officer for the Homicide Department of the Berlin Kripo.

He reached for a sharpened pencil. "Where, Willi? Who? And when?"

"Several homicides, in fact. Here in Poland."

"Warsaw? But you're there."

"I am, dear fellow, but it's not Warsaw I'm talking about. And it's not something I have the time to handle, although I confess I'd love to take a crack at it. It's in a place called Zin. Do you know what that is?"

"I don't even know *where* it is."

"Actually, it's one of those double-barreled unpronounceable Polish names. . . . I have it here in front of me somewhere.

Zinoswicz-Zdroj. In our inexhaustible Teutonic wisdom, we've shortened it to Zin. Southeast of Posen, direction Breslau. Not too far from the old border."

Paul envisioned the map. "Willi, that's out in the middle of nowhere. Potato fields, peasants, and potholes. I hope you're drunk, although at six o'clock in the morning it's unlikely." He checked his rush of annoyance. "Are you still a lieutenant colonel, or have you disgraced yourself and made major?"

"Colonel, dear boy," Willi said smugly.

"I was afraid of that. Look, you may drink schnapps with Himmler himself, but we've shoveled horseshit together. Shared, if memory serves, Jacqueline and what's her name, the redhead, on rue Saint Denis. I know secrets from your unsavory past."

"Nothing that *they* don't know." Willi gave a barking laugh. "This won't take long, not for you. And think how glad you'll be to get back."

Paul was suddenly curious. "Who's been done in? And why me?"

"Because I want to keep this in the family. And because you're a genius at what you do. As for who . . ."

The line crackled ominously, as if the connection were about to be broken. Willi cleared his throat, pitched his voice more sharply.

"A couple of important Jews, and one Polish SS lieutenant."

For a moment Paul was silent. Then he said, "This sounds like the sort of practical joke we used to play on each other at the academy."

"Can you speak up?"

"I don't believe you!"

"It will all become clear when you get there. Bring your woollies—Poland is cold. I'll have travel orders drawn for you . . . ready tomorrow." A burst of static obliterated his next words.

"Willi!"

". . . connection is ghastly. I'll call later today . . . priority . . . details. Heil—"

"Auf Wiederhören," Paul muttered angrily into a dead telephone. "Until later."

2

Zinoswicz-Zdroj: January 1943

Some ten weeks before the telephone call that threatened to separate Paul Bach from his cluttered desk on Werd'scher Markt in Berlin, a Ukrainian guard at Zin discovered a note wedged next to the wooden trough in a shadowed corner of Block B, one of the workers' barracks. The note was torn into four pieces and then crumpled, but the guard bent to one knee on the cold dirt floor, assembled it, and attempted to read it. The language was unfamiliar to him.

Dutifully he marched across Roll Call Square, crunching through thick white snow almost as hard as ice, then veered left past the gas tanks and water tower toward Commandant Kirmayr's bungalow. The winter sun had risen, but that was only evidenced by a whiter patch of sky in the swollen gray cloud band that suffocated the camp like a blanket and seemed virtually to isolate Zin from the rest of the world. It might very well snow again, the guard thought . . . and he hoped so. When it snowed there was less work to do.

The time was a few minutes before eight o'clock on the morning of January 13, 1943.

Outside the administrative bungalow, SS Lieutenant Rudolf Stein was smoking a cigarette with the commandant's aide-de-camp, Sergeant Zuckermann. Both men stamped their feet impatiently and blew clouds of vapor into the cold morning air. It was an unwritten rule that no one enter Commandant Major Kirmayr's quarters before precisely 8:00 A.M., in the event that the commandant might have spent the night with his new Jewish whore. There had been two or three in succession last winter to keep the commandant warm but so far this year only one. Jewish whores was the label that Stein attached to them.

The Ukrainian guard saluted sloppily. With a brief explanation of its origin, he handed the note to Lieutenant Stein, a scrawny scholarly looking young fellow with weak eyes and a receding chin. It was too cold for the lieutenant to take off his gloves and fish inside his greatcoat for his gold-rimmed glasses. He held the paper close to his nose in the shadowless morning light.

"I thought it would be in Yiddish," he said, annoyed.

He was not a scholar. Dismissing the guard, Stein glanced at his watch. He uttered a whistle of relief, opened the door, and jumped quickly inside the bungalow. He stomped his boots loudly on the pine floorboards—not only to shake off the clumps of snow but to warn Major Kirmayr of his presence. The outer office was empty, the bungalow silent. Not even a snore . . . not even a moan of morning passion.

"*Cold* in here, Zuckermann!"

The young blond sergeant bent immediately before the potbellied iron stove and began to work a bellows energetically upon the ashes of last night's fire. In a few minutes, with the aid of some fresh pine logs, a cheerful blaze sprang up. As the heat poured forth, both men bent eagerly to warm their hands.

A short time later the commandant shuffled from his bedroom, wearing a royal blue silk bathrobe (a Christmas present from his wife back in Rosenheim) over gray long johns and heavy gray woolen socks. He was a heavyset man in his fifties with a round face and an unhealthy pallor. Lieutenant Stein had often thought that he looked like a sick squirrel.

At his side, in a shapeless sack of a dress, was his latest Jewess. A bold one, Stein decided, recognizing her as the wife of the kapo in charge of the dental commando. She was in her early twenties, pale, black haired, and well curved—rather appetizing if you were so inclined.

Major Kirmayr's brown eyes were still clogged with sleep. "Well, Rudy?"

Rudy Stein related the tale of the finding of the note, which he then spread in its four intersecting pieces on the surface of a table stacked with manila folders and metal trays. The commandant snapped his fingers in the direction of his sergeant.

"Get some tape."

Zuckermann strode to the desk and came back with a roll of brown tape that the commandant had used to seal his own Christmas presents sent back to Germany. Kirmayr carefully assembled the quarters of the note upside down, then with greater care licked and applied the tape. After he had sipped some fresh water to rid his mouth of the taste, he studied the note a second time.

"Bella . . . translate, please."

To Stein's ear it sounded less an order than a polite request. I suppose, he thought, if you fuck them and they show some enthusiasm, you can't help becoming a little fond of them. He had never been tempted. He loved deep-breasted blonde peasant women on a bed of pine needles in the forest and was grateful for what his sixteen-year-old cousin had done for him in a glade of the Schwarzwald when he was fourteen. There was something about these dark Jewesses that struck him as unclean.

Bella Wallach glided across the room. She wore a pair of thick socks, one of the many pairs shipped by the doting Frau Kirmayr back in Rosenheim. Her golden eyes never wavered. Bending with a youthful grace that was apparent even under the floppy dress, she glanced at the note.

But she looked up quickly. "It's in Hebrew. I can't read it."

The commandant wheeled on Zuckermann. "Get the rabbi. He works with the gold commando."

Ten minutes later the sergeant returned with Rabbi Jacob Hurwicz, a cadaverous creature in his early thirties. An ugly horizontal pink scar seamed the rabbi's forehead. He brought with him a stench of bad breath and old sweat, so that the three Germans instinctively backed away. Shivering from the cold, he edged as close to the stove as he dared. But the cold came from inside and was a coldness that only food could cure.

Commandant Martin Kirmayr, dressed now in his black woolen SS duty uniform, face flushed from a splashing of ice water at the sink, sat at his desk sipping a mug of hot coffee and munching some wheat biscuits. On the desk in front of him stood framed photographs of his two married children and the fair-haired, smiling, vacant-eyed Frau Kirmayr.

Lieutenant Stein ordered Rabbi Hurwitz to translate the note.

The rabbi held it between bony, crooked fingers. While he studied it, a wan smile appeared on his face. At the same time the scar on his brow creased with confusion.

"You find it amusing?" Stein demanded.

"Yes, Lieutenant," the rabbi said. "Amusing . . . that's the right word."

"Be so kind as to share the joke with us."

The rabbi, a Pole from the city of Czestochowa, spoke fluent German. "The Hebrew is very fine," he commented. "Whoever penned this is an educated man, and he has wit. I would say—"

"Translate!" Stein yelled.

Clearing his throat by way of apology and stretching his absurdly long, narrow neck, Rabbi Hurwicz translated as follows:

Dear Jacob,

I find your bunk area in a deplorable condition. You are a prime example of the lamentable failure of the Third Reich's correctional system to rehabilitate its residents.

Remember, work makes you free. Neatness is rewarded, too.

"*That's* what it says?" Stein asked. His jaw dropped.

"Yes, Lieutenant," the rabbi replied.

"There's no signature?"

"None. Look, you can see."

"You've translated precisely? Left nothing out?"

"Not a word, Lieutenant. Naturally, there is room for interpretation, and some synonyms might equally apply. *Sad* for *lamentable*, for example. Hebrew is a complex language . . . its vowels are omitted from the written text, which sometimes causes confusion. Even double meanings. For example—"

"No examples," Major Kirmayr interrupted. He ordered the rabbi once more to read the note aloud while he gazed fondly out the window at his little fenced-in patch of garden where two shivering Ukrainian guards were hacking with shovels at the snow.

"Who is this Jacob?" Stein demanded.

The young rabbi shrugged. "Lieutenant, there are probably thirty Jacobs in this camp. *My* name is Jacob."

"This one seems to live in Block B."

"It's a common name. Jacob was the second son of Isaac, the father of the twelve patriarchs. Any Jew from Germany, Poland, Bohemia, Galicia—even the Low Countries—"

The commandant growled. "I don't give a damn who the note was addressed to. I want to know who *wrote* it."

No one could guess. A Jew . . . but which one? There were five hundred who lived in the camp. After a fruitless ten minutes of debate, the discussion was tabled.

Rabbi Jacob Hurwicz returned to his job of weighing and classifying gold. Bella Wallach returned to her job of bundling hair. Sergeant Zuckermann was ordered to brew a second pot of Brazilian coffee. The diminutive Lieutenant Stein, gloved, fur-hatted, armed with whip and Walther pistol, began his regular morning inspection of the camp facilities accompanied by his pet dog, Wolfgang, a brindled cross between a Doberman pinscher and Spanish mastiff. The Jews in the camp called him Prince Rudy . . . the Prince of Darkness.

Commandant Major Kirmayr slid the anonymous note into a file marked "Miscellaneous: To Be Inspected for Refiling on the 15th Day of Each Month."

He quickly forgot about it, which was a mistake.

3

Berlin: April 1943

Captain Paul Bach shuffled papers on his desk. After the call from Warsaw he found it difficult to concentrate.

Telephone the glazier, one note said. He had to make sure a bombed-out window had been replaced in the sitting room of his apartment on Claudiusstrasse. Another scribbled note reminded him to inquire about his overdue ration tickets for the coming month of May. His allotment for the family entitled them to four hundred grams of meat a week, when available; a quarter kilo of butter, five eggs, five apples. The SS provided vitamin pills, which he gave to Ushi and Erich. Milk—no ration tickets necessary—was so watered-down that it looked blue. Berliners lived on a diet of potatoes and beer, cabbage and black bread. Paul grew tomatoes on his balcony in summer, but they were sad specimens.

Sometimes, when he could afford it, he ate out on the Kurfürstendamm. Alone at the Schultheiss or the Kempinski; otherwise the Café Hilbrich. The waiter would clip ration tickets from a chain around his neck. Widows, lonely wives—or young women who had blossomed, he thought, in a time when the young men who should be courting them were dying on the steppes of Russia or choking in the sands of the Sahara—if he fancied one and had enough tickets, he took her to dinner at the Hilbrich, which was chic. The women were grateful for attention.

Last November he had volunteered to care for the six-year-old twins of a nurse on the second floor of his apartment building. Her husband, a tank commander, was dying of third-degree burns in a

23

military hospital in Stettin. Sweet girls . . . they called him Uncle
Paul. For Christmas the widow, Greta, had delivered a plum pud-
ding. She was a chatty, ivory-skinned young woman of thirty. Now
he spent most weekends in her bed, or his if Erich and Ushi were off
parading.

He was not in love with her but used her, he realized, as she used
him. Afterward he would smoke a cigarette and wonder, "Why am I
here?" Habit not motivated by love or duty was a crime against
one's destiny . . . if one still had a destiny at forty. But a private
crime. The punishment was unwritten—unclear.

The morning wore on, crammed with conferences on pending
investigations, decisions on whether or not to seek prosecution. A
twenty-year-old soldier, home on convalescent leave from the
Afrika Korps, had shot his drunken uncle, a '14-'18 veteran who
wore the Iron Cross Second Class. The boy had immediately confessed and dictated a sworn statement. "My uncle was disrespectful
toward my uniform and all authority. He repeatedly insulted the
Führer's military abilities."

"Recommend prosecution," Paul wrote—almost certain it
would be vetoed by the SS Police Court-Martials. Would my father
have approved? The old police inspector, killed along the Somme
in the first war, had been fond of quoting from Euripides. "The
man who sticks it out against his fate shows spirit, but it's the spirit
of a fool. . . ."

He kept thinking about the telephone call from Warsaw . . . and
Willi Dietrich.

"Smart and lucky," Willi had once said.

Paul and Willi had ridden with such success for the Equestrian
Club of the Prussian Civil Service that they ended by representing
Germany in the '24 Olympics. It was their first trip to Paris. Paul
on his big bay gelding placed sixth in the high jump at Long-
champ. Willi, the following day, won a bronze medal for the
Weimar Republic in cross-country with hurdles.

All night after that triumph, in company with two young French
equestriennes, they toured the *boîtes* on both banks of the Seine. At
dawn, as the sun crept above the rooftops of Montmartre, a

drunken Willi threw an arm about the shoulder of an equally drunken Paul.

"Brother mine forever," he said hoarsely, "your brother has come to an interesting conclusion. *Cher ami,* you are more intelligent than I am. . . . I guessed that years ago. And you're more dedicated, too. But I am smarter. And luckier. So let's see which of us goes farther in this crazy, quite delightful world."

They had seen. In the spring of 1925 Inspector Heller, their commandant at the Kripo and a booster of the National Socialist German Workers' Party, invited them to a fund-raising dance at the Adlon Hotel. The Nazi cause was in the doldrums. Its Austrian immigrant leader had just spent six months in prison following an aborted uprising in a Munich beer hall.

"I think, if we want to stay on Heller's good side," Willi said, "we'd better go. Besides, he's got a niece in town from Mecklenburg. He says she's a knockout."

"You believe him?"

"He's the commandant!" Willi, laughing, thumped the kitchen table in the little flat they shared in Wilmersdorf. "His word can't be questioned."

At the dance they were introduced to Inspector Heller's niece, Marlene, and her best friend, a curly-haired girl named Sylvie. "The ugly one's yours," Willi whispered.

"Which is the ugly one?" Paul had already gained a reputation for his devotion to logic; he was not known for sparkling humor. "God, they're *both* beautiful!"

Willi chuckled. "You take the little brunette with the tits. They say opposites attract. I'll dance with the blonde."

The following June they honeymooned with their brides at twin chalets on the Tegernsee. A year later each became godfather to the other's firstborn son. Paul, in love with Sylvie and their two children, watched from a measured distance as torchlight parades goose-stepped down the Kaiserdamm, trumpets blared, Brownshirts clashed with Communists, and Blackshirts clashed with everybody. The former Corporal Hitler—"that gutternsipe," as he was then termed by Paul and Willi—shouted, "We need a superfluity of national fanaticism!"

Bewildered and amused in equal parts, Paul concentrated on his wife's soft thighs, the right school for Erich, Ushi's ballet lessons, the rigor of his work. He was fascinated by human frailty and angered by evil. He wanted the world to be orderly. A policeman, he thought, is sometimes all that stands between peace and barbarism. He solved a difficult case: Two Jewish girls in the Wilmersdorf section were raped and bludgeoned to death. The murderers turned out to be a pair of young factory workers—instructors in the Hitler Youth. Paul's handsome Nordic face appeared, heroic, on the front page of the *Berliner Tageblatt*, but the Nazi paper, the *Völkischer Beobachter*, labeled the indictment an outrage.

When the men were convicted and guillotined, Willi threw a party for Paul and got drunk. "You're unpopular in certain quarters," he confessed. "I invited Commandant Heller, but he wouldn't come. Mumbled something about Jew lovers being not quite his cup of tea."

"I have no love for Jews," Paul said, downing a brandy. "I hardly know any. I love . . . justice. A natural harmony."

"An eye for an eye?"

"I don't need the Bible to spell it out," Paul said. He was not a religious man. His family and his work were his religion.

"Heller says you're a cold fish."

"Heller can go screw himself."

Willi was promoted to assistant detective-inspector; it took Paul another two years to reach that grade. The following year, 1933, the coalition government fell and the corporal from Austria, now a German citizen, became Chancellor of the Reich. On a Sunday under a blue February sky, riding their horses in a trot through the Tiergarten, Willi said, "We've got to join the Nazi party."

Paul tugged on the reins, brought his bay to a halt, and demanded to know why.

"For the same reason we went to that dance at the Adlon. Expediency. But it brought us luck, didn't it? And if we wait too long, we'll miss the boat. Generally speaking, boats should not be missed."

"Willi, you forget. We're police officers in the Prussian Civil Service. Above politics!"

"No longer possible, dear fellow!" Willi cried out, winking. "This is the dawn of a new age, didn't you know?"

The young Paul frowned. He knew the slogans—the Nazis had shouted them through megaphones on every street corner. Germany would be delivered from the bonds of Versailles; men in tattered old army coats would no longer beg for soup and bread. Not each for himself but all for all: the inner freedom inherent in obedience. Everyone would jog before breakfast, hear tales of Wotan and the Valkyrie by blazing campfires. Women would be able to throw away their makeup, which was French and decadent. To the women the party faithful handed out sheets printed with ground plans of the ideal two-family dwelling: six rooms, two baths, garden, and attic—flag with swastika rippling above the front door. More women had voted for Herr Hitler than men.

"The most effective political instrument in Germany," Willi said dryly, "has always been a lieutenant and ten men. And always will be. Marlene's with me completely."

They were walking their sweating horses back to the stable. "Where politics is concerned," Paul explained, "Sylvie and I agree to disagree."

"I think we're obliged to do it. Not only the party. The SS."

"Willi!" Paul drew a quick breath of cold air and warm horseflesh. "You're *serious*."

"They're not as antiintellectual as you like to make out." Willi, a neatly built young man with jet black hair and a charming smile, puffed thoughtfully on his cigarette. "Heidegger's our most eminent philosopher, and he took a public oath to support Hitler. With the exception of our ivory-towered Berlin, all the universities are the strongholds of the party. Do you know who Himmler got to join the SS as honorary members? Prince Wilhelm of Hesse—Prince von Hohenzollern-Emden—the grand duke of Mecklenburg. The list goes on. These are not bums, Paul, like the ones you sent to the guillotine. These are the elite."

It reminded Paul of what they said back in '23, when a few million marks couldn't buy a loaf of bread. "The inflation is desperate but not serious."

The ascendancy of the Blackshirts, he believed, was serious, but not desperate. They were the natural outgrowth of the vigilante brigades that had roamed Germany after the armistice; then the brownshirted SA, marching under the banner of the National Socialist Party Gymnastic and Sports Section. The SS, the Protective Squad, originally Herr Hitler's private police force, wore black. On their caps they pinned the silver Death's-Head insignia. Their ranks seemed to be filled with young slum toughs and bored farm boys; their leaders were hot-eyed idealists and bitter ex-soldiers, with a smattering of cranks who pursued quasiscientific racial theories.

Reaching the stable, Paul inhaled the sweet smell of hay. "Maybe the party . . . just maybe. I understand what you mean about not missing the boat." He shook his head. "But not those simpletons with their death's-heads and their damned Kith and Kin Oath. 'We believe in God, we believe in Germany, which He created in His world and in the Führer Adolf Hitler, whom He has sent us.' One of those kids quoted that to me—the ones who butchered those Jewish girls in Wilmersdorf. You go ahead, Willi. Plunge in. I'll observe, if you don't mind, from a slightly loftier perch."

But Willi nagged him for another month, so that Paul began to feel that his perch was a bit too lofty, the air too rarefied. He had been an armchair socialist, but they had voted in the Reichstag without a dissenting vote to approve Hitler's policies. If the Nazis indeed embodied the German will, if they could end inflation and debt and bring about their goals of "work, freedom and bread," perhaps it was wiser in the end to belong. With a hearty endorsement from Commandant Heller, he filed his application. In a few weeks both he and Willi received their membership books and red lapel buttons. Whatever unpopular prosecutions Paul may have conducted in the past, he was Aryan a certifiable five generations back and possessed of a head shape flawlessly conforming to Aryan ideals. He was also, at the age of thirty, an assistant detective-inspector in the Berlin Kripo.

Within a year, under the guidance of the Prussian minister of the interior, Hermann Goering, a reorganization of the security services began to take place, and the Kripo was subsumed under the Police of the Greater German Reich and the State Protection Corps.

28

"It's a labyrinth," Paul muttered. "Who reports where? Who gives the orders? I don't like labyrinths. I like *order*."

Heinrich Himmler, a rising star, urged that the corrupt police from the old regime be placed under the control of "the best sons of the people"—the Blackshirts. All Kripo officers, including Paul and Willi, were elevated automatically into equivalent ranks in the SS. "Congratulations," SS Inspector Colonel Heller said to them. "You will draw new uniforms and new insignia."

They were not asked if it was agreeable; they were not required to attend a single indoctrination meeting. A year later they were awarded their black-hilted SS service daggers, to be worn at all times sheathed and hooked to the left side of the Sam Browne belt. The inscription on the steel blade read, "My honor is my pledge."

"I didn't join the SS," Paul grumbled, feet up on his desk as he cleaned his fingernails with the point of the dagger. "The damned SS joined *me*."

Willi Dietrich took one step farther. An organization had been formed to replace the old Department 1A of the Prussian Political Police. Meant to be an arm of the SS, it possessed almost sovereign power. It was called the *Geheime Staatspolizei*, or Gestapo.

"That's for me," Willi said. "If there's going to be another war—and most of these idiots think that's the answer to all of our problems—I don't want to flop in the mud of some trench. I want to swim with the fast fish. How about it?"

"You're mad."

"Smart and lucky, dear fellow. Take my word for it."

After a while, in the office on Werd'scher Markt, Paul pulled a military atlas from the shelf where the coffee mugs were stored. He opened it to the map of Poland. The prewar border, erased in 1939, was less than two hundred kilometers from Berlin. Posen—the Poles called it Poznań—lay to the east on the road to Warsaw.

He looked up Zin in the gazeteer of cities and towns and found Zinoswicz-Zdroj. Only a hamlet between the Warta and the Oder Rivers. Maybe two hundred people, if they had survived the blitzkrieg. Not even on the main railroad line.

He was sure he had heard some mention of it but could not recall in what context. Willi would tell him when he called back.

A couple of important Jews and one Polish SS officer. A Pole? What the hell did that mean to the Gestapo? And the Jews? For a decade they had been persona non grata in the Third Reich— reviled, boycotted in business, even beaten on the streets by the SA and occasionally sent to the work camps at Sachsenhausen and Dachau. The camps were located near quarries. Paul had been invited a few times but had always found an excuse. He knew what prisons were like; his job was to populate them with rapists and murderers. The camps were for enemies of the state—Communists, antisocials, degenerates, and malcontents. Paul had read some of the protective custody orders.

"State Police evidence shows that his/her behavior constitutes a danger to the existence and security of state and people, because *He has abused his clerical position to make defeatist remarks concerning the strength of our armed forces. . . . It is feared that she would continue her illegal Marxist endeavor. . . . Although a Jew, he has persisted in flying the Reich national flag from his parlor window. . . .*"

Lately there was a new scheme: resettlement in the East. A somewhat mysterious term, its details known only to the party brass . . . but probably more of the same. Factories and quarries hidden in the marshes of Poland, where the RAF bombs were unlikely to fall. So at least the poor souls wouldn't be buried under rubble, like Sylvie. Perhaps the Jews were lucky. Perhaps there was such a factory at—what was it?—Zinoswicz-Zdroj.

There were other rumors, but Paul gave them no credibility. Why destroy a source of free labor? Stupid! Why kill anyone who wasn't trying to do the same to *you?* That would be a rupture of all harmony, a barbarous insanity. Lately, after the defeats at Tobruk and Stalingrad, people were becoming hysterical. They would believe anything.

4

Zin: February 1943

During the night a silent snowfall swaddled Zin in a white coat. In the morning the Ukrainian guards chose up sides and threw snowballs at each other. By the end of the day a second note appeared, this time on the frozen dirt floor of Block C—not crumpled or discarded but in full view for anyone to read. It chastised those Jews who failed to observe the Sabbath.

"You are already in hell," the accuser wrote, in the same scholarly Hebrew. "How will you get to heaven if you don't obey the Law?"

More snow fell. The air a man drew into his lungs felt like ice. A third note—in Yiddish, as if the writer no longer trusted the scholarship of his audience—was found on the body of a man who died in his sleep in Block B.

Another one who won't spend next year in Jerusalem. Avenge me, comrades!

Lieutenant Werner Vogl, a tall young man of twenty-four whose skin had the healthy glow of a child's, stamped through the hard-packed glitter and brought the sheet of onionskin to the administrative bungalow.

The commandant sighed. He ordered all three notes translated into German by Rabbi Hurwicz, then typed by Sergeant Zuckermann, who used only two fingers and corrected mistakes by pounding out a series of xs. The translations were stamped with the date in purple ink. Commandant Kirmayr opened a new manila file, labeled it with a large blue question mark—he tried to keep a sense of humor—and inserted it in the top drawer of his filing cabinet. Someone was committing a series of relatively harmless pranks. But if a resident of Zin could commit a prank . . . what else might he be capable of doing?

That question, which the commandant's mind dimly formulated only for a moment, was answered early one icy February morning when a fourth note appeared, this time printed in German and stuck with a yellow thumbtack to the wood of the barracks that housed the eighty Ukrainian conscripts. It rattled and flapped in the cold north wind.

> Sons of Russia:
>
> Has it not occurred to you that your masters will not tolerate any witnesses? When the task is completed, you will never again see the sun rise above the beloved Sea of Azov.
>
> Is there no hope? The question answers itself.

"Damn him," Kirmayr muttered.

Lieutenant Stein was on leave in the Schwarzwald. The Polish camps were officially labeled hardship posts, and officers accumulated one week's leave a month. Kirmayr consulted with his second-in-command, Captain Dressler. But Karl Dressler was an accountant more than a staff officer. He spent his spare time doing crossword puzzles mailed to him daily by his wife in Dortmund. Once a week, to relieve the monotony of camp life, he drove with Lieutenant Stein to the German officers' brothel in Posen.

"A malcontent," Dressler said airily. "When Rudy gets back, he'll take care of it."

A few days later the commandant reviewed Dressler's monthly summary of shipments to Germany. For January: twenty kilos of gold, sixty-six carats of diamonds, seventy-five thousand czarist rubles, and four thousand three hundred dollars in cash; one freight carload of medicines, one of artisans' tools, two of valises, two of hair packed in bales, three of shoes, four of bedding, twenty-five of mixed clothing, and seven of miscellaneous items—fountain pens, combs, dolls, baby carriages, china, wallets, umbrellas, eye-glasses, cigarette lighters, and toilet articles.

The report contained other statistics, and Kirmayr suddenly noted that there had been thirteen suicides in the month of January—seven more than the average.

He had developed a theory. Without a margin of hope to which the residents could cling, the camp could not continue its smooth existence. You could starve them, whip them, periodically kill some of them if it was absolutely necessary . . . but you had to offer them hope. My Jews, he reflected, are not the kind to commit suicide. If they are, then I've chosen poorly. Worse, I'm not running this place the way I want to run it. The way I *must* run it if I'm to survive.

He thought back to the building of the camp in the autumn of 1941. It had been a barren stretch on the edge of a birch forest where only stunted potatoes grew. He witnessed the construction of the railway spur, the foundations of the barracks, and had lived in a field tent until the first batch of Ukrainians built his bungalow. He remembered in the beginning, with the winter convoys of '42, all had been chaos, panic, brutality. It can't go on this way, he thought. He soon encouraged a small orchestra, allowed limited sexual contact, turned a half-blind eye to mild bribery, occasional religious worship, contraband food. Anything within reason to soothe their minds, keep them busy in their spare time—*give them hope.*

"Thirteen suicides in January? I can't afford to lose one more man," the commandant murmured.

Lieutenant Stein, back early from his leave, adjusted his glasses. He thought this was nonsense. They could choose replacements from among the thousand or more who arrived almost every day but Sunday—although lately the numbers had slacked off because of the snow and the winter holidays back home. But the commandant had his odd ideas.

"What do you suggest, Herr Major? A reduction of rations as punishment?"

"Rudy, you don't understand. We are only forty-odd German soldiers commanded by six officers—one of them a Pole!—plus those eighty slovenly Bolshevik turncoats. We depend on our five hundred Jewish residents. They're trained specialists! They eat little enough as it is." Kirmayr shook his head glumly, glancing at the photograph of his smiling wife, knowing that she would approve. "If I had my way, I'd give them *more* food. Pep them up. Make them stronger, not so dejected."

Stein cleared his throat. "May I make one more recommendation, Major?"

He had done a bit of investigating into the suicide problem on other occasions and discovered an interesting aspect. "They all hang themselves. A man stands on a chair or a stool, loops his belt around a beam and then ties it around his neck. But the chair still has to be kicked away. That's not so easy. The man himself is either too weak to do it or liable to change his mind at the last second. So he needs someone else to kick the chair away. Do you see?"

Kirmayr wrinkled a veined nose. These were the kinds of details he preferred not to hear about. They made his stomach clench.

"What is your proposal, Rudy?"

Stein leaned across the desk, eyes narrowed. "Suicide can be defined as self-murder. If another party is necessary for the act, he becomes an accomplice to murder. Murder is a crime. The customary punishment is death. We have only to enforce it."

Kirmayr shook his head in disgust. "You must have led a very prosaic life," he said, "before you came to Zin."

Stein, the youngest son of a failed pig farmer, had worked in a country tavern in the Black Forest. He had hated the need to be polite to the most demanding, drunken customer in order to get a decent tip. He was in love with his older cousin who had seduced him in the woods; but she was married now and had two children. The Hitler Youth, the National Socialist party, and then the SS had shown him the path to freedom. On a previous occasion he had said to the commandant, "My life as a man didn't begin until I wore a uniform. A uniform changes you entirely. What you were inside,

34

you can now proclaim on the outside. Seven years ago, when I was eighteen, the thought of this job would have frightened me. But now I see it as a kind of liberation."

Kirmayr had jibed at him. "And what happens to your liberty when our job is done? This camp is small potatoes. There aren't an infinite amount of Jews."

"A bigger camp. Maybe Russia." Stein smiled thinly. "I'll do whatever is asked of me. Like you, Major."

Kirmayr had then let out his breath in an unbidden groan. Without meaning to, his question had voiced his deepest fear.

"Do I have your permission, Major? To announce that aiding a suicide will be defined as murder?"

The commandant's mind drifted, as it often did these days. "Let's hope that March is kinder," he said. "Perhaps the cold weather demoralized the residents. I hate the cold. Snow is for penguins, not human beings. Every winter before the war my wife and I took a long holiday from the pillow factory. To Greece . . . usually Rhodes. Greek cheese, Mediterranean skies . . . that's my idea of heaven. Not snow and ice. Now, of course . . ." He sighed again.

"Talk to them about spring," he said wistfully. "It's just around the bend. Tell them that by April they'll feel the sun on their backs. The sun is a life-giving force." He reached for a bottle of Schladerer pear liquor. "Rudy, no more talk of suicide and murder! What about a good schnapps and a game of chess?"

Stein was not a skilled chess player, but the commandant was worse. Kirmayr put a record on the gramophone—Walter Gieseking playing the first movement of the Emperor Concerto. He hummed along. An icy wind rattled the windowpanes. After a dozen moves he placed Stein's queen en prise. Stein moved a bishop.

"My dear Rudy," Kirmayr chortled, "you've overlooked something."

"Damn! I was listening to Beethoven! I was only thinking about attacking your king. . . ."

"Take the move back. Otherwise, you're lost."

"Certainly not." Stein folded his arms; behind the gold-rimmed glasses, his eyes glittered. "Concentration is part of the game. I moved the bishop—there's nothing more to do."

With a sigh, the commandant captured the queen and marched on to a dull exchange of pieces and a checkmate.

It's the price I have to pay, thought Prince Rudy, for letting him believe he runs the camp.

"A staff car and driver will be placed at your disposal at oh six thirty hours tomorrow. You'll report to SS headquarters Berlin, Prinz Albrechtstrasse."

The telephone had rung a few minutes after eleven. This time Willi was being more formal. Someone's standing over his shoulder, Paul thought, or else they're recording the call on a dictaphone.

He was to proceed directly to the resettlement camp at Zin and there report to the camp commandant, SS Major Kirmayr, who would be expecting him and would provide all necessary facilities and information.

"Understood. But did you say the resettlement camp at Zin? Not the factory or the village?"

"It's a small camp," Willi said calmly. "Between you and me, it has an uncertain future. But it's part of a network, so for now it has to function."

The radiator hissed and knocked in the corner of his office. "Can't you tell me any more, Willi? There may be files and equipment I'll want to bring from Berlin."

"Totally unnecessary. Just use some discretion."

Paul liked nothing of what he heard. No files . . . just discretion. He had been a criminal inspector for too many years—it was too late to start playing games. Starting on the streets as a traffic cop in navy blue uniform and puttees, he had moved up to the Riot Squad, curbing the excesses of Nazi demonstrations and Communist street rallies, then earned his stripe as a junior inspector in the battle against cocaine smuggling, pimping, and prostitution. When the Nazis came to power, that all ended; you had to give them credit. Paul hunted down kidnappers, murderers, a gang of white slavers operating out of Alexanderplatz. He thought of himself as an inexorable force, embodying harmony and reason and restraint.

You kept the world tidy. You couldn't do that if you didn't know where you stood and within what logical process you occupied a necessary niche. Investigation to discovery; discovery to indictment. After that the judiciary took over. You had to have faith. You didn't go banging off from Berlin to the middle of nowhere in Poland, to a labor or resettlement camp or whatever it was, without understanding the means at your disposal and a belief that the process was still sane.

"Willi, if I find the man or men who are responsible . . . what exactly do you want me to do?"

"Turn them over to Commandant Kirmayr," Willi replied promptly. "He'll take care of the rest."

Summary execution. It was wartime. No opportunity for the dull niceties of law forged over centuries. My father must be turning over in his grave.

"Is this an assignment that I can refuse?"

"That you can *what*?"

"I'm sure you heard me."

"Don't be a fool," Willi said. A moment passed while he seemed to be marshaling his thoughts. "I see what you mean. You might refuse under certain circumstances in your capacity as a criminal inspector. However, as a serving officer of the SS, you don't have that privilege."

"You're ordering me to conduct the investigation."

Willi's lighthearted voice had a cutting edge. "I'm only a colonel in the Gestapo. A mere functionary. I have no direct authority over the Berlin Kripo. It's our dear Commandant Heller who gives the orders."

"And you've spoken to him?"

Willi didn't reply. Paul imagined him seated at his desk in Warsaw, cigarette holder with an unlit cigarette clamped between white teeth—he had given up smoking years ago but still needed the feel of something in his mouth. "Paul," he said at last, rather amiably, "I ask this of you as a personal favor. Settle it with Heller. I've told Major Kirmayr that you're on your way. I told him you were a genius."

"That was rash of you."

"Not at all. I know my man. I'm counting on you, Paul . . . and I have to go. Good luck. *Heil Hitler.*"

This time the line was not dead. The call was being recorded. The connection was without a hint of static—a priority line. *"Heil Hitler,"* Paul said. Then there was a click.

He's left me the way out, Paul decided, whether he meant to or not. And I'll take it.

5

Zin: February 1943

The camp at Zin, encircled by two rows of barbed wire, was constructed on a north-south grid and divided into two areas—an upper and lower camp. The upper camp, on a military map, resembled a chinless human face with a grotesquely beaked nose protruding in an easterly direction.

The main gate, railway station, and hospital were at the base of the neck. Three square redbrick buildings that appeared to be warehouses stood just inside the barbed wire at the nostrils of the beak. The four workers' barracks formed a quadrangle surrounding Roll Call Square—they were located at the lower cheek of the human face. A row of conjoined rooms assigned to privileged kapos was a slim appendage between the westernmost Block C and the smaller Block D, which housed the thirty Jewish women.

Above Roll Call Square was a second quadrangle of long pine buildings and individual huts, called simply the north quadrangle. On three sides it housed the Jewish kitchen, laundry, hair depot, tailor shop, machine shop, coal cellar, bakery, dental commando, shoemaker shop, jewelers' workshop, carpentry unit, and storage sheds; the western quarter consisted of offices, the German kitchen, enlisted men's mess and officers' mess, and, in a separate stone building still under construction, a new armory. Farther north, leading to the barbed wire, lay the camp farm, a small electrical plant, and a large woodpile.

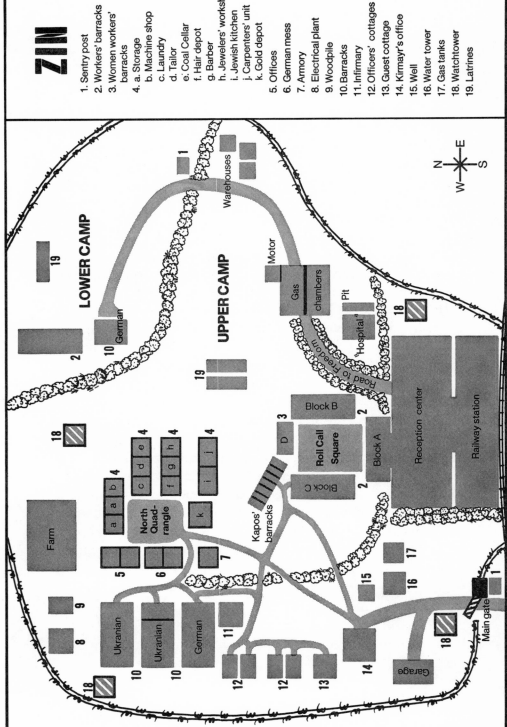

ZIN

1. Sentry post
2. Workers' barracks
3. Women workers' barracks
4. a. Storage
   b. Machine shop
   c. Laundry
   d. Tailor
   e. Coal Cellar
   f. Hair depot
   g. Barber
   h. Jewelers' workshop
   i. Jewish kitchen
   j. Carpenters' unit
   k. Gold depot
5. Offices
6. German mess
7. Armory
8. Electrical plant
9. Woodpile
10. Barracks
11. Infirmary
12. Officers' cottages
13. Guest cottage
14. Kirmayr's office
15. Well
16. Water tower
17. Gas tanks
18. Watchtower
19. Latrines

LOWER CAMP

UPPER CAMP

Warehouses

Motor

Gas chambers

Pit

"Hospital"

Road to Freedom

Block B

Block A

Block C

Roll Call Square

Reception center

Railway station

North Quadrangle

Kapos' barracks

Farm

Ukranian

Ukranian

German

Garage

Main gate

German

N
W — E
S

In a descending row at the back of the head—the western perimeter—were the Ukrainian barracks and mess, the German enlisted men's barracks and their infirmary, the semidetached brown-and-white Tyrolean-style cottages for the six officers, a similar guest cottage, and finally Commandant Kirmayr's half-timbered white bungalow, which also served as the camp administrative office. Gravel paths led through a gorse hedge (so that the Germans might have some privacy) in the direction of Roll Call Square. At the base of the skull, hard by the main gate, were the well, water tower, garage, and one of the four wooden watchtowers.

The emptiest part of the fifty-acre kingdom was the rocky plain sloping between the windowless brick buildings and the farm—an ochre landscape littered with overturned tree stumps whose gnarled roots, stretching toward the sky, resembled the mutilated arms of buried trolls. In the middle of this desolation were two wooden latrines for the prisoners. The plain was bounded by another gorse hedge, which ran slightly downhill for several hundred meters, like a coat of dark green fur along the beak of the face. The hedge divided the upper camp from the lower camp.

The two enjoyed mutual access only by a gravel path that led from the railway platform to the front doors of the redbrick buildings and then from their back doors to the lower camp. The first part of this path was fenced in, like a chute, with barbed wire that had been heavily laden with transplanted shrubs, twigs, and seasonal flowers.

The Germans had given the path a name. Now even the Jews used it, too. It was called Freiheitstrasse—the Road to Freedom.

A tall Jew, wearing hobnailed boots and a baggy gray military uniform, stepped off the first of the early morning trains that pulled off the railroad spur onto the siding at Zin.

It was a small train bearing a mixed bag of Austrian, Czech, and Polish Jewry—twenty cattle cars, their wooden sides chalked in white with the exact number of passengers. The trip had begun in Vienna, skirted the Carpathians through Brno and Ostrava, stopped at Cracow, and then turned northwest toward Zin.

A flawless slate blue sky smiled down, but a wind that might have been born in the ice floes of the Baltic sliced across the sunny fields to kick up pebbles on the rail bed. Polish children, taking a shortcut from some farms on their way to school in the village of Zdroj, shouted gaily and waved their caps from beyond the barbed wire fence. A few of the German soldiers waved back.

At Commandant Kirmayr's orders, the arrival site had been designed to look like a tiny village station such as one might find at a holiday resort in the Alps. The camouflage commando had erected a barrier of brambles and bushes so that the majority of the camp was shielded from view. The long southern wall of Block A facing the railroad tracks was painted a bright rosy pink. Pinecones or available flowers were festooned about the slats of its green boarded windows. False doors had been painted on the wall and hung with signs that said Stationmaster, Men's Toilet, Ladies' Toilet, and Tickets. A timetable next to the ticket door announced the departure of trains for Posen, Berlin, and Prague.

This new Jew alighting from the train in his rumpled gray military uniform was one among three or four hundred, but Mordecai Lieberman, Jewish camp leader and kapo of the welcome commando, noticed him immediately. Lean and tall, he stood a moment alone with shoulders thrust back, hands planted in a lordly manner on his hips. His clean-shaven face was narrow, wolflike, with thin lips and hard green eyes. In his middle thirties, Lieberman guessed.

The newcomer gazed about him with great intensity. He seemed to be thinking, "What a zoo! What can it mean?"

He's about to find out, thought Lieberman.

All the members of the welcome commando were snatching bundles of food and clothing from the new arrivals, crying at them to remember the numbers of their porters. But the tall man paid no attention. He carried no bundle of his own, only a scarred leather briefcase. Lieberman broke through to him at the door of the cattle car.

He clutched the stranger's arm above the elbow. It felt like a thin bag of rocks. He said, "When they ask, tell them you're a carpenter."

42

The man recoiled slightly at Lieberman's breath, but his cold eyes never blinked. He nodded one time.

Lieberman quietly exulted. Here's a mensch, he thought. He asks no questions. He has the eyes of a killer.

This may be the one I've been waiting for.

Mordecai Lieberman was a short gray-haired Jew in his late forties. Over the Christmas holidays a typhus epidemic had carried away the former appointed leader of the Jewish workforce, and Captain Dressler was assigned the task of selecting his replacement. His first choice was a grizzled Austrian cavalry major who wore the Iron Cross from the '14-'18 war. But the major declined the post.

"Captain Dressler, I don't choose to spend what little time is left to me acting as a collaborator. Surely, as a soldier, you understand. If you would be good enough to lend me the use of your pistol, with a single bullet . . ."

"I'll accommodate you," Dressler said. But he had been an accountant. He did not share the same military traditions. He ordered the major to be clubbed to death on Roll Call Square by Lieutenant Hrubow and a squad of Ukrainians.

Mordecai Lieberman was among the Jews who witnessed this. Some minutes later Dressler approached him and offered him the position of Jewish commandant. Lieberman said, "I would be honored, Herr Captain."

"Splendid."

Dressler was a burly man. With two fingers he raised Lieberman's chin and then slapped him twice across the face with all his strength. Tears sprouting from raw eyes, Lieberman crumpled to the dirt, prepared to absorb further punishment. He had no idea what he had done wrong.

But that was the end of it.

Dressler wheeled on the assembled prisoners and shouted, "This weeping old man is your new leader! He's the best you've got. Obey him, as he obeys me!"

The train from Vienna and Brno disgorged its cargo into the flailing wind. SS soldiers waved whips cored with umbrella wire.

Lowering the scarf from his face, one of the young Germans standing near Lieberman called out in broken Polish.

"Smell! Good country air! Clean and fresh!"

Some of the babies on the train were frozen stiff. Under Lieberman's direction the welcome commando, with numbered red patches sewn on their knees to avoid being mistaken for new arrivals, began piling up the bodies. The bath attendants led women and children down the busy path of Freiheitstrasse. A father, parted from his family, prayed loudly, "Purify our hearts, oh Lord!"

Jews of the welcome commando tagged along next to the parade crying out in Yiddish, "All clothes off, please! Don't be shy, ladies—no one will touch you! You're going to shower in nice hot water! Tie your shoes together! Leave all food! Be sure to take along all valuables!"

Lined up below the tracks, the little camp orchestra played a polka. Women ripped at their clothes. Money had been sewn in secret pockets and jacket linings, diamonds baked in bread or hidden at the bottom of matchboxes. The naked women seemed to walk on tiptoe, unsure of their balance. A child strayed in the wrong direction. One SS soldier quickly took him by the hand, whispered something in his ear—so that the child giggled—and guided him back toward his mother on Freiheitstrasse.

The women, children, and old men moved toward the showers. Just at the moment when they might have begun to doubt—when they were peering numbly over their shoulders at their husbands, fathers, sons, and brothers lined up in front of the final selection committee—they were subjected to Commandant Kirmayr's masterstroke. As they passed by some frozen rose bushes, they were handed bars of soap and fresh white bath towels.

"Hope!" the commandant had proclaimed to his officers on the day he had hit on the idea. "They must have *hope* until the very end. That way, it's easier for them. And the last thing we need is an epidemic of panic."

The long wooden platform soon became littered with hundreds of tins of meat and vegetables, fat and fish, jars of preserved fruit and jams. The black earth of the ramp was pink and yellow with cakes. Heaps of clothing—furs, chesterfields and raglans, coats and muffs, silk blouses and crinolines, ladies' marriage wigs, slips and girdles, sturdy walking shoes and brocaded high heels—rose like colorful hills. Here and there was an artificial limb, a violin case, a pile of books neatly tied and tagged with the owner's name. A chinchilla coat spread atop one pile of blankets and Persian carpets, its silver gray fur glistening in the sunlight, rippling in the wind as though the beast still lived.

The men from the train milled in confusion. Their prayers soared above the tumult.

Mordecai Lieberman was used to this; he heard but didn't hear.

Lieutenant Werner Vogl, in charge of arrivals that week, bundled in his greatcoat with blue eyes streaming tears from the cold, called out firmly.

"Those willing to work, step forward!"

Some held back, frightened to make any choice at all. Lieberman, busily sorting cardigans from smoking jackets, noted with satisfaction that the tall green-eyed man in the rumpled military uniform was among the first to volunteer. *Yes*, he thought again, *this is the man.*

6

Berlin: April 1943

Death by suffocation of a seventy-six-year-old woman on Landstrasse. Granddaughter the confessed perpetrator. The old woman had been suffering from cancer of the bowel. "I was only putting her out of her misery," Fräulein Ganz had stated.

"Prosecution," Paul wrote in his neat, almost crabbed handwriting, *"will probably result in acquittal on the grounds of euthanasia. Nevertheless, premeditated murder has been committed. The law insists on a reckoning. Indictment for second-degree murder recommended."*

He signed his name in triplicate to the forms and tossed them into his Out basket. Then he walked down the overheated corridor to General Heller's office, bypassed the secretary, and knocked on the thick mahogany door. He had worked under Heller for fifteen years and knew that the commandant always ate his lunch alone so that no one would see the contraband wurst and buttered loaves of white bread that he brought to Werd'scher Markt in his old leather attaché case.

Paul waited a full minute so that the commandant could clear up his desk and remove the grease-stained napkin from his collar. Then, as expected, a gruff voice called, "Come in! What are you waiting for?"

Heller's niece was married to Willi Dietrich. Heller had come to Sylvie's funeral. Since Paul had returned from Russia, the relationship had cooled, but he had not questioned the reason because he knew that the commandant was more than occupied in coping with an irritable wife, four daughters who all wore the Cross of Honor of the German Mother, a score of grandchildren, and a mistress who was the wife of a U-boat captain stationed in Brest.

"You've brought the Ganz report?" Heller leaned back in his leather chair, belched, then smiled and patted the bulge of his stomach beneath his uniform.

"No, General. But it's finished."

"Not important. Are you ready to leave? You want the rest of the afternoon off?"

"That's what I came to talk to you about."

"Take it," Heller said, misunderstanding. "Go home. Enjoy the April sunshine. Poland is not so mild," he added, echoing Willi Dietrich.

"Am I correct, General, in assuming that Colonel Dietrich called you from Warsaw and explained the assignment that's been offered me?"

Heller allowed his double chin to bob twice up and down on his throat.

"In that case," Paul continued, "could you explain it to *me*?" In rapid order, Heller looked puzzled, upset, then stolid. "Sit down, Bach."

Paul lowered himself into a yellow chair and crossed his legs. He sniffed, smelling smoked pork. Through the window he saw a streetcar rattling by. He heard a traffic cop's whistle blow. He waited; so did General Heller, but Paul was more skilled at it. The general broke the silence.

"Multiple homicide. A case that falls under the jurisdiction of the general government of Poland. Military, not civilian. According to Dietrich, no one there is capable of conducting a speedy investigation. He requested you. That's simple enough."

"And the victims?"

"Jews necessary to the war effort. More important, a Polish SS officer named Hrubow. Under the command of some—" The general glanced at a notepad near his telephone. "A Major Kirmayr. Commandant at—" He peered down again. "Zin."

"What is Zin?" Paul asked.

48

The general looked up. There was an expression in his milky blue eyes that suddenly fascinated Paul. The eyes were intense yet somehow blank. A glaze seemed to cover whatever window supposedly led to the soul.

"The place you're going to," General Heller said, "is in western Poland. That's all I know. Your services have been requested by Gestapo Headquarters Warsaw. You'll be under Dietrich's orders. When you get back here, you will tell me that you have successfully—or, let's hope not, *un*successfully—completed the assignment." The general's voice rose a notch from its customary quiet wheeze. *"That's all I want to know.* Do you follow me, Bach?"

"And if I request permission to refuse the assignment?"

"Refuse?" Again he echoed Willi Dietrich.

Paul patiently explained what Willi had said, and not said, but what they all knew: that a Gestapo colonel attached to the general government of Poland could do just about what he pleased, but in theory he had no authority over the Berlin Kripo, who operated as an independent arm of the Central Security Office of the Reich under the friendly umbrella of the SS. The order to conduct an investigation outside the Berlin jurisdiction could come only from the chief inspector, General Heller himself.

"Which leads me to request," Paul said formally, "that I be given your permission to refuse the assignment."

The general stared at him with blinking eyes. They were not hostile. They showed, if anything, a hint of dulled regret.

"Why?"

He said, with what he had convinced himself was perfect accuracy, "It's irregular. I'm led to understand that if I find a suspect worthy of indictment, he'll be turned over to the camp commandant. There won't be any trial. Just summary execution."

"Will you take my advice?"

"I'd be grateful for it."

"Forget your request. Go to Poland and do your job as well as you can."

"If I go," Paul said, straightening his back, "I go as a representative of the Kripo. As a professional. But—"

Heller stayed the rest of Paul's protest with an uplifted palm.

Frowning, he swayed his bulk up from the heavy leather chair and lumbered to one of the freshly painted yellow steel filing cabinets that lined the far wall of the office. He started to bend, then changed his mind and tapped the bottom drawer, an unlabeled one, with the toe of his polished boot.

"You know what this file is, Bach?"

"No idea, General."

"Personnel. A file on every man and woman who works here. There is a duplicate of this file at Prinz Albrechtstrasse."

Number 8 Prinz Albrechtstrasse housed the Central Security Office of the Reich, in the premises also occupied by the Gestapo.

"There is a file on me," the general said, kicking the drawer again, so that it clanged. "There is a file on everybody. Obviously on you, too. In your file, Bach, there exists a photocopy of a letter you wrote to General Eicke. You remember General Eicke?"

Paul nodded, although the question was rhetorical. General Theodor Eicke had commanded the Waffen-SS Death's-Head Division that spearheaded the German advance into Russia in 1941.

"The date of your letter, I believe, is January 1942," said General Heller.

"December '41," Paul said calmly. "By January I was back here in Berlin, in the hospital."

"And the original letter, the one you wrote in ink, is at Prinz Albrechtstrasse."

"I see."

"Do you? Do you remember what the letter said? Need I read it to you?"

"That won't be necessary," Paul said.

Paul's platoon had been west of Demyansk on the wooded banks of the Lovat River. Under a sunny December sky, they were digging frozen German corpses from the snow.

The corpses were mixed Wehrmacht and SS General Eicke's Death's-Head Division, both under the command of Army Group Center. A single blizzard had covered them in less than three hours. After a few days of sun, the snow had begun to melt. The eyes thawed first. One moment, Paul thought, they looked like marbles, the next moment they ran like jelly. The mouths gaped open as if they yearned to speak, but they were choked with ice. . . .

Late November had been wonderfully quiet; a week's rain and fog made all advance impossible. The men played skat in the bunkers. Paul wrote letters to his children.

> Dear Erich and Ushi . . . I hope you're studying hard. Not just what the school requires but what excites you. Almost all of the world is waiting there for you in books. . . . you have only to decide what part of it to make your own.
>
> I wish I could tell you where I am and what kind of a life this is. The censor would strike it out. Have you read *War and Peace*, by Count Tolstoy? There is a copy somewhere in the sitting room. It's most instructive, especially the parts about Napoleon, the emperor of France, who thought he could conquer the world. . . .
>
> Warm thoughts, love, kisses and hugs, from
>
> Your father

Six months of continuous fighting had driven the German armies to the edge of exhaustion. Battles were fought in gloomy forests, vast swamps, open plains crisscrossed by a bewildering network of rivers and streams. Ivan, Paul realized, had an expendable population. Partisans operated behind the German lines killing men with gasoline bombs. In December, counterattacking behind massed formations of T-34 tanks on a five hundred-mile front from Kalinin to Yelets, twelve Russian armies under Marshal Zhukov slammed Army Group Center into the ice. The Führer's response was predictable.

"No retreat."

"That's enough," Paul called. His men had been hacking for an hour with their shovels. "Load the bodies in the truck. We'll take whatever we've got to the command post."

He wanted badly to go there. He had lost his gloves, and the cold steel of the Schmeisser seemed to suck at his bare thumb and index finger. The Death's-Head Division had a supply of fur-lined gloves and thick coats. They ate the best chunks of beef. Paul's men wore expensive Swiss watches that had been shipped last month, un-accountably, from Poland.

The truck bounced down a muddy road that knifed through a desolate gray plain, past hedgehog bunkers and overturned tanks that looked like giant beetles. In the clear air the plain flowed endlessly to a pale horizon. Russia was too big. By then it was obvious to Paul that you could never conquer it. You couldn't even comprehend it. Napoleon had found that out.

A ruined village and the onion tower of a church rose from the snow like a mirage. They came to the command post. From a distance they heard the dull hum of airplane engines. Paul's men looked up uneasily, fearing another strafing by Stormoviks.

"Messerschmitts," Paul said. "You can unload the truck. I've got to find a pair of gloves—then we'll liberate some grub."

He trudged down the dirt road, hands thrust deep in his pockets, toward the supply depot. In the glaring sunlight a gang of people were gathered by a ditch under the leveled rifles of a dozen SS soldiers and their lieutenant, all wearing the bony death's-head on the collars of their coats; on the other collar was the green patch of the Einsatzgruppen. The Einsatz were special units first organized to follow the German armies into Poland to round up Jews and place them in the fifty-five designated ghettos. With the invasion of Russia their ranks were expanded and they were issued new orders: "Liquidate all gypsies, all racial inferiors and asocials, all Soviet political commissars attached to the Red Army, all Jews."

Some Wehrmacht soldiers from General von Seydlitz's 290th Infantry Division stood in a huddle to one side, shivering. Their lieutenant was arguing with the SS lieutenant. Paul approached slowly, skirting a puddle of mud.

The gang of people, he realized, consisted of Russian civilians: about a hundred peasant men, women, teenage children. Seated nearby were a dozen flat-faced, coatless Russian soldiers in dirty foot bandages. They looked immune to the cold. Behind them a Volkswagen van, engine revving, spat vapor into the frosty air.

All I want is a pair of new gloves, Paul thought.

The argument between the two lieutenants grew sharper.

"You're out of your mind!" the Wehrmacht lieutenant shouted. "A *hundred* commissars?"

"The rest are partisans!" the SS lieutenant shouted back.

"The women? The children?"

"They fight, you idiot. Get out of my way!"

Both lieutenants were young. The one wearing the Einsatz patch had rosy cheeks and a baby face; he kept his jaw thrust forward. The Wehrmacht officer was taller, darker, harder looking, with a ragged stubble of black beard. The Einsatz lieutenant wheeled around angrily on his sergeant, who had approached from the van.

"What's the problem *now*?"

"It's not working right. We calculated ten minutes per batch. It's already half an hour." The sergeant clucked his tongue. "They're still jumping around inside like kangaroos."

By then the Wehrmacht lieutenant had spotted Paul. He realized that Paul wore no Einsatz patch on his collar.

"Captain!" he called. "These people are being murdered. The Ivans are prisoners of war. They surrendered to my platoon. The civilians came along because their village was under our artillery fire. On behalf of General von Seydlitz, I strenuously object."

Paul's hands were freezing. He knew that the Einsatzgruppen were under orders not only from General Eicke but from Reichs-führer Himmler himself, who had conceived the extermination corps and stressed repeatedly that its rank-and-file members did not share any personal responsibility. He and the Führer bore the burden. Moreover, according to new regulations, regular Wehr-macht units could be ordered by the Einsatzgruppen to aid them in their work. Refusal meant courtmartial and a firing squad.

"There's nothing I can do," Paul said, drawing numbing air into his lungs. It felt like fire. "Be glad you're not involved. If you don't like what you see, file a protest with General von Seydlitz."

The Wehrmacht officer scowled.

Babyface from the Einsatz said coldly, "Thank you, Captain."

Without a reply Paul headed for the supply depot. As he passed the van with its engine running, he heard muffled grunts, the sound of fists beating on metal walls. His stomach churned. In his mind he repeated his words to the lieutenant. *There's nothing I can do.*

A friendly corporal showed him a selection of sheepskin gloves, cowhide gloves with rabbit-fur lining, and double-layered woolen mittens. Paul chose the sheepskin.

On his way back to the truck, unavoidably he witnessed the final part of the execution. The Einsatzgruppen had given up on the van with its inefficient carbon monoxide ducts. They lined up the peasants and shoeless soldiers along the length of the ditch. The bearded Wehrmacht lieutenant was nowhere in sight. Smart fellow, Paul thought. And lucky. Babyface stood to one side, puffing hard on a cigarette. The rosy color had drained from his cheeks. But he gave the order to fire. The harsh chatter of the Schmeissers was so normal to him that Paul barely heard it. He had seen men killed. He was not shocked by the sudden rending of cloth and flesh, the red spray. The Russian women died cursing. The Russian men and children died stolidly, as if death was a natural conclusion to an unsatisfactory life. The faces of the SS soldiers who pressed the triggers were filled with the disinterest of boys pulling the wings off flies.

Most of the bodies tumbled obligingly backward. The soldiers booted the few stubborn ones into the ditch with the rest, and its walls ran sodden with blood. By then Paul was gone.

The snow froze again during the night, so that the following day it groaned and crackled. Paul's platoon sat around the bare trees, oiling and greasing their weapons. Artillery grumbled off to the left, falling on the light-skinned bunkers; an experienced soldier in Mother Russia knew they were the worst places to be during a barrage.

After a breakfast of acorn coffee and cold mutton, Paul hunched down on the fender of the truck next to a twig fire and began to compose a letter to SS General Eicke.

He detailed the massacre of the day before.

Then he wrote: "A lieutenant of Attila the Hun once asked the barbarian king where their forces would strike next. Attila is supposed to have replied, 'Wherever there are people whom God hath cursed.' Attila broke every human law. He slaughtered women and children. He took no prisoners. It was said that grass never grew again where the Hun cavalry passed. And the judgment of history is clear. God's curse fell on Attila as well."

He added some respectful phrases, signed the letter with his name and serial number, then stuffed it into his kit bag to be delivered later that day to regimental headquarters.

Two minutes later, with no warning, a single artillery shell struck the other side of the truck, demolishing the engine, killing four of the platoon, and mangling Paul's left arm. A boot had been blown off, too; there was shrapnel in his thigh. He lay there for some hours while his toes froze. He dreamed of fresh oranges and his dead wife in her gray uniform with the twin runes, a Christmas tree from his childhood, his father's laughter . . . but the dream was all muddled up and made no sense.

When he woke up in the field hospital the stump of his arm was swathed in clean white bandages. The sleeve was neatly sewn with black thread. He felt no pain—it was as if the arm were still there. Thank God, Paul thought. He hadn't known if he could go on. Now, for him, the war was over. Under the circumstances, a left arm seemed a reasonable price to pay.

After that, for a while, he had wondered what happened to his missing kit bag, with his children's photographs and the letter to General Eicke. And now, in Commandant Heller's office, he knew.

7

Zin: February 1943

The clouds drifted south toward the Moravian Heights. The sun glittered off fields of melting snow. At Zin, whose name General Heller was destined to scratch on his memo pad some six weeks later, an order defining suicide as murder was posted on the walls of all four Jewish barracks. But in the cold week that followed, two men tied belts around their necks and found accomplices willing to kick away the chairs.

An informer named Guttman scurried through the starlit darkness to Lieutenant Hrubow in the Ukrainian barracks. The next morning, under a blue, diamond-hard sky, one of the accomplices was hauled from his job at the pig farm and dispatched to the camp hospital.

The hospital was a clapboard building with a large red cross painted on the front. The red cross could be seen from the railway platform, and it gave men hope.

SS Captain Dr. Lustig, a tall lantern-jawed man of forty-two who wore a caduceus on his peaked cap to indicate his medical status, reigned there. He sat most of the day on a brown velvet sofa—outdoors in the summer sun, indoors by the wood stove in winter—drinking French wine, writing to his children back in Württemberg, and reading novels about the American West by Karl May, a nineteenth-century writer who had never left Germany. Lustig identified completely with May's hero, a Rhineland doctor named Sternau who battled savage tribes of Comanches and bloodthirsty bands of Mexican revolutionists. Lustig dreamed of one day going to Arizona, where he would smell sagebrush, hunt buffalo, and sleep under the stars.

Lustig's Ukrainian helpers wore faded red cross armbands on their black jackets. A pit filled with burning sulfur ran the eastern length of the shack. When a patient arrived, the Ukrainians undressed him and then called for Dr. Lustig, who would put down his novel and then shoot the patient in the back of the neck. The Ukrainians booted him into the pit for cremation. Documents, letters, and snapshots were also burned in the pit by members of the garbage commando.

The second accomplice to murder was hanged on Roll Call Square by Lieutenant Stein. Commandant Kirmayr sat in his bungalow during the hanging and wrote a letter to his wife in Rosenheim. The woolen socks, he said, kept his feet toasty on even the most bitter cold day. He hoped to see her in the summer—with luck they might spend his holiday in the south of France. The hand that gripped the gold fountain pen was trembling.

But now it will stop, he thought. Now they will understand that I have limited powers of mercy.

A few days later, in the clarity of a frosty dawn, the Jews in Block A rose from a night of mutterings and groans. They were wedged body to body on triple-decker wooden bunks; if one man turned over in his sleep, it was usually obligatory for every man to turn. In the pearly light their red-rimmed eyes beheld a man hanging from a beam. It was Guttman, the informer. A wooden stool sat to the right of his dangling bare feet.

On the stool was a note in Yiddish written on white onionskin. It said, "What else? Of two solutions, a Jew always chooses the third."

Cheeks drained of color, the commandant planted a finger in Lieutenant Stein's thin chest. "This man mocks us. What does he think he is—the Angel of Death?"

"I don't think it was a suicide," Stein said resolutely. "I think Guttman was murdered."

"So what? By your new definition, it's the same thing."

One hundred and fifty men lived in each block. Stein selected ten at random from Block A and had them brought to the coal cellar, in the north quadrangle, where he always conducted his interrogations.

None of the ten revealed who had written the note. "They swear they were asleep," Stein reported to the commandant.

"Do you believe them?"

"With some I was very persuasive."

"So it's still a mystery . . . and not one that amuses me. Keep digging, Rudy. I hold you personally responsible for the unmasking of this man."

But then the suicides ceased. Stein met with Kirmayr one evening for a game of chess. Beethoven boomed throughout the cold night.

"You see, Major? It was only a matter of their realizing that we were serious."

"But may I point out that you still haven't found Guttman's murderer?"

"For all we know," said Stein, moving a pawn carelessly into the line of the enemy bishop, "he may be one of those who died in the course of my investigation."

With a sigh, Kirmayr snapped up the loose pawn. "God willing," he said.

Mordecai Lieberman hunted his man down on the same evening of his arrival and found him in Block A. He still wore the baggy gray uniform, but he had lost his leather briefcase. He stood tall and aloof against a wall, surveying with stony eyes his fellow residents, who huddled in little clumps on the damp dirt floor or on the wooden bunks, talking softly or praying. Several half-naked figures jostled for position under the trickle of water from a punctured gasoline tin. A wooden trough along the far wall served as a toilet. There was no drain. The level of urine rose steadily throughout the night. It was emptied by the garbage commando at dawn.

Lieberman introduced himself as the camp leader. "Appointed, not elected. Did you get the job as carpenter?"

The man nodded, squaring his shoulders. "It seems they're expanding their facilities."

"It will be an armory. What is your real profession?"

"Officer in the regular Czech army. A member of the Athletic Union of Prague. Captain Avram Dobrany, at your service."

As he spoke these words, Dobrany almost stood to attention. Lieberman laughed with rare warmth; for the second time in one day, he seized the newcomer's sinewy arm. "A *captain!* You have no idea how you'll be at our service! You're a Jew, aren't you?"

Dobrany took the question seriously.

"A Czech. My father was Lutheran and died when I was a youth. I was born into the Hebrew faith by virtue of my mother." He coughed. "That is to say, she was a Jew."

Lieberman opened his mouth to say something caustic, then changed his mind. Mother, father . . . who cared? You needed only one Jewish grandparent to be awarded the yellow star. The Czech Jews considered themselves to be an elite, generally as well-to-do as their German counterparts and equally happy to believe they had been assimilated. They viewed the Polish Jews as a rabble of lice-ridden peasants. Regarding the lice, thought Lieberman, they're correct. He had never known an anti-Semitic louse.

"You fought in the Czech army?"

Dobrany shook his head. "I served four years with the French Foreign Legion. I fought there. I have . . ." He hesitated, then shrugged. "I *had* the Médaille Militaire. It was in my briefcase. But they promised to give it back to me when I leave."

Still another one, thought Lieberman, who's sure that *it could never happen to me.* He would deal with that in a moment. Meanwhile he was impressed. A man with a past . . . maybe a criminal!

"When you got off the train, I saw no one with you. You're not married?"

"My wife and son were taken by the Czech SS a few days before I was detached from duty. They're going to a non-Jewish camp elsewhere in Poland. My commandant arranged all that." He gazed over Lieberman's shoulder at his shrunken blockmates wearing their *tfillin* and murmuring their prayers. Most were silent, staring only into space. Once again Dobrany's face clouded.

"Herr Lieberman," he asked politely—"what exactly is this place?"

At last, thought Lieberman. It takes them a while, but even the ones without eyes eventually ask. He cleared his throat, dug in his heels.

"A death camp, Captain Dobrany."

Dobrany's high forehead creased with vexation. "Please! We were told it was a labor camp. For some, a transit camp."

"To heaven." Lieberman waved at a pack of stick-thin Jews bent in one corner near the trough. "You see how they pray for admission?"

"I'm a straightforward man," Dobrany said coldly. "I don't like riddles."

Lieberman saw that he was dealing with a man whose experience was somewhat out of the ordinary. He was a Czech, not a Pole. He was not even sure he was a Jew.

"I apologize, Captain. Let me go back a bit and tell you what happened here. Otherwise you won't understand."

The Germans, he explained, had come to Poland as conquerers of an alien people—"It wasn't like the Sudetenland, where they were liberating all those ethnic Germans. But we were Jews, we were used to being conquered. We were experts at survival—we thought. 'If a goy hits you,' my mother used to say, 'bow your head and he'll spare your life.' It usually worked with the Poles—with the Germans, how different could it be? After all, they were the inheritors of Kant, Goethe, Mozart. We knew there were a million Jews in Germany who spoke of Herr Hitler as "our Führer."

"And they were clever," Lieberman said. "They understood something of our nature. If the SS had marched into Poznań and announced that they were going to kill us, imagine the result. An uncontrollable riot. We were docile, but we weren't dead between the ears. So instead they distributed identity cards. White cards, pink cards, yellow cards, pale green cards, workers' cards, non-workers' cards, cards for families of those who carried each other kind of card. We thought workers' cards were best . . . until the holders of the workers' cards were taken away one morning to a place called Treblinka. A labor camp, we were told. Then a girl escaped from there and made her way back to Poznań. She was lame and hysterical. She was only twenty-one, but her hair had turned gray like mine. She told us they were killing all the Jews at Treblinka. Skilled workers! Carpenters, bricklayers—all! Not possible! We decided she wasn't right in her head.

"But soon they began to play a game called Freedom of Choice. You know that game, don't you, Captain? In the ghetto, which we hadn't had for a hundred years—which *they* created to make it easier for them to control us—they would line up a thousand or so Jews and say, 'Everyone, go either to the left or to the right. You are free to choose.' No one had the slightest idea which path went where. Those who went to the left that day were taken away . . . never seen again. To Treblinka, Zin, Auschwitz—who knew? Who wanted to find out? Those who had gone to the right, like myself, congratulated themselves on being clever yids. Then, on another day, we had to choose again—right or left. But this time those who went to the right were the unlucky ones."

Lieberman calmly continued, as if he were relating a new version of how Columbus blundered upon the Americas.

"Eventually I chose wrongly. Who can win all the time if you flip a coin? I came here to Zin in a train with my father and four hundred other bad gamblers. I then discovered that the girl who came back from Treblinka was not crazy. I had no guide. I *saw*. Zin is a small camp. The others I've mentioned are better known. Your wife and son have gone to one of those. Wait, Captain, please . . . don't protest. You think I'm half-cracked, but indulge me."

The captain looked as if he were ready to throttle his informant. His eyes glowed like translucent emeralds; his hands clenched and unclenched.

But Lieberman continued implacably.

"I was allowed to join the workforce here. They needed bakers then. I told them I was a baker—I learned quickly to roll dough. Then I got sent to the welcome commando. I'm now a specialist in meeting trains. There's a turnover, but the commandant believes all his residents are specialists. I've heard him say to Captain

Dressler, 'I want to reach a point where we don't have to do anything. Not even press a button or blow a bugle. Our role is not to do but to *be.*' Such organization! There are kapos who head each workforce, which we call commandos. We have furriers, shoemakers, jewelers, garbagemen, girls who wash clothes. Name it, we've got it."

Lieberman's voice grew a shade shriller, like a blade turning on a whetstone. "But our main job, Captain—other than recovery of anything that's valuable—is extermination. We help to kill the Jews who come on the trains. The Germans supervise. When our job is done, there will be no more Jews left in Europe. That war will be over. They will still have to finish the other war, against England, Russia, America, but that's of small consequence to us. They will have won their war against the Jews."

During the last part of this recitation, Avram Dobrany had turned gradually paler. Lieberman noticed. He twisted one more screw.

"They use gas," he said. "You heard us tell them it's a shower. But it's gas. Then we bury them in the lower camp. Forgive me, Captain. You asked what this place was."

Dobrany began to blink rapidly. He suspected, Lieberman thought, but he didn't believe. And from the way his eyes grew gradually cooler and his head inched slowly backward on his shoulders, Lieberman understood that in his heart he still chose not to believe.

Lieberman, although he had never heard Commandant Kirmayr elaborate his favorite theory, would have endorsed it heartily. Hope keeps us going . . . in the wrong direction. Hope, here, is an enemy.

Dobrany's tongue flicked across thin lips. "I have a letter in my pocket from the colonel of my regiment in Prague—a testamentary letter to faithful service."

"You'll pardon my vulgarity, but you can use it to wipe your ass."

Dobrany battled to keep hope and sanity. "The war will be over within a year. The Russians are advancing—the Americans are going to invade this summer at Calais."

"By then, Europe will be no more than a cemetery."

In a trembling voice, Dobrany said, "How is that possible?"

"When the weather is better," Lieberman continued, unrelenting, "Zin will work to its maximum capacity. That means two thousand Jews a day. Stripped. Gassed. Burned. Buried. We are very efficient. Their death means our life."

"We?"

"I told you, but you don't believe me. We—the Jews. I, the others. Now you."

Dobrany repeated, this time with anger, "How is that possible?"

"When there are no Jews left, they'll destroy the camp. They'll plow the ground, plant potatoes. No evidence—unless you dig six feet under to find the ashes. Knowing the Germans, there may not even be any ashes. They'll ship them to the Rhineland for fertilizer."

The captain thought for a while, knuckling his weather-lined forehead. Then, as Lieberman anticipated, he shook his head. He thrust out his jaw.

"You exaggerate, Herr Lieberman. In times of stress, people have that tendency. But even if part of it's true, there's an obvious solution."

Lieberman's heartbeat quickened. "Such as?"

"Escape."

"To where?"

"Switzerland is still neutral."

"Captain, the neutral Swiss closed their border to us last summer. The right to sanctuary, they explained, extended only to prisoners of war and deserters. Also to the politically oppressed. But not to Jews. Not even," he said, "to Czechs born into the Hebrew faith."

Dobrany hunched his shoulders like a medieval ghetto Jew in kaftan and pointed hat. He was not aware of it. At that point Lieberman thought, *maybe he's ours*. Still, he had more to explain.

"Some have tried to escape. Maybe one in ten gets beyond the barbed wire. But alone in the forest, in winter, you can't survive. There's no food, there are wolves. In summer the Poles are all over the place. They turn you in quicker than you can say *'Sh'ma Yisroel.'* If you're still alive and they don't beat you to death for the sport of it, you're shipped back here."

"So you believe we're all doomed," Dobrany said.

"All of us, yes . . . if we do nothing. Most of us . . . if we do something."

"And what is it that you propose to do?"

Lieberman leaned forward—he believed he had his man. Why waste time? He spoke quietly, but his voice vibrated with intensity.

"Revolt. Attack the Germans. Destroy them. Then escape together, in a group . . . however many of us are left."

"Attack them?" Dobrany's green eyes grew tight and hard.

"You like those words?"

"If you're serious."

"I have forgotten what it's like to make jokes."

Dobrany arched his spine and inspected his companion from head to toe, then peered into his face as though he were alone in a laboratory looking through a microscope at some specimen pinned to a table. It was clear from his expression that he was not impressed with what he beheld: this scrawny, gray-haired, middle-aged Polish Jew with a carbuncle on his neck and a crippled right hand with two fingers missing.

"You have a plan?" he inquired politely.

"We don't even have guns. If we had them, we wouldn't know how to use them," Lieberman said. "But we can get guns—we know how to do that. And you can teach us how they work. You can help us make up the plan."

"You want me to lead your revolt?"

Lieberman raised his gnarled hand; he had lost the two fingers to frostbite that first winter in the Poznań ghetto. "We don't know your capabilities yet. We already have a committee, a leader."

"You, Lieberman?"

"I'm too old. I'm forty-nine. Before the war I was a bookseller. A member of the Socialist Worker party . . . an armchair Zionist. Big deal. Our leader is younger. More energetic."

"I'll have to meet him," Dobrany said.

"Of course. He'll want to meet you, too."

"Does your group have a name?"

It had none, but Lieberman made one up on the spot. "The Jewish Revolutionary Army of Zin."

"Very stirring." The captain wasn't sure whether to laugh or cry. He wrinkled his thin nose. The trough along the wall had begun to stink more than he could bear. A man nearby, too weak to walk, had loosened his bowels and fouled his pallet.

"I'll need some time," Dobrany said, "before I make any kind of decision."

Time, thought Lieberman. Time heals. Time kills. Maybe I was wrong—maybe this is not the man I looked for. But one will come.

Berlin: April 1943

General Heller sank once again into the soft leather of his chair.

"The point is that *I*, my dear Captain!—and Colonel Dietrich, who got wind of it as soon as the Gestapo began its investigation—stood up for you. I said, 'I need this man! One-armed or not, I don't give a damn. He can be of service to the Reich at what he does best. Who knows under what circumstances he wrote that foolish letter?'" The general thumped his desk, so that the ashtray and water pitcher shook. "I'm too old to go to Russia, for which I'm not about to shed tears, but I pointed out to some Gestapo major—a pleasant enough fellow, thank God—that battle fatigue on the Demyansk salient was hardly uncommon. So they dropped it, you understand, but didn't drop their memory of it. Do they ever do that? I doubt it, *Captain*. Haven't you ever wondered why you're still a captain? You should be a major by now, at least. Hasn't that ever troubled you?"

"Only when I pick up my pay envelope," Paul said truthfully, with no attempt at humor.

Still, General Heller smiled.

"I've tried to do my job," Paul added.

"And you have! In a first-class manner! Never doubt that! If you hadn't . . ." Heller's smile faded and was replaced by that same look of regret that he had registered before when Paul inquired about the nature of the camp at Zin.

"From time to time," he said, "I'm asked questions about you. Quite a few years ago, with more zeal than foresight, you prosecuted two members of the party for the murder of a pair of Jewish girls. I remember the case perfectly. A misplaced sense of duty, one might say. Bad luck for you. But it's in *there*." His eyes flicked to the bottom drawer of the filing cabinet, then back to Paul.

"I've been instructed," he concluded, "in the event of any irregularities in your behavior, to report to Prinz Albrechtstrasse."

"I see," Paul said.

"Do you see? That's good! That's *excellent!* You see you have to go to Poland. Of course—that was obvious from the beginning. To a professional such as yourself, just another job of work. I hope you also see that no matter what you find in this place, a first-class job of work is required of you. This is Gestapo business. No shilly-shallying. *No failure.* Well, that's hardly likely, is it? I can't remember when you couldn't crack a homicide. I have faith in you, Bach," he said, for the third time echoing Willi Dietrich.

"But," Paul replied, "when I return, you don't want to know the details of the case."

The general wobbled his porcine head in firm agreement. "I wish you a safe journey." He considered for a moment, then opened a desk drawer and took out half a blood sausage wrapped in waxed paper. He pushed it between two stacks of paper across his desk, toward Paul. "A little bon voyage present. When you eat it, think of me. Think of what I've told you. Think of how pleasant it is these days, despite the bombs, to work here. In Russia, or Dachau, or in front of a firing squad, it's not half as pleasant. Not half, dear Captain!"

8

Zin: February–March 1943

God apparently took no notice of Commandant Kirmayr's prayer that his tormentor had died in the course of Lieutenant Stein's investigating the death of Guttman, the informer. The Angel struck again—a blow that made Kirmayr sick to his stomach.

Captain Dressler's favorite informer was a widower named Margulies, a former member of the *Judenrat*, the group of Jewish elders appointed by the Germans to govern the population of the Warsaw ghetto. He was best known then for an editorial he had contributed to the local ghetto newspaper on the subject of cooperation.

"In our every effort," Margulies wrote, "it is our obligation as Jews to prove that the prejudice about our unfitness for manual labor is absolutely false. We must cease complaining. We must increase our common output, which will increase our rights, including our right to exist peacefully."

After that he was elevated by the Germans to vice-chairman of the *Judenrat*. But his zeal to cooperate, as it turned out, had its limits. He was shipped to Zin after the discovery that he had tried to withhold the name of his retarded granddaughter from the selection committee. He was not a man without principles.

Margulies had been the bookkeeper for a large Warsaw jewelry store, and Captain Dressler immediately awarded him the post as kapo of the gold commando. Gold, jewelry, and clothing were the most valuable by-products of the resettlement scheme. In the first fiscal year of Zin's existence, the profit on gold alone was forty million reichsmarks.

Captain Dressler corrupted Margulies in the space of ten minutes' discussion.

"In this place, Pan Margulies, it's every man for himself. A jungle, Pan Margulies." He used the Polish term of respect.

Dressler explained that a special housing unit existed for certain kapos, with private rooms. "If you notice a new woman who appeals to you, just let me know. We're in favor of marriage. We understand a man's needs."

After Margulies became kapo of the gold commando, pilferage failed to decline, although he quickly weeded out several men he deemed risky, gave the list to Dressler, and they were sent to the hospital. But Margulies kept the most detailed books that had ever been kept. Printed in black ink in perfectly ruled columns, they were a joy for Dressler to behold. Momentarily, he was satisfied.

In late February two young sisters named Leah and Anneke Wijnberg arrived with a train from Belgium. A blushing Margulies appeared before Captain Dressler, who frowned at his proposal.

"You can't marry them both, Pan Margulies."

"I'd like to get to know them a little better before I make my choice."

"That's different. I'll have Lieutenant Stein speak to the sisters."

Margulies now shared a tiny room with the girls from Brussels. One March day he returned for his lunch break. He had a private supply of cheese and tinned sardines that he bought from the Ukrainian guards, who seemed to love gold more than life. He no longer even ate kosher. Bella Wallach, the commandant's mistress, knocked on the door after the bugle call ending the day's work to visit the Wijnberg sisters.

She screamed.

Margulies was spread-eagled on one of the bunks, eyes popping from their sockets, tongue black and extended. A note from the murderer accepted responsibility. It was not easy to define its tone.

It said: "Nothing to get excited about. Only another dead Jew."

Captain Karl Dressler was enraged.

"My most valuable worker!" he bellowed to Commandant Kirmayr. "Kapo of the gold commando! How dare he say, 'Only another dead Jew'? I can't replace this man!"

70

"Try your best, Karl," Kirmayr said moodily. After seeing the body he had gone to the toilet to throw up.

"This is not a suicide, Major, which you and Rudy can redefine to suit your separate purposes. This is not an unpleasant jibe at the Ukrainians. This is a *real murder.*"

"I understand." The commandant straightened his shoulders. "I joked when I called this man the Angel of Death. Now it's no joke. Whom do you suspect?"

"The sisters couldn't have done it. Their hands couldn't even go around the old lecher's neck."

"Do something, Karl. I want results."

Karl Dressler made efforts, but he discovered nothing. In a few days, desperate to make sure that the collection and classification of gold went smoothly, he appointed Rabbi Hurwicz as Margulies's successor. Although he could not be used as an informer, the rabbi was totally conscientious. He was slow, and he kept poor records, but to Dressler's surprise, the rate of pilferage declined dramatically.

It occurred to Karl Dressler that Margulies may have been a skilled thief as well as a lecher. Maybe the Angel was right, he thought. *Only another dead Jew.*

Another snowstorm struck the camp. Several Jews in the gravel commando, which worked outdoors all year around, contracted pneumonia and were put out of their misery at the hospital. When they were stripped of their clothes, Dr. Lustig found a few sheets of onion skin paper folded neatly and concealed in a torn boot. It was no longer possible to identify the owner.

But Lustig brought the evidence to Dressler, who brought it to Commandant Kirmayr, who popped the cork on a bottle of Crimean champagne.

"To the Angel of Death," he toasted. "Late and unlamented."

Zin: April 1943

A few minutes before six o'clock, a lone man walked slowly from the direction of the German barracks toward Roll Call Square. In the pockets of his coat he carried a dozen gold wedding rings and assorted bracelets. The penalty for their unauthorized possession by Jew, Ukrainian, or even German was death.

He kept his hands deep in his pockets to keep the gold from jingling. No wind blew today. Any sound in the frozen silence of the early April afternoon carried freely across the compound. The man's heart beat in a rising tempo. His head was lowered against the bite of the air, but his eyes pressed with fierce concentration against their sockets, searching for any sign of danger. He kept his steps as deliberate as possible through the melting snow.

He seemed to be heading for Block A, but at the last moment he veered westward on a muddy path toward Block C and increased his pace. He dared not look behind him now. He had already seen two German soldiers emerging from the hedge that led to the water tower. They would take no notice of him unless he took undue notice of them. He hesitated a few seconds but heard no noise from inside the barracks, so he leaned his shoulder against the wooden door and shoved it open. The barracks doors had no locks. The Germans, afraid of contagious diseases, entered them only if it was absolutely necessary.

The sun had already begun to set behind massed gray clouds. Inside it was shadowed and chilly. The man moved swiftly across the dirt floor toward the rear wall.

Then his heart heaved drunkenly. A flashlight flickered directly ahead of him. The beam shone in his eyes, then skidded down and across his body. But he was not blinded. He saw that the flashlight was gripped in the hand of SS Lieutenant Hrubow.

Hrubow was a Pole who had served in the Red Army. Because he spoke fluent Ukrainian, he commanded the eighty-man detachment that helped the Germans keep order at Zin. The Ukrainians wore makeshift black uniforms sewn by the Jews in Zin's tailor shop; therefore the Jews called them Blackies.

Hrubow was a middle-aged man with a broad Slavic face, a pockmarked skin. His narrow blue eyes glinted with alarm. He was bent to the floor on one knee. One hand grasped a carbine propped against the wall. The dirt at his feet had been gouged and ripped at

72

by some sharp instrument, so that there was a ragged hole some four inches deep and two feet in diameter. The man who had just entered the barracks understood instantly what had happened.

"It's all right," he said in German.

Hrubow raised the beam of his light once again, but not aggressively, to inspect the man's face.

"What are *you* doing here?"

"Looking for Grudzinski. The commandant wants to see him."

"Who is Grudzinski?"

"How should I know? Some Jew."

The other man now could see clearly what lay partially uncovered in the crudely scooped-out hole—a cache of gold coins, packs of grimy Polish zlotys bound with rubber bands.

Lieutenant Hrubow faced a cruel choice. He could offer to share the booty and then worry that he would be betrayed. He could report his discovery to Kirmayr, for which he would receive a commendation and a few extra days' leave. Or he could kill the intruder, make up a story to account for it, face the consequences . . . then slit a hole in his own mattress to store the treasure.

This thought process showed plainly on his simple face. With an exaggerated sigh, Hrubow rose to his feet.

"Wait," the other man said. "I want to show you something interesting." He dug into one pocket and took out a handful of wedding rings. Hrubow reached for them, but the man let them fall tinkling to the dirt, cursing at his clumsiness. Knees cracking, Hrubow crouched to pick one up.

The other man also bent, one hand flashing inside his boot to grasp the bone haft of a knife. He smelled sweat, old wool, the sudden exhaled odor of sauerkraut and rotten teeth. He spun Hrubow around. Hrubow grunted, flailed his arms, cried out softly, gurgled in protest. His murderer flung him in the dirt to avoid the spray of blood.

He dragged the lump of dead flesh to another wall, then returned, out of breath, sliding his boots to smooth the path and wipe out the trail of blood. For a minute he hesitated, then made his own difficult choice. He placed the horde of gold and money back in the hole, scooped and kicked the dirt back into place, and tamped it carefully down. He ran to one of the windows that looked out on Roll Call Square. No one was in sight—he still had time. He worked for five more minutes, putting everything in order.

Removing his other boot, he took out some sheets of folded onion-skin paper and the stub of a pencil. He scribbled a note, which he tucked under Hrubow's lapel.

As he emerged into the gloomy air, a clear bugle call from the watchtower behind the Ukrainian barracks signaled the end of the workday at Zin.

The Jews in Block C returned from their jobs to find a dead man lying on the dirt floor. Some shuddered and others wailed. The Blackie's neck and chest were soaked with blood.

"Don't touch the body. Don't touch anything. . . ."

"Call someone!"

"*You* call someone. I see nothing. . . ."

Some brave or foolhardy soul finally ventured into the twilight and was lucky enough to find Lieutenant Vogl. The young lieutenant was a tall, robust young man with soft eyes and healthy skin. He carried no whip, and sometimes he doled out extra margarine to the prisoners. He liked boys and was currently doting on one fair-haired muscular Dutch youth whom the other Jews referred to with a sneer as Blondie.

"Lieutenant—a terrible accident! By all that's holy, I swear to you we don't know how it happened! Come!"

Lieutenant Vogl rushed to the barracks and examined the accident, which consisted of an SS officer's throat cut from ear to ear.

"*My God . . .*"

Vogl soon discovered a folded note, in German, tucked under the lapel of the lieutenant's greatcoat. It said in so many words that Hrubow had been doomed to die from the moment he set foot in Zin. "I am just helping him a little bit."

Commandant Kirmayr conferred that night with his officers at an emergency meeting in the administrative bungalow. This time there was no bottle of champagne on the oak table.

"So! Now we know that we're dealing with a lunatic—and a dangerous one. An SS officer has been murdered! A Pole, but still . . . he took the oath. Who's next?"

The commandant felt quietly desperate. One day the camp would close. If he had less than a perfect record, he could count on a transfer to the Eastern Front. Poland was cold, but Russia was even colder . . . and Poland was safe. If he listened to the advice of Rudy Stein and Karl Dressler, he would not have a single Jew left to do the job at hand.

"The murderer's among them," Stein said grimly, "and there's only one way we can be sure to eliminate him. Get rid of them all."

It was a simple solution, and Kirmayr considered it for most of the next day. He went for a walk under a raw gray sky, his teeth chattering. But he decided that it would open the door to total chaos. Warm weather was coming; transports would be increasing. Five hundred new men would have to be selected and trained—the camp's entire operation would stagger to a halt. How would he explain that to Berlin?

He reached a decision. An elegant one, he believed. Let someone else take the responsibility. If it doesn't turn out well, how can they blame *me*?

He put in a call to Gestapo HQ in Warsaw and eventually stated his problem to Colonel Willi Dietrich.

"You're absolutely right," Willi said, sealing Paul Bach's fate as well as that of the commandant. "It's serious. You're not equipped to handle it. You're lucky you reached me. I know just the man to help you."

9

Berlin: April 1943

A milky early-morning fog, which the slanting April sun failed to disperse, cloaked the streets of Berlin. With narrowed eyes, Paul settled into the leather front seat of the chauffeur-driven Mercedes staff car as it eased through the streets on the way to the autobahn. They passed through a desolate area of ruined apartment houses, then a gutted electrical plant. The tracks of an S-bahn station rose into the air like a huge twisted paper clip. A repair crew was already at work, hammers ringing. They crossed a bridge where the Spree crept over broken remnants of docks. To the south the industrial district of Neukölln still smoldered. The air smelled as if a million cigarettes had been left to burn themselves out in a giant ashtray. A copy of the *Völkischer Beobachter* spread on the back seat of the car had a banner headline: ANOTHER CRIMINAL ACT BY AMERICAN PILOTS.

The driver, Lance Corporal Albert Reitlinger of the SS Motor Pool, maneuvered the car smoothly among the potholes. He was a thin and taciturn young man wearing a black leather raincoat. He had dark hair, a chin covered with acne, a somewhat high-pitched voice. He placed a thermos flask on the front seat between them.

"Coffee, Captain?"

"Later, Reitlinger. It was a short night. I need some sleep."

The bombers had come early, a few minutes after ten o'clock. Paul had been in the midst of washing the dinner dishes when the new sitting room window blew in from concussion, ripping right through the blackout curtain. It would take a week to replace it, and he would be picking slivers of glass from the carpet and plush sofa for days.

"Damn it, Erich! That window arrived this morning! I left you a note to tape it."

"I forgot," the boy muttered.

"Did you read the note? It said *right away.*"

"I told you. . . . I forgot."

Paul snatched blankets, a bottle of water, and some magazines. With the other tenants they thumped down the wide staircase with its oak bannisters. His apartment on Claudiusstrasse was on the top floor under the laundry room; he had five rooms and a surrounding balcony to grow his shriveled tomatoes. The old cellar, where tenants used to store trunks and furniture, had been remodeled to make an air raid shelter. The support beams were reinforced; there were sturdy wooden pillars and an iron door.

Ushi had taken a Red Cross first aid course at the League of German Maidens. She seemed to enjoy the raids, especially if someone suffered a minor cut or a friend had the time to bring a gramophone and records. The day after a raid the children's heads drooped at school. Examinations were postponed. There was talk that if the bombings worsened, the schools would have to be evacuated and the children moved to the country.

"How was school today?" he asked Ushi, when they had settled in a corner on their blankets.

"All right, I guess."

"What did you learn?"

"Nothing special."

It was a dialogue that took place with wearying regularity. Paul had almost given up.

"Can't you be a little more specific, Ursula?"

Ushi sighed and began to pick at her blonde braids. She was an angular girl of thirteen, just beginning to bud. She looked exactly like Paul and bore no resemblance to her mother.

In a flat voice she said, "We learned that when the Führer was in Landsberg Prison for trying to awaken the sleeping German people, his spirit was unbroken. This was the time he wrote *Mein Kampf*, the most important book of our time. He also exercised every morning and evening, because he knew that a sound body is the key to a sound mind. He was never depressed. He knew that there are always some setbacks on the road to victory. He . . . let's see . . . after that, he . . ." She shrugged her thin shoulders. "I forget the rest."

A cigarette would have helped, but smoking was forbidden in the shelters. "And your music class?" Paul asked.

"It was all right, I guess."

He asked no more questions. The girls at the middle school listened to lectures on Wagner, Beethoven, and Richard Strauss. Mendelssohn, Offenbach, and the other Jewish composers had been banned. The other subjects were Modern Geography, Modern German History, German Religion, and German Literature. Brecht, Freud, Mann, Kautsky, Marx, Remarque, and Zweig had not only been banned but thrown on bonfires. A special course was taught at all levels on the life of Adolf Hitler. Erich, at his gymnasium, enjoyed the same curriculum plus New Biology, German Mathematics, and German Physics. Einstein had not been banned, merely refuted and driven across the Atlantic to the enemy.

And for this, Paul thought, I have to pay hard-earned reichsmarks.

Two afternoons a week Ushi and Erich went to meetings of the League of German Maidens and the Hitler Youth. On Saturdays they backpacked or marched in torchlight parades, trumpets blaring, carrying huge billowing banners. Dwarfed by the stark architecture of the Olympic Stadium, they listened to lectures on "The Historical Danger of the Jew" and "The Aryan as the Creative Force in Human Development." The concentration camp, they were told, did not bear a German patent. The British had developed them in the Boer War and still maintained them in Egypt. They were necessary in wartime to segregate potential saboteurs.

"German boy! German maid! Temper your strength in battle! Be quick like a greyhound, tough like leather, and hard like Krupp's steel!"

For this, Paul thought, I pay in other ways.

The crunching sound of the bombs came from afar. Paul edged closer to Erich, who sat cross-legged on an army blanket wearing his tan Hitler Youth uniform, reading an article in Paul's SS magazine, *Das Schwartze Korps*. You didn't need to subscribe; it always arrived in the mail on time. He scanned the page over Erich's shoulder and saw an excerpt from an early text of Joseph Goebbels.

". . . Never do the people rule themselves. The mass is victorious? What madness! Just as if I were to say: marble makes the statue. History is a sequence of virile decisions. If the most courageous hold the helm . . . who shall cast the first stone?"

When Erich had finished, he looked up at his father and smiled. That smile said all. He believes, Paul thought. He let out his breath and said, "I'm leaving Berlin for a while. To Poland. I've arranged for Greta to look after you. Do what she tells you, Erich—please." He gave some details. "Is there anything you need before I go?"

"No, Father," Erich replied calmly, returning to his magazine.

They were glad he was going, he realized later in the darkness of his bedroom. At least, they didn't care. They had their own lives.

And tomorrow, Poland. I tried to get out of it. I did my best. If I had refused, I'd be going to Sachsenhausen, not Zin—and as a prisoner, not a captain.

Based on previous detrimental remarks concerning National Socialism as well as handwritten correspondence to a high personage criticizing the conduct of military operations in a war zone, and in particular a current unwillingness to do his duty as a state official, it is feared that his behavior constitutes a danger to the existence and security of state and people. . . .

Do what has to be done, he thought. Do it quickly and well. You're a professional. Pay the price . . . whatever it may be.

Wolkowysk: April 1943

Head bobbing against the pillow he had made of his greatcoat, he dozed in the staff car for almost two hours. The car heater pumped stupefyingly hot air into his face. He raised his head once when they crossed the old border into Poland and a second time when they skidded slightly on a sheet of ice. The road had narrowed to two lanes. Patches of snow lay like soiled white handkerchiefs on drab tableland.

The road passed through a village that ended in a railway crossing. Corporal Reitlinger pumped the brakes, easing the Mercedes to a halt. A freight train blocked the crossing—a group of Polish Order Police commanded by an SS sergeant were herding about fifty people into one of the freight cars.

Paul woke as the car slowed. "Where are we?" he muttered. "What's going on?"

The clouds had retreated to the horizon and the vault of Polish sky was as blue as the cupola of a Byzantine church.

"Sir, the village is called Wolkowysk," Reitlinger replied smartly. "A small delay. Some people being boarded on a train. Coffee now, Captain?"

"Yes."

The coffee erased the rottenness from his mouth. He massaged the leg that had been struck by shrapnel. "I've got to get out and stretch this damn thing."

"With your permission, Captain," said Reitlinger, "may I relieve myself?"

"Every soldier's privilege," Paul declared. "I'll join you."

Side by side near the railway crossing, the officer and his driver planted their boots in the weeds that lined the embankment. The yellow streams arced brightly in the morning sunlight, trickling down toward the tracks. "Always piss on a downgrade," Paul said, "and make sure the wind's at your back. That's the main thing I learned in Russia other than to eat snow. Now what the hell is going on over there?"

He peered into the sun. The train was an old relic with a wheezing engine, longer than he had realized—some thirty cars, most of them windowless boxes with padlocks dangling on latches. Wehrmacht soldiers with Schmeisser submachine guns sat on the roofs, legs swinging boyishly, faces tilted to catch some of the sun.

The Order Police formed a cordon around the train. A few of the doors slid open. From one of them Paul heard sounds of evident distress.

He buttoned up and walked slowly down the track to where the police had begun to prod the village people into a freight car.

"Line up in pairs!" the SS sergeant cried. "Warm meals when you arrive!"

The men and women looked baffled. They carried chamberpots and bundles. Children clutched at the legs of mothers whose babies were wrapped in shawls and pressed to their bosoms. An old man, bearded, wearing a black skullcap, hobbled by on a crutch. Jewish peasants, Paul realized. He had never seen any. The Jews of Berlin were—had been—prosperous.

"May I ask what's going on?" Paul said.

The young black-uniformed sergeant snapped his head around. Then he saw the Death's-Head patch, the sun glinting off the six parallel silver threads of rank, the twin runes, the Eastern Front medal, and the missing arm.

"Jews in transit," he said cordially.

"Yes? To where?"

"East." The SS sergeant was a trim young man with black hair. "My job is to get this group moving—the train's behind schedule. The ones aboard have come from Silesia."

"In closed freight cars?"

The sergeant's cordiality ebbed a trifle. "It's not an Easter vacation, Captain."

From the open cars some corpses were unloaded and stacked among the weeds like cords of wood. A woman leaned out of a door. "Is there water?" She tore off her wedding ring and thrust it toward a nearby Polish policeman. "Give us water, please. . . ."

Paul's hand dropped to the canteen at his hip. Before he could move, the policeman had shoved the woman back into the freight car with the barrel of his carbine.

From among the group of peasant Jews a woman and a bald young man darted from the pack, howling. Paul understood some of the Yiddish—something about a lost child. The sergeant's sweating men hacked at the peasants with truncheons and rifle butts, prodding them toward the black cavern of the railway car.

"Not quite full! Keep them coming!"

The bald father fell to his knees, thumping his fists in the dirt. A Polish policeman jabbed at his spine. The man pounded the earth as if it had swallowed his child. The mother had vanished inside the train. The sun poured golden light, throwing rich shadows. Paul stared. It was brutal. . . . it was disorderly. It made no sense. He moved forward and found himself in the midst of the mêlée. He had no idea what he meant to do. Nothing, he realized. He was just drifting, buffeted by the sweating, shouting policemen.

"Captain!" The sergeant reached him. "You're in our way!"

"Who is the authority here?" Paul demanded.

"I am." The sergeant tugged inside his overcoat and produced the Silver Warrant identity disc of the Gestapo—they required no outward insignia.

"This is how you do things?" Paul waved at the tumult.

The Gestapo sergeant said wearily, "Captain, don't provoke me. You should know better."

He brushed past Paul. The lost child appeared from the weeds where the bodies had been stacked, toddling with outstretched arms. A Pole snatched it up, hurling it like a stuffed toy into the open boxcar door. The father stumbled after it, shrieking. The sergeant crashed the door shut and padlocked it. Shadowed faces pressed to a tiny window cross-hatched with barbed wire.

The sun blazed from the faultless April sky. At a shouted order, the train began to rattle out of the siding. Not quite sure how he had got there, Paul reached the staff car. Corporal Reitlinger picked nervously at the skin of his thumb.

"Are you all right, Captain?"

Paul wrenched open the car door before the corporal could leap to do it. He dropped into the leather seat, heated by the sun. His hand rested on the dashboard, quivering.

"More coffee, sir?"

"You saw?"

"A trainload of Jews," Reitlinger said quietly. "They pick them up at many stops en route. Everything is scheduled in advance."

"For what purpose?"

"Resettlement, Captain."

"Do you *know* that?"

"For what other reason? Those Jews have done nothing to deserve being killed. They were peasants, Captain. I'm sure they're being put to work somewhere. A camp like Sachsenhausen."

Reitlinger's face was terribly young and unlined, but his brown eyes were as troubled as those of an old man's.

"You were at Sachsenhausen?"

"No, Captain." Reitlinger turned the ignition key and the engine caught, rumbled, purred.

"There were corpses in that train," Paul said. "A woman begged for water—she even offered her wedding ring. I wanted to give her the water, but I had no chance."

Reitlinger frowned, his hand resting on the throbbing gearshift. "Captain, that SS sergeant was Gestapo. They're in charge of all transport."

"So he told me," Paul said.

"He has the right to arrest you. If you interfered, you would have been risking your life—and for what? They would still have loaded the train."

Paul sipped the lukewarm coffee. There's no point to this discussion, he thought. Done is done. Not done is not done—in this case, perhaps, thank God. He reached for the map above the dashboard clock.

"You had better drive on, Reitlinger. I want to reach Zin before it's dark."

Zin: April 1943

A weak red sun vanished below the birch forest. A pale sunset licked at the horizon line. The evening wind blew chill as the staff car rolled down a dirt road to pass through the gates under the sign that said *Arbeit Macht Frei*—Work Liberates You. A German sentry stepped out of his box. He examined their ID and pointed the way to Commandant Kirmayr's administrative bungalow.

Reitlinger swung the Mercedes smoothly down the gravel path. An odd-looking place, Paul thought. Circling the camp on the dirt road he had seen a farmyard with pigs and chickens, barracks, a water tank, a Red Cross hut, a coal pile, and stables. He was reassured; there was normal life being led, work being done; the people were cared for. It reminded him of one of those Hitler Youth summer camps where people staggered awake at four in the morning to do calisthenics, take hikes and holy oaths, sing the "Song of the Nibelungs" and learn the formation of character.

But for the surrounding barbed wire and the four watchtowers. And the smell . . .

The smell tainted the purity of the evening wind. It wafted lightly to Paul's nostrils—sweet, slightly rancid, like old pork fat mixed with burned sugar. Gazing at the sturdy wooden barracks, the Tyrolean-style cottages with Teutonic motifs woven into the designs, the snow-streaked quadrangle surrounded by sheds and workshops, the square brick buildings that seemed to be warehouses, Paul wondered where the smell was coming from.

10

Zin: April 1943

"He's a soldier," Mordecai Lieberman said. "A former legion-naire. No doubt an expert in death. He'll inspire the others with confidence. He'll make nails that have heads."

At the precise moment that Paul Bach's car passed through the camp gates, Lieberman huddled in a corner of Block B with two other men—Stephen Wallach and Aron Chonszki. Together they constituted the committee to head the recently named Jewish Revolutionary Army of Zin.

Lieberman was cooking stolen rice on his little kerosene stove, a gift from the commandant following his appointment as camp leader. He had declined the offer of a room in the kapo block; he dreaded being cut off from his people. A lookout had been posted at the door. The trough had just been emptied, but the barracks still smelled of old urine and mold. Rats scurried in the beams.

"Can we trust him?" asked Chonszki.

Stephan Wallach spat in the dirt through a great gap in his front teeth. "What is the difference, Lieberman, between leading a revolt and organizing it? An organizer is a leader, and vice versa. You would like this goyishe Czech to take over from me?"

"He's a Jew."

"From what you told me, he doesn't know it."

"You're the boss, Stephan." Lieberman knew he was dealing with a man of delicate sensibilities and a recently crushed ego. A

87

sufferer. Wallach had lost not only most of his front teeth but his wife—it was no longer a secret that Bella slept with the commandant.

"But do you know how to throw a hand grenade?" Lieberman asked. "How to aim a rifle? Can you make a Molotov cocktail, or whatever it's called? Neither can I. . . . I'm not even sure what it *is*. Dobrany can teach us. He can work out a plan that we're capable of carrying out, considering all our weaknesses."

"So can I," Wallach said. He tapped his shaved skull. "It's all up here."

"They teach you that at dental school?"

Wallach, after studying orthodontic surgery for four years at the University of Vienna, had briefly practiced dentistry in Berlin. When he and Bella alighted from the train at Zin on a cold December day, he whispered to her, "This is a rabble. They'll need technicians. Let them know you're a journalism student. . . . they may have a camp newspaper. If not, suggest that you start one."

He had marched confidently up to the German lieutenant in charge that day. The lieutenant's appearance—the slight, almost boyish body in its neatly pressed black uniform; the pale face dominated by squinting eyes and gold-rimmed bifocals—gave him the look of an intense young scholar.

"May I be of service here?" Wallach inquired in his excellent German, his breath a cloud in the glacial air. "I'm an experienced dental surgeon."

"Open your mouth and let me see your teeth," Lieutenant Stein replied.

A little puzzled, Wallach obeyed.

Stein drew his Walther pistol and smashed the butt end into the dentist's mouth, knocking out most of his front teeth. He looked down at the young man who lay writhing in the gray slush that spattered the platform.

"Now you're just an ugly Jew."

Stein then gave the new dentist a job as assistant kapo of the dental commando. Wallach was handed a pair of pliers. As the dead were carted from the gas chambers to the lower camp for cremation and burial, the carriers would pause long enough on their yawing march for two operations to be performed. Members of the hair commando would shear off all hair. Then one of the dentists would examine the mouth of each corpse and extract all gold teeth and bridges.

For a trained surgeon like Wallach, each such operation took less than a minute. Murmuring Kaddish for the dead, he dropped the teeth in a basin. When full, the basin was carried off by a former Leipzig pediatrician to the dental commando hut, where other Jewish former doctors and dentists cleaned and classified its contents before turning them over to the gold commando.

The evening after his first day's work, Wallach was introduced in a dark corner of Block B to Mordecai Lieberman. He soon sensed that the older man had bottled up inside him a hatred and a lust for revenge that was more seasoned, although not more keen, than his own. There was no need for him to ask Lieberman, "How is this possible?" In the space of a day Stephan Wallach had aged ten years. He knew.

"What can we do?" Wallach demanded. "I beg you!"

"Are you afraid to die?"

"I want to live," Wallach said passionately, "but I have no fear of death."

A delighted Lieberman sketched out for him what they could do. Soon after that, Wallach was elected the leader of the little committee. An olive-skinned man in his late twenties, he held his mouth now perennially curled back over his missing and chipped teeth, the result of Rudy's pistol butt.

Wallach's young bronze-eyed wife had been selected over a month ago to give sexual service to Commandant Kirmayr. When Wallach heard of it, he confronted Bella in the north quadrangle outside the hair depot, where she worked at sorting gray from brown, long from short, then bundling it for shipment to factories that made bedding and hair-yarn socks for U-boat crews. He demanded to know if the tale was true.

"True, false . . . what's the difference."

He drew back his hand to strike her, but some weariness in her expression, some iron sense of purpose shaded by a tragic resolve, stopped him.

"How could you do such a thing?" His hand fluttered impotently in midair. "I would rather die!"

"But I would not."

Wallach suddenly remembered that this was his wife, the woman he loved. He had to comfort her; he still loved her. He thought he saw a way.

"He took you by force," he said grimly but with a little catch in his voice.

Bella was stubborn. Not cruel, but determined not to warp her vision and lose touch with reality. "Then," she said, drawing a painful breath of the cold air, "he would have had to kill me. The commandant does nothing by force. He has Prince Rudy for that. He asked me."

"And you just said *yes?*" Wallach nearly choked.

"Words to that effect."

"You gave in? You spread your legs for him without a struggle?" He spoke that way to hide his pain. His cheeks paled; his lips drew farther back across his cracked teeth so that he looked like a ferret. *Behold, you are consecrated to me by this ring according to the law of Moses and of Israel.* He remembered breaking the glass under his foot to recall the destruction of the temple. What was marriage now but another destroyed temple?

". . . You didn't plead for your honor?"

"Stephan," she said wearily, "you know as well as I where we are. Do you think there is such a thing here as honor?"

"For you, there's none. . . ."

"But I may survive," Bella said, refusing to lower her head in shame. "Probably not . . . still, now there's a small chance. And those who survive can serve."

"You're no better than Blondie!" he suddenly raged. He was too bruised, not only by what she had done but by her apparent determination to justify it, to see any shades of meaning. "Vogl feeds him sausage and egg brandy and sticks his putz you-know-where." He jabbed a finger at Bella, then withdrew it as if he had been burned by a flame. "A whore, like him! Not for money. For favors!"

"Blondie's not as bad as you think," she said.

Wallach let out a low groan and stalked off, shivering, through the snow past the kitchen toward Roll Call Square. He felt that he had never been so cold in his life. Aron Chonszki's bulk rose before his dimmed eyes.

"Stephan—" Chonszki blocked his path, gripping his arm with a huge hand that had the strength of a bear's paw—"are you all right? You look terrible!"

"Fuck you, Shoelace. Let go!" With a desperate surge, Wallach shook his arm loose from the powerful grip.

Chonszki hated the nickname and colored a little at the curse. But he was a good-natured young Jewish Hercules, with wide blue eyes and broad, Slavic cheekbones. He believed that Wallach was his friend and leader.

"I saw you talking to your wife. Has anything bad happened?"

"My wife? No more! God forgive her!"

Wallach burst into sobs. He rushed off awkwardly toward the barracks, head buried in his hands.

Chonszki stared after him, starting to feel like a fool. He had obviously said something terrible. He wanted to help now, but he was not clever enough. An oaf, he thought dismally. I've never been anything else, except a thief. . . .

Among the Jews, Chonszki was a rarity. He had been a butcher in Poznań. But in his youth he had run with a renegade gang of teenage Poles who broke into shops at night and stole bicycle tires, penknives, even radios. They accepted him because he was strong and knew no fear. One night the gang had been caught by the Polish gendarmerie. The other boys were given suspended sentences, but Aron, a Jew, served a year in a reformatory. Upon his release he was a frightened, thick-necked youth of fifteen who went to work in his father's butcher shop and scrupulously weighed every veal chop and bag of soup bones to the exact gram.

Because he now worked with the welcome commando and knew how to steal small parcels of food from what was always heaped on the ramp of the railway platform, he was still in remarkably good health. He could bend the blade of a shovel with his bare hands, and his trapezius muscles were so rounded that he almost looked hunchbacked. But his fellow Jews had given him the nickname of Shoelace.

In the early days of Zin the shoes of the doomed were tossed haphazardly in a common heap. Soon the Germans realized that this system made for chaos when the shoes reached Berlin and had to be paired. They ordered the arriving Jews to tie their shoes together neatly with their own laces. Aron Chonszki began to notice that in the frenzy of the selection process the knots were poorly tied and often came apart. Anxious to please his new jailers, he made it his business to rush around and retie the laces, firmly double-knotting the bows with his sausagelike fingers so that the shoes would never separate.

Sergeant Grauert, Lieutenant Stein's aide, noticed his zeal and said merrily to him one day, "Chonszki, I'm creating a new commando. The shoelace commando. It's going to be a one-man commando . . . and you are the kapo."

From then on, to his shame, he was called Shoelace.

Mordecai Lieberman understood that Chonszki was an artless man who lacked that typically Jewish quality of struggling between the horns of a dilemma and undertaking what is logically impossible. In his father's butcher shop in Poznań he had wielded his cleaver expertly through yielding flesh—why chop at bones? Lieberman had been one of his customers. Chonszki still addressed him by the Polish honorific—Pan Lieberman.

Chonszki was tireless and faithful. He could be trusted to do simple things, and he took it upon himself to feed Lieberman and act as a kind of bodyguard. He swore allegiance to the revolt.

"I know I'm not a real leader," he said quietly. "I'm not a hero.

But when the time comes, Pan Lieberman, I'll do whatever you ask. You can count on me."

Lieberman affectionately rumpled the black hair of the young Jew. We don't need heroes, he realized. We need sacrificial lambs.

An inky cloud obscured the moon. "Pleasure before business," Commandant Kirmayr said, smiling broadly.

Wearing his duty overcoat and dagger, black boots glistening with mink oil, he showed Paul to the guest cottage. The sitting room and bedroom were furnished with coal stoves, dark red Bokhara rugs, a ritual portrait of the Führer, and framed watercolors of Alpine slopes. The draperies were rose-colored damask of the type common to brothels and old ladies' parlors. The bathroom contained furry brown towels, a bar of French soap, and a big bottle of amethyst bath crystals.

Paul wandered into the kitchen, whose shelves were stocked with tins of butter and smoked herring, jars of rosebud jelly. Such delicacies, he realized, I can't even buy today on the Ku'damm.

Linking arms, Kirmayr ushered him through the darkness to the administrative bungalow next door. A fire sizzled in the iron stove, making the air smell sweetly of burning pine. They sat in leather dining chairs under the shadow of a cuckoo clock that had been transported to Zin by a Hamburg lawyer who had not survived the final selection at the railway siding.

A stack of records and a gramophone lay on a table next to a stuffed squirrel with glass eyes and a nut between its paws. Wooden shelves bolted to the wall were filled with the commandant's recently acquired collection of Meissen china. His ceremonial SS sword hung on the wall.

Kirmayr treated his guest to a meal of roasted capon and potato pancakes prepared in the officers' kitchen. He pulled the cork on a bottle of Mâcon '34. After dinner he set out a decanter of thirty-year-old Napoleon brandy and two crystal goblets that sparkled like fire. With a blunt fingernail he tapped the polished dinner table.

"The best Polish oak. I hadn't been aware that Jews were such

fine carpenters. Jewelers and furriers, yes. That's in their tradition." He chuckled with mild embarrassment; he knew he talked
too much when he was drinking. "I appreciate fine things. Have I
mentioned our factory in Rosenheim?"

Paul's cheeks were also flushed from the wine. "No, Major."

The commandant explained that he and Frau Kirmayr operated
a small establishment that manufactured the finest goose down
pillows on the continent of Europe.

"The down, as you may know, covers the skin of the goose. The
feathers cover the down." Goosedown, he emphasized, was far
superior to duckdown: less greasy, lighter, and cleaner. Down was
altogether superior to feathers. The best geese came from Hungary,
and it was a Kirmayr tradition—"unbroken even in wartime!"—to
use exclusively Hungarian geese.

"I inherited the business from my father, who had a partner
named Grossman . . . a Jew. Grossman, unfortunately for him, was
politically unreliable. He criticized National Socialism. He was
packed off to Dachau way back in '35." Kirmayr raised an admoni-
tory finger. "Not because he was a Jew. Our pastor went, too. So did
dozens of other priests in Bavaria. So did our mayor, a Communist.
Which brings me to a vital point, Captain. I despised our mayor,
the Bolshevik, but I had the greatest respect for Herr Grossman and
his entire family. We had Jewish girls in the factory—among our
most conscientious workers. In my school as a youth I sat cheek by
jowl with I don't know how many Jewish boys. What did we care?
They went to their synagogue on Saturday, we went to our church
on Sunday. That's absolutely all."

Kirmayr downed his second cognc in one gulp, caught his
breath, then refilled the glass.

Paul still saw the woman at Wolkowysk, begging for a cup of
water; the missing child, hurled through the air . . . He forced his
cheek muscles upward in what he hoped was a sympathetic smile.

"The reason, Captain . . . the reason for your most welcome
visit . . ."

During dinner the commandant had recited at random, almost

teasingly, certain details of his problem. He did so again now, jumbling dates and events but somehow managing to end with Lieutenant Hrubow's gruesome death in a Jewish barracks.

"With no discernible motive! Obviously this fellow's a lunatic!" Kirmayr calmed himself, clutching his goblet of cognac in both hands. "I've often heard that lunatics are the most difficult criminals to catch. One can never predict their next move. Isn't that so?"

"Often true," Paul said.

"Lieutenant Stein has a theory that the murders are part of some plot to get rid of Jewish informers and those officers who are overzealous in their duties." The commandant raised a bushy eyebrow. "And what is your theory, Captain? Whom do you suspect?"

"I've just arrived," Paul said, making an effort not to sound annoyed.

"But surely you must have a theory."

"It's a mistake to theorize before one gathers hard information."

"But there are so many clues! Have you ever heard of Sherlock Holmes?"

"Conan Doyle is one of my favorite authors," Paul said archly.

"The incomparable Holmes would have a field day, Captain. Please don't be offended. We know that the murderer is a Jew. He writes Yiddish and Hebrew, even German. The notes were found in different barracks, so he's got to be a man with a certain freedom of movement. He strangled this Margulies with his bare hands—ergo, he must be strong. He slit the throat of our Polish lieutenant—he knows how to use a knife. He's ruthless. Doesn't that narrow it down for you?"

"It may, once I've examined your list of prisoners . . . and if everything you've told me is a fact. I assume nothing. I don't even assume," Paul added, "that your avenging angel is a Jew."

Kirmayr reddened slightly. "Surely you're not serious."

"He might be Ukrainian. He might even be German. Didn't you say he was a lunatic?"

"One of *us*?" Kirmayr looked aghast.

"It's also possible that it's more than one person. And, since I gather there are women in the camp, he may be a she."

"Bizarre . . ."

"There I agree. But don't be discouraged, Major. The more bizarre an event is, the less mysterious it proves to be. Featureless crimes are the most difficult to solve, just as a featureless face is the most difficult to identify. I am paraphrasing Holmes. These murders committed in your camp are hardly featureless."

The commandant poured himself another cognac. He glanced at Paul's glass, noted that it was still nearly full, then fell back heavily in his chair.

"I'm sure you'll succeed, Captain. You're a professional, but I'd like to offer you as much help as possible. I'm going to appoint Lieutenant Vogl as your coinvestigator."

"I won't require a coinvestigator, Major."

"Surely, as a newcomer . . ."

"I've brought my own assistant," Paul said, inspired. "Corporal Reitlinger has been billeted in the enlisted men's barracks."

The commandant looked a shade downcast, but then he brightened. "I had one more thought, Captain. Penetrating the minds of these Jews is no easy task. Have you had dealings with them in Berlin?"

Paul heard the cuckoo clock begin to chirp the hour.

"That was not my job, Major. That aspect of police work is handled by the SA, the Gestapo, and the Economic and Administrative Department of the SS. I have nothing to do with the camps."

"In Russia you were not connected with the Einsatzgruppen?"

Paul said coldly, "I was a reserve captain of infantry posted to the Death's-Head Division. My orders were to fight the Red Army. Usually to the last man."

Kirmayr raised both chubby hands in a placating gesture. "And I admire you. At the risk of sounding boorish, may I state that I also envy you. You've done what a soldier is meant to do."

"Lose an arm?"

Kirmayr flushed. "I didn't mean that at all. . . ."

96

"A soldier is meant to die for his country," Paul said. "I haven't done that either."

"Captain, you misunderstand me. . . ."

Paul realized he was sweating. He reached behind him to open a window a crack, and once again he smelled the putrid scent borne by the damp night wind.

"The point is this, Major. Like you, I'm not a soldier by profession. I'm a homicide investigator. Your duty is to run this camp. Mine, at the moment, is to find a murderer."

"Still, it occurred to me that you might benefit from the knowledge of certain Jewish residents. I have one in mind, a man utterly loyal to the functioning of this camp. His name is Hurwicz—a rabbi. He translated the notes of which we've spoken. I'm told he's famous for his powers of logic."

Paul now realized that all Kirmayr had in mind was a way of getting firsthand information as to the progress of the investigation. And why not? He had nothing to hide.

"I'll be glad to use him in some capacity, Major. As I see fit."

The commandant knew he was up against a stubborn man. He would not push it farther. He had been impressed by his visitor from the moment he had stepped out of the staff car and so smartly saluted. From the oval head and thatched blond hair to the missing arm as proof of dedication and sacrifice, Captain Paul Bach was the model of a clean-cut, elite, superior German SS officer. And yet behind the wintry façade, Martin Kirmayr sensed something hidden. He contemplated the observant gray eyes, the austere mouth and jaw. Kirmayr fumbled for a while in an effort to sum up his impression, and then he hit on it.

Here, he thought, is a man much like myself, a fundamentally decent man scarred by events over which he has little control. He keeps his counsel until he feels on safe ground. Superficially a stiff-necked Prussian, whereas I'm a good-natured Bavarian to the bone . . . but in this struggle we're brothers. I can rely on him. I can trust him.

"In the morning," he said, "you'll see all there is to see in Zin. I tell you in advance that you may be shocked."

He paused, and Paul realized that he was being put to some sort of test. A reply was necessary—the pump had to be primed.

"I'm aware of that, Herr Commandant."

"But not fully aware," said Martin Kirmayr. "Very few back home are fully aware. We're forbidden to tell our families . . . did you know that? Even my wife doesn't know. Women have more sensitive souls than men. If they ran the world, I've often thought it would be far better. Why should they sit in the cave? Why should we do all the hunting?"

He had slurred his words. He's drunk, Paul realized. And so would I be if I were in his boots. Find the Angel, he thought, and *go.* He had begun to understand General Heller's words.

That's all I want to know.

11

In the barracks Mordecai Lieberman tried to concentrate on Wallach's words, but his mind drifted. Night and day he had one recurrent dream. White parachutes were floating down on the camp from a blue summer sky. Voices were shouting in English to the Jews that they were free.

God forbid, he thought, we should still be here in summer.

Then he remembered something his father had said to him on the day they arrived at Zin. In the hot train they had been so thirsty they licked each other's sweat. Lieberman's wife and children had already been taken to Auschwitz. His mother had vanished; they thought she had been picked up in the ghetto during an unannounced selection. His father, a retired mathematics teacher, was all he had left.

The welcome commando shouted at them to guard their valuables. "Stay with me, Papa!" Lieberman cried. "God forbid we should be separated. . . ."

The old man answered, "All sentences that start with 'God forbid' describe what is probable or necessary." He blinked wet eyes. "Goodbye, my dear Mordecai."

In a few moments he joined the others for the walk through the sunshine down Freiheitstrasse.

Many months later, in the winter, the day after he had been appointed by Captain Dressler as Jewish commander, Lieberman in his capacity as kapo of the welcome commando met an early-morning train. He was anxious to create a good impression on the Germans. He shouted angrily at both his fellow workers and the new arrivals. The train had come from Koszalin on the Baltic and passed through Poznań.

He was shouting at an old woman who had her back to him, telling her to undress more quickly. Her brown wool dress lay on the ground, but she was fumbling at her corset with stiff fingers, trying to undo the snaps. Suddenly something about the shape of her gray hair bun and the flab of her shoulders seemed familiar to him. He realized it must be his mother.

He rushed up to her and laid a trembling hand on her arm.

"Please give me a minute, sir," she said calmly, in German, turning to face him. "My fingers are so cold."

The old woman only resembled his mother. But it was too late; she had seen the expression that shriveled his features.

"What's the matter?" she asked, switching to Yiddish.

"I thought you were my mother," he murmured.

She digested his mistake. "Then you can tell me. Are we going to die here?"

Lieberman paled. "Don't ask that."

By then she had managed to unsnap the corset and twist it to the ground. She stood naked before him, with sagging gray breasts and bloated thighs reddened by the marks of the elastic. She lowered her shaky hands to cover her gray genital area. But her eyes, he remembered even now, were a remarkably clear blue.

"And you? You're a Jew. You're alive."

"I work here."

He was conscious that one of the German soldiers was watching him and that this dalliance with the woman might result easily in the loss of his job, his position as commandant, perhaps even his life. Yet he could not even begin to tear himself away.

"You see what I do," he murmured in shame, glancing over his shoulder at the same time. The German still had not moved; he was tapping his whip against the side of his boot.

Then he felt the old woman's hand touch his wrist. He had a slight shock, perhaps from the cold.

100

"You could be my son," she said. "Promise me you'll stay alive."

The words burst from him. "I promise, Mama!"

"Now I'll go. I don't want you to get into trouble."

For a moment he watched as she trudged toward the Road to Freedom, buttocks swaying. Then he bent quickly to search her corset for anything of value. He found a fine diamond engagement ring and dutifully handed it over to Sergeant Zuckermann, making the collection. He wanted to cry, but no tears came. No one cried at Zin—it would be a flood to drown the earth. He spoke to no one of his wife and four children; he hardly dared think of them lest he collapse with grief.

But the image of the old woman refused to leave his mind. He had loved his mother and father. But not since he was a child had he ever thrown himself into their arms and told them. For doing, he thought, there's always a reason to postpone. For dying, there's always time.

I'll keep my promise. I'll live . . . and more. From that moment on he resolved to preach the doctrine of revolt. How else could he keep his promise? It was not a conscious decision. By the railway siding it had been made for him with no effort at all.

He heard the rain gently tapping on the roof of the barracks. He turned to Wallach and Chonszki and said, "I'm going to speak to this legionnaire. Soon. No . . . forgive me. Not soon. Tomorrow!"

"We don't even know him," Wallach said. "He could be an informer. You can't tell who's a man and who's made of jelly until Prince Rudy raises his whip. I have my reasons to hate these bastards. This Czech has none—not yet."

"Not so loud . . ." Lieberman put a hand on Wallach's arm. He was a man who liked to touch people; he drew strength from knowing they were flesh and blood, even if the flesh dwindled day by day.

He was also a little startled by what Wallach had implied, that you had to have a personal reason to hate the Germans. It's not enough, he wondered, that they're gassing us by the trainload?

But at the mention of the word *informer,* he had turned to cast a quick glance at one of the bunks near the door. The lean young

Dutch Jew they called Blondie lay apart from the other men, hands clasped behind his head. His eyes were closed. Maybe he was sleeping . . . maybe not. His pectoral muscles rose and fell. Now and then he clenched his fists. He had close-cropped whitish yellow hair, a bladed nose, and cauliflower ears. The veins stood out from his forearms. His stomach was ribbed with muscle; he did dozens of sit-ups at dawn.

Lieberman had no idea what kind of life he had led in Holland, whether he had been a student, a worker, a bum. The Dutch Jews had been lawyers and businessmen, doctors and schoolteachers. Few spoke Yiddish. They arrived at Zin eager to please. Those who survived the selection soon sank into despair. The Germans took special pleasure in degrading them, turning them into informers. The Polish Jews avoided them.

Blondie's isolation was worse than most. When he arrived at Zin he was assigned to the transport commando—carting bodies from the gas chambers to the lower camp. He spoke to no one. His movements became slow and apathetic; he walked in his navy blue pea jacket with his heels turned inward, like an old drunk. It was obvious that despite his youth he had lost the desire to live. Then he met a thin, quiet Dutch boy named Pieter, a dreamer. They arranged with the block kapo to sleep in the same bunk.

Through Pieter's tender attentions, Blondie recovered.

After Pieter died, Blondie began sleeping with Lieutenant Vogl. He wore clean clothes and a pair of good cast-off German boots and took hot showers in the lieutenant's bathroom. For practical purposes, that was all Lieberman needed to know. He felt pity—it was a difficult idea for him to live with, that a Jew could be a pansy.

"He can't hear us," Chonszki said.

Wallach scowled. "Informers have big ears. Especially this one." He turned to Lieberman and spoke more quietly. "What did Dobrany say when you put the proposition?"

"He was a little confused. Maybe I rushed him too much."

"And since then?"

"Not yes, not no," Lieberman admitted.

"Lieberman, you're amusing." Wallach shook his head in

friendly disgust, then gritted his fractured teeth. They had other, more important matters to discuss, he said.

He set forth his plan. At the chosen hour, on some unnamed future date, the Jews would attack the Germans and the Ukrainian guards. Destroy the camp. Organize the escape of all prisoners. The new armory would be completed in about a week—when the time came they would break into it and take whatever weapons were needed. They would need a few pistols in advance. And gold, to bribe the Blackies for the pistols.

"Meanwhile," said Wallach, "you and I and Shoelace will each recruit five men. None of them will be told who the other members of the committee are. So if one man is caught, we won't all face disaster."

"Wonderful," Lieberman said. He scratched at some scabs on his scalp under the short gray hair. "That's a start. Your other ideas, I confess, still sound pretty vague to me."

"The idea is to kill as many Germans as possible," Wallach said savagely. "Starting with Kirmayr! There's nothing vague about that."

"Not vague. But wrong," Lieberman responded. Color rushed to his sunken cheeks. He had first voiced the cry of revolt, although many men had nibbled at the edges of the unthinkable long before his statement. He had given up his leadership to Wallach, a younger, stronger man. But he had never surrendered his surge of comprehension at the railway siding.

"The idea of the revolt is not to kill Germans," he said. "That's necessary—of course we'll do it. The idea is to live to tell what happened here. Do you remember Massada? The Temple was in ruins and Judah had ceased to exist. A handful of Jews defied the Romans. They all died. But if Joseph ben Mattathias hadn't written about it in *The War of the Jews*, who would know? Stephan, listen!" He raised a calloused hand that formerly had lifted nothing weightier than a book. "Maybe we'll fail . . . maybe we'll all die, too. But what we do must appear as a symbol of the Jewish people. Like Simon Bar Kokhba, who destroyed the army of Emperor Hadrian —against all odds, all logic. Like the Maccabees, who rose up against the Seleucids. No earthly power has ever been able to destroy us!" He grew more passionate; he was unable to control himself. "Our submission here wasn't cowardice. We are a people obsessed with God. We thought it was God's will. But I no longer believe that. The world must know that at the bottom of the abyss, in the pit of hell, *we refused to descend farther.* Let them say that when the Jews found the spirit to resist, the means to fight back— *nothing on earth could stop them.*"

Chonszki unhappily studied one huge palm. "If we all die, Pan Lieberman, what's the sense of it?"

Lieberman calmed down. He was a man, he knew, who often went too far.

"Let's not be too pessimistic, Aron. Maybe I exaggerated. But if it must happen, at least we won't die massacring our own people. Let me explain our problem," he continued thoughtfully. "The reason we haven't been able to act is because we saw the Germans as our masters. We still do. They convinced us that no one else cared about us. Maybe they were right. And maybe *revolt* is the wrong word. The Germans are not our masters—*I can never accept that!* We have to see them as our enemy, dedicated to our destruction. Then it's not a revolt. It's a war to the death! And we must fight a *battle.*"

Wallach had begun to fidget. "Lieberman, you think *I'm* vague?"

"For a leader, Stephan, yes, you're vague. I'm not the leader. However, I do have a specific idea that I'd like to mention . . . if it doesn't offend your leadership."

"Go ahead," Wallach said cordially.

"The women must be made part of this battle, or whatever we now call it. Therefore we need a woman on the committee. Stephan, I nominate your wife."

"*No,*" Wallach said immediately.

Lieberman leaned forward again. "Bella's smart. She's young and strong, and she's in the best possible position—God forgive her." He winced at the double meaning, but in his excitement he plunged ahead. "She'll know whether the Germans are getting suspicious. Whatever she doesn't know, she can find out. And we may need copies of the commandant's keys for the new armory. Your wife can get them."

"She is no longer my wife," Wallach sadly reminded him.

"Then you've got no problem," Lieberman pointed out. "Let's not argue. I propose a vote. Obviously you're voting no. It's up to you, Aron."

Swept along by Lieberman's enthusiasm, Chonszki nodded his heavy head up and down, slowly at first, then emphatically. He kept his eyes averted from Wallach.

"It's settled. I'll speak to Bella tomorrow." Lieberman was pleased. "Stephan, you are our leader. It's for you to say if the meeting is over. Is there anything more on the agenda?"

Wallach's dark eyes were flooded with a sorrow that only he could comprehend. He shook his head, and the meeting of the Jewish Revolutionary Army of Zin was adjourned.

A short time later Blondie, whose real name was Leo Cohen, yawned and swung smoothly down off the bunk. He sauntered out the door of the barracks, breathing the frosty air deep into his lungs. The stars possessed a thrilling brilliance.

Leo Cohen had no watch. Possession of a watch at Zin was punishable by death. But he could tell time by the stars. A year ago, when he was eighteen, he had dreamed of seeing those stars over Palestine; he had been an apprentice seaman then aboard a Dutch freighter sailing to Le Havre and Hamburg. Pieter, whose bunk he had shared after his arrival at Zin, was the son of a Reformed rabbi in Rotterdam. Friends and lovers, they had joined Hashomer Hatsaïr, a Zionist youth group that hoped to populate Palestine with Jewish workers and farmers.

"To hell with rabbis and intellectuals," Cohen had said to Pieter then, in Holland. "Let them split hairs and argue. We will *do*. Some day . . ."

At Zin Pieter worked on the camouflage commando, gathering brushwood and pine branches to stuff among the barbed wire. One February morning, after a night when it had been too cold to sleep, he slipped into the woods and dozed off against a birch tree. A

Ukrainian guard found him and dragged him back to the compound as a gift for Lieutenant Stein.

Stein was particularly hard on anyone he suspected of homosexuality.

"A sleeping Yid? Take down your pants, pretty boy, and let's see what you've got that makes you so irresistible."

In the freezing morning Stein began to lash Pieter across his naked buttocks with a whip. He had done this before to other Jews—he never stopped until his victim was too weak and torn to be of any further use in the camp. The hospital was the next and last stop.

Pieter screamed. Realizing he would die, he stumbled halfway to his feet, raised his head, and spat in Stein's face.

"*Wolfgang!*" Stein cried, summoning his dog.

The brindled Doberman was the size of a calf and had the powerful shoulders and brisket of a mastiff. His jaws were at the level of a man's groin. He could be petted by the Jews when Stein was absent, but the shouts of his master maddened him. He had been trained by Stein to rip at a man's testicles and penis.

Pieter's screams soon stopped. He lay quivering in the dirt while the Jews who had been forced to watch shut their eyes. Stein finally shot the wrecked boy in the back of the neck.

Leo Cohen, after the meeting of the committee, crossed the starry compound toward Lieutenant Vogl's bungalow. His hands were thrust deep in the pockets of his warm pea jacket. The Ukrainian guards knew him now. They smiled at him, pursed their lips, and made lewd gestures with their fingers. Leo Cohen—Blondie—blushed, but his step never faltered.

Vogl, tingling with anticipation, heard the light knock and opened the door.

The cuckoo clock stopped its warbling, and the little bird appeared at the door to chirp his final note. The commandant raised a warning finger at his guest.

"You should also be aware, Captain, that I am not responsible for the existence of this camp. I built it with mixed feelings, but they turned to joy because I was able to conquer those feelings. '*L'homme c'est rien, l'oeuvre c'est tout . . .*' so said Flaubert. We're grown men. We relish challenge. But in a sense—I've given this a great deal of thought—we are pitifully vulnerable to challenge. Do you understand?"

Paul nodded without replying. The commandant's face looked chalky in the lamplight.

"I administer the camp. I don't select those who come here. I don't decide what happens to them. Those are orders that come from above. Not from God, because then we could disobey them, but from our superiors in Berlin, who have powers that would make God blush. We're all soldiers. All doing our duty, as you pointed out." He wagged a cautionary finger. He was very drunk now, Paul realized. For what he's saying—if he said it to the wrong man—he could be shot.

Kirmayr's eyes narrowed. "Here's a favorite party slogan. 'The Jews are our bad luck.' But they had their own bad luck, too. They stood in conflict with a self-respecting Germany. They were too powerful." He poured more cognac, splashing a bit onto the table. "My nephew wanted to study law—this was back in the late '20s, when there were six million unemployed. So my brother took him to the Ministry of Justice in Berlin. They walked along a corridor, and my brother asked his son to read the names on the office doors. Mendelbaum, Levy, Ginsberg . . . almost all the names were Jewish. And it was the same then for the medical profession, the big newspapers, the banks, the stockmarket. That was their bad luck— their mistake. That wasn't *right*. There should have been more Germans in control."

"I'm a Lutheran by birth," Paul said, "but I'm a German. Those Jews were also Germans."

Kirmayr seemed not to hear. There was a little sad croak in his voice. "So my nephew joined the army. He lost both legs at Stalingrad."

It's time, Paul decided.

"I arrived here in the dark, Major. So far I've seen nothing. What do you do with the Jews who come on the trains?"

"That's another question." Kirmayr downed the cognac in one swallow. "We haven't got enough to feed all of them, so obviously we can't keep them indefinitely. We'd need a camp half the size of Poland. They would starve to death." He shook his head earnestly, then looked up. His eyes were suddenly pink veined. "Nobody in Germany had *any* idea. Ten years ago if you'd said to somebody on the street, 'We're going to kill all the Jews!' you would have been laughed at! Right, Bach? Wouldn't you have laughed at such a notion?"

I might have laughed, Paul thought. I might have made that mistake. But no one *did* say it—not to me.

"I've studied this," Kirmayr said. "Originally they wanted to put into practice an old Polish plan outlined by Marshal Pilsudski. One-third to be eliminated . . . the old and the feebleminded. Logical. One-third to be allowed to assimilate. One-third to be resettled elsewhere. They decided to create a Jewish state in Madagascar. Can you imagine? Down there among the baboons! Then the province of Lublin, here in Poland. The Poles screamed, 'Why us?' The Americans didn't want them—they already had too many. The French and the British have always hated them because they could outmaneuver them in business. So . . . what could we do? It was only when nothing else worked out that they decided . . ."

His eyes had turned from pink to a speckled lobster red.

"What did they decide?" Paul asked.

Kirmayr clenched his fist around the nearly empty cognac bottle. "I believe that there are good Jews and bad Jews. Good Poles, bad Poles. Good . . . whatever. The world over. Isn't that right? I try to help the good Jews who come here."

"How do you do that, Major?"

He seemed surprised, as if the question was naive. "I employ them. If they weren't employed, they'd be disposable. I feed them. I feed Bella. I fed . . . it doesn't matter who. Let me tell you an interesting story. At the beginning here I discovered that the Polish workers had ration books that allowed them an egg a week, so much fat, so much meat. I had an idea. It occurred to me that if every damned Polish worker had the right to ration tickets, then our Jews, who were in Poland and working a lot harder than the Poles, also had the right to ration books. So I told Dressler to go to the town council in Poseń. Told him to get five hundred ration books for our residents."

"And what happened?"

Kirmayr laughed sheepishly. "The Poles were flabbergasted. Dressler was a German SS officer. They had to agree. But they complained to someone at Gestapo HQ. I was reprimanded—a slap on the wrist, thank God. Colonel Dietrich in Warsaw thought it was funny. I suppose it *was* funny. The ration books were confiscated. Still, for that period our people received their fresh egg every week. Hot oatmeal. Artificial grapefruit marmalade . . ."

Paul heard his own voice as if from a distance—a telephone call from far away. "How many have you killed here, Major?"

"How many have *I*—"

"Not you personally."

Kirmayr swirled the last of the cognac in his crystal goblet. The lamplight reflected in the liquid created amber and golden flashes. He stared at them, seemingly hypnotized. "You have to ask Dressler," he muttered after a while. "He's an accountant. I rebuilt our pillow factory in . . . when my father died. I joined the party, the SS. I have a talent for building and organizing. I served two years at Buchenwald. . . ."

"What if you had refused, Major?"

The commandant swayed in his chair. "All men must die. Our common fate. Throughout history, whole peoples have been sacrificed so that more vigorous nations might emerge from the slime of human confusion. The process . . . is beyond one man's control. . . ."

"When you were assigned to Buchenwald," Paul said doggedly. "Or given command here. What if you had refused?"

Kirmayr drew a finger across the folds of his throat. "Or the Eastern Front. I'm fifty-three. I might not have been as lucky as you, Captain. A left arm is less than my nephew's legs. Less than a life." He reached for Paul's nearly empty glass. "You're not drinking. I'll get another bottle. You Berliners are such snobs . . . you think the air in Berlin is purer than anywhere in the world."

"I've had enough," Paul said.

The commandant shoved back on his chair, planted his square hands on the wooden arms, and tried to spring to his feet. But he was too drunk. He fell back, thumping a fist on the oak table, so that the cognac glasses rattled.

"This camp is nothing." His voice was a rough gargle. "A pimple on the map of Poland. The smallest one we've got. At Auschwitz they're building night and day. Room for two hundred thousand Jews. A city! This place hardly counts. And yet . . . it exists. We must do our job." He groaned. "That damned murderer is ruining my life. . . ."

Tears ran down Kirmayr's cheeks. Paul was unable to tell if they flowed because he considered himself worthy of blame as a murderer or because the other murderer was ruining his life.

The lamplight cast phantasmal shadows. The reek of alcohol mixed with the scent of crackling pine. Dropping back into his chair like a stunned ox, the commandant gave a last shudder. His soggy eyes closed; the lids fluttered to a stop. His head lolled on the silver-threaded shoulder of his uniform. He began to snuffle, then snore.

Rising unsteadily to his feet, Paul wrenched open the window. He felt a wave of dread as palpable as the shock of cold air that burst into the room. The cuckoo began to chirp the hour of midnight.

12

Avram Dobrany slept fitfully. He dreamed of his little son on the day he had taken his first steps, laughing all the while at his father, and then of the *souks* in Marrakech and the sweet-sour smell of roasting lamb. He woke shivering in the middle of the black night and gazed around him at the congregation of sleeping, festering skeletons.

I don't belong here, he thought frantically. A mistake's been made. *This has nothing to do with my life. . . .*

He was a soldier, a fighter. Throughout his life, little else had meaning.

In 1924, unable as a Jew to qualify for the Prague Military Academy, he traveled by third-class coach to Marseilles to enlist in the French Foreign Legion. He was eighteen years old. The recruiting sergeant, an ash-blond German, studied the brief application and the whiplike, hard-eyed young man who dropped it on his desk.

Dobrany had used his own name. He was not fleeing from any crime.

"Jewish?" the sergeant asked.

"Does it matter?"

"Not to me. What matters in the legion is that you follow orders. If I tell you to kiss my ass, will you do it?"

"Only after I've signed the papers."

The burly blond German sergeant laughed warmly, clapped him on the shoulder, and bade him welcome to the legion.

Dobrany fought in Morocco, in the last battle of the Atlas, against El Glaoui. When his lieutenant and sergeant were wounded, he led his platoon in a sweep through a *wadi* to wipe out a nest of Berber sharpshooters. He was awarded a corporal's stripes and the Médaille Militaire.

On leave in Tangier, he walked into a café on the Petit Zócalo and ordered a pastis. A drunken Polish legionnaire standing at the bar said, "Give me a cigarette, Jew."

"Are you talking to *me*?" Dobrany asked, amazed.

"Kiss my ass," the Pole said in disgust.

Dobrany smashed a bottle across the Pole's face, blinding him in one eye. He was reduced to the rank of private, shipped to France, and given six months' detention in the legion prison near Port Saint-Louis.

Upon his release and the return of his medal, he deserted. He made his way back to Prague, where he enlisted in the Czech army as a common soldier. After four years he was permitted to enroll in officers' candidate school. By the time he made captain, he knew it was as far as he would ever go.

It no longer mattered. He was a leader of men, a respected officer. He had married a Christian girl with a good income; he had a Christian son who one day would attend the military academy. To the world in general he thought, "Kiss *my* ass."

But on his papers, as the Czech SS discovered during a routine check in 1941, was the word *Hebrew*. He was not allowed to travel with his combat unit to the Ukraine; instead he was given a clerical job in a military hospital near Ostrava. In early 1943 he was stripped of his commission and sent across the border to Poland.

By the end of his first month at Zin, he had inspected the camp thoroughly with a keen and practiced eye. He understood prison life and believed he understood men. He watched the way the Jews shambled from the barracks to their jobs. Their clothing, which had once proclaimed each man's self-image, was a common gray, baked by dust, rotted by damp. These aren't men, he thought. These are shades, zombies, walking dead. They can't even look you in the eye.

He did his job with hammer and adze, dressing timbers for the

112

armory. He refused to eat the warm water with coarse roots floating in it that passed for soup, the black bread that was mostly sawdust and made your stomach howl, the hunks of potato crawling with grubworms. In a hollow heel of one boot he carried a handful of small diamonds, a legacy that he and his wife had divided on the eve of their separation in Ostrava. He traded a diamond with a Jew in the tailor shop for dollars and zlotys. A Ukrainian guard regularly delivered to him loaves of white bread, cans of sardines. An apple cost five dollars, a pint of vodka twenty. Ham, which the Jews wouldn't touch, was only twenty dollars a kilo. Dobrany bargained until he knocked the price down to fifteen. He ate alone in a corner of the barracks.

The Pole in Tangier felt free to insult me. He thought I wouldn't fight back because Jews are natural victims.

Not I. The Germans look at me; they know it. Even the one they call Prince Rudy avoids me. He sees a soldier. He respects what he sees.

Revolt against the Germans! Attack them with guns! Five hundred emaciated Jews . . . civilians who had never touched a trigger in their lives . . . Pigs would fly, and the day of the Messiah was at hand. What counted in a battle, Dobrany knew, was the number of weapons that could be brought to bear on an enemy, the discipline of the common soldier, the daring of the officer corps.

Lieberman was a dreamer, an agitator. A man is known by the company he keeps. The people here, he reasoned, must be special cases—malcontents, the dregs of Polish slums, perverts like Blondie, maybe even Bolsheviks. *They help to kill their own people.*

When the trains came each morning, Dobrany stuffed bits of oily cotton in his ears to avoid hearing the mewling of those who walked up Freiheitstrasse toward the brick chambers.

The trick was to wait. Eat well, keep your head down. If things turned sour, escape. A soldier knew how to live in the forest, how to forage food and cross borders. How to survive in enemy territory.

If it had to be done, he would do it. Alone.

Paul woke to the drumbeat of rain on the roof. The air was cold and damp, and a dull gray light bled through the damask curtains. His

113

head felt stuffed; his temples were swollen. He looked around him, trying to adjust his senses. Not Berlin. No Erich and Ushi to prod off to school. Zinoswicz-Zdroj, Poland. They kill people here. He peered at his watch in the dim light. Midnight? Noon? He held the crystal to his ear. A silence . . . a faint roaring, as of the sea. Time had momentarily broken down.

A moment later someone knocked firmly on his door.

"Reitlinger . . . it's you?"

"I have breakfast, Captain."

Rain dripped from Reitlinger's field cap. He carried a tray with steaming coffee whose aroma instantly assailed Paul's nostrils—real coffee, not made from chicory or acorns. Toast and blackberry jam. Paul began to sneeze—three rapid, draining bursts. He clutched at his forehead.

"What's the hour?"

"Just after six. You slept well, Captain?"

He nodded. Partly true. A brief, deep sleep. No air raid, no need to stumble down to the cellar. The bed had been firm, the pillow soft. Probably down from the Hungarian goose—far superior to feathers.

He remembered hauling Kirmayr from the table to the bedroom, awkwardly twisting off his boots, then spreading an eiderdown over the lump of snoring flesh. A human gesture, what any man would do for any other man. The commandant could quote Flaubert; he was not altogether a lout. The commandant had found a way to anesthetize whatever horror it was he faced.

Paul had weaved through the darkness to the nearby guest cottage. He pissed, brushed his teeth, climbed between the icy sheets, and slept almost instantly. The body makes its simple demands. In the black night he woke, heard the wind and a guttural rumble of thunder. He swallowed a Luminal pill in order to sleep. But he lay there during the storm, sneezing.

I must do my job. Find the murderer, then get out. To have no choice is a blessing. To have no choice is to know exactly what to do.

In the morning he sipped his coffee and spread the jam thinly on the toast. In wartime one developed habits of frugality; they were hard to give up.

Corporal Reitlinger said, "A Lieutenant Vogl is waiting outside. And there's another man hanging about. A Jew. He claims that the commandant ordered him to assist you."

Paul remembered Kirmayr's need to keep himself informed. "His name is Hurwicz?"

"Correct, Captain. A weird-looking bird."

"Give me ten minutes. Then bring the lieutenant in first."

Reitlinger ushered the imposing figure of Lieutenant Werner Vogl into the bungalow. By then Paul was dressed and wiping away the lather from his shave. Through the barred bathroom window he could see two women hurrying by on the path to the kitchen, chattering at each other like magpies. Rain fell thinly on their shorn heads. A milk white fog shrouded the distant forest.

Paul inspected his visitor. A vain young man—clean fingernails, uniform spotless. Jackboots glistened beneath a light spattering of mud. Dark-haired and good-looking, Vogl had blue eyes and a cleft chin that no doubt drove women wild. Paul detected a certain weakness in the face.

"You wanted to see me, Lieutenant?"

"Commandant Kirmayr suggested that I might be of assistance to you."

"There's been a change," Paul said. "Corporal Reitlinger is my assistant. Rabbi Hurwicz is going to act as my guide. But I'm pleased that you dropped by, Lieutenant. There are some questions you can answer."

Paul waved the ruffled-looking lieutenant to a chair beside a hammered-copper smoking stand. When he sat, his gleaming boots stood like stovepipes in front of him. Then Paul ordered Reitlinger to bring in the rabbi.

Hurwicz's appearance was startling; he was the first Jew here at the camp whom Paul had seen at close quarters. He wore baggy brown trousers, torn shoes, and a stained oatmeal-brown jacket wet enough to cling to his skin. Under it he had no shirt. He was so gaunt that it was possible to count the ribs. His flesh was the color of a dried lemon, his lips thin and blue. He had a scar on his forehead that looked like a miniature horizontal South America and a hooked nose as in the caricatures of Jews that used to appear on party posters.

RECOGNIZE THE TRUE ENEMY!

Set in deep caverns, his dark eyes were a little mad. His neck was a narrow white pole to which his head, wobbling precariously from side to side, seemed poorly attached.

"Good morning, Rabbi," Paul said cordially. "Sit down. Do you speak German?"

Rabbi Hurwicz wobbled his head up and down. "German, certainly. Also Polish, Yiddish, Hebrew. Greek, Aramaic, Russian." Most of the rabbi's teeth were fractured or missing, so that his open mouth resembled the merlons and crenels of a battlemented castle.

"For the moment, listen and observe. I'm going to ask the lieutenant a few questions." Paul directed his attention once again toward Vogl, leaving the rabbi to stand and wobble. The offer of a chair had been declined.

"Smoke if you wish," Paul said. "Be at ease." Vogl nodded and remained rigid. "I understand from Major Kirmayr that it was you who discovered the body of the last victim."

"Not quite true, Captain."

Vogl took a deep preparatory breath, then settled more comfortably in the chair, crossing his sturdy legs.

"The body was discovered by a group of Jews who live in Block C. They had just returned from work. I was at my post on the square, prior to roll call, when they rushed out and informed me. I then entered the barracks and was shown the body."

This was familiar to Paul. He felt at home when he was asking questions, probing, sorting out facts from fancy and evasion. A homicide inspector devoted most of his thinking life to the sins of others. Those sins were in friendly territory. If it was sown with mines, they could blow up only in someone else's face. Or so he assumed.

It's going to be all right, he thought. Last night I was drunk. The commandant even more so.

"The man was an SS officer . . . is that correct?"

"Yes, sir. A Polish lieutenant named Karel Hrubow. Mother was Ukrainian. Age at death, forty-two—married with five children. Former officer in the Warsaw Order Police. Conscripted into the Red Army January 1940, served in a Ukrainian artillery unit. Captured by the 56th Panzerkorps near Demyansk in March 1942. Volunteered for service in the resettlement program, accepted in the SS, and arrived Zin July 6, 1942. In command of the Ukrainian unit here. Satisfactory work record."

For all I know, thought Paul, Karel Hrubow may have loaded the shell that blew off my arm. The world is small.

"Excellent, Vogl. Did you know the man well?"

"Captain, we have little contact with the foreign personnel."

"Describe what you saw when you entered the barracks. Leave nothing out, no matter how trivial."

Werner Vogl was the son of a disabled World War I veteran, a drunkard who did odd jobs in a suburb of Düsseldorf. Whenever his son displeased him, he struck him across the face with a beer bottle. Young Werner fled home at the age of sixteen, joined the National Motor Corps, and was seduced by his local commandant. He applied for the SS. He passed the test that proved that his blood had been pure since the year 1750 and that there was no disproportion between his legs and his body, and vigorously denied any history of homosexuality. He swore the Kith and Kin Oath, completed a term in the Labor Service and then the Wehrmacht, further swore that he would marry "solely if the necessary conditions of race and healthy stock were fulfilled," and finally received his SS dagger and silver death's-head signet ring.

Posted then to Bucharest, he led a pleasant life as the aide-de-camp to an SS colonel in charge of deportations. He enjoyed the company of both young men and women in Romania. Because of his expertise in his field, he received the assignment to Zin. Like Major Kirmayr, he abhorred visible brutality, but he prided himself on an attention to detail.

In a precise, slightly mincing voice, he related the tale.

About twenty Jews had been present by the time of his arrival in

Block C, huddled by their bunks. More kept arriving. None stood near the body of the dead SS lieutenant, as if they might be held responsible. All appeared "scared out of their wits," according to Vogl. The body sprawled on the dirt floor of the barracks, about a meter from the south wall. Lieutenant Hrubow lay flat on his back. His open eyes held a reproachful expression. His carbine and bayonet lay in the dirt at his side. Blood had soaked his black greatcoat, his jacket, even his undershirt. His throat, Vogl said, had been slashed from ear to ear with a knife.

"You found the knife?" Paul asked.

"No, it wasn't there."

"Then how do you know he was killed with a knife?"

Vogl shrugged. "What other weapon would a Jew carry?"

"You're telling me that the Jews here carry knives?"

"Certainly not. But with a little enterprise, I'm sure one could be found."

"What about Hrubow's bayonet?"

"Detached from the carbine. Captain Dr. Lustig examined it carefully under a microscope. He found no trace of blood."

"Lustig is a qualified doctor?"

"As I understand it, he had a small practice near Dortmund. A country doctor. Quite dedicated."

"You said that as soon as you entered you saw that Hrubow's undershirt was soaked with blood. How is that possible? Was his greatcoat open? Unbuttoned?"

"I believe so."

"His jacket, too?"

"Also unbuttoned, as I recall."

"He wore a helmet?"

"A hat. It was on the floor near the body."

"What kind of hat?"

"Made of leather and rabbit fur."

Paul looked up keenly. "The kind that has a strap and buckles under the chin?"

"Yes, Captain. That's general winter issue."

"The date, Vogl?"

"Sir?"

"When did the murder occur?"

"Exactly a week ago."

"Do you recall the weather that day?"

"All the men's teeth were chattering when they told me what had happened. It was cold. Very cold."

"The Jewish barracks are not heated during the day when the men are at work?"

"There's no heating at all."

Rabbi Hurwicz had effaced himself completely. His eyes were nearly closed. He may be asleep on his feet, Paul thought. A nerve in his cheek jumped from time to time, as if a tiny animal lived beneath the yellow skin.

Paul turned his back, lit a cigarette, and stared out the window. Unheated barracks in the Polish winter. Well, they were prisoners . . . more disposable than most. Everyone in Germany was cold these days. He heard Reitlinger cough, and Vogl scuffed his boots on the carpet. The rabbi, he realized now, had not remarked on his surroundings or even inspected the opulence. He was indifferent.

Get on with it, he thought.

"Lieutenant—did you say there was blood in the dirt near the dead man's body?"

"I didn't say that. In fact, hardly any blood. That surprised me."

"Yet his chest was soaked with it. He lay on his back. His head was straight up, facing the ceiling. Think a moment."

"Twisted to one side, I believe."

"Which way?"

Vogl paused to consider. "Is that significant?"

Paul hadn't been facing Vogl; now he looked at him squarely. "I'd be grateful if you'd just answer my questions. Leave the significance to me, Lieutenant. Try to picture the scene in your mind. If you don't remember, say so."

"I remember that his head faced the wall. So . . . yes, it was twisted to the left."

Paul filed that away, then asked, "Who has access to the barracks during the day?"

"We do. The Ukrainians do. A Jew might, if for any reason he was excused from his work detail."

"Jews from other barracks as well?"

"Few of us are aware which Jews live in which barracks. The block kapo is responsible for keeping track of his men. But it's a lax system. The commandant is not strict." Vogl smiled sheepishly in apology.

"Do you have a record of men excused from their work details on that particular day?"

"Captain, we're too busy to keep those kinds of records."

"Let's get back to the blood. There was hardly any in the dirt near the body. Was there blood elsewhere? On the floor . . . or on a bunk?"

Vogl thought for a while. "I didn't notice any."

"You looked?"

"I didn't see any reason to look. The man was dead. I was only concerned with keeping the Jews from becoming more hysterical."

Paul had begun to pace the carpet, but now he stopped abruptly. "How do you feel about the Jews, Vogl?"

The tall young lieutenant's head jerked back a fraction; he looked startled. His eyes flicked for a moment toward Rabbi Hurwicz. The rabbi's scarred head drooped on its stalk of a neck. But Paul noticed that his eyelids had begun to flutter.

"I don't understand the question," he murmured.

"It was a very simple question. Answer as you please."

Vogl sucked in some air and stubbed out his cigarette in the metal stand. "I have no particular feeling for them as a group. The Führer has designated them as an inferior race. In general, that's true. There are exceptions. I've seen mothers separated from their children—they literally tore their hair, as any normal mother might do. They don't all have bulbous noses and beady eyes. Not all the rabbis have black beards, as you can see."

"I had a black beard," Rabbi Hurwicz said from the corner. "It's not permitted to grow it again. If it was permitted, it would be gray."

"Thank you, Rabbi," Paul said. "Please allow the lieutenant to finish."

120

But Vogl shrugged. "What more is there to say, Captain? I try to treat them as human beings."

"What form does that treatment take?"

Vogl reddened slightly.

"Never mind," Paul said. "I'm not trying to entrap you. . . . I'm just trying to find out how things work around here. Let's get back to Lieutenant Hrubow. Why would he have entered the Jewish barracks during the day, when the men were at work?"

Vogl regained his normal healthy color.

"Any number of reasons. To check on neatness. To search for contraband. To look for a particular person. Hrubow may have seen something through the window. That's what I believe—that he saw something out of the ordinary, entered, and was killed."

"But Hrubow was armed. Was there any sign of a scuffle?"

"None."

"Time of death. Was it ascertained?"

"It couldn't have been more than half an hour before I arrived. The blood was still trickling."

"Are you telling me there was no autopsy?"

"Captain, we have no facilities for autopsies. There are sometimes two thousand deaths a day in this camp."

The figure quivered on the edge of Paul's mind like a malignant bubble, trying to force an entry . . . then faded . . . burst, evaporated. *Two thousand a day.* He felt a stab of pain in his temple.

Get on with the job.

"The rain's stopped," he said. "We'll visit Block C."

Commandant Kirmayr tapped his gold fountain pen on the oak surface of his desk to call the meeting to order. A craze of tiny veins reddened his nose.

"You may sit, gentlemen."

The damp morning pressed against the window panes. The wood stove blazed, providing cheerful warmth. Captain Dressler, Captain Dr. Lustig, and Lieutenant Stein took their places on hard-backed chairs drawn into a straight row, as in a schoolroom. Sergeants Zuckermann and Grauert, Corporals Mannheimer,

Hirsch, and Munzing, stood at ease behind them. Only Lieutenant Vogl was absent.

"Today at lunch," Kirmayr said, "you will meet SS Captain Bach of the Berlin Kripo, whom I had the pleasure of dining with last night. A most competent and perceptive man. Vogl is already with him. The captain is here to do the job at which we have all so far failed. He's going to find the murderer of Lieutenant Hrubow. You will all cooperate."

The officers nodded solemnly.

Kirmayr hawked and spat some phlegm into a tissue that he took from a box on his desk. He crumpled the tissue before tossing it in an arc into the metal wastepaper basket a few feet away on the floor. He smiled at his success.

"Furthermore, gentlemen . . ." This was not easy for him to say, and he had been too jaded to prepare a precise statement. He raised his voice.

"Furthermore! When the captain leaves here for Berlin, he will report to his superiors. He's taken no oath of silence. He will no doubt discuss what he's seen with both friends and colleagues. I want him to have a good impression. I want him to say, 'Zin is a model camp. Efficient. Humane. Run by dedicated men.' Is that clear?"

Again the officers nodded. The commandant looked directly into Lieutenant Stein's olive brown eyes and saw through the magnification of his lenses that they were utterly blank.

"Rudy, I'm talking particularly to you. I want you to be careful. Discreet. No incidents in public. No punishment other than what's absolutely necessary . . . and even if it's necessary, I'd rather you postponed it. If discipline demands some action, do it so this captain doesn't get wind of it."

"Yes, Major."

"That applies to all of you." Kirmayr struggled to his feet. For a moment he felt dizzy, but he recovered.

"I commend you all. I've heard Reichsführer Himmler say privately that what happens here is a chapter of history that will never be written. By comparison a soldier's job in battle is often easier—he faces an armed enemy, not a defenseless, whimpering Jew. To do our work," Kirmayr added, "and still retain our fundamental decency—and we *have*, gentlemen!—is a triumph of which every man in this room can be proud until the day he dies." He fought for breath. "You may go now."

13

Their boots made sucking sounds through the mud. An opaque black mass of clouds had formed in the skies. The clouds seemed riveted together by iron chains.

Lieutenant Vogl threw open the door to Block C, and Paul stepped inside, followed by Vogl, Corporal Reitlinger, and Rabbi Hurwicz. Paul stared for a minute at the tiers of slabbed wooden bunks, the tongued-and-grooved pine walls, the single slop bucket in a far corner, the trough that served as a toilet. The cold air was rancid with the odors of feces and old sweat. Paul wondered, how could they stand it?

"Show me exactly where you found the body, Lieutenant."

Guided to the spot, he bent to one knee and studied the earth. A week had passed. But he stayed pondering for several minutes, trying to reconstruct what had taken place. Then he rose and walked slowly down the aisles, between the three-tiered hutches and along all four walls, eyes lowered to the dirt. At one point near the north wall, directly opposite and as far from where the body was found as possible, he paused for half a minute.

When he had finished his tour, he confronted Werner Vogl.

"The other murder, I understand, did not take place in a barracks."

"That's correct, Captain. The kapo, Margulies, was strangled in his private room."

"How do you know he was strangled?"

"His throat was badly bruised. His tongue was blackened and sticking out. His eyes looked like fried eggs. I didn't see any other signs of violence."

"Did you look for them?"

"I'm sure he was strangled."

"Vogl, answer the question directly. Did you examine the body?"

"He was wearing clothes, sir. We never took them off. Of course, eventually they were taken off. But not by me."

Paul sighed; he would have to examine the remains himself, and he was no expert in pathology. He asked where the bodies of Margulies and Lieutenant Hrubow were buried.

Even in the gloom of the barracks, it was possible to see the color slip from Lieutenant Vogl's cheeks. He raised his jaw defiantly. "In a common grave, Captain, in what we call the lower camp. That is to say, a grave common with many others."

Paul let out his breath. "How many others?"

Vogl shrugged, as if to say, there's no longer any way to tell.

"The bodies are coated with quicklime to aid decomposition," he explained. "Then they're burned. You can no longer separate one from another."

"Splendid, Vogl. A technological triumph."

Paul spun on his heel and strode out the door. He recognized instantly that the root of his anger was absurd. One chance for technology had merely been defeated by another. If you killed them, did it matter what you did to them afterward? The dead surely didn't care.

In his lifetime Paul had mourned a wife, fallen comrades, his parents. He remembered many years ago, at the breakfast table, Sylvie had read aloud a newspaper account of a famine in India. Hundreds of thousands dying of starvation and typhoid. Bodies being carted to the Ganges for mass cremations. Paul had been preoccupied then in tracking down a rapist in the Hallensee district. He kept chewing his poached eggs.

Sylvie had said, "Don't you *feel* anything? A million people in Calcutta have nothing to eat. . . ."

"I don't know any of their names," Paul replied stolidly. "I haven't looked into any of their faces."

That still held true.

Lieutenant Vogl and the others followed him out the door into the chill of the compound.

"Where are the two thousand?" Paul asked, with a calmness that belied his feelings.

"I don't understand, Captain."

"The ones who will die today."

"The trains begin to arrive at about eight-thirty."

"How are they killed?"

"Carbon monoxide."

"Show me."

He would never understand why he had asked. Because to do my job I need to see everything, he thought. But that was not true.

With Reitlinger at his side and Rabbi Hurwicz wavering in his tracks, he tramped after Werner Vogl through the mud of the square, then through a gate in a barbed-wire hedge and down a shrub-lined gravel path leading from the railway platform. The Road to Freedom was raked and smoothed every day. They were heading toward what Paul had assumed yesterday were windowless brick warehouses.

Vogl showed them one of the three gas chambers while Rabbi Hurwicz waited outside.

A suction pump first drew most of the air from the room, a four-by-eight meter rectangle. The diesel motor, taken from a Russian tank and housed in a nearby shed, then pumped carbon monoxide through hoses connected to the shower heads. The inside brick walls were scarred with claw marks. The floors were tiled and slanted toward a hermetically sealed back door. The room smelled of vinegar that had been used as disinfectant. Outside, a ramp led to a loading platform crowded with large wooden carts that had been requisitioned from Polish peasants.

"In the main," Vogl said in his mild voice, "it's the most humane method yet devised for rapid mass liquidation. The guillotine is quicker on an individual basis, but it's impractical for large numbers. The firing squad—considering the numbers and the slowness involved—brings up a panic factor. Besides, these are not military prisoners."

127

He proceeded to sketch for Paul the history of killing that had led up to what he termed the most humane method.

From the outset of the program to solve the Jewish question, there had arisen certain psychological problems for the executioners. Once the classic method of the firing squad had been dismissed as inappropriate, it had been replaced by a single bullet in the back of the neck. The victim would kneel before a ditch that he himself had dug, the pistol would be fired, and he would fall into his grave. Simple and quick. This had been tried for a few months in some marshy fields outside Warsaw, but the SS soldiers who did the job began to complain of lack of sleep.

"They had bad dreams," Vogl said. "They truly suffered."

It was *the necks*. The muscular necks of the men—the slender white necks of the young women. The wrinkled necks of the old that reminded a man of his parents . . . the frail necks of children, even the fleshy little necks of babies. The memory of the necks began to haunt the executioners. The soldiers began to miss the targets at point-blank range. A bullet would plow into a shoulder or slice off an ear or even strike the earth.

"Then someone in Berlin devised the method of a van in which the exhaust pipe fed carbon monoxide into the back of the vehicle, sealed with a steel door. The van had only to be driven some few miles to a mass grave. Upon its reaching its destination, the occupants would be dead."

But it led to the same problem as the bullets in the backs of necks. When the truck was unloaded, the spectacle of the victims, who usually died in agony, proved indecent. Again the German soldiers complained.

Paul remembered the van at Demyansk.

"Finally," Vogl resumed, "a solution was reached, and here you see it in operation. It allows for a large number of victims to be treated at the same time—it offers a swift and relatively painless death—and it provides manpower from among the Jews themselves to take care of their own dead. No German soldier need suffer. I've heard there's a new gas called Zyklon B, even faster, that they're using at Auschwitz, but we haven't got it yet." He waved a hand at

128

the brick buildings. "This is the heart of the camp. The camp couldn't exist without these gas chambers, and the gas chambers couldn't exist without the camp. A perfect marriage."

Vogl's urbane voice had droned at him as from a great distance, but still Paul had heard every word.

"And the bodies?" he asked.

"They're taken in those carts to the lower camp."

"Show me the lower camp."

The wind gusted more sharply, so that from afar the boughs of the forest rustled. They walked under a lead-colored sky past the stench of latrines, down a gentle slope into a misted landscape, then through a barbed-wire gate in yet another hedgerow guarded by two tired-looking SS soldiers who nevertheless jumped quickly to attention.

Here there were smaller barracks, one for Jews and one for guards, in a large field. Two giant excavators stood in the gray mud. Their steel arms ended in sets of teeth that were agape like the jaws of beached sharks. The earth seemed to be steaming. Two open ditches, six feet wide and perhaps a hundred forty feet long, ran parallel toward the forest. The forest looked darkly mysterious, like the forest in children's fairy tales where evil creatures lurked. The sweet aroma of charred flesh swirled through the mist.

"The burial commando are in their barracks," Vogl explained, stuffing his hands in his pockets. "They can sleep until the trains come."

Paul felt the earth move slightly beneath his feet. A chocolate brown bubble the size and shape of a truck tire rose obscenely from the earth a few yards away, then burst with a soft prolonged hiss like that of a helium balloon. The swift smell of putrefaction that wafted toward them was nearly unbearable. Paul took a step backward.

"What is *that*?" he cried.

Vogl cleared his throat. "We must be standing on a grave, Captain. . . . the gases from the bodies expand and rise. Don't worry—it stops after a minute or two."

Paul shut his eyes for a moment, then opened them and glanced at Reitlinger, who looked pale. But Vogl seemed fine; if anything, his face was ruddier than in the barracks. The rabbi had also shut his eyes, but his lips were moving.

Paul, when he had recovered his composure and assured himself that he would not throw up, asked to be shown where Margulies had lived and died.

Margulies's former room, in the low pine building reserved for kapos, had been inherited by Rabbi Hurwicz. It was furnished with a small rickety table, a wooden chair, and a narrow cot on top of which lay a threadbare blanket and a gray pillow. A rusting metal sink with one faucet for cold water leaned at an odd angle against the wall. The floor was covered with wooden planks, and a light bulb of low wattage hung from the ceiling by a black wire. The wooden door had a sliding metal bolt on the inside. A small window let in some threads of gray light. The room smelled of mold and rat droppings.

The rabbi again declined to sit. Paul lowered himself to the cot, the springs sagging under his weight. "You live here now, Rabbi?"

"Yes, Herr Captain."

"Was the room furnished the same way when Margulies occupied it?"

The rabbi's obsidian eyes popped a little.

"You were never here," Paul inquired, "or you don't know?"

"The kapo didn't invite me to visit."

Lieutenant Vogl interrupted. "I believe that there was a second bed and two more chairs."

"And the door had the same bolt?"

"I think so."

"You're assuming, Vogl, or do you know?"

"I remember the bolt. I came here to examine the body with Captain Dressler a few minutes after it was discovered."

"And in this instance who discovered it?"

"A Jewess named Bella Wallach. A protégé of the commandant."

Paul remembered the name. He hesitated a few seconds before he said, "I want to talk with her."

"When, Captain?"

"Right now."

After Vogl left, Paul rose and took several turns around the room, moving in concentric circles and thumping his boots on the floorboards. As he did so, he watched the rabbi's face, but it revealed only boredom. Then he sat down on the single wobbly wooden chair and lit a cigarette. He glanced up at Reitlinger, who had regained the color lost during the tour.

"Corporal? Any conclusions?"

"About what, Captain?"

"For the moment—even though it's difficult—let's confine ourselves to the question of Lieutenant Hrubow's murder. What have you learned?"

"Well . . . it seems clear that when the lieutenant looked through the window of the barracks, he saw something unusual. He entered. The assailant, who was probably in hiding, leaped out at him, and cut his throat. That's my general impression. But I haven't the slightest idea what the motive could be."

Paul shook his head. "Don't worry about motives, Reitlinger— they turn up in good time. And never trust to general impressions. Concentrate on observable details. The goal in any investigation is to isolate probable facts from embellishments and theory. Forgive me if I'm being pedantic. The truth is I like to remind myself from time to time . . . because I forget, too."

He inclined his head and touched the breast of his uniform with his hand. Then he looked up smartly. His voice grew firmer.

"Lieutenant Vogl's suggestion that Hrubow spied something through the window is nonsense. I looked through those windows. They're filthy, the glass is of poor quality. From outdoors, in daytime, you can't see deeply into a room unless strong lights are burning. There's the dimmest kind of electricity in there. So when Lieutenant Hrubow entered the block, it wasn't because of any immediate suspicion. He had another reason."

Paul turned toward Rabbi Hurwicz, having noted that his head was wagging up and down in agreement. He had thought the rabbi was half-asleep.

"You agree with me, Rabbi?"

"Agree?"

"With my conclusion."

"What conclusion?"

Paul grew a little annoyed. "Rabbi, Commandant Kirmayr asked me to accept your help in this investigation. The commandant tells me you're a famous logician. I've been under the impression, however, that you're not interested."

The rabbi shrugged nonchalantly. "I made one or two observations. . . . maybe they're right, maybe they're wrong. We say, 'Out of snow you can't make cheesecake.'"

"What did you observe?" Paul asked, not bothering to hide his impatience.

Rabbi Hurwicz was a little frightened by this overbearing, hatchet-faced SS officer who had nothing to do with the running of the camp but was nonetheless poking his thin nose and one arm into every conceivable place, asking more questions than a yeshiva student. He carried no whip and made no threats. But they were all unpredictable.

A logician? The rabbi did not consider himself a logician. He was a scholar of Torah and Talmud. He understood that the Talmud and its commentaries were not logical treatises. They were Halakah—the Law. To interpret them correctly required a mastery of divine intent and human capability, not of reason. To believe one had that mastery required a stubbornness that went even beyond faith.

In the city of Czestochowa, long before he reached Zin, the rabbi's grasp of such intent and capability had been tested by events that he privately believed made Job's trials comparable to those of a mouse with a runny nose. His first significant decision took place in 1940, a year after the German occupation of Czestochowa.

The resettlement program had already begun. Several young members of the rabbi's congregation approached him at the scruffy makeshift synagogue in the ghetto. They asked if it were permissible for them, as Jews, to purchase forged baptismal certificates from the Polish black market. They intended to pass as Christians, flee to the forests, and join the partisans.

Despite his own comparative youth, the rabbi was used to providing answers to many such *she'elot*—questions on fine points of Jewish law. But this was a particularly thorny one. Except for the three grave sins of murder, incest, and idolatry, it was axiomatic in Halakah that every commandment of the Torah might be violated to save a human life. But the rabbi also knew the mitzvah that commanded a Jew to be unafraid of any danger in the proclamation of his true faith.

"Let him be killed rather than violate the Torah," Rabbi Hurwicz replied, quoting Maimonides.

His young petitioners argued that in this instance if they didn't violate the Torah they would probably die. Halakah, they felt, therefore allowed them to save their lives. And in their hearts, while they were fighting with the partisans against the enemies of the Jews, they would still be faithful to the God of Israel.

But the rabbi shook his head. There was no way around the Law. The first purpose of the baptismal certificates would be to convince a gentile that the bearers were not Jews.

"It is an apostasy." He paused, stroking his face with spidery fingers. "And consider this, children—if you do escape to the forest, how can you be sure it will save your lives? You may die from starvation, or in a battle. Worse, you might be caught by the Germans before you get there. On the other hand, if you allow yourselves to be resettled in the East, you don't *know* that you will die. Without such certainty, the Law may not be violated."

The young Jews grudgingly accepted the authority of this response. They were unlucky: they were among the first to be rounded up and sent to the new camp at Auschwitz-Birkenau. Auschwitz was a labor camp. Birkenau was a killing center.

But the rabbi's next and most celebrated decision took place in August 1942, when the Germans decided to evacuate the Czestochowa ghetto, where thirty thousand Jews still survived. The German commandant announced that five thousand special white cards would be issued to the Judenrat, the Jewish ruling council. These cards were to be distributed to the most skilled workers and craftsmen and their families. The chosen ones would remain in Czestochowa; the rest of the Jews would be resettled.

The Germans had set up machine guns around the ghetto so that no one could escape. Thousands of men and women stormed the offices of the Judenrat, demanding and begging to receive the white cards. Windows were broken; files were shattered.

The members of the Judenrat literally tore their hair. How could they choose? Why only the workers and craftsmen? What about the Judenrat itself, the doctors and scholars, the pious youths who were the hope for the future? Should certificates be given to every member of a craftsman's family, including sick children and doddering grandmothers?

It was too painful to decide, and they summoned Rabbi Hurwicz. They asked of him a *she'elah la'Halakhah u'lema'aseh*—a question that demands an immediate response to a desperate situation.

Who should receive the white cards?

"Render a judgment in accordance with Torah," the Judenrat begged. "Whatever your ruling, we swear to obey it."

The August heat gripped the little room in a vice. Sweating profusely, Rabbi Hurwicz replied, "My beloved friends ... how can I determine the Halakhah in such a grave matter? Even when we possessed the Holy Temple, a capital matter such as this required determination by the whole Sanhedrin. Here am I in your office, without any source books and without the necessary clarity of mind because of these awful circumstances. I need ... time."

A rock struck the window. Glass sprayed through the room, badly cutting the rabbi's forehead. The men wrung their hands. "If a decision isn't made right now," they cried, "all of us will die!"

When he finally grasped the full urgent nature of the problem, the rabbi fell into what many described as a trance. He turned white as snow. He sat on the wooden floor in the stifling room, his long neck bowed. Tears dripped from his eyes, mingling with his sweat and the blood from the gash on his forehead. The tears were so hot and copious, witnesses said later, they sizzled as they struck the floor and formed a pink pool.

At last, in a trembling mellifluous voice, the rabbi gave his response.

"'Neither shalt thou stand against the blood of thy neighbour,'" he whispered, quoting Leviticus. "But also in the Talmud it is written—'Who can say that your blood is redder than his?'"

The rabbi meant that there was a contradiction in Halakah. Even at the risk of his life, a man must attempt to save his neighbor's life; but since mortal men cannot know whose life is the more valuable, a man cannot be compelled to do so. This contradiction had precise bearing on the matter of the white cards. He then quoted a Talmudic precedent.

"A group of Jews is confronted by gentiles who say, 'Give us one of your number. We're going to kill him. Or else we'll kill *all* of you.' The *Tosephta* says, 'Let them not deliver a single Jewish soul. However, if the gentiles make the choice, and if that man is guilty of a capital offense, he may be delivered lest the others be killed.'

"But now," said Rabbi Hurwicz, "We have a situation where those who are to be sacrificed are not specified at all. And it's clear that they've committed no capital offense. And who is to say that the holders of the white cards will truly be spared? They may also be resettled in the near future. On the other hand—"

"Rabbi . . ." One of the Judenrat, about ready to faint from the heat, interrupted as gently as possible. "The Germans gave us an hour. The time is nearly up. Our own people are out of control. You've heard our *she'elah*. Who gets the cards?"

The rabbi groaned, and fresh blood sprouted from his wound to mix with his sweat.

"I thought I'd made that clear," he said in a soft, desperate voice. "No one may seize a chance to live at the expense of others. The cards must be returned to the Germans. We will all leave Czestochowa together." Then he cried out, as Abraham had cried out to God and man, "Shall not the Judge of all the earth do justly?"

When the Judenrat returned the cars to him, the German commandant in the city was almost as touched as he was annoyed. But he bowed to the Jewish madness.

In the following week the entire population of the ghetto was divided into groups for transport to the various camps. Most of the craftsmen went to Auschwitz to staff its score of factories. A white sticking plaster covering his forehead, Rabbi Hurwicz stood nearby as the last of his congregation was herded aboard horse-drawn carts for the bumpy ride to the railway station and then to Zin. He was considered a strange man even in Czestochowa. He had not yet married, despite the many eligible young women thrust his way by the marriage brokers. But now, when he saw the women and children being led off to slaughter, he was not sorry for his celibacy.

Tears glittered in his eyes. Old and young alike kissed the hem of his black coat or his thin white hands and asked his blessing. After their first outbursts of rage had cooled, after they had contemplated a fate that seemed inevitable no matter how they twisted, squirmed, or schemed, they had forgiven him. They knew that without his instructive piety, they would be like sheep being forced to their knees under the ritual knife. Now, at least, they were like Jews.

The rabbi understood perfectly. History had reduced all *she'elot* to a single *she'elah*—how to sanctity God's holy name and die as a Jew.

14

Paul had never known a rabbi, although one had lived down the street from him on Claudiusstrasse in an apartment block inhabited mostly by Jews. That one had been middle-aged, a queer-looking duck with milk white skin and a black hat that seemed to perch on his head rather than fit it. The whole apartment block had been cleared out in '42 while Paul had been in Russia; when he got back the Jews had simply been gone.

The word *gone* had now taken on another meaning for him.

"Rabbi, I know you're not a trained investigator. But you've been ordered to help me. I'd be glad to hear what you think about the murder of Lieutenant Hrubow."

Outside the window, rain slanted down in the gray morning. Rabbi Hurwicz began to finger his beard. After the paths of decision he had trod in Czestochowa and since, here at Zin, this seemed like child's play at a Purim festival.

"You really want to know my opinion?"

"If you please," Paul said curtly.

"I think," he began, raising one crooked finger on his left hand, "that if the murderer didn't enter the block before the Blackie—pardon me, the lieutenant—then either the Blackie entered before the murderer"—he raised a second finger—"or they entered together." As Paul watched, he raised a third finger, signifying another possibility. "If they entered together, the chances are they were friendly. But would one friend kill another? Why? Only for

137

one of two reasons. Greed is the first. Jealousy the other." To account for them, he wiggled two fingers on his right hand.

"But who here owns anything worth killing for? Greed is far-fetched." One finger curled down. "Jealousy is more ridiculous. To be jealous, you have to be in love. No one here has the energy. It follows that they weren't friends—and therefore they didn't enter together."

The second finger of his right hand curled down. "Which brings us to the next possibility—that the murderer entered the block *before* the Blackie. If that happened, then either the murderer buried himself away successfully and then jumped out like a wild man from his hiding place to do this terrible thing . . . or else the Blackie, as soon as he entered, laid eyes on the man who was going to kill him. . . ."

The two digits of the rabbi's right hand shot once again into the air to account for the alternatives.

"Where could the murderer hide?" he chanted. "He couldn't dig a hole and jump in. There's no furniture. He could hide behind a bunk! Yes, that's obvious. Where else? Nowhere else! But the nearest bunk was five meters from where the body lay. Was the murderer barefoot? It was a cold day. So he was wearing shoes or boots. Could he move silently? Was he a cat? Not possible! Surely the Blackie would have heard him coming and would turn in time to use his rifle, which we know he was carrying. So it follows that he wasn't hiding anywhere. Therefore, if the murderer was in the block first, the Blackie saw him right away. A chance meeting? When two men bump into each other by chance, only two things can happen—" Fingers were fluttering now in all directions. "They talk friendly, or they argue and maybe come to blows. If they talk friendly, one doesn't wind up cutting the other's throat, unless they're business partners. But no one's in business here. And if they don't talk friendly—if they argue and fight—and one, God forbid, dies, there are signs of a struggle. The lieutenant said that wasn't the case. So it wasn't a chance meeting. An appointment? If it was a Jew, how could he make an appointment? He doesn't have a watch.

If it wasn't a Jew, why would he make an appointment in the barracks?"

Now, in triumph, the rabbi raised and vigorously shook an altogether different finger of his left hand—his pinky. "So . . . Captain! You see? *It's obvious!* The murderer wasn't there when the Blackie entered. The opposite is true. *The Blackie was there first!*"

Paul was astounded by the galloping process of thought he had been allowed to witness. Some of it made sense to him, some of it didn't. But that was no longer the point.

"Remarkable," he said quietly. "That's also the conclusion I reached . . . although by a somewhat different method."

"Ah! You mean the hat and coat."

"Exactly." Paul's eyes gleamed. "Rabbi, you knew all along. It was a very cold day, according to Lieutenant Vogl—"

"And why should he lie?"

"—which suggests that if Lieutenant Hrubow had unbuttoned his coat and his jacket to the extent that he did, he hadn't just entered. He was there for quite some time."

"Good, Captain!"

"But why? What was he doing there on a cold day that he need unbutton his coat *and* jacket?"

"Obviously, some kind of work. Certainly not just loafing. Otherwise, why would the *pogromchik* take off his nice warm hat?"

"Why, indeed?" Paul asked, delighted.

For Rabbi Hurwicz it had been an interesting distraction. He had not thought once of his real problem: whether Halakhic law permitted him to use potato peelings to make the contraband matzoh for the upcoming Passover holiday.

"What else did you conclude?" Paul asked—and coughed politely. "Tell me quickly, if you don't mind, before the lieutenant gets back."

The rabbi frowned. He would have preferred to explain his deductions in detail, lest they appear frivolous. But he knew better than to contradict an order from a German officer.

"If the Blackie—pardon me, if the lieutenant was killed where his body was found, there would have been blood in the dirt. There wasn't. So it follows that he was killed somewhere else in the block. He was dragged to where they found him. You knew that already, Captain. You sniffed around."

Paul ran his hand across one smooth-shaven cheek. "Rabbi, you're a very observant man."

"Eyes I've got. And ears. You, Captain, asked the right questions. In a million years I couldn't think of such questions."

"I have a few more," Paul said quietly, "if you don't mind."

"Why should I mind?"

"What kind of man was Margulies?"

Rabbi Hurwicz sighed. "He forgot he was a Jew."

"He had many enemies?"

"That's possible."

"And friends?"

"That's unlikely."

"Now that you live here, in the same room he occupied, do you bolt the door from the inside?"

The rabbi murmured, "No, but who knows? Margulies might have had reason."

"Such as?"

"Who knows?"

"And for whom would he be likely to unbolt the door?"

Rabbi Hurwicz started to speak, then clamped his mouth shut. But he could not prevent his gaze from shooting to the door—the door that Margulies had unlocked to admit his murderer. It was unlocked now. At that moment Lieutenant Vogl knocked loudly and entered with Bella Wallach.

Zin: December 1942

Stephan had brought a supply of food with him on the train from Berlin. The journey took four days; the boxcars sat unmoving at a siding somewhere just inside the Polish border. Through a single barred window the Jews saw nothing but snow and ice and denuded trees under a white sky. The landscape was utterly silent.

The temperature fell to ten degrees Fahrenheit. The Jews clung to each other like lovers. Stephan gave away all his food to the children. A young mother died, and Bella clutched the baby under her shawl and tried to warm it against her cold breasts. During the second night the baby froze to death. Stephan wept as he recited the mourner's Kaddish.

But even then, and even upon their arrival at Zin, if someone had told Bella that she might survive by becoming the mistress of the German camp commandant, she would have lifted her chin and said, "No—I will *never* do that."

Stephan was struck in the mouth by Stein and sent to the dental commando. Bella and a few other young women were also chosen to live. They were led across the slippery ice to the German infirmary. Laid naked across a wooden table, they were probed rectally and vaginally by the gloved fingers of Captain Dr. Lustig. Three young German soldiers wrapped in greatcoats sat around another table by the coal stove, drinking from liter bottles of beer and offering observations as to the size and shape of breasts and the matching color of pubic hair.

Still naked, trembling from the cold, the women were herded to a hut in the north quadrangle. A slender Jewish girl named Tzippora, whose face was the color of stale bread, sheared off Bella's hair with a steel scissors and then depilated her body. Bella was given a rag of underwear made from coarse dusting cloth, a gray dress, old shoes without laces, a tattered blanket. She and the women were escorted to Block D and assigned places on the bunks.

The next day one of the new women was discovered to be pregnant. She was taken away. Two other girls of eighteen were sent to the Ukrainian barracks. Three days later, disheveled, frothing like rabid bats, they received the coup de grace from Dr. Lustig at the hospital. Bella was assigned to work at the hair commando, bundling the sacks of tresses that were sheared by Tzippora.

Her second morning at work, she and two others, under a steel gray December sky, trundled an ox cart full of hair sacks to the railroad depot.

A train had just arrived, originating in Yugoslavia. On board, among several hundred others, was an American lawyer named Ackerman, his blonde wife and pretty daughter of seven. The family had been stranded in Belgrade under a kind of house arrest at some South American embassy. Ackerman wore a belted camel's hair coat and a Tyrolean hat with a feather. He jumped off the train shouting that a serious mistake had been made. At worst he deserved to be a prisoner of war; at best, as a member of the diplomatic corps, he should be repatriated to the United States. And despite his name, he was not Jewish.

"If you want proof," he said boldly to Lieutenant Stein, "let's just the two of us step behind that ticket office over there. I'll take down my pants."

After a moment's consideration, Rudy said, "That won't be necessary. I believe you."

"Then you have no right to keep us here." Ackerman blew a burst of vapor into the cold air.

"Is your wife Jewish?" Stein asked.

"Episcopalian! From Richmond, Virginia!"

"Forgive me," Stein said. "You're right—there's been a mistake. I'll speak to the commandant immediately, and he'll arrange transport to Berlin." He turned to Corporal Munzing. "Meanwhile, take this gentleman and his family to the American camp. Deliver them to Dr. Lustig. Tell him they're to get immediate special treatment."

The Ackermans were marched over the crunchy white snow to the hospital.

It was then that Bella realized what everyone at Zin realized sooner or later: There were to be no witnesses.

One morning, a month later, Major Kirmayr noticed her. He rarely ventured into the compound. He was little more to Bella than a squirrel-faced, middle-aged, somewhat melancholy man glimpsed behind barbed-wire hedges.

Kirmayr had Bella brought to his bungalow in the early evening. Wearing a bulky Scandinavian sweater and sheepskin-lined slippers, he sat at his desk sipping a schnapps. There were pouches under his eyes. He looked like a businessman after a tiring day at the office, except that at his waist he wore his black-hilted SS dagger and a Walther PPK pistol in a shiny holster with a buttoned flap. After he had studied Bella for a minute or so, he smiled and asked her if she spoke German. She hesitated, then said, "Yes."

"You are married?"

Bella's heart pounded. She shook her head vaguely.

"Fräulein," he said cordially, "I'm a simple and direct man. These winter nights are lonely. If you'll share one or two with me, I'll be kind to you."

Bella immediately agreed. Later to Leo Cohen she said, "No one on this earth—no one!—may say, 'I will never do that.'"

The demands on her body were minimal. The commandant was not a satyr. More than anything he suffered from lack of tenderness in his present surroundings. He explained to Bella that he wished her to lie behind him in bed at night, naked, so that he might feel her warmth. He would be grateful if she would stroke his back in a gentle circular motion until he slept. Then she would be free to put on a nightgown and move to the other side of the double bed.

On the third occasion of Bella's presence, the commandant, in the cold blackness of early morning, woke her with tentative kisses on the neck and a hoarse muttering. Gradually she realized that the time had come. She shut her eyes.

Afterward he plunged instantly back to sleep. In the morning he fed her hot buttered biscuits and Brazilian coffee. He provided her with heavy socks, woollen panties, and a silk brassiere. The socks she wore; the underwear she gave to Tzippora.

When the commandant asked her why she had done that, she explained calmly that she knew the underwear came from the luggage of dead Jewish women. Kirmayr was not angry, only embarrassed at the faux pas. A few days later he handed her two new sets of underwear with Polish labels, wrapped in tissue paper with a receipt from a lingerie shop in Poseń.

He loved Beethoven and Verdi, sunsets, a rough joke. He reduced work hours in the slack season. He told Bella the story of the Polish ration cards. He turned a half-blind eye to the fact that many of the

Jews, against camp regulations, covertly practiced their religion. He had never struck a prisoner.

These so-called kindnesses clarified something for her. The Germans' sin was in their refusal to be human. The killing machine was only a product of that denial. One day they might be punished for murder but never for their lack of human feeling. That was not illegal. For that, who would indict them?

But like a parrot on a thin wire, the commandant clung to the vestiges of his humanity. One day, Bella thought, if he survives, he will say and believe, "I never killed a single Jew. I helped them. Under those ghastly circumstances, I did all I could."

If he survives. By then the revolt had been blueprinted. Bella had been given her assignment: to kill Martin Kirmayr.

He was not evil, she believed, only weak. Some nights, while he shifted and snored, she lay next to him, sweating, wondering if she could truly do it.

Zin: April 1943

Paul was surprised and a little disturbed. He had expected the Wallach girl to be attractive; she was the commandant's protégé—from among the arriving Jewesses he could have chosen whomever he liked. Beauty was a quality one failed to associate with Zin, yet—not very tall, black-haired, round-armed, with a tiny waist and flaring hips—she was a young Jewish beauty.

"I feed Bella," Kirmayr had said.

Twenty-one, Paul guessed—if that. She wore a dark blue woollen dress and a good cloth coat. Her skin was creamy and looked soft as a pillow. She moved into the room warily, like a jungle cat.

Her eyes were feline, too: almond-shaped, a dark gold color, glaring at him as if he were a hunter and she the prey. But even her fear was not enough to mask her hatred. Dare she look at the commandant that way, Paul thought, she would certainly fall from grace. He was intrigued. Was she so secure that she could reveal such a feeling? Or unaware that it showed?

He asked Reitlinger and Vogl to leave. Now that he had the rabbi's services, he no longer needed Reitlinger. He had never needed Vogl.

"I'll be frank with you, Fräulein Wallach. If you'll be the same, I won't bother you for very long. I have only one purpose here. To find a murderer."

"That will be easy, Captain."

He understood at once. A clever woman, he thought, and bold. He began to smile politely—to show her he was neither angry nor an enemy—then realized that such an expression, in response to her statement, was fulsome. He moved the muscles of his face so that his expression was once more frozen in neutrality.

"I'm looking for a specific murderer. In civilian life I worked as an investigator for the Berlin police. I still do."

"I am also from Berlin," Bella Wallach said. Her tone softened a shade.

"Oh? Yes?" It was extraordinary, in these circumstances, that they were about to begin the kind of conversation that two citizens of the same city might have while sitting at a Saint-Tropez café or waiting for the ski lift at Kitzbühel.

"May I ask which district?"

"Grünewald. On Brahmsstrasse."

"Very pretty. I know it well. I live in Bellevue, on Claudius strasse."

"I had a close friend who lived around the corner from you, on Holsteiner Ufer. Her name was Lanke . . . not Jewish."

"I knew very few of my neighbors," Paul admitted. "Although I got to know them better after the air raids began." He smiled. "You were a student?"

He drew her out slowly, asking friendly questions, gradually putting her at her ease with the realization that he intended no harm. He was skilled at it. She began to talk freely.

She had attended a Jewish middle school in Grünwald, she said. Summers she worked for a Yiddish-language newspaper; she had hoped to go on to the university at Freiburg and study journalism. Her father worked for the Deutsche Bank. But after Kristallnacht in

1938, when nearly all the synagogues were destroyed as punishment for a Jew's assassination of a German Embassy third secretary in Paris, her father was fired. He found a job in a Berlin factory that manufactured canned heat for soldiers to warm their meals. She was seventeen then. A year later the whole family sewed on the yellow star. Her mother had to surrender her winter coat and stylish suits with narrow skirts; her father was not allowed to buy tobacco for his pipe.

"Jews, as you know," Bella said coolly, "could own no bicycles. No telephones. I had to give up my radio. My school was closed. It became a very odd life. I was bored. We had to share the apartment with two other families who had lost their own. One of the men couldn't keep his hands off me. I was unhappy. I decided to marry."

"And then?"

By then she seemed to be wondering why she had spoken so openly. "Captain, do you care?"

An attractive young woman, he thought. She reminded him of Sylvie, except that her hair was darker, her eyes gold brown rather than blue. He cared and realized that in his present position it was simple minded to care. But he was a creature of habit. She wasn't a suspect; she was just a witness. He had started out to interrogate her about Margulies, but when he discovered a fellow Berliner, his questions had veered off course. Nevertheless, they served a purpose.

"I would like to know."

"My mother and father were sent to Sachsenhausen," Bella said stolidly. "It was the nearest camp to Berlin. Then my sister and brother—they're younger than I. My husband and I were lucky for a while. He was a dentist. Jews still had cavities. However, last December we came here."

"What happened to your husband?"

He was aware of her hesitation. "He is kapo of the dental commando."

"*Here?*"

She nodded.

"I see." Paul was nonplussed; he glanced at the rabbi, who had partially closed his eyes again. It was not a very unusual story for the rabbi. She had told it calmly, yet for that very reason the flesh on Paul's forearm had risen. And a deeper chill touched him.

He had never really looked at Jews in any clear light—he realized now he had always been a little uneasy with them. In restaurants in Berlin you saw them grouped at a table, wolfing food with such unflagging enjoyment, laughing—too loudly, it seemed—flinging their arms about in excessive, un-Germanic gestures. But he sensed the quickness that flickered in the dark eyes behind the subtle smiles. If you had to deal with them, there was always that unspoken hint of superiority. Non-Jews were *goys*. The word had a harsh, derogating sound, although *Yid*—their own name for themselves—was not much more melodious. They kept to themselves. Christian women might be dallied with for pleasure, rarely married.

"We want to be part of you," they seemed to be saying, "because it makes life smoother for us. But we know things you'll never know. In business, in friendship, we'll always choose one of our own above you."

Let them go to Jerusalem, America, wherever they want to go, he had thought. He remembered Willi Dietrich once saying, "They're not all that anxious, dear boy. Zionism is a movement of one Jew sending a second Jew to Palestine on a third Jew's money."

I never much liked them, Paul now realized. I never really knew them. They made no effort to get to know me. *But I never thought of killing them.*

He became aware, to his annoyance, that he had shut his eyes. When he snapped them open he saw that the Wallach girl was staring at him with surprise.

"You're shocked," she said slowly.

He said nothing. But it was true. At his thoughts; at what she had so readily told him. What we've done to these people can be neither forgiven nor stopped. There was nothing *he* could do except turn on his boot heel and walk out of Zin, order Reitlinger to drive him back to Berlin. An act of avoidance, neither cowardly nor bold. And he would have accomplished nothing except his own ruin.

Get on with the job.

"I understand," he resumed, "that you are the commandant's protégé."

Her eyes hardened again. "I sleep with him. Just as Blondie sleeps with the lieutenant."

"Who is Blondie?"

"His real name is Leo Cohen."

"And which lieutenant do you refer to?"

"The one who brought me here."

Paul now understood certain of Vogl's responses. What Vogl did was of no interest to him. What Bella Wallach did . . . there, *interest* was the wrong word. The right word eluded him. Does it matter that she resembles Sylvie? That's foolish.

"Frau Wallach, I have some questions about Margulies."

"Of course, Captain."

"You discovered his body?"

"True."

"Did you know Margulies?"

"I knew him."

"Tell me about him."

She hesitated, as if about to plunge into an icy pool, then spoke in clipped, tense syllables.

"He had a position of authority—he abused other Jews, informed on them. He couldn't accept that he was a victim. He lost his moral sense. You had said to him—not in so many words, but it was clear enough—'If you want to survive, copy us.' He thought, 'I'll show them I'm as strong as they are.' He misunderstood what it means to be strong."

She glared at Paul, as if he was responsible. His eyes said, *I wasn't here.*

Now that she became aware of her intensity, she lowered not only her gaze but the level of her voice.

"He asked to share this room with two girls from Brussels. They told me the things he insisted they do. I would blush to repeat them, and I no longer blush easily. The girls were—are—my friends.

148

They are younger than I, only nineteen and seventeen. That day I came here to comfort them. The door was open. I found Margulies on one of the beds, strangled to death. I remember thinking, *Swine, you deserved this.* Then I cried, because it occurred to me that at one time he may have been a good man . . . someone's father. I called a guard, and Captain Dressler came."

During this recital Paul had listened carefully, mulling certain phrases. If Margulies had lost his moral sense, he wondered, what had Bella Wallach lost? Her husband was here at Zin. By sleeping with Kirmayr, surely she had compromised herself beyond repair. To survive. If so, why condemn the dead Margulies?

"When you knocked on the door that day, you found it open. Were you surprised?"

"I suppose so. I don't remember."

"Didn't Margulies usually lock it?"

"I don't know. I didn't come by that often."

"Where do the Belgian girls work?"

"In the laundry."

"But you thought they'd be here."

"The bugle had blown."

"Tell me what you saw when you entered this room. Leave nothing out, even if it seems trivial."

While she talked, Paul watched her face and the movements of her body that illustrated her words. He had questioned enough witnesses to trust his instincts. He sensed that she was lying about something, but what it was he couldn't tell.

When she finished, Paul remained silent, looking at her calmly, hoping to provoke her into saying more—what she had not meant to say.

But she was stronger than he had expected, and canny. She waited patiently for him to continue.

He approached from another angle.

"You worked for a Jewish newspaper. You speak and write in Yiddish."

"Of course."

"Yiddish is your native tongue?"

"No. German. My father mistakenly believed he was a German citizen. Yiddish is the common language of Jews."

"You all speak it? Write it?"

"All speak it." She explained that it was a folk language, born in the Rhineland in the twelfth century. "Like a bastard—a German father, a Hebrew mother. The Jews spoke German, but they wrote it with Hebrew letters. When they moved eastward into the Pale, they added Polish, Russian, Lithuanian. They began to speak it, too. Anyone with an education can also write it."

"You're very knowledgeable, Frau Wallach."

"I'm a Jew. I read books."

"In Hebrew?"

"A Jew prays in Hebrew. Unless he's a scholar he reads it indifferently. Few can write it. Certainly not well enough to write the first two notes left by the murderer." Her eyes glinted. "Is that what you're driving at?"

"Perhaps," Paul said.

"You've seen the notes?"

He wondered why she asked, but ignored the question and turned to Rabbi Hurwicz.

"What about Margulies, Rabbi? If what Frau Wallach says is true, he made serious mistakes. But he was still a human being. Do you draw any conclusions?"

"He was a frightened man," the rabbi said.

Paul understood. "True. The bolt on the door is fairly new. You don't need a bolt. Apparently Margulies did. I'm sure we'll find it was attached at his request. He wanted privacy. He was frightened . . . as you say. You doubt he had friends. For whom would he have unlocked his door?"

The rabbi shrugged bony shoulders. "For Captain Dressler. For any German or Blackie. Or for *dee shayne maydelach*. The Wijnberg girls," he said sadly.

Paul observed him for a moment. "And if they happened to be here, wouldn't the Wijnberg girls have opened the door for one of their friends?"

"Even if they were not here," the rabbi said, brightening, "Margulies might have done the same."

Paul turned on Bella Wallach in time to catch the chafe of anger in her eyes. Their catlike gaze had been fastened on Rabbi Hurwicz.

"Would Margulies have opened the door for you, Frau Wallach?"

He saw a shadow of fear. It's natural, he thought. She's being interrogated by an SS captain. Her fear is not evidence of any guilt. He looked at her hands. They were small and white, with little dimples at the wrist: too chubby to be beautiful. Her nails shone without polish.

They were not hands that could have fastened on Margulies's throat to end his life of betrayal.

"Yes, he might have opened it for me."

"Or for anyone else who was a friend of the Wijnberg sisters. I'm not accusing you of anything," Paul said. "Thank you for your time, Frau Wallach. I may want to ask a few more questions later, but for the moment you can go. I enjoyed our talk. It's a pity we didn't meet under other circumstances . . . that would have been more pleasant. When the war is over, I hope you can return to Berlin. It was a wonderful city. I'm sure one day it will be so again."

She stared at him as if he were a half-wit. He had no idea what had prompted his last remarks. It was more than good manners. A yearning, a refusal to believe.

Bella Wallach would not return to Berlin. She would die at Zin. If not tomorrow, then when winter was over and the commandant no longer required the warmth of her round arms. If not then, then when the camp closed. For the first time it dawned on Paul what all the others knew: There would be no witnesses.

Her eyes blazed with scorn. Not only for me, he realized, but for her death. And yet she must be burdened by the will to live. If not why had she chosen to share the commandant's bed?

He glanced at his watch. Nearly eight-thirty. According to Lieutenant Vogl the trains would be arriving soon. Paul decided that was not something he wanted to see.

Bella Wallach is lying to me, he thought. But about what?

_____ **15**

Zin: January 1943

Until just after her summons to the commandant's bed, Bella
knew Leo Cohen only as Blondie, Lieutenant Vogl's pansy. It had
been of no interest to her what path to survival any Jew chose at Zin,
unless it was that of an informer. Already the women whispered
that she fell into that category, and they had begun to avoid her.

In that case, she thought, maybe I've misjudged Blondie. Maybe
they all do.

A cold mist fell, somewhere between rain and snow. They met
one morning on the rocky field outside the latrines. Both were
leaving. The women had no separate latrine, but Bella was beyond
embarrassment. The Dutch youth spoke her name. She turned, a
little startled, and marked that his penetrating gray eyes revealed a
sense of amusement.

"Leo Cohen," he said, introducing himself.

"I know who you are."

So young, she thought—younger than I. And so blond. His hair
was very nearly white. He could be one of *them*. But she had heard
the tale of his lover's death.

Cohen said, "I know who you are, too."

"Then what do you want?"

"I am not only a homosexual, Frau Wallach. No more than
you're only a whore."

At the word, her eyes flashed. How did he, of all people, *dare*? She
groped for a retort, but her hand seemed to move of its own
accord—she reached up and slapped his face.

Cohen touched his reddening cheek with his fingers. He

153

accepted the blow as his due. But he noted that she had made no move to leave.

He said calmly, "Perhaps you misunderstood my meaning. I have no reason to insult you."

"I don't care about your reasons. I don't care what you are."

He never lowered his direct gaze. "I didn't mean that I liked women. I never have. I've tried, but without success. I couldn't do what was expected of me. I'm not happy about it, but it's a fact. I meant that I choose to make love with Werner Vogl for the same reason that you sleep with the commandant. I despise Vogl. But I choose to prolong my life as long as possible."

She digested that while she studied the carved line of his lips and tried to read what was in his eyes, aware that he examined her with the same care. The first part of his confession, she realized, had not been easy for him.

"So?"

The rain trickled down his neck. "Do you believe me?"

"Let's say that I'm willing to believe you. What difference does it make?"

"I'm a Jew, like you. Do you trust me?"

Yes, she thought, surprising herself. I do. There was something in the simplicity of his words that moved her. We're both young, both fighting to live. Both a little desperate.

"I'm cold," she said. "Please tell me what you want."

The gravity of his face softened into a boyish smile. He said quietly, "I've been watching you. I have a proposal to make. I need your help. Can we be friends?"

Zin: April 1943

Gold and pistols. The words danced elusively at the edge of Mordecai Lieberman's mind. We need both. But the gold first, to purchase the pistols.

A train chugged into the depot on a foggy morning. A small load of French Jews had come from Paris through Bar-le-Duc and Mosel. Their Yiddish for the most part was poor; Lieberman's

French was nonexistent. He tugged at coat sleeves and neatly wrapped bundles and all but knocked one protesting old man's homburg from his head. Prince Rudy was watching.

"Mais, M'sieu, on nous a dit . . ."

Lieberman stubbornly shook his own gray head. "Bring all valuables with you!" he shouted. "Remember the numbers of your porters!"

But inwardly he wept.

The greatest turnover in the camp was in the welcome commando; unless a man steeled himself against human feeling, it quickly destroyed his last shred of sanity. The haulers of bodies, the cutters of hair, the wrenchers of teeth, dealt with only the dead. The welcome commando cajoled, bullied, and lied to the living. Somehow it was worse. During the suicide epidemic, although the commandant had not realized it, most of those who hanged themselves were men who met the trains. It was not the cold that unhinged them.

Aron Chonszki got through the morning by refusing to look anyone in the eye. He busied himself knotting shoelaces. It was only later, in the barracks, that he clenched his fists in agony.

"God is blind," he had once sobbed, beginning to beat his knuckles against the side of his head. "If He could see, He would crush me like a bad bug. Pan Lieberman, I'm too ashamed. . . . I don't think I can continue. . . ."

"You have to, Aron," Lieberman replied with all the unfelt certainty he could muster. Holding the butcher in his thin arms, he felt the huge body shudder, as if gripped by fever. "God is shocked and frightened but not blind. You know what we have to do. We dare not fail Him."

Lieberman survived by constantly reminding himself of his promise to the old woman he had mistaken for his mother. To each trusting Jew he directed down the Road to Freedom toward the gas chambers, he vowed, *I will avenge you. I will live to tell the world how you died and what they made us do to you.*

He spoke those words silently to the old man who had lost his homburg hat and was about to lose his life.

Gold and pistols . . . nothing else mattered now.

When the last carload of French Jews had been sorted, he excused himself from the detail. He was the camp leader, meant to see that everything went smoothly in all quarters. He walked purposefully past Block A across the mud of Roll Call Square, past the carpentry shop and the kitchen to the little square hut that housed the gold commando.

The German guard on duty outside knew him.

"I must speak with the kapo," Lieberman said, doffing his cap. "Important camp business."

In a few minutes he had immersed himself in the shadows of a cluttered corner of the hut, talking in rapid-fire Yiddish with Rabbi Hurwicz. The dentists and porters were already beginning to arrive with their trophies—inlays, francs, dollars, bracelets, wedding rings—gleaming dully. The rabbi's helpers, all former jewelers and goldsmiths, knew far more about the metal than he did and were busily sorting it into small piles. The attention of the German guard inside the hut was wholly absorbed.

"Lieberman!" the rabbi said urgently. "God whispered in your ear. You knew I needed you."

Lieberman was momentarily confused. He thought it was *he* who had come to ask a favor and a mighty one. "But . . . yes, Rabbi . . . what can I do?"

The rabbi's eyes glowed like a stalking tiger. "You're a practical man. A good Jew. 'Rejoice in God, righteous ones!' So far, Lieberman, you've never failed me."

He meant that not only was Mordecai Lieberman his factotum among the camp population, he was also his provider. When Rabbi Hurwicz first reached Zin, he learned that many of the religious Jews were avoiding work on the Sabbath. From time to time Lieutenant Stein dispatched such offenders to the camp hospital. For that same reason no other rabbis were then resident in the camp. They had all gone up in smoke or down in quicklime.

Rabbi Hurwicz immediately buttonholed Lieberman, the new camp leader, and swiftly explained that the matter of Sabbath labor performed under duress was not governed by a Talmudic prohibition but by a rabbinical one. He would permit the men to work on the Sabbath. Lives would be saved . . . for a while.

Lieberman, rejoicing, spread the news. After that he arranged candles to be stolen for Chanukah services. On Purim, to commemorate the Jews' escape from Persian tyranny, he bribed a Ukrainian named Taddeus for a cupful of vodka; it passed from man to man. With a special pleasure the rabbi intoned the words of the *Megillah.* "Cursed be Haman, who sought to destroy me. Blessed be Mordecai, Mordecai the Jew. . . ."

Soon, on the first night of the Passover holiday, it would be required to tell the story of the Exodus from Egypt, drink the Four Cups of wine, taste bitter herbs, and sip from a dish of salt water— above all, to eat unleavened matzoh. For the entire eight days no one might eat or even possess any leavened substance. Such a person according to Torah "shall be cut off from Israel."

One of Lieberman's minions had already stolen a small quantity of wheat for the matzoh, which was now hidden under the floorboards of the rabbi's room.

"I've solved all the problems for Passover," the rabbi said despondently, in the shadowy corner of the gold commando hut. "All but one . . ."

Lieberman said, "Tell me quickly what you need."

But Rabbi Hurwicz was in no hurry. "The mitzvah calls for 'the wine of the country,' so I've decided that we can use tea sweetened with saccharine. Bravel, in the kitchen, stole the saccharine for me. The tea he'll get, too. Salt is everywhere. There are all kinds of awful things growing in the commandant's garden that will do for bitter herbs. Bella will provide."

Lieberman shuffled his feet impatiently. "Splendid."

"And you, my dear Mordecai, provided the wheat."

"So what do you lack?" Lieberman glanced cautiously over his shoulder at the brawny young German guard, but he was bent over the table watching the Jews weighing gold inlays.

"There isn't enough of it," the rabbi groaned.

Lieberman groaned also—in despair more than sympathy. "The man who stole the first bag," he said, "risked his life!"

"Lieberman! There are five hundred Jewish souls to be fed!"

"Not for five thousand," Lieberman replied hotly—a bit more hotly than he intended—"could I ask this man to risk his life a second time!"

"Listen to me, Mordecai. I spoke to a student named Prager, from Vilna. He told me that last Passover, in the ghetto of Vilna, they mixed potato peelings with the flour. That stretched the supply—enough to bake matzoh for ten thousand people."

"Potato peelings are like salt! There's plenty, if you know where to look."

"Prager looked. Prager found. But what they did in Vilna is one thing. What fulfills the mitzvah is another. Maybe in Vilna they had clean potato peelings. . . . I'll give them the benefit of the doubt. Our potato peelings, however, are *filthy*!"

"So we'll wash them, Rabbi. In nice, clean water. Maybe even snow," he said gloomily.

Rabbi Hurwicz sighed. "Under my floor I have the *Shulhan Arukh,* which codifies the dietary laws. If you mix water and potato liquid, it could leaven the flour we will grind from it. It's forbidden!"

Lieberman wagged a finger. "Could leaven the flour. But not *will* leaven the flour."

Sadly, the rabbi said, "Dear Lieberman, you wouldn't ask your friend to steal a second bag of wheat—he might lose his life. But you ask me to risk that the flour might become leavened by washing the potato peelings. 'It is this divine pledge that hath stood by our fathers and by us also.' How could I do such a thing? If it turned out badly . . . we would all be cut off from Israel, and it is *I* who would be responsible!"

Not for the first time Lieberman silently asked himself, *Dear God, if you really loved the Jews, why did you make them the chosen people?*

He realized that Rabbi Hurwicz could not be swayed by any argument of expediency. In Czestochowa he had refused permission to use the forged baptismal certificates and had ordered the white cards returned to the Germans. He would certainly give up his life before he contravened the Law in the smallest detail. The Law in such a time of darkness was the only rock upon which a Jew might lean.

So he believes, thought Lieberman, and he is right. But, in what I have to do, I'm right as well.

He said at last, "Rabbi, this is a difficult problem, so I can't solve it for you with a snap of the fingers. I'll come up with something. Meanwhile, I have a favor to ask of *you*."

The rabbi's gaunt yellow face glowed. He considered his problem solved. He had faith that Lieberman was capable of doing anything he chose to do.

"Ask, Mordecai. I'm your servant."

"I need gold."

"Gold?"

"Yes . . . gold. A lot of it."

The delight had faded to terror. "You want me to give you gold?"

"Yes, Rabbi," Lieberman said patiently.

"*Steal* it?"

"It's not stealing. It's already been stolen from *us* . . . from other Jews. I want some of it back."

"I can't do that," the rabbi said. He clenched his bony hands to his chest as if he anticipated Lieberman's forcing them open to release hidden treasure.

"You just said, 'Ask, Mordecai. I'm your servant.'"

"But not for that. Not to steal! For you it might not be stealing. The gold hasn't been entrusted to your care. You forget, I'm also God's servant. For me it would be stealing."

"From the *Germans*?"

His black eyes widened in dismay. "Mordecai—that's worse!"

"Worse than what?"

"To cheat a gentile," the rabbi explained with patience that now exceeded Lieberman's, "is even worse than cheating a Jew. It brings Israel into contempt. It desecrates the name of Israel's God."

Lieberman ground his few remaining teeth. He knew that Rabbi Hurwicz was quite serious. An argument that would easily sway any other man would be of no use.

But now that the crisis seemed past, the rabbi grew curious. "Why do you need gold, Mordecai?"

Lieberman had been wondering whether to tell him about the revolt. Eventually he would have to know. But if a man—a Jew—even a rabbi—refused to steal what had been stolen by murderers from the live and dead bodies of other Jews . . . how would he react to a plan that had at its core the murder of the murderers? Theft was a minor sin. Murder was the most grave.

Lieberman had no idea what to reply. Then the devil whispered in his ear.

"It's all right," the rabbi said softly, before he could speak. "You don't have to tell me. What I don't know can't hurt me."

"Rabbi . . ." He looked over his shoulder, then whispered, "I need the gold to buy the second sack of wheat for the matzoh."

The last bit of color fled from Rabbi Hurwicz's cheeks, leaving them like the belly of a dead carp.

"Without it—"

"Yes! I understand."

If a man is destined to drown, thought Lieberman, he'll drown in a spoonful of water. He waited for the rabbi's decision.

After a minute of pained contemplation, Rabbi Hurwicz heaved a sigh. What tortuous thread of logic had blazed back and forth at the speed of light through his extraordinary brain, Lieberman could not even guess.

"I can't do it, Mordecai," he said with soft anguish. "God would never forgive me. I would never forgive myself." He glanced over Lieberman's shoulder at the men busily working. The chink of gold was like hard metallic music in the little room. The German guard, smoking a cigarette and enveloped in a blue haze, observed every movement of the sorters.

"But . . . I can turn my back. Behind my feet is a wooden crate. It's filled with bracelets. The best quality, I'm told. I beg you not to steal any of them. But if you do," he said pitiably, "I won't see it."

He turned his back right away, in a jerky motion, as if even a second's hesitation might force him to renege on his decision.

Lieberman was equally fast. In a few seconds he had plunged his left hand into the crate and shoved four thick bracelets into the seat of his pants. Don't let them jingle, he prayed.

"Goodbye, Rabbi. I have to go."

"And the wheat for the matzoh?"

"Soon! I'll take care of everything."

He walked toward the door of the hut smiling foolishly. He was aware of the smile, but no matter how hard his muscles strove, he could not tear it from his lips. The face, he thought, is the most dangerous informer.

The narrow-eyed young German guard ground out his cigarette in the dirt. He moved a step to block Lieberman's way.

"Finished?"

"Yes, thank you. All is well. Thank you—"

"I have to search you," the guard said. "Take off all your clothes."

Lieberman felt his bowels loosen. He took a sharp breath. "You know who I am?" he said angrily.

The guard laughed. "I know who you think you are, Herr Lieberman. You won't like it if I tell you who you really are. Do as I say."

You never knew which tactic would work. Now he began to wheedle. "Please, I'm in a hurry. . . ."

"In a hurry? Why?" The laughter faded. The German fingered his truncheon. "Do what I tell you. Don't waste my time, you fool."

Lieberman squeezed his bowels silently, with as much force as he could, so that thin wet feculence squirted down his cheeks and dripped down the back of one leg. The odor rose like a bullet. He felt a wave of shame, and his face turned a mottled crimson and pink.

"The reason I'm in a hurry . . . I couldn't control myself . . . a terrible thing happened. . . ."

He bowed his head, as if for a blow, and turned slightly so that his buttocks faced the German.

"Get out," the guard snapped, wrinkling his nose and spitting in the dirt at Lieberman's feet. "Filthy Jew!"

Lieberman bolted out the door. He rushed across the wet earth to the latrines. Holding his nose with one hand, he washed himself with the other.

Then he walked slowly across the rocky field to the watchtower behind the farm. A cold wind bit through his jacket. Taddeus, the Ukrainian who had sold him the vodka for Purim, manned the machine gun.

Ten minutes later Lieberman's business was finished. He quivered with joy. The steel of a Mauser pistol burned like an icicle against his chest. The Jewish Revolutionary Army of Zin had secured its first weapon.

Paul blew his nose again into a white handkerchief, then thrust it back into his pocket, where it lay wetly against his buttocks. The officers' mess gave off a stench of perfume, sweat, and alcohol. All drank a schnapps before the meal, beer and Rhine wine with the sauerbraten and boiled potatoes.

Captain Karl Dressler, sitting opposite Paul at the table, spoke in a leaden monotone. He had a massive head whose facial muscles seemed paralyzed. His blue eyes were lifeless and glassy. He had been an accountant in some small Hessian town, then joined the SS in 1936, and soon helped keep the books at Dachau.

"It's no secret," he told Paul, "that the commandant and I disagree on who is responsible for these outrages. The commandant thinks the murderer is a lunatic. I don't." He speared a hot boiled potato with his fork. "Have you read *The Protocols of the Elders of Zion?*"

"No," Paul said.

"You should, Captain. It was written by a high-ranking Russian Jew, privy to their every secret. It's a book that greatly influenced the Führer. *The Protocols* proved beyond any doubt that the Jewish worldwide conspiracy was directed to frustrating the mission of the Teutonic race. The tribe of Levi was meant to manipulate the governments of Europe into their debt. The tribe of Aaron was given the task of vilifying the Christian Church. The tribe of Isaac had to undermine the military class and the national patriotism it

162

represents . . . and so forth. Most instructive. Here at Zin," Dressler continued unblinkingly, "the Jews reap their reward. This Angel of Death, as the commandant so poetically styles him, takes a sick form of revenge. He strikes at an officer who is only doing his duty. He strikes at one of his own kind who was useful to us. Weed out the malcontents, Captain. Among them you'll find your man."

Dressler was insane, Paul realized.

But in Germany they had said the same things: not only at Brownshirt rallies but in university seminars, over office desks, and at dinner parties. Blabbering theorists, witless bureaucrats; the young parroted them to be stylish. It will pass, Paul had thought, like adolescence. You emerge one day, chuckling, "Was I really like that? Did I believe such garbage?"

Once, in 1938, after a law had been passed against "decadent art" and German troops had occupied the Sudetenland, Paul had idly considered leaving Germany. Perhaps Paris . . . but what could he do there? He wondered if the Swiss Police would have any room for him in their organization. He kept wondering for another year as the Wehrmacht occupied Slovakia and then blitzed Poland, but by then it was obviously too late. The war was insane, but he saw how the young people's eyes glowed with pride when they strolled in their smart new uniforms down Kurfürstendamm and through the Tiergarten.

He had lost his appetite. Halfway through the meal he pushed away his plate of sauerbraten, lit a cigarette, and gazed at the portrait of the Führer hanging on the wall above Kirmayr's head. We joked about him. We were right. But we thought it was enough to joke.

"I believe it's part of a plot," Lieutenant Stein muttered. "The murderer's no fool."

"Things are quiet now," ventured Vogl.

"Maybe he's escaped," said Dr. Lustig, puffing on a cigar. "We had two escapes yesterday, in one of the freight cars going back to Berlin. Maybe this man was one of them. If so, he'll turn up. They always do."

Rudy Stein was in charge of all discipline at Zin. But no one had told him of these last two escapes. He realized immediately that it was part of the commandant's hopeless and unnecessary plan to present to Captain Bach an idyllic vision of how Zin worked.

It had been Stein's policy that for every escapee, ten prisoners would be escorted to the hospital. I can't go that far now, he thought. But they've got to know that we're on top of them.

"With your permission, Major, I'd like to give the population a little lecture on the subject of escapes."

Kirmayr looked back warily. "A lecture, Rudy?"

"It will be instructive. I may even be able to persuade some of them to help the captain in his investigation."

"The captain has all the help he needs," Kirmayr said. "Our task is to cooperate. If he asks, give him the facts. No theories!" Patting his lips with a snowy napkin, he beckoned to Paul.

"If you've finished your meal, Captain, I have something interesting to show you."

The commandant opened a creaking wooden gate. At the rear of his bungalow there was a small green plot of land ringed with barbed wire and a sign that said ENTRY FORBIDDEN TO ALL.

"You don't look well, Bach. Hay fever?"

Paul nodded. "I haven't had it since I was a child."

"I can help you. Here is my garden. Rosemary, ginseng, and garlic, horehound and aloe, ferverroot, camomile, many others. I get all my cuttings directly from our own institute in Berlin."

Paul knew that the SS had offices whose concern was Germanic archaeology and ancestral research, alchemy, and astrology. The commandant's passion, following the example of Reichsführer Himmler, was medicinal herbs. Their joint ultimate purpose, Kirmayr explained, was to remove all artificial medicines from apothecary shelves; to wean the German people back to the use of natural products and health-giving herbs.

"I'm going to make up a tea for you. You can drink it or inhale the steam—it cures both cold and allergies. I developed it myself. You see, Bach . . . here at Zin, in the midst of everything else we do,

164

we have the opportunity to help humanity. More than the opportunity, we have the obligation."

He was also insane, Paul realized.

The water boiled and the commandant steeped the tea leaves. It was black Ceylon pekoe, which Kirmayr prized. It had arrived in a Jewish suitcase on yesterday's train from Berlin. He wondered how the Jews came by it . . . surely it was no longer imported from Britain. But you never knew. In wartime, the commandant thought, fortunes are made.

Bach had gone back to his bungalow, sneezing. Kirmayr had dismissed Sergeant Zuckermann until dinnertime; Zuckermann was by the barbed wire, kicking a soccer ball back and forth with Sergeant Grauert and Corporal Munzing.

"Some tea, Rabbi?"

The rabbi's thin neck swayed. Kirmayr tried to keep his distance, hating the way the rabbi smelled of moldy clothes and rancid sweat. He sat down in his swivel chair and began to spin lazily from side to side.

"I understand you've already met with Captain Bach. Toured the camp with him, discussed certain matters. Lieutenant Vogl has informed me," he explained.

Rabbi Hurwicz nodded. The aroma of the tea dizzied his senses.

"I've been cooperative with you, Rabbi." Kirmayr stopped spinning and poured the tea carefully into two Meissen cups. "I know of the services you've held. I did nothing. I let most of your people avoid work on Saturdays. I allow no reprisals. One of your important holidays is next week—isn't that so?"

About such a matter the rabbi was not permitted to equivocate. He nodded again, warily.

"Commemorating the escape of your people from Egypt, yes? From Pharaoh? The Red Sea parted for Moses. Actually it was the *Reed* Sea, which explains the phenomenon—yes?"

"Passover," said Rabbi Hurwicz.

"And of course you plan to hold services."

"If God allows it," the rabbi said.

The commandant sipped the hot tea, then cleared his throat. "Without intending to be coarse, Rabbi, I might point out to you that God isn't the only one whose permission you need. Let's say what's required is a quiet order to Lieutenant Stein."

The cup of tea warmed the rabbi's hands. He bowed his head and inhaled the fragrance rising from its surface. He had not yet dared to taste it.

"Captain Bach is searching for the man who murdered our Lieutenant Hrubow, and also your countryman, Margulies—a former member of the Jewish ruling council in Warsaw, I'm told. That man must be caught and punished. Do you agree?"

The rabbi swayed his neck, nodding. On that point his awareness of secular justice and his vision of the Law were in agreement.

"Of course you'll help the captain in every way possible," said Kirmayr. "It's your responsibility as a man of God. In addition, you will report to me daily. Whatever you see, whatever he tells you, I want to know. That's also your responsibility as leader of your flock. Rest assured, your holiday will pass without incident. Is this entirely clear? Do I have your word, in front of God?"

The rabbi had no choice. Once again he nodded.

"Drink the tea," Kirmayr said. "It's delicious."

16

The dove gray sky was slowly darkening. Searchlights atop the barracks surrounding Roll Call Square cast a yellow glow. The wind no longer blew, but the air was cold. The prisoners squeezed against one another like a herd of sick sheep. Ukrainian guards ran up and down the rows and files, tapping crops against their thighs. They sought out the block kapos, who scribbled figures in pocket-sized notebooks.

Lieutenant Stein was in charge of roll call. The counting took forty minutes.

"That's very fast," Kirmayr whispered to Paul, from where they stood in the shadows of Block C. "Rudy usually drags it out for all it's worth. Winter or summer makes no difference."

Cap drill followed. At a command from Sergeant Grauert, caps were whipped from heads and slapped against thighs. Whips cracked in the chill air.

"Not bad!" Grauert yelled. "But not good enough . . ."

Cap drill lasted twenty minutes, until the five hundred caps, slapping against five hundred thighs, made one report like the crack of a distant cannon.

Then Lieutenant Stein mounted a wooden platform in front of the shivering mass. He raised his hands for silence, although there was not a sound. Wolfgang crouched at his side like a monument, licking one paw.

"This is a special occasion at Zin!" Stein cried. "We have a distinguished visitor who's come from Berlin to serve our needs. Allow me to introduce Captain Bach of the Berlin Criminal Police!"

Like the director at a summer festival, he waved his hand to where Paul stood flat against the barracks wall with Commandant Kirmayr.

"Do you want to say a few words?" Kirmayr asked.

"No, Major."

Stein turned back to the Jews. "In honor of Captain Bach," he called out, "we will now sing the camp anthem."

Without hesitation the prisoners began to march stoutly in place. Necks rigid, backs straight, faces grave, they burst out in a military rhythm, bawling the German words to the song as loudly as possible while their slippers and shoes slapped against the wet earth of the compound.

> The workers' voices rise
> O'er the fields and trees
> We toil for bread and glory
> Until we fall to our knees.
>
> Our world is here at Zin
> Where work is the noble way
> Our cares are left behind
> Our task is to obey.
>
> We toil for bread and glory
> Rather than quit we die
> And we will never leave . . .
> . . . 'Til destiny winks an eye.

They sang hoarsely, out of tune, like drunken men in a bar at two o'clock in the morning.

"Not bad," said Stein, who had written the words to the melody of the "Horst Wessel" song. "But we'll do it once more. I want to be moved by your singing. I want Captain Bach to be moved. Sing from the very bottom of your hearts, as if you would wake the dead with your sincerity."

The mass of men stomped and shouted. The veins on their wizened necks swelled with blood. Tears sprang to some eyes.

Stein was satisfied. Then he launched into a speech.

"Today I was told there were two recent escapes from the camp. This has also been brought to the attention of Captain Bach, and although he has made no comment, I'm sure it made a bad impression on him. Why should anyone want to escape from here?" He raised his hands in the twilight, as if he were a preacher exhorting his congregation.

"If you fail, you'll be hanged. If you succeed, you'll be caught and brought back here—or someplace worse. I can see by your expressions that you don't believe there are worse places, but I assure you it's true. Our commandant is a humanitarian. Zin is like the bottom of a well during a fierce storm." He thrust a hand toward the east. "Our armies are locked in mortal combat with the Bolshevik hordes. We are winning! Never doubt! But the cost in human life is terrible. Does that affect any of you here? Anyone who does his work merits bread and glory. Think of our song! Its words are true. Only the shirkers are punished. Only the unfit are eliminated. That's not something I made up—it's the basic law of nature. Some of you have read Darwin. Work or die! A blind wolf, a crippled lion—neither survives for long. And now," he said, "let me illustrate. . . ."

Descending from his wooden box with Wolfgang trailing behind, he began to prowl up and down the ranks of Jews. Finally he halted in front of the upright figure of Avram Dobrany, former legionnaire and captain in the Czech army.

"You seem to be new here," Stein said. "I don't yet know you." With an exaggerated air of puzzlement, he bent, but not far down, to Wolfgang's ear.

"Mr. Wolfgang, have you ever seen this dog? Am I correct? Is he a new dog?" Wolfgang turned and licked Stein's thin lower lip. "What? I thought so. Thank you."

Hands on the hips of his black uniform, Stein straightened up, raising himself slightly on his toes, to address Dobrany again.

"My good and faithful friend confirms that you're a new dog. Introduce yourself."

Dobrany had anticipated such a moment. He knew he was not entirely immune. He had known Germans in the legion. Outcasts and scum like the rest, they were also victims of the Junkers military tradition and caste system. If they were enlisted men, they followed orders without question. If they were officers, they instantly respected any man who gave the outward appearance of blind and rigid obedience.

In that sense, Dobrany theorized, although the Germans at Zin literally held the whip hand, they were fools. I'll show this little martinet. I can play by his rules and go him one better.

He stood stiffly to attention in the military hobnailed boots he had brought from Ostrava, eyes steady and unblinking, back like a steel ruler, chin tucked tightly into his corded lean neck.

With razor-sharp precision he cried out, "Dobrany! Avram! Number 30829! Begs respectfully to report!—*sir!*"

Stein stared at him with reproach, then raised his riding crop. "I called you a dog. You didn't bark." He slashed the crop across Dobrany's knifelike nose.

Blood flowed down the Czech's face, which grew instantly white. He had to lower his eyes. He knew what they would reveal to Stein. The veins in his forehed stood out like blue twine. He was unable to recover from the shock.

Stein took one step to the side and reached up to smash the knobbed handle of the crop into Dobrany's ear. Dobrany staggered. His eyes bulged in their sockets.

I can kill him with my bare hands, he thought.

"Bark, dog!"

The lips moved, yet no sound issued from his mouth other than an agonized gargle, a bubble of humiliation.

"You're angry," Stein said, only mildly reproving, as if he were scolding a child for interrupting a conversation. "No, no, no." He struck him again lightly, across the buttocks. "Bad doggie."

But if I kill him, my own life is at an end. . . .

170

"Woof, woof," Dobrany said at last, in a hoarse whisper.

Stein's crop whistled once more through the dark air, drawing blood from Dobrany's neck.

"Louder! Like a good, obedient dog."

Dobrany's face was snowy with pain, but not from the blows. If he didn't strike back, he was no longer a man. But he had heard the story of what happened to the Dutch boy, Pieter, and the urge to live still ruled him.

In a strangled voice he cried, "Woof, woof!"

"Louder! I want the world to hear. Mongrel! Toy soldier!"

"WOOF—WOOF—WOOF!"

"Much better." Stein bowed his head in mock appreciation, then adjusted his glasses. "Now step to the front of the doggie battalion. Wait there for me."

Dobrany, eyes lowered so that no one could see his tears, half-marched, half-shambled to the designated place. Lieutenant Stein continued his inspection of the ranks until he halted in front of Leo Cohen. Tensing his muscles, Cohen waited to be struck.

But Stein only smiled coolly.

"We all know *you*, Blondie. A very special puppy. You don't need to bark for me, and I certainly don't intend to mark your pretty face. Someone we both know would be too upset. Yes? No, you don't have to agree. Just step forward with the other dog."

In front of the mass of waiting Jews, Stein studied the two men he had selected. Neither was a large man, but both were tall with sloping shoulders that narrowed to lean waists. They hardly belonged with most of the Jews, whose bodies, clad in rags, had been whittled down to the essence: bones packaged in skin. Their eyes were almost incapable of meeting a forthright gaze.

But Paul Bach's attention had been captured by the one called Blondie. To his surprise, Blondie's head swiveled on the muscular neck to return the look. Paul realized he stared into an old mirror. The crooked nose, thick mouth, and cool gray eyes, the jutting bones, were the same. It's me, he thought, twenty years ago.

A single vague star blinked between the clouds. Stein once more addressed his audience.

"I've told you that I'll illustrate Darwin's law. The fit survive!

171

The fit are content! The fit don't want to escape! These two"—he indicated Avram Dobrany and Leo Cohen—"seem to be fit. They will lead you in exercises to improve your physical stamina."

He gave his instructions.

Dobrany and Cohen began to jog in place. They kept it up for five minutes while the rest of the Jews aped them as best they could. Before the time period was over, half a dozen men slumped to the earth. They were taken away by the Ukrainians.

"Enough," Stein called easily. "Knees bent . . . hands up! Hop, my bunnies!"

Dobrany and Cohen hopped; so did the mass. A dozen more sprawled in the dirt and were dragged away.

"*Major* . . ." Paul spoke sharply.

"I made a mistake," Kirmayr said quietly, "but I can't interfere now. What's done is done."

"That's for the legs," Stein shouted. "This next one is for the abdomen. It requires cooperation!"

He showed Dobrany and Cohen what he had in mind. Cohen bent to hold Dobrany by the ankles, while the Czech placed his hands behind his neck and sat up, touching elbows to knees. "You two needn't continue," Stein said. He handed his riding crop to Dobrany. Grauert gave his to Cohen.

"Go among the doggie battalion," Stein instructed them. "If you see a lazy mutt, give him a hard one with the crop."

The Jews paired off and began their struggle to do the situps. Stein followed Leo Cohen down the first row of gasping men.

"Here, Blondie . . ." Stein pointed to Mordecai Lieberman, who lay flat on his back, unable to rise. "Don't you think this dog is shirking? He's your illustrious leader—he must be fit. So do your duty."

Cohen slashed the crop cruelly across Lieberman's thighs. Lieberman uttered a sigh. His body shaking as if in the grip of fever, he raised himself slowly and managed to touch one elbow to one knee.

In front of Block C, Paul again turned to his host. "Is this necessary, Major? Does it achieve anything?"

"I don't like it," the commandant replied, "but it's a mistake to interfere with discipline."

Paul made up his mind and took the first step on his road. "You asked me to say a few words to the men. May I do so now?"

"Of course, Captain! I'm delighted . . ."

He hurried forward to jump up on the wooden platform. It was fully dark now, but the square and the hundreds of squirming bodies were illuminated by the searchlights mounted on the barrack roofs.

"That will do!" Paul cried out. "You may stop!" His breath came in quick bursts. "Stop! I am impressed—I am satisfied. Lieutenant! You may dismiss the company."

Stein regarded him balefully with the same expression that Paul had seen in the eyes of the Gestapo sergeant at Wolkowysk. *Another Jew lover?* But Stein was not Gestapo. Paul was a superior officer, a distinguished guest. He turned to the Jews.

"You heard the captain," he said. "One last bark to show your appreciation for his kindness. Then you are dismissed."

A great *woof* rose from five hundred throats.

17

In his bungalow Paul switched on a lamp, then walked into the kitchen. A bottle of schnapps stood on the shelves with the jelly and tins of herring. He poured a glass half-full and drank greedily, letting it burn his gullet and then fill his stomach with heat. The glass was icy in his fingers. He put it down on a table in the sitting room and began to poke at the fire.

The cry of five hundred barking men still rang echoing in his mind.

Corporal Reitlinger knocked on the door. "Can I do anything for you, Captain?"

He turned, almost angrily, from where he knelt at the stove. But his anger was not directed at his corporal. "You can answer a question, Reitlinger. We had a conversation at that village where the train stopped. You told me you thought the Jews had done nothing to deserve being killed."

Young Reitlinger cracked his knuckles at the side of his greatcoat. "I remember."

"Do you still think that?"

"Yes, Captain."

"You also said they were boarding that train to be resettled. This is my question, Reitlinger. . . . Did you *believe* what you were saying?"

"I wanted to believe it," the corporal said.

He stood up, retrieved his drink and swallowed it. "You can go now, Reitlinger. Thank you."

He poured another drink.

"Don't you feel anything?" Sylvie had accused at the breakfast table. To feel too much is to be vulnerable. He had never been a friend of suffering. He had wanted to meet the challenge of his work, enjoy his children and his private pleasures. Sex beneath an eiderdown... Mozart on the gramophone, Rilke by the fireplace... decent wine, evenings with friends. Maybe a week at Tegernsee in August, the slopes of Kitzbühel in February.

And what had Sylvie felt? An SS clerk, a typist in the pool. Not inducted, but a volunteer. For all her breakfast-table concern over the brown-skinned millions in Calcutta, he thought, if it had been Jews starving, she would have said, "They deserve it. Their relatives all have gold in Zurich banks."

Perhaps, after Kristallnacht, that was what she *had* said. Paul had neatly blotted it from his mind.

She had believed all the claptrap about the perfect home with the perfect adoring Aryan children—believed that she and the rest of them were forging the future of the Fatherland against the Slavs, who had weakened the bloodlines of Europe and let their land go fallow; against the decadent French and the imperialist British, who had sold out to the American dollar; and above all against the Jews, who were oppressing decent people everywhere. The Führer had taken upon himself the burden of securing happiness for the common folk; his genius would shine like a torch for a thousand years.

Paul had only sighed, ignoring all that. *We agree to disagree.* In this manner, he thought, we pass the years without fraying the edges of our comfort. Hadn't he known, without having to go there, what went on at Sachsenhausen and Dachau? What Bella Wallach had told him about the Jews losing their winter coats and radios was not news. Reitlinger wanted to believe. So did he. We ignore what we don't have to face—what we choose not to face.

And Erich? Ushi? There I am truly delinquent. Culpable... but as usual, unarraigned.

He poured a third glass of schnapps.

And now it had come to this. To Zin. A truth too poisonous to be swallowed whole. *Two thousand a day.* He sank his head in his hand to blot out the light. For the first time in his life, he suffered from more than a personal sense of loss. He suffered because others suffered. And we, he thought—my people—inflict it on them. He wanted to cry out in rage.

What kind of men are we that we can do this?

Stein was a barbarian. Dressler a fanatic. Vogl memorized dossiers, lectured on death, expiated his sins in the arms of his blond Jewish lover. The commandant cultivated health-giving herbs, fed his Bella, drank himself to a numbed sleep. The Jews extracted gold teeth and bagged hair—carted bodies, covered with shit and blood, to the lower camp. They burned and buried them. They whipped each other on command. They barked like dogs.

All mad, he thought. All but one. That one, the one it was his duty to find and hang, may know exactly what he's doing.

He had a new vision of his quarry. Not a madman. A desperate man plotting a desperate move.

Lieberman limped past the women's barracks toward the latrines. A cold half-moon shone from a clear black patch of sky. The two wooden shacks stood on the slope of ripped-open field between Block B and the barbed-wire hedge isolating the lower camp. The latrine served as a meeting place to exchange gossip or shreds of news from the outside, barter stolen cigarettes for a piece of white bread, or just rest. The Jews had become used to the smell. The Germans avoided it.

Lieberman was almost as puzzled as he was weary. Why had the captain done that?

The commandant had tried to get them Polish ration cards, but that was to increase productivity. Vogl never whipped a Jew, yet didn't hesitate to usher pregnant women toward the gas chambers with the smiling assurance that "in a few minutes you'll feel wonderful." The captain's dismissal of the doggie battalion seemed to fall into another category.

Long ago Lieberman had stopped thinking of the Germans as human. But once upon a time, he knew, each of them had been a child, a child who feared its father's hand, yearned for its mother's warmth—a child who would weep if its pet was run over in the street.

Some must have children of their own. When the children bruise their knees roller skating, don't they kiss away the tears? Don't they make love to their wives and sweethearts, as we once did? A tenderness must be there.

How had they lost it? What fogging of the mind? What alchemy of the heart? He wanted badly to know the answers, but none came readily.

Perhaps, he thought, I should ask the captain.

From the darkness of the latrine, Dobrany appeared. The Czech had wiped most of the blood from his nose and cheek, but in the blurred moonlight Lieberman could see the raw welts on his neck from Rudy's whip. The inner part of his ear was swollen and purple.

Lieberman asked, "Are you all right?"

"Talk into my other ear," Dobrany said. "I can't hear out of that one."

Lieberman's body ached fiercely. His stomach quivered; his legs felt like sacks of rocks. He sat down on the dirt.

"Are *you* all right?" Dobrany asked.

"Not so good. My *kishkes* hurt. You know what are *kishkes*?"

Dobrany ignored him. "I wanted to kill that bastard," he said quietly.

"Wolfgang would have had your *kishkes* for supper. Now you know what are *kishkes*."

Dobrany gazed moodily out at the forest. They could hear branches creaking in the night wind.

"May all Stein's teeth fall out but one. So he'll still be able to have a toothache." Lieberman tried to grin. He explained: "An old Yiddish curse, which I don't think they use at the Athletic Union of Prague. But you did the right thing tonight, Dobrany. You barked very nicely."

Dobrany scowled. "I couldn't have used a whip on you. There I draw the line. That Dutch faggot hit you as hard as he could."

"If he had refused or been more delicate," Lieberman said instructively, "Rudy would have obliged. Rudy cuts to the bone. Blondie did the right thing."

Dobrany had hardly been listening. He still stared at the swarthy forest beyond the barbed wire. Lieberman now realized that some terrible struggle buffeted his mind. His lips were twisted back, and his fist was clenched. He began to gasp.

"What is it, Avram?"

Dobrany still struggled. Finally he found words.

"I didn't believe you," he said hoarsely. "About the camp. About my wife . . . my son . . ."

Lieberman reached up again, with more warmth, to clasp the other man's cold hand. "Don't think about that. It will drive you crazy. And I understand," he said quietly. "I also had sons."

"I loved my son . . ." Dobrany wailed. He shoved his knuckles into his mouth and bit on the flesh to stop himself from saying more. He was a man ashamed of deep feelings.

Lieberman was silent a while in sympathy. But it was necessary to speak.

"Avram, listen to me. Survival is a great talent. You showed it tonight when you didn't strike back at Stein. Don't be ashamed of what you did. And don't brood too much. They've been killing our sons and our fathers for four thousand years, ever since we were trapped in no-man's-land between Babylonia and Egypt. A Jew lives in no-man's land. Try to think as a Jew. You *are* a Jew. Do you know that now?"

"I'm a man. That's enough."

Lieberman wanted to debate that but checked himself. He wanted something else even more.

"Avenge your son," he said angrily. "Strike at them! The revolt—the battle!"

"I will," Dobrany murmured. "I swear on the life of my little son."

"You'll advise us?"

"That's what you want of me?"

"What do *you* want?"

"To fight with you. To lead you."

"You see, Avram? Jewish history! At the right time, the right man always appears." He glanced over his shoulder in the darkness to make sure they were beyond earshot of the men filing to and from the latrines.

"Tomorrow night in Block B," he said more quietly. "After soup. Don't be late!"

18

Rain fell vertically in a fluid gray wall that ripped at the earth and created a river of mud flowing from Roll Call Square past the latrines to the lower camp. The land sucked greedily and began to throw up green shoots. The trains were delayed. A dozen Polish whores were brought from Poznań to service the Ukrainians. When the rain eased, the skies over Zin resembled a sponge soaked in dirty oil. Pale lightning flickered over the forest. Grauert and Zuckermann kicked their soccer ball back and forth in the puddles, splashing their faces with mud and laughing like children. The trains began to arrive on time. Two yellow butterflies with brilliant red dots on their wings played around the waterlogged carts that were trundled down Freiheitstrasse.

Paul's sinuses dripped. During the day he drank pots of the commandant's bitter herb tea and at night, before sleeping, half a bottle of Polish vodka. He finished his box of Luminal tablets.

Some nights he lay totally still, listening to the drop of rain, the buffet of wind, and the bark of distant dogs. Other nights he entered a maze of dreams in which he fended off mutilated forms, skeletal phantoms, shrieking birds. He woke once to find flecks of blood on his pillow. In the foggy daylight, when he ventured into the camp, the same images passed before his eyes. They itched and burned so cruelly, without relief, that he wanted to tear them from their sockets. They were always inflamed.

He interrogated Germans and Jews alike. Could you tell the face of a man capable of murder? He had read quasiscientific analyses that offered theories, but long ago he had come up with his own disturbing answer. The face of a murderer looks like the face of any man I might pass on a sunny day strolling down Kurfürstendamm.

One morning the commandant knocked timidly on his door. He inquired as to his health, invited himself to a mug of herb tea. Thumped his bulk down on the sofa, picked some dead skin off a thumb . . . then cleared his throat.

"Bach, how is it possible? Haven't you come across any clues? Hasn't anyone pointed a finger? Haven't you got, at least . . . a *suspect*?"

Paul shrugged. "Major, I think you have the wrong idea of what a homicide investigation involves. You think it's peering with a magnifying glass at footprints in the mud . . . the discovery of a woman's silk handkerchief hidden behind a bureau. Well, sometimes. Most of it is note taking, examination of records, the use of paid informers, the wearing down of shoe leather while you hunt for people who usually give you no help whatever. Drudgery . . ."

He hesitated, then chose. "Let me give you a typical case. It happened a few years ago. The daughter of a rich industrialist," Paul said, "was snatched off the street in Grunewald. A ransom was asked and paid, and then the little girl was found floating face down in the Spree. Tragic. The father finally came weeping to the police, and I scoured the neighborhood and dug up a ten-year-old boy who remembered seeing a car stop that day and a little girl dragged in. He also recalled that the car didn't have a Berlin license plate, but he couldn't remember where in Germany it came from. He thought the car might have been of a foreign make but didn't know which. A lot of maybes. Now pay careful attention, Major. There were two ransom notes. The first was made up of printed words cut out from newspapers and magazines. The second note, telling where to leave the money, was printed in common blue ink. No fingerprints." Paul asked, "How would have you proceeded?"

Kirmayr stroked his cheeks, then shrugged. "I'm not a detective." He tilted his head forward. "What did *you* do?"

"We compared the print in the first ransom note to the typefaces in various newspapers all over Germany. We finally got a match in
182

the *Dresdener Zeitung*. So my men and I moved into a Dresden hotel. Every day we went to the automobile licensing bureau. We compared the printing on the second ransom note with the printing on application forms for licenses of foreign-made cars. We went back ten years. No match. So we thought, 'Maybe the boy was mistaken, maybe it wasn't a foreign car.' We started in again on German-made cars. By the end of each day, none of us could see straight. The printing started to blur—we could easily have missed what we were looking for. After two weeks we gave up and went back to Berlin. Tails between our legs, so to speak."

"You mean you never found the murderer?" The commandant seemed more disappointed than shocked.

"Patience, Major. A year later we picked up a young Berliner on suspicion of robbing a jewelry store. He drove a Skoda, a Czech car, with Berlin plates. It wasn't my case, but someone at the Kripo mentioned it to me and let slip that the man had a girlfriend in Dresden, a prostitute. I dropped in on this fellow in his cell and asked him to fill out an application for visiting privileges. He printed it, of course. I compared that with the old ransom note in the file on the unsolved kidnapping. A perfect match! The ten-year-old boy had been right about the foreign car but wrong about the plates . . . the kind of mistake anyone could make. After a day or so without sleep under the lights, the fellow confessed. He and his girlfriend from Dresden were guilty." Paul brought his hand down on the back of his neck, meaning that they had gone to the guillotine.

"But—that was all just luck!" Now the commandant was shocked more than disappointed. "And coincidence!"

"Yes," Paul said, shrugging, "it was dumb luck and coincidence . . . if that's how you look at things."

"If your friend hadn't spoken to you—"

"You *need* a bit of dumb luck, Major. And sometimes you can make your luck if you're diligent, listen well, and keep an open mind. Now, if you'll excuse me, I have work to do . . ."

Arms were waving and spittle was flying in the darkest corner of

Block B. After yesterday's terror of the roll call, Lieberman thought it was a good sign. It was as natural for Jews to argue as it was for lice to bite.

Dobrany arrived from Block A. He nodded politely to Stephan Wallach. He looked Aron Chonszki up and down, impressed by the former butcher's physical stature, but his eyes clouded when he peered into the open, broad-boned Polish face. He knew the story of how Chonszki had acquired his nickname. A peasant, he thought. The dentist is a wild-eyed wreck. And Lieberman is an old man before his time, lucky to be alive.

"I wish to help you," he said.

The welts on his face and the swollen ear now gave him good credentials. Lieberman brought out some black bread, and Dobrany offered a ten-bladed Swiss pocketknife to cut it. Wallach dug a bit of margarine from his coat pocket, Chonszki a slab of stolen liverwurst.

"Let's talk while we eat," Wallach said. "Lieberman—report."

Lieberman had been recruiting. He had his five men—Porzowski of the burial commando in the lower camp, Mashlik in the bakery, both from Poznań; Pinchas Levy, the carpenter; Jacob Bomberg in the tailor shop, which made fur-lined winter coats for the Germans; Rabinowitz the locksmith.

Chonszki then gave his list, and it was approved.

Stephan Wallach's eyes shifted from one man to another. He had not yet spoken to anyone, he said. He had been busy making a plan. The first object of the revolt, he explained, would be to mount an attack on the administrative bungalow—to kill Commandant Kirmayr.

"Because," he said, clenching his fist, "what you try to do in a battle is first eliminate the enemy leader. When that's done, the rest of the Germans will panic."

Dobrany so far had said nothing. But now he interrupted. "Wallach, the commandant is not the military leader. That's Stein. And even if we start out by killing both of them, it won't lead to any victory. These are SS soldiers in the camp. The Blackies all fought in Russia. They think of us as dogs. They'll slaughter us."

But with Bella cuckolding him, Lieberman realized, Wallach no

184

longer cared if he lived or died. He felt a rush of sympathy, but he readjusted his thoughts.

"Before we go on," he said, "I have a proposal. A new member of the committee. We were lucky to get Captain Dobrany. Now we need one more, to increase our strength."

"Who, Pan Lieberman?" Chonszki asked.

"Leo Cohen."

"Blondie?" Chonszki's blue eyes widened. "He's an informer!"

"He sleeps with Vogl. That makes him a pansy, not an informer."

Dobrany frowned. "We had faggots in the legion. You never know what they'll do next. They can't be trusted."

"I share your prejudices," Lieberman replied. "And that's all they are. Bella explained this to me. Blondie hates the Germans as much as we do and for good reason. What he does with Vogl is his insurance policy. It can be of use to us. He'll be like a spy . . . a male Mata Hari."

They argued for ten more minutes. Chonszki at last voted with Lieberman, but Dobrany refused to change his mind and Wallach sided with him.

"That settles it," Lieberman said, relieved. "I'll go get Blondie."

"It's two against two!" Wallach protested.

"Your wife has the fifth vote, Stephan."

He excused himself and limped away toward the far end of the block where Blondie slept when he was not with Lieutenant Vogl. He heard moans and snores, the sounds of stealthy chewing and low voices. Gathered in a group, the Jews resembled a clump of exhumed skeletons, almost indistinguishable from each other. Some had lost their memories. Some spent hours staring straight ahead with no sign of life. If the time came, they would let themselves be led to the hospital without protest. Lieberman gazed at the boils and oozing sores, the palsied limbs, the dulled and terrified eyes, and understood the depths to which they had fallen. He experienced a sudden despair. We're fooling ourselves, he thought. They have beaten us already.

Then Leo Cohen entered the block from outside. His cheeks were flushed; his youthful eyes were clear and gray.

185

Lieberman greeted him politely. "I forgive you for whipping me yesterday, Herr Cohen."

"Thank you, Herr Lieberman."

"I would have done the same."

"Maybe not," Cohen said.

When he brought Blondie back to the others, Dobrany said coolly, "We met at roll call. You understand who we are? What we intend to do?"

"Bella told me everything."

"And you're with us?"

Cohen raised an eyebrow. "You see me here, don't you?"

Lieberman ignored that and rubbed his hands together as if he were about to carve an exceptionally fine roast. "So now let's give the floor to our military expert. Have you had time, Captain, to think up any strategy?"

"Yes." Dobrany spoke dispassionately. "The most important thing in our favor is the element of surprise. The Germans think of us as subhumans. An armed revolt is inconceivable. We can go quite far without arousing their suspicions . . . provided we continue to bark."

In the course of planning his solo escape, Dobrany had carefully studied the terrain. The birch forest was only a mile distant, but the four watchtowers were equipped each with a heavy machine gun. "We'll need a major diversion. I don't yet know what. Something that draws as many of the enemy as possible to one part of the camp and also captures the attention of the machine gunners so we can get at them. Now let's work backward to preparation. . . ."

He discussed the accumulation of food, then of weapons. "To buy them both, we need gold. And Polish zlotys, to survive when we get out of the forest—however many of us are left."

"I have enough." Leo Cohen spoke quietly, but they all heard.

"Of what?"

"Gold. Zlotys."

Wallach hunched forward. "How much?"

"About eighty thousand zlotys. Maybe fifty thousand dollars in gold. Most of it is twenty-dollar coins."

"Where did you get all that?"

"It grows on trees, Herr Wallach, if you know where to look." Cohen let out a short high laugh, revealing a silver tooth.

"And what did you plan to do with this little nest egg?" Lieberman asked. "Go into competition with Rothschild?"

Cohen hesitated, then said, "I planned to do exactly what you're doing. I didn't know about this group until Bella told me. Then I realized we had the same idea. It was obviously necessary to join forces."

Lieberman's little gray head jerked back as if he had been lightly slapped. "You planned an escape?"

"We called it an uprising."

"How many of you?"

"Eventually, all. Right now I have Jozek from the gravel commando. Prager and Wohlberg from the farm. Engel from the machine shop. A dozen others like that."

"And who is the leader?"

Cohen blushed. "I am, Herr Lieberman."

Why, Lieberman thought, should I be the only one with good ideas? Why did I see a mass that had to be cajoled? Why did I ever think a pansy couldn't be trusted? He wanted to dance with pleasure.

He knew three of the four men Cohen had mentioned. They were all under twenty-one. Lieberman had wanted more experienced men who could be counted on not to do anything rash. But Cohen's group had certainly kept its counsel. With him and Dobrany, Lieberman thought, we have a chance. We are not beaten.

"You have guns?" Dobrany asked.

"Not yet. But we worked out some tactics. I have an idea for the diversion."

"Give it to me. In my good ear, if you don't mind."

"A fire in Vogl's bungalow. I can start it. It will bring everyone running, especially if Vogl's there and screaming his head off."

Dobrany considered for a minute and then said calmly, "You'll have to kill Vogl."

"I understand," Cohen said, with an even icier calm.

Dobrany seemed satisfied. "It's not a bad idea. It may bring the guards down off the watchtowers. . . ."

It was settled that the revolt would take place in the early evening—still light enough to find their way into the forest, soon dark enough to hamper pursuit. They came to the question of fixing a date.

Chonszki blinked nervously. "There's no hurry. . . ."

"There's a lot to do," Wallach agreed.

Lieberman understood. They would be in the vanguard; they were deciding the date of their death. Now, however wretchedly, they lived. But each day they waited brought more risk. If any of them were caught with a pistol or gold, even a knife, he would be tortured for information. Whipped in the coal cellar, hung by his feet on Roll Call Square until his brains burst.

"Can't we be ready in ten days?" Lieberman asked.

Dobrany shook his head firmly. "I need a month."

Lieberman nodded his acceptance. "Tomorrow," he said, looking destiny in the eye, "I'll give you all cyanide pills."

19

Zin: April 1943

Late the next afternoon, in a light drizzle, Lieutenant Vogl and Corporal Munzing drove to Breslau in one of the camp's supply trucks. They did this at least twice a week, always returning the following day at noon. Munzing had a girlfriend who worked in Breslau as a waitress, and he always vanished immediately. Vogl, the camp supply officer, went to a cinema or cruised the soldiers' bars, then slept at the Wehrmacht barracks. In the early morning he met Munzing and they would deal with the list of chores typed out on onionskin paper by Captain Dressler and Sergeant Zuckermann.

Soon after the truck bounced through the camp gate, Leo Cohen got word to Bella. At seven o'clock, when darkness fell, she slipped out of Block D and splashed through the puddles as if on her way to a rendezvous with the commandant. Once the departing searchlight beam plunged her dappled figure into even grayer vagueness, she veered off the gravel path and scratched with her fingernails on the door of Vogl's bungalow.

Cohen let her in, slid the bolt, then folded her into his arms. He could feel her quickly beating heart.

Zin: February 1943

The rabbi had been mistaken. It was possible to be in love at Zin. Leo Cohen could have explained it to him. It required only opportunity, desperation, and the recklessness of youth.

He loved Bella long before the first time they lay together in

189

Vogl's bed. But he would never have dared to say what he felt. For that, he thought, I am not worthy or capable.

Then one day, talking quietly in the darkness outside the latrine, she said to him, "Have you never been with a woman?"

"I didn't say that, Bella."

"You had a girlfriend once?"

"No, not that way. Never."

"Then—?"

"I went with women. Twice, maybe three times. I paid them. In Le Havre and Southampton. It wasn't good. . . . I told you that."

"But there was no one you ever loved?"

"I loved Pieter," he said simply. "I knew him in Rotterdam. We wanted to go together to Palestine and work in the desert. And before that, when I was much younger, I loved an older man. He was thirty—he seemed older. I was sixteen. He was the mate on my ship. He wasn't a kind man, but I couldn't help myself."

Even in the darkness he could see her deepening frown.

·"It disgusts you?" he asked.

"Yes," she admitted. "I can't help it. But not a great deal, and it makes no difference. Would you make love to me?" she asked suddenly, bravely.

"If you would let me," he said, with a catch in his voice. "I would try. But I couldn't promise anything. Although . . ."

"Although—?"

"Never mind," he said, coloring a little. "But you're not serious, Bella. You're making fun of me."

"No, I'm not. I'm serious. I want to do it."

"But why?" He shivered.

"I'll tell you afterward. I'm a Jew," she said, mocking his first words to her. "Do you trust me?"

"With my life," he replied gravely. "You know that. You risk everything for me."

"Not for you, Leo."

By then Stephan had renounced her, saying, "In the sight of God you are no longer my wife." In that sense she felt free. Lieberman had brought her into the revolt committee; she had told Leo and begun to convince him to join his little group of young Jews with the older ones in Block B. In that sense she felt doomed to die.

A few evenings later, with Vogl gone to Breslau, they met in the bungalow. Next door, Wolfgang growled and barked. She could feel Leo's nervousness.

"He always barks," she said. "And Stein is with the commandant tonight."

"It's not that."

"One thing must be clear," she said to him. "I don't love you. I want no talk of love. And you mustn't pretend anything. I accept that you don't love me, either."

"But perhaps I do," he said quietly.

She touched his lips with her fingers. "You're very young."

"So are you."

"I was married," she said bitterly. "I know what love is."

A murky light sifted through the drawn damask curtains. The searchlights swept the compound. They had sipped a small glass of Vogl's egg brandy—for courage. She lifted her dress, letting it spill to the carpet. Cohen drew his breath sharply at the sight of her white thighs, the round white breasts and little hard buds. The whores he had known in port towns had reeked of flowery perfume. Bella smelled of sweat, of musk and youth.

He had worried, because she was married and so young, that she would be cold and ungiving.

When he undressed, she stroked him gently and told him how beautiful he was. It was true: he was lean and corded with muscle like a runner.

She took him quickly, firmly, without shyness or much preparation. But she cried out in her passion beneath him, and he had to clap a hand to her mouth. She bit his thumb.

Later she said, "Was it awful for you?"

"Bella! No!"

"I didn't think so. . . ." She smiled slyly.

They were sprawled on the bed, exhausted. When they were at last apart from each other and putting on their clothes, he said, "But if not from love, Bella, then why?"

"Does it matter why?"

"You promised you'd tell me. To me it matters. Is it just for pleasure?"

"It's a reason."

"The only one?"

"No. To catch at straws. To feel alive, Leo, while there's time."

But he somehow understood that there was even more. Perhaps the other thing was more difficult to say. Perhaps it was only he who felt it, but he doubted that. He glanced down at the outlines of the lieutenant's bed, which she had smoothed to its former neatness, tucking in the hospital corners. He had loved Pieter, and they had clung to each other in the dark of the barracks like wasted souls, touching and soothing and shedding tears even as they felt the desire that sprang from gratitude. But here, on this bed, he had let himself be used like a piece of meat.

"And to be clean again," he said.

In the darkness he felt Bella's cold fingertips press his cheek, trace the outline of the bone with wordless agreement. With love, he might have thought, had he dared.

Zin: April 1943

In Captain Dressler's office, Paul completed his examination of the camp records, the dossiers on personnel, the various commandos, and certain Jews. The records were scanty. Even the bureaucrats here had no time to do a decent job. The turnover, he realized, defeated them.

He had already satisfied himself on one point regarding the murderer's notes: they seemed to have been written by a single right-handed person. In the first two notes, printed in Hebrew, the strange spidery characters moved from right to left across the page; it was difficult to compare them to the ones written in German. But the margins, the spacing between words and lines in all three languages, the use of the same onionskin paper and soft pencil, argued for the same author.

"Dressler," he asked, "besides yourself, which Germans in the camp have access to a supply of this onionskin?"

"Any of them," Dressler said. "It's used in every office, every detail."

A search made no sense. If I had to hide it, Paul thought, it certainly wouldn't be under my own mattress. Any fingerprints had been bruised or already faded in the air. He considered handwriting samples, but the murderer of Margulies and Hrubow would be clever enough to disguise his hand. He thought of the Dresden kidnapping case. If I could study old documents printed by the Jews, I might find a matching style.

But there were no applications for admission to Zin.

Among what the commandant called "the resident population" was the man he sought. He ruled out the rabbi, whose devotion to Mosaic law would stand like a barred oak door before the possibility of taking human life. He ruled out Bella Wallach and the Wijnberg sisters. Women who used knives on hated husbands or fathers always stabbed; he knew of no case where a woman had cut a man's throat. All three women lacked the physical strength to have strangled Margulies.

He let the concept of motive nibble only at the edge of his mind. The question of *cui bono*—whom did it profit?—was too vague. When he found the man, motive would become clear. Then he would be free. Free, at least, to go.

After talking to Dressler, he walked back to his bungalow through a light rain. He was depressed as never before in his life. If he could, he would have effaced himself from the surface of the earth, crawled into a warm hole, slept forever. He realized what he was thinking. He understood now why a man committed suicide: he could not bear one more day of self-torture.

Free to go . . . but go where? Back to Berlin and pretend that he had not seen what he had seen. Forget about Zin—the Road to Freedom, the windowless brick buildings with claw marks in the walls, the lower camp with its stench and shifting earth. But to forget would be impossible. If possible, then unforgivable.

But what can *I* do? He asked himself that question over and over. He remembered what Reitlinger had said at Wolkowysk: "If you

193

interfered, you would have been risking your life—and for what? They would still have loaded the train."

Here at Zin he had no power to interfere. And even if he tried, if he could find a way—what would it accomplish? Perhaps in stopping the exercises at roll call he had saved the lives of a handful of men. But he knew their lives were not saved; their death was only briefly postponed. Their suffering would go on. And in the end there would be no witnesses. None, he thought, except us.

And when the war is over, will we go before the tribunals of the world and proclaim our manhood by recounting this tale? Will we confess? Boast? Deny? He no longer understood the mentality of his own people. He knew only that they committed a crime beyond belief or punishment . . . *and they were unaware of it.*

Such thoughts led him nowhere other than an abyss of self-disgust. The only thing that could save him, he decided, was his work. Where it would lead, he had no idea. But perhaps to an unforeseen answer.

He cleared the table and once again assembled the collection of notes, both the originals and the typed translations, while Reitlinger kindled an oak fire in the stove. The room was cozy and warm, the drapes drawn to cut off any view of the gray sky and compound. Paul unscrewed his fountain pen, and digging into his briefcase, took out a small black Kripo notebook with a swastika on the cover. He opened it to a fresh ruled page.

The notes are the key, he thought. What kind of man am I looking for?

In the first note the writer had chided a fellow prisoner for the sloppiness of his bunk. Was he himself neat? The note seemed self-consciously witty, striving for irony. He had a streak of vanity.

Paul's pen scratched across the page.

The first two notes were written in Hebrew. The Angel was scholarly. And religious? In the second note he spoke of "the Law"—in the third he referred to "next year in Jerusalem." Paul had queried the rabbi as to whether that was a practical thought or a quotation, and the rabbi had explained the concept of the yearning for the rebuilding of Zion.

But in the third note, Paul decided, the tone subtly changed.

194

Avenge me, comrades! the Angel wrote—in anger. Or was that ironic, too?

In the fourth note, pinned to the Ukrainian barracks, he had written, *you will never again see the sun rise above the beloved Sea of Azov.* Paul had checked an atlas in Dressler's office. Had the murderer studied geography or been to Russia? Did the Ukrainians reminisce in front of the prisoners, in a language they could understand?

He wrote again in his black book.

The fifth note, in its way, was even more revealing than the first four. *Of two solutions, a Jew always chooses the third.* The note had accompanied a suicide. Upon such an occasion, who would have the taste for an aphorism? A comedian? No, this man is bitter. He uses wit to mask his feelings.

The sixth note, pinned to the body of Margulies—*Only another dead Jew.* Grisly. Mocking. But if you listened for accents, enraged. A man had been murdered, but the murderer was also an accuser.

The seventh note, found on Lieutenant Hrubow's body, echoed the first message concerning the Ukrainians' fate at Zin. *"Er wär sowieso gestorben—Ich helf ihm nur ein bisschen."* (He would have died anyway—I am just helping him a little bit.)

Crude, Paul thought. No trace of the former elegance. No anger. And *wär* was grammatically sloppy; *wäre* would have been proper. The earlier note that had been written in German was longer, yet couched more cleverly and with no grammatical errors.

He understood something now. The first six notes were deliberately conceived and written in advance. The note on Hrubow's body had been scratched hastily—as if the harried murderer had nevertheless felt obligated to take responsibility lest it fall on someone else. He was a man of some moral backbone. And the murder of Lieutenant Hrubow had not been planned.

"He killed Margulies because he intended to," Paul murmured, "but he killed Hrubow because he *had* to." He reconstructed the scene in his mind. Late afternoon of a cold April day. The Jews are still at work. My man enters the barracks for a purpose that has nothing to do with Hrubow. But Hrubow is there; he's taken off his fur hat, unbuttoned his coat and jacket. They see each other. They

195

talk or they don't talk . . . and my man kills him, getting close enough to do it with a single slash. From behind, so he won't be spattered with blood.

He drags the body to another part of the barracks. He takes time to smooth out the path and any sign of where the murder took place.

Why bother?

And why was Hrubow's bayonet detached from the carbine? It was not the murder weapon. Paul had checked with Dr. Lustig, who swore he had examined it carefully under his microscope. Blood was a tenacious substance.

Paul looked at what he had written in his notebook.

Neat (?) Young (?)
Writes good Hebrew and Yiddish, erratic German.
Scholarly. Religious (?)
Angry. Bitter. Wit to mask feelings.
Knows Russian geography (?)

He added two entries. "Strong"—he had strangled one healthy man and dealt with another who was armed. "Freedom of movement in the camp."

He scanned the translations. Sergeant Zuckermann had methodically stamped them all with the date of discovery. Paul scribbled a final caveat.

"Arrival at Zin—no later than Jan. 24, 1943."

He lit a cigarette, then paced the carpet for ten minutes while it burned itself out in the glass ashtray, leaving a wet brown stain and an odor that made him choke. He opened the door. The rain had stopped. Reitlinger lounged against the wall of the nearby infirmary, talking to one of the German corporals. Behind them in the lower camp, a rich red blaze rose toward the gunmetal sky. Neither man seemed to notice it.

Paul's hand squeezed the hilt of the dagger sheathed at his side.

He beckoned to Reitlinger, who moved quickly forward.

"Find Rabbi Hurwicz," he said. "Tell him I want to question some of the prisoners. I'll give him their names."

196

20

Reitlinger waited outside, and the rabbi took up a chair in a corner. Paul could hear his raspy breathing, the bubble of the tea as it passed his lips, the soft shuffling of his shoes like a boa constrictor on the Bokhara carpet. The wood stove gave off a steady red heat.

The blond young Dutch Jew sat in an easy chair, drinking his tea and munching on French biscuits, legs planted hard in front of him, eyes peering defiantly from the fine-boned face with its floppy ears and bladed nose. In the warmth of the bungalow, he had taken off his pea jacket. Under it he wore a ragged shirt and loose brown trousers. His boots were caked with mud. For the first time Paul noticed a small blue Star of David tattooed on Leo Cohen's right wrist.

How little I know of him, he thought. How little I know of any of them.

He questioned Cohen easily about his job with the gravel commando, his movements about the camp, his feelings for the dead Margulies and Lieutenant Hrubow. The answers were terse, youthfully flippant, and edged with irony—what Paul had expected. In Cohen's eyes he saw an icy contempt. Here, he thought, may be the Angel of Death. As a man, he qualifies.

His youth will betray him, Paul decided.

"You speak Yiddish, Herr Cohen?"

"Poorly."

"And write it?"

"The same."

"Hebrew?"

"A few words, that's all."

"And yet your German is very good."

"I was a merchant seaman. I sailed often to Hamburg and learned German. I sailed to Southampton and Le Havre—I learned some English and French. *Bloody fuckin' bastard. Merde alors.* There was nowhere to sail to learn Hebrew."

"But I'm told by the rabbi that you were a member of Hashomer Hatsaïr. Its object was emigration to Palestine. You would have needed to know Hebrew. Isn't that so?"

Cohen glanced briefly at Rabbi Hurwicz. The look contained a flash of perplexity, confusion at even such a small betrayal. Then it vanished as quickly as it had appeared.

"I studied a bit, but only conversationally."

"Do you speak it here?"

"I had a friend. He tried to teach me. His name was Pieter."

"Was?"

"He's dead."

"Did you ever sail to the Black Sea, Herr Cohen?"

"Never that far, Captain."

"Before the war, Dutch merchant ships didn't sail to Odessa and Sevastopol?"

"Some did," Cohen said. "Not mine. It was a small freighter. North Sea and Channel trade."

"Or to Rostov?"

". . . Rostov?"

"On the Sea of Azov."

Cohen's eyes flickered uneasily. "They may have sailed there, Captain. I wouldn't know."

"You have the Star of David on your wrist. Is that allowed in your religion?"

"A folly," Cohen said. "I was sixteen. All sailors are tattooed. We docked in Antwerp, and my shipmates got me drunk. In any case, I'm no longer religious." It seemed more of an accusation than a statement.

198

"You lost your faith?"

"I never called it faith. Faith is for rabbis and children. I called it a belief in a reasonably interesting God."

Paul wanted to keep him talking, draw him out. He recalled a phrase from one of his conversations with Rabbi Hurwicz. "You don't believe that the fear of the Lord is the beginning of knowledge?"

"I never did." Cohen hesitated, then thrust out his jaw. "Before I came here," he said, "I saw the connection between God and this world. That's not difficult for a sailor. In a North Sea gale, whether you're aware or not, you pray. I also believed that God had created man in His own image. Therefore He was irrational, changeable. Vengeful, even merciful, on occasion. But, like men, He could not be relied on. Prayer is an instinct, not an intelligent action. In that respect I was not a good Jew."

"But you no longer believe all that," Paul persisted.

Cohen leaned forward in his chair, gray eyes glinting with flecks of blue. "Do you want to know why, Captain?"

"If you'll tell me."

"Why should I?"

"I didn't say you had to."

Given the choice, as Paul suspected, Cohen chose to speak.

"I was picked up at the docks one morning in Rotterdam by some of your SS and the Dutch traitor police. I was sent here. I wasn't joyful at the idea, but I didn't shit my pants. My parents and little sister had already gone some months before. They had sent postcards from Auschwitz. They were working hard, they wrote, the food was 'tolerable,' the general treatment 'correct.' I believed all this. I didn't look for a way to escape. It wasn't even a terrible journey—for the Dutch Jews they provided real railway cars. I thought, well, my family's waiting for me, the war can't last forever, and I'll still be young. So I reached Zin, not Auschwitz. It's Hell, Captain. You may have noticed." He paused. "Do I bore you? Why do you want to hear this? Are you a sadist, Captain?"

"I want to hear it," Paul said, "because I want to know."

"And I want very much for you to know," Cohen said, with surprising heat. Any levity had vanished. "No German has ever asked me before . . . not even Lieutenant Vogl. I consider it a great opportunity."

He leaned forward on the edge of his chair. "When I arrived here, I realized instantly that the postcards were a trick. My parents and sister were dead. I might have become a drowned man if it were not for my friend Pieter. I knew him from Hashomer Hatsair in Holland. He rescued me. Then he fell asleep on his job. As punishment, the lieutenant shot him."

Paul was silent a moment, tapping the rim of his empty teacup. "And because of that," he said slowly, "you lost your belief in your God. . . ."

"Does it seem unreasonable to you?"

"No. I'm asking for a confirmation."

"It didn't happen that way," Cohen said. "I'll tell you the truth, Captain—you deserve to know. I lost my belief within the first twelve hours of my arrival. I told you I nearly became a drowned man. On the train with me there were hundreds of children. Dutch children, Belgian children, some Polish children who got on at Poznań. They were taken away immediately and killed by the gas. My first job here was to haul bodies in carts to the lower camp. That job is always given to the young and strong, for as long as they last."

His eyes were as hard and milky gray as opals. "Try to imagine this, Captain. I could not have done so. I had never believed for a single moment that such a thing could happen on the surface of the earth. You see, I believed that God and man alike had set limits to the degradation of human beings. A storm at sea that takes the lives of innocent sailors, a war in which men maim and slaughter other men, the murder of a rich man for his money, or a brutal husband in revenge—all that was terrible enough, but it was still *human.* You could whip and kill, even torture for a purpose, however perverted it might be—and it was still in some way human. It had been done before, for centuries, by so-called civilized peoples. But I had never conceived in my worst nightmares that human beings would be capable of taking three hundred little children and calmly—*calmly, Captain, without the slightest anger, and not in revenge*—gas them to death. Can you comprehend it, Captain? Can you picture that scene in your mind? I doubt it. . . .

"But I *saw* it," Cohen said. One foot began to tap uncontrollably on the carpet. "So I collapsed, began to drown. I no longer saw a reason to live in this kind of world. It was not just hell here. The world—the *world*, Captain—had become hellish."

The image of the event that young Leo Cohen described rose up in Paul's mind—then, as Cohen had predicted, faded. His mind refused to allow it sufficient purchase. Now he understood why he had visited the gas chambers and the lower camp but not the railway station upon the arrival of the trains. To see the mass of living, who in minutes would be the dead, would be unbearable. *I don't know any of their names. I haven't seen any of their faces.*

"But you recovered," Paul said, drawing a shaky breath.

"I was hauled from the water," Cohen replied, more calm now, "and brought back to life, thanks to Pieter. Thanks to the love of another human being. And I have survived to this point, as you see. But without God."

"Your friend, Pieter . . ." Paul said quietly. "You said the lieutenant shot him. Lieutenant Hrubow?"

"No. Stein did that."

"You're positive?"

"Would I forget, Captain? If you doubt me, ask him. He won't remember Pieter's name—there have been so many. He may remember a boy who fell asleep on the job with the camouflage commando. It was on the twenty-second of February. He may remember that his dog tore off Pieter's testicles."

"You have a good memory, Herr Cohen."

"For such things, yes."

"Can you remember, for example, when your train left Holland?"

Cohen's silver tooth glittered in the light of the crackling stove. "I spent my nineteenth birthday on the train, passing through Westerbork. We left Rotterdam on February sixth. It was just starting to snow."

"And how long was the train journey?"

"A week. Exactly seven days, almost to the hour."

"So you arrived here about February fourteenth. Two months ago. Are you sure of that?"

Cohen nodded absentmindedly, as if it was of no significance.

But to Paul it was of significance. The Angel's first note, concerning neatness in the barracks, had been discovered on January 24. The third note—*Avenge me, comrades!*—had been found pinned to the body of a man who died on February 12. If Cohen was telling the truth, he had not yet reached Zin.

When the youth had gone, Paul turned to Rabbi Hurwicz. His eyes were nearly closed, and he rocked a little, back and forth, on his wooden chair.

"Rabbi . . ."

"Captain?" The eyes remained hooded.

"Do you remember when Leo Cohen arrived in the camp?"

The rabbi, who had been concentrating on Passover, instantly brought his mind to bear on the problem. He remembered the Dutch boy, Pieter, who had sought him out and asked permission to read the *Haphtorah* on the Chanukah sabbath. That was in the month of Kislev. By Purim, on the fourteenth of Adar, he was dead.

This other one with the tattoo on his wrist certainly hadn't been here for Chanukah. The rabbi made it his business to talk then with every Jew in the camp, requesting his presence for at least the kindling of a single candle in the menorah. But for Purim, yes. I remember his voice reading from the Megillah. An awful accent. For The Fast of the Tenth of Teveth? No, he wasn't here. But for The Sabbath Relating to the Shekels—yes. He asked to be included in the service. He was mourning for his friend.

"He arrived," the rabbi announced to Paul, "in the first part of the first week of Adar."

Paul was bewildered. "Rabbi . . . what is Adar?"

"The first part of the first week of the month of Adar was in the middle of February, according to your calendar. It was snowing. I remember it like yesterday."

"So he told the truth. . . ." Paul spoke aloud, but to himself. "He could not have written the notes."

202

"Not the first ones," the rabbi said, trying to be helpful.

Paul thought for a while.

"Thank you, Rabbi. You can go now."

He called Reitlinger back inside.

"Get a shovel and pickax," he said. "Wrap them in a blanket so they don't attract attention. Then meet me outside Block C."

"I talked too much," Cohen said later, thinking of his meeting with the captain from Berlin.

The gray evening light had begun to fade. It was often colder in the barracks than outside, and the men wore their coats. They lived in them, slept in them, shared them with their lice.

Lieberman nodded. "The captain has a problem. He has a conscience. In Germany that's gone out of style. It's like having a tail."

But Cohen shook his head. "No living German," he said, "would trade the pain of his conscience for even a Jewish toothache."

Lieberman understood the younger man's unwillingness to accept the captain's humanity. If you accepted that, it restored a shred of your faith. It gave you a margin of hope. But for what they were going to do, neither faith nor hope was required. Not even desirable. Animal cunning, blind desperation—that was all they needed.

The revolt committee met now on every possible occasion, going over the plans. On this occasion Chonszki had stolen some rancid cheese and shriveled onions from a train that had arrived from Thessaloníki. After they ate, Lieberman dug into his pocket and produced five small glass vials that were shaped like bullets. He juggled them in the palm of his hand.

"Bella already has hers. You can't just swallow. You have to bite the glass. You'll cut your lips . . . but you won't feel any pain."

The others nodded absentmindedly and dropped the cyanide capsules into their pockets, except for Wallach, who still held his between thumb and forefinger. An indecipherable sound broke from his throat.

"Stephan . . . ?"

"I think we have better use for these."

"Then tell us."

"Bella could put one in Kirmayr's coffee. Cohen could do the same to Vogl. The others . . ." Wallach grinned. "We'll just shove them down their throats."

"They will be shot," Dobrany said.

"You mean later, *if* we do this thing. I mean now."

Lieberman spoke gently. "Stephan, if you killed the commandant now, you can kiss our plans goodbye. Rudy would wipe out the camp. We are replaceable."

"You're preparing this revolt as if you were studying the Talmud. And it won't work," Wallach muttered. "They'll find out, someone will inform, and then it will be too late." He raised the capsule in front of their eyes. "A waste!"

Lieberman thought it was better to placate him. "Avram, will it be possible, on the given day, to let Stephan shoot the commandant?"

"No," Dobrany replied, disgusted. "Every man will have a job that suits him, that he can do correctly, quickly, without emotion getting in the way. I don't want to discuss this any more, do you hear? This is how it will work. . . .

"There are three phases to the operation. Preparation, execution, and escape. Without perfect preparation, execution will be a disaster. Without precise execution, escape simply cannot take place. So although escape is the aim, preparation is the key. Preparation is *now*, and right up to the minute that Cohen lights the fire in Vogl's bungalow."

He discussed weapons. He and some men in his unit had already bribed two Ukrainian guards for pistols, which they had claimed would be used for individual escape. The price for each had been six hundred dollars in gold.

"I felt like a housewife in the market bargaining for onions. The Blackie asked eight hundred. I offered four. He yelled. I yelled. Finally we compromised. I thought, what's money? Our friend Leo is richer than the Bank of Prague."

"Where do you have the pistols?" Lieberman asked.

"Hidden. Better that you don't know where."

"And rifles?"

204

"I'll get them," he said coolly. "Let me explain. . . ."

He gave them the timetable. In the early evening the guards at their machine guns would be lured down from their towers—a false message from Prince Rudy, a flash of gold in the hand. Cohen would start the fire. The watchtower guards would be killed, their weapons seized. Dobrany would do the same to the guards in the armory: He would pass out rifles and grenades. Specific men under his orders, already armed, would kill Stein, Dressler, and Lustig. "And Bach, if he's still here. Leo will take care of Vogl. Bella, the commandant."

Chonszki's unit would cut the telephone wires and immobilize the vehicles that might try to reach the Wehrmacht garrisons at Poznań or Breslau. Cohen's men would mount the assault on the lower camp. Bella would organize the women, who would be armed with knives and scissors. Wallach's unit would destroy the barbed-wire fence behind the farm. Lieberman's group would be responsible for sifting the men in an orderly manner through the gap in the wire.

"Many will be hysterical, unable to respond to a command. I'm sorry to say we'll have to leave the badly wounded behind. In that matter . . ." He paused, staring coldly at Stephan Wallach. Throughout his lecturing, Wallach's eyes had been half-closed. Now he yawned.

"Do I bore you?" Dobrany demanded.

Wallach looked up with a strangely mild expression. "What do you want?"

"I want you to wake up! Do you know what it is that you have to do?"

"It won't work," Wallach said calmly. "We'll be slaughtered. We're Jews. They're *men*. Don't you see it?"

He voiced a fear that all had once felt. They had been told they were subhumans. They had been made to act that way. For a while they had forgotten that they were men.

Lieberman said quietly, "Stephan, if we don't resist . . . who will ever want to be a Jew again?"

"Who would want to be a dinosaur?"

"Stephan . . ."

"A billion years ago, the last dinosaur died. The world evolved without them. Who mourns them? The Jews are the dinosaurs of the twentieth century."

"*No,* Stephan . . ."

After the meeting was over, Lieberman was drawn to one corner of the barracks by Dobrany, Cohen, and Chonszki.

"We'll watch Wallach at all times," Dobrany said calmly. "He's of no use to us anymore. The threat is that he might become of use to the Germans. If there's any chance of that, we'll have to silence him. We can make it look like a suicide. Let them blame it on the madman who killed Hrubow."

"No. He suffers," Lieberman tried to explain. "He still loves Bella, but he's too proud to talk about it. He can't help himself."

"That's the point," Dobrany said. "A man who can't help himself can't help anyone else."

"Is that a reason to kill him?" Lieberman shuddered. His bowels twisted in pain. "There are times here when none of us is completely sane. . . ."

He looked to Leo Cohen for help. Cohen said calmly, "Herr Lieberman, all we intend to do is watch him, to make sure."

Chonszki also nodded.

A fool throws a stone into a pond, Lieberman thought, and ten wise men can't recover it.

Dobrany said, "We'll do it in shifts."

Lieberman, intent on reaching the latrine, had just stepped out of the block when someone hissed his name from the shadows. Peering intently at the wall of the women's block, he saw an angular form that resembled a grounded huge dark bird more than a man.

"Rabbi . . . ?"

"The wheat, Mordecai. Did you get it?"

Lieberman felt another rumbling at the pit of his stomach. He was too upset to do anything but tell the truth. "I lied, Rabbi," he said hurriedly. "I needed the gold for something else."

"Lieberman . . . you *lied?*"

206

"But it doesn't matter—"

"Doesn't matter? Doesn't matter that you lied?" The rabbi's voice rose hysterically. From somewhere in the opaque night the bolt of a carbine snicked.

"Not so loud, Rabbi. It matters that I lied. I feel badly about it. But it doesn't matter that I didn't buy the wheat."

"And the five hundred Jews who must eat matzoh? To *them* it doesn't matter?"

"The other evening, when I was sitting there doing those exercises, a thunderbolt came to me. There are plenty of potato peelings—yes? And potato peelings mixed with the flour can stretch the supply—yes?"

"But not if they're dirty!"

"I know you can't wash them. That could leaven the flour. The *Shulhan Arukh* is firm on that point. So . . . we'll *wipe* them clean! With nice dry cloth! Cotton or wool, even silk, whatever you think is best. We'll scrub the peelings until they shine like gold!"

He immediately regretted the use of that word, but the rabbi was thinking other thoughts; he was not a man to bear a grudge when there was a problem to be solved.

"In Vilna," he mused, "the chief rabbi ordained that clean potato peelings fulfilled the mitzvah. So if they're to be wiped with cloth, the *cloth* would have to be clean. . . ."

"Clean and dry! Practically new! Touched only by Jewish hands. I swear it to you!"

"Where will you get it?"

Dear God, Lieberman thought, we know that you will provide, but why don't you provide *until* you provide?

"Rabbi, the Talmud says that when a student knows that his teacher is able to answer him, he may ask a question. Otherwise, he should not. So don't ask," Lieberman said quietly.

Rejoice in God, righteous ones. In the darkness of Block D, the rabbi embraced and forgave his helper, who then wrenched away from him in misery, thinking still of Stephan Wallach's possible fate, and fled to the latrine.

21

Lieberman was cleaning up near the railway platform the next morning when, once again, Rabbi Hurwicz hobbled up through the mud, shadowed by Corporal Reitlinger.

"Mordecai. The captain from Berlin wants to see you."

They called Paul that to set him apart from the others. But not too far apart. You could smell vodka on his breath now, but he still displayed the bearing of the perfect Aryan. It reminded Lieberman of a saying that had made the rounds of the ghetto in Poznań. "The ideal German is muscular like Himmler, slender like Goering, tall like Goebbels . . . to sum up, a blond beauty like Hitler!"

But the captain was here for a purpose: to find the murderer of Lieutenant Hrubow. You had always to bear in mind that he was a professional.

"He wants *me?*" Lieberman asked. "What for?"

The rabbi said slyly, "Maybe, Mordecai, he thinks you're the Angel of Death."

They were walking now toward the guest bungalow, with Reitlinger leading the way. Lieberman frowned.

"Tell me, Rabbi . . . does the captain from Berlin make any progress?"

"He talks to people." The rabbi spread his hands. "He writes a lot of notes . . . obviously he has a terrible memory. He does a lot of sitting and sneezing. He asks me questions about Passover. I don't think he's very enthusiastic about his work. I doubt if they've sent us one of their best men."

"Good!"

Rabbi Hurwicz glanced up. "But we'll find the murderer, Morde-cai . . . don't worry."

It was an obligation on pain of death to do what the Germans requested. It was a further obligation, on pain of losing your soul, not to do it well. The rabbi, even though he refused to steal gold from the Germans, had been willing to turn his back.

I must have misheard him, Lieberman decided.

In the bungalow he sat in a soft chair with his feet scuffing at a real carpet. Not for a long time had he been so comfortable. The captain offered him tea and biscuits with jam. The stove cast a baking heat. Lieberman's face grew flushed. He had forgotten what it was like to live as a human being.

The interrogation began innocently. The captain, who looked gaunt and red-eyed, thinner than when he had first arrived, sat behind his desk and asked questions about life in Poland before the war. Like a job interview, Lieberman thought.

Did he have any family left? Had he read Thomas Mann? Was he fond of the Wijnberg sisters? How long had he held his post as Jewish commandant? Did that give him free run of the camp? Did he read and write Yiddish? Hebrew?

Lieberman answered patiently, honestly. He knew quite well where the captain was heading, but he decided he had nothing to fear.

"You're a religious man, Herr Lieberman?"

"From time to time," he replied, "I believe in God."

"Here?"

He sighed, but Paul waited patiently, so at last he said, "It's just my opinion. I'm not a geographer of God's wanderings. But I believe that except in dire emergencies He is much too far away to be of much help."

"And you don't consider this to be dire emergency?"

"Suffering, here, is not a dire emergency. It's the law. You have to deal with the law as best you can."

"You knew Jacob Margulies, Herr Lieberman?"

"Not well."

"You weren't friendly with him?"

"I disliked him."

"Enough to have wanted to kill him?"

"The circumstances would have to be extreme."

"Such as what?"

"For me, they didn't arise."

The captain tacked in another direction. "You've had military training, Herr Lieberman?"

"I was a bookseller. When I was young, Jews were not invited to serve in the Polish army. So the answer is no."

"You've traveled?"

"Here and there."

"To Russia?"

"God forbid."

"But you've studied Russian history."

"I read a book or two."

"Do you know where the Ukraine is?"

"Who doesn't? From Kiev down to the Black Sea."

"And the Sea of Azov?"

Lieberman thought a moment, then shrugged. "A northern arm of the Black Sea."

"Why do you shave, Herr Lieberman?"

"I beg your pardon. I don't fully understand the question."

"I asked why, in a place such as Zin, you bother to shave. Why take the trouble to keep up appearances?"

"I'm a neat man by nature. I don't like to let myself go. I've noticed . . ."

"What?"

"A matter of survival," Lieberman said cryptically. Then he thought, why not? He's just fed me tea and herring. An honest answer won't kill either of us.

"What I noticed a long time ago, no matter how absurd it may seem to you, Captain, is that if you don't keep yourself clean, you lose the will to live. Or perhaps when the will to live is lost, you stop caring about being clean. It's the old story of which came first, the chicken or the egg, and the answer is 'Who cares? I'm hungry.'"

Lieberman was rambling, pleased to air his thoughts to what he considered an interested and intelligent listener, even if he was German. At the same time a soft voice whispered to him, "Are you crazy?"

But he resumed.

"Now that you've been here a while, Captain, you may have noticed that there's no paper of any kind in the barracks. So, please forgive the expression, those who are doomed to die stop wiping their asses. We call them the drowned. They say, 'I can do nothing. I'll just walk around in my own filth until the inevitable happens.' However, Captain, I and others have a little rag or a piece of cloth—in my case, a scarf—which we use for that purpose. I wash it out and keep it tied around my ankle for emergencies. The demands of the bowels are absolute. Forgive me for being so specific, but you asked. Well, you asked about my shaving, but it's the same thing. To please someone? No. I shave for the same reason that I carry my scarf. To feel a little human. Feeling human, I have reason to live a little longer."

Now he wondered if he had gone too far. But he had noticed that throughout his explanation the captain had been deeply attentive. Maybe even moved. Was he imagining it?

The interrogation then took an unforeseen turn. Lieberman wondered later how it had been possible. Had *he* invited it? The captain leaned forward across his desk. With his one hand he pinched his temples beneath the thatch of blond hair.

He looked up, and there was pain in his eyes. "Herr Lieberman, have you never asked yourself *why?*"

"Why what?" Lieberman said uneasily.

Paul said, "Why we do this to you. How we are capable of it."

Lieberman was instantly distressed. He felt there must be some trap about to spring. This man talks to me now as an equal, as one human being to another. It's not acceptable.

212

"Captain . . . that's a question of . . . I would rather not . . ."

Paul nodded. He had ventured into deep water, and the man he pulled with him wore chains. He let go. His gray eyes grew veiled. To busy himself, he poured more tea into the cups. But Lieberman saw that his hand was shaking.

"You knew Lieutenant Hrubow, of course."

"Yes." Relieved, Lieberman let out his breath and accepted the second cup of tea.

"You had contact with him?"

"Some."

"Can you describe him?"

Lieberman hesitated. No, he hasn't quite let go.

"A beast, Captain."

"In what way?"

He scratched at some lice migrating through the gray stubble of his hair. What is there to lose?

"A beast exists in every man, Captain. Maybe it's a hangover from when we had tiny brains and could survive only by smashing the skulls of other animals with the thighbone of a dead baboon. Lieutenant Hrubow unchained his beast. He beat Jews to death with shovels. He seemed to enjoy it. During the winter, with Lieutenant Stein's permission, he met some of the trains. He and his men selected a few of the prettier women. They were made to undress and lie down in the snow behind the Ukrainian barracks. After a while Hrubow explained that there was a way to get warm. Those who didn't oblige were shot. The others, after they did what was required, were told they had earned a hot shower. You understand what that meant?"

Paul nodded. He knew there was a way to get through to Lieberman, to find out what he needed to know. It no longer had anything to do with the murderer of an SS lieutenant. Paul had another and deeper need.

"Hrubow was not a German," he said. "He was a Pole. Half-Ukrainian."

"True."

"He let loose the beast, you said. How was *he* capable of it? Did he so hate the Jews? Had he no human feeling?"

Lieberman understood. A clever captain, he thought. Perhaps he truly needs to know. Anything is possible.

Lieberman could not resist.

"For the Poles and the Ukrainians, Captain"—he laid the stress gently on the nationalities—"the Jews were easy to dislike. Throughout history Jews have always been welcomed by sophisticated nations. We were philosophers, healers, traders, mathematicians—even, in our own land, warriors. We lived quietly, bothered no one. But in the end we were always kicked out. You know why? We were too independent. We never cared to rule. Worse, we would never convert. Usually we blended in, if it was allowed, but we always remained Jews. We had survived so long, while other great empires collapsed and died. That was almost unnatural. We were not only easy to dislike. We were easy to hate."

"To dislike and hate is one thing," Paul said. "To kill is another."

"There's a more primitive explanation," Lieberman continued, warming to his subject. "I read somewhere that all animals are territorial. When their territory and its food supply is threatened or they think it is, they look to blame someone else. They don't dare accept that they haven't measured up to the planet's demands, that they may be headed for inglorious extinction. They require an enemy to make their terror more specific. The enemy need only be of a different species. The baboons, when they haven't got enough bananas, blame the mandrils. The mandrils blame the monkeys. The white monkeys blame the brown monkeys. Even the brown monkeys blame another tribe of brown monkeys who live over the hill and say, 'They're so pushy. They take females from our tribe. They're eyeing our bananas. Look! They're not at all like us. They're submonkeys. Let's kill them.'"

"But the Poles and the Ukrainians are human beings," Paul said quietly. "Not animals."

"A higher order, Captain, with a higher capacity for destruction. That's the great lesson of the twentieth century. That's what we've learned here at Zin and elsewhere."

"A man is capable of thinking for himself," Paul said stubbornly.

Lieberman grew inwardly angry at some of the unspoken assumptions. It was then, he later decided, that he made his crucial mistake.

"May I take the liberty of asking *you* a question, Captain?"

Paul nodded.

"What would you have done if you were a Ukrainian under Lieutenant Hrubow's command?"

"I would not have hacked a prisoner to death with a shovel, Herr Lieberman. Or raped a Jewess in the snow."

"You would not have wanted to. But suppose you were ordered to do so? Or ordered, as a German soldier, to work here in the camp?"

Paul remained immobile, unblinking, like a statue carved of flesh-colored stone.

"And you are here," Lieberman said, clenching a fist without realizing it. "Doing your job, following your orders. I understand. If not, they would shoot you. You want to live, Captain. We all do."

Paul said quietly, "If I were a Jew in this camp, Herr Lieberman, I would not follow orders. There is no way out of here. You know that."

It was a terrible thing to hear.

"So what would you do?" he flared, forgetting where he was, to whom he spoke. "Become a drowned man? Take the bullet in the back of the neck from Dr. Lustig?"

"I would rise up in revolt," Paul said softly.

Lieberman made a violent gesture, as if he were thrusting off some assaulting creature. He half-rose from his chair. It was too late to check himself, to draw back.

Fool, he thought. You forgot to bark.

His fists were still clenched, but he summoned all his wits and self-control. "Our sages," he said stiffly, "have taught us to love the Lord in the punishments that He sends us, as well as in the mercies that He grants. . . ."

Sitting attentively on the edge of his own chair, Rabbi Hurwicz bobbed his head up and down on its thin stalk. A few minutes later the interrogation ended and Lieberman was politely dismissed. There was no more Paul could learn. He had seen the shock of recognition in Lieberman's stricken brown eyes.

I wasn't looking for it, Paul thought. But it was there.

Lieberman hurried across the barren stretch between Roll Call Square and the north quadrangle. The sky was gray and layered with clouds. Some crows squabbled for space in the dead field beyond. He had got word to Leo Cohen earlier in the day to meet him at the latrines, and now, because of the captain from Berlin, he was late.

I'll tell no one what happened, he decided. It'll only make them crazy with worry. Let me do the worrying. I've had more practice than any of them. Certainly the captain doesn't suspect. It was a wild shot, no more.

Cohen was waiting for him at the latrine.

"Wait," Lieberman said. A squad of German soldiers passed by, smelling of tobacco and wurst, en route to the lower camp. Their shouts to each other were like the echoes of a cannibal chant. Lieberman frowned and waved his arms in the air, as though complaining about something in his capacity as camp leader.

When the soldiers were beyond earshot, he said, "I have good news. I can get a rifle. A Mauser in good condition."

"Where? From who?"

"Taddeus. He's the Blackie who has the afternoon shift on the north watchtower. I spoke to him this morning at the railroad depot."

"You trust him?"

"I trust his greed. He's saving up to buy a farm in Kirovograd when the war is over. We've got more business on the calendar."

"How much?"

"You'll have a fit. Four thousand dollars, all in gold."

Cohen whistled through his teeth. "A lot! You couldn't bargain?"

"I did. He asked five."

"How will he account for it's being missing?"

"It won't be missing. They have two rifles all the time, locked in a steel box, at each watchtower. No one opens the boxes. He has an extra key."

"It's worth it," Cohen decided. "When do you need the gold?"

"Tomorrow night at the latest."

"On the Sabbath? Herr Lieberman!"

"Don't mock. This is a matter of life and death—it's permitted. He'll hold the rifle for me all Sunday afternoon. After that he promises nothing."

"You'll have the money," Cohen promised.

He left Lieberman then and made his way to the hair depot in the north quadrangle. In the rear of the hut, the Ukrainian guard dozed by the open grate of the coal stove. Bella was absent on an errand. Tzippora came to the door.

"I have a message for Bella," Cohen said. "Please tell her it looks like it will snow at eight o'clock."

Tzippora stared at him as if he were crazy.

"Snow? At eight o'clock?"

"Yes. I promised to let her know. Don't forget—at eight o'clock."

Some ten minutes later, when she returned to the hair depot and Tzippora told her of Cohen's visit, Bella blushed with pleasure. The message meant that Lieutenant Vogl had gone to Breslau and she was to meet Leo Cohen in the bungalow at eight o'clock.

Tzippora smiled wanly. "Will it really snow, Bella?"

Bella flushed more deeply. The other women in the hair depot began to laugh—a low, hoarse sound, more like the semicrazed laughter of old crones than the bright sexual laughter of nubile young women. They know, Bella realized. If they don't know, at least they suspect. And it seems to please them.

At first she had worried that there would be anger if they suspected her duplicity. They had shunned her for a while after she had become the commandant's willing mistress, but then after a time their lassitude had overcome that resentment and she was treated with an indifference that was normal at Zin. The women at

Zin were shadows. She had hardly anything to do with them. They were quiet and neutered creatures, robbed of femininity. Almost all of them had stopped menstruating after a month in the camp. They began to believe that even if they survived, they would never bear children.

An hour after Bella returned to the hair depot, Sergeant Zuckermann came by, his breath smelling of brandy. He drew Bella aside and told her formally that the commandant requested the pleasure of her company that evening.

"At what hour?" she asked, trying to sound pleased.

"Seven. When the bugle blows. It's a special occasion . . . but I'm forbidden to give you any details. Don't be late!"

Bella bit her lip, nodding. She had no way to tell Leo.

22

A shuffling, perhaps. A soft, rustling sound . . .

Paul woke at dusk from a short and uncomfortable nap with the memory that his sleep had been somehow disturbed. A sepulchral light still filled the room. He walked from his bedroom into the sitting room of the bungalow. His lower back ached. He stretched from side to side, then backward, then touched his toes and let the weight of his head hang to separate the disks of the spine.

When he raised his eyes, he saw a sheaf of white paper on the floor by the front door. Slipped through while I slept, he realized. That's what I heard.

The onionskin was folded neatly into thirds, like a business letter. He lit the oil lamp and rekindled the fire in the stove. His movements were unhurried. He settled into the easy chair. He handled the paper with some care, but his heart beat raggedly.

A long letter, written in German cursive script, so he had no way to compare the handwriting with the other printed notes. There was no date.

At the top of the first page was a single printed word:

PETITION

Dear Captain,

I address this to you personally. I believe that you are an intelligent man. You are not against progress or change. You have an open mind.

You may have observed, since your arrival in our camp, that we here are dedicated to a threefold creative purpose: Death, Efficiency, and Recovery.

That is to say, it is the purpose of Zin to achieve death in the most efficient manner possible and recover from death whatever may be of value to those who still live.

Our death, therefore, constitutes a paradox. It is actually a contribution to life.

The gold from our teeth, the diamonds on our fingers, the currency from our purses, buy guns for the soldiers of the Reich. Our coats keep the citizens of Berlin warm. Our skin on occasion is made into lampshades by whose light scholars study in Heidelberg. Young couples in Munich make love on mattresses stuffed with our hair.

You yourself, Captain, although you believe you dream on a pillow stuffed with down from the Hungarian goose, rest your cheek nightly on the hair of two dozen of our dead women.

Many are made happy and comfortable by our death.

Your countrymen have lunch after cremating us. No one is ever sick.

Nausea is a state of mind.

In that spirit, Captain, I take the liberty of offering the following suggestion which will increase the efficiency of our death/recovery process:

Our camp has existed for one year. During that time some 300,000 Jews have passed through here. Their freshly slaughtered corpses have been burned and buried. But this contravenes our basic purpose.

It is reasonable to assume, even acknowledging the existence of larger killing centers such as ours, that in the future at least another 300,000 Jews will be killed at Zin. (In 1936 the Jewish population of Europe was approximately ten million; if Germany should conquer Great Britain and the United States, a further six million Jews will have to be added to that original figure.)

Although the average healthy human body weighs 70 kilos, the average weight here at Zin is probably closer to 55 kilos. Still, that

220

is considerable tonnage when multiplied by the minimum estimated future number of 300,000.

It reaches a total of more than 16 million kilos.

The percentage of fat in the body mass of a human being (including a Jew) is 23 percent. The percentage of muscle is 38 percent.

The total of edible meat is more than 10 million kilos.

Calculating the weight of the healthy heart to be approximately 300 grams and that of the liver to be 1400 grams and adding lungs, kidneys, and brains (average weight per body: 1600 grams), a further one million kilos is available for processed military rations and pet food. The human intestine could be salvaged for the wrapping of sausages made from human blood, of which an approximate total of 2 million litres may theoretically be retrieved.

Do not wince, Captain. It is a logical suggestion. Remember, nausea is a state of mind.

Think how many more brave soldiers and currently disadvantaged citizens of the Third Reich would be made healthier and happier through our contribution. It is literally the last gesture we could make.

In the name of the holy trinity of Death, Efficiency, and Recovery,

I subscribe myself as

Your obedient servant,

The Angel of Death

Under an empurpled sky bruised with rain clouds, as Paul read the Angel's petition, Stephan Wallach slouched between the two camp quadrangles toward the commandant's bungalow. A wind blew from the marshes bordering the Oder River. A few drops of brackish rain began to fall, and a crust of thunder formed like a scab upon the silence.

Men drifted back from their work details to the dampness of the barracks. They moved softly through the mud. Wallach was one among many. But the last brittle strand binding him to that world of other men had frayed, then parted with no sound. From ten thousand rictal mouths he had wrenched bone and gold. Once he had recited the mourner's Kaddish: "Magnified and sanctified be His great name in the world which He created according to His will. . . ."

But no longer. God was dead, too. Adoring a dead God, he thought, is a sin.

Lieberman had once said to all of them, "We must live to tell what man is capable of doing to man. Perhaps this is just the beginning of man's possibilities."

"No, Mordecai . . ." Wallach spoke aloud. The rain began to fall more strongly as he tramped along. "Even if we live to tell them, and that's unlikely . . . who will believe? And if some believe, even if some weep and some mourn, in the end you know as well as I that they'll all forget. For the troubles of others, Mordecai, we feel bad. Then it's time to pay the rent . . . eat . . . make love . . . sleep. Live and forget."

To exist one day beyond the boundaries of Zin, Wallach had decided, would be insupportable. They had taken away his profession, his wife, his honor. Everything but his body was dead. He would let them have his body, too. He would demand that they take it. But in dying he would sanctify dishonor with vengeance.

Passing through the hedge separating Roll Call Square and the German officers' bungalows, he placed his feet on the gravel path leading to Commandant Kirmayr's bungalow. He removed his cap. The rain on his head cooled and soothed him.

The rain slanted in delicate lines through the searchlights' fuzzed warm glare. Lights also burned inside the administrative bungalow, like the lights of a cottage on the outskirts of a small town.

For a moment a terrible pain scissored Wallach's heart. A yearning . . . but a yearning equaled pain. At a distance he heard the throaty murmur of Bella's voice, as if she were stroking a cat, soothing a child.

Was it a dream? Was it real? His heart beat rapidly. He tried to calm himself.

He became conscious of a lengthening shadow across his path, a streak of pewter gray against silver gray. He glanced around . . . but it was only another Jew, shoulders hunched, head bent, slogging wretchedly through the rain toward the barracks.

Wallach moved forward in the darkness, and there came to him, framed rectangularly, a vision of the commandant's aide seated at a table under the hot glow of a lamp. Sergeant Zuckermann drank from a metal flask. No matter. It had to be *now*. Wallach reached inside his damp trousers and gripped the cold haft of a knife.

From behind him he heard a hiss.

"Stephan!"

Amazed, he turned. The Jew in the rain had straightened to his full height and was approaching at a rapid pace.

Wallach recognized the hawklike face of Avram Dobrany. Even in the shadows, something thin and bright glittered in his hand.

Paul's flesh felt clammy. He let the petition drop to his lap. He stood, and the pages of thin onionskin fluttered to the carpet.

One detail—as foul as the bubble that had risen underfoot in the lower camp—rose noxiously in his mind. Not possible. Not true.

He walked to the bedroom where he had slept. The pillow still bore the imprint of his head. Under the white cotton case with its pink hand-stitched roses lay the malevolent object.

He tore the case loose and flung it to the floor. The pillow itself was covered with gray sacking. If he wanted to know, he had only to slit it with a kitchen knife.

He was conscious of a rising ache in his throat. He clutched the plump gray thing and brought it closer to his face, inch by inch. He began to sneeze. It was the pillow. He was allergic to what was in the pillow. Down from the Hungarian goose . . . or the hair of dead Jewish women.

He kicked open the back door of the bungalow; he crashed it angrily against the timbers. A misty rain fell in the twilight. Crimson fires burned in the lower camp, lofting a pink cloud into the eastern sky. The air smelled of wet earth, greening trees, sweet charred flesh. He drew back his arm to hurl the thing over the barbed-wire fence. . . .

His angle of sight let him see beyond Captain Dressler's quarters next door to Werner Vogl's bungalow. The back door creaked slowly open in the evening. No light burned inside, but the lamplight behind Paul flowed across the dark wet gravel and illumined the worried face at the door—the face of Leo Cohen.

Paul had no time to react, not even to wonder. He heard a cry of alarm from the other direction, from the commandant's bungalow.

Bella had crossed the compound through a sea of clinging mud. The gray wool of the sky seemed to press down on her bare head.

Leo will realize what's happened, she thought.

"It's a special occasion," Kirmayr said, after he had greeted her. "I hope Zuckermann didn't tell you, but it's my birthday. I'm an Aries—the Ram. Have you studied astrology?"

"No," Bella said.

"Aries people are impetuous, kind, and truthful . . . but you know that about me already, my dear." Dusk had already fallen, and they sat in the leather chairs in his bedroom while Sergeant Zuckermann kept a vigil in the office. Rain began to patter on the roof, making a hushed sound.

"Since there's no way for you to have gotten me a present, I bought one for myself in Breslau. A zither! I was a member of a zither club in Rosenheim. I didn't bring my zither to Poland, and I've missed it. Meanwhile, I have a present for you—on *my* birthday." He laughed; the idea seemed to strike him as witty. "A dress. From a store in Breslau," he assured her quickly.

"Thank you, Herr Commandant."

"Martin." He made the correction as he always did, for she never used his Christian name.

"I'm sorry."

"One day you'll slip. You'll see—you'll call me Martin."

Bella forced a smile by a slight widening of her cheeks. "I'm sure it will happen."

"That will make me happy. When is your birthday, my dear?"

"In early October."

"Libras are intelligent, calm of soul, and quietly passionate." He chuckled warmly. "Shall I show you the dress?"

224

He rose, but a sound intruded—the sudden sharp scraping of a chair in the outer office, followed by a yelp from Sergeant Zuckermann. With a quizzical look the commandant turned.

"Zuckermann?"

Boots thudded on the pine floor. The door, already ajar a few inches, was flung open. Zuckermann, his finger curled around the trigger of a carbine.

"Major! You're all right?"

"Of course! What's going on?"

Zuckermann leaped back into the office.

With admirable speed Kirmayr snatched his pistol from the holster he had draped on the arm of a chair and charged after him, with Bella following. He slowed his pace as he neared the open door leading to the porch and the gravel path. Zuckermann seemed to have vanished.

Soft rain still fell in the buttery evening. The commandant waved his pistol in front of him as a talisman, a warning to whatever evil might lurk.

But there was none. His eyes adjusting to the rain-soaked darkness saw only the familiar low outlines of the German barracks, the workshops, the water tower and hedge—and then, off to the left, the shadowy form of Zuckermann bent to one knee on the glistening stones. He moved slightly to one side until the commandant realized that a body lay facing him on its stomach. Less a body than a bundle of gray rags. But still a body.

"Zuckermann! What's going on?"

"A Jew, Herr Commandant! He's dead!"

The commandant marched down the steps, flourishing his pistol like a baton, and demanded to know what had happened.

The stupedied, vodka-drinking Zuckermann had been sitting at his desk—checking reports, he claimed, from the quartermaster division in Poseń. He had heard noises outside: a shout, then the sound of a scuffle in the rain.

"I didn't want to disturb you, Herr Commandant. I went first to the window. Two men were arguing. One was trying to get up to the bungalow. The other seemed to be holding him back. Then you called me."

Zuckermann had plucked a carbine from the gun rack above the filing cabinet. During the time he jumped into the major's office, he had lost sight of what was going on outside the bungalow.

"And when I got here, there was only one man left. This one." He nudged the body with his boot.

"Turn him over," Kirmayr ordered.

The body was so slight that Zuckermann was able to flip it with one hand, as if it had been a loosely filled sack of bones from some archaeological tomb. A fierce white face glared up at them above a band of flowing dark red. The mouth gaped over broken teeth. The right hand, flung across the chest, gripped a long-bladed knife. Even in death it refused to let go.

"Look! Where is Bach? *Bach!*" he shouted. He pointed down. "He was . . ." He heard steps behind him. Bella, at his shoulder, threw a hand to her mouth to keep from screaming. "I know this man," Kirmayr said. "But not his name."

Zuckermann responded at last. "Kapo of the dental commando . . ."

The commandant was unable to make the necessary connection. When Bella arrived, they had taken her gold wedding ring. After the first lie, she volunteered nothing. The commandant refused to discuss Bella with any of his officers.

"Who did this to him?" he asked.

"It was too dark, Major. I couldn't see."

Like a shade from the underworld, Paul Bach appeared out of the night, clutching a bundle under his arm.

But it was all wonderfully clear to Kirmayr. My death at the hands of a madman, he realized, would have meant retribution—a bloodbath not beyond the imagination of the quick-thinking Jew who had rushed up to interfere. Kirmayr laughed in the rain. He clapped a hand heavily on the shoulder of Captain Bach, who dropped his bundle in the mud and bent to one knee by the body.

Kirmayr also bent. He pried loose the fingers of Wallach's dead hand and seized the knife. He raised it high above his head as if he were about to stab the corpse.

"Do you understand, Captain? The knife that killed Hrubow! He meant to kill me, too! *This is our man!*"

226

Paul looked quickly up at Bella. The yellow glow of the searchlights stabbed through the rain, placing her eyes in caves of shadows. Rain slid smoothly down her cheeks, masking any tears.

Let her be, Paul thought. He wheeled on Kirmayr, thrusting a finger toward the body on the gravel.

"And who killed *him*, Major?"

Kirmayr laughed nervously. "Does it matter? Dumb luck ... like Dresden! Get rid of the body, Zuckermann." He nudged Wallach's body with the toe of his boot, then turned back to Paul. "Bach, come inside with me! I'm soaked. So are you."

But Paul refused to move. He seized the pillow he had dropped in the mud. *"What's in this?"* he shouted, then sprang and twisted the knife from the commandant's grasp.

Kirmayr stared at him. "Bach, have you gone insane?"

With one slash Paul slit the muddy gray sacking. Reaching into the guts of the pillow, his hand came up clutching a matted clump of shorn gray hair. He had expected it, but it was no less a shock. The words he had read in the letter were only words—a grim promise, a grisly fantasy. What he clutched in his hand was real. He flung the handful into the commandant's face, the hair fluttering like feathers in the rain that dripped from the night sky.

Kirmayr grew pale. "How dare you?" he whispered, more stunned than angry.

"Hypocrite!" Paul cried. "Pig!"

He had gone too far. Kirmayr was shy about flaunting his authority, but to accept such an insult in the presence of witnesses was unthinkable. I could shoot him, he realized, and no one would dare deny me the right. His fingers touched the slippery coldness of his pistol grip, but the touch frightened him. He had never in his life fired a weapon to wound or kill.

His voice quivered.

"Consider yourself under arrest, Captain. In your quarters!"

Then, embarrassed, he turned his back and rushed up the stairs to his bungalow, leaving Paul, Bella, and Sergeant Zuckermann standing in the rain over Wallach's body.

23

Late the next day Cohen delivered the gold to Block B. It was in a small gray bag made of the same sacking that had covered Paul's pillow of hair.

Lieberman sat on his bunk gazing at the drizzle that fell so silently in the steel-colored afternoon. He grieved for Stephan Wallach. In another world, he thought, Wallach had no doubt gravely warned that you must brush your teeth after every meal. A Jewish husband, meant to be a father of scampering children with Bella's golden eyes. He had not been ready to tear teeth from the dead, to ache from the pain of his wife in the arms of a German officer who was not even aware of his name.

He shivered first at his vision of what had happened . . . and then at what might have happened if Wallach had reached Kirmayr. If Dobrany with his Swiss knife hadn't stalked him like a hunter following a mad dog, they would now all be dead. Stein would not have hesitated.

He focused on Leo Cohen. The little bag of twenty-dollar coins was bulkier than he had anticipated.

"Where can I hide it?" he asked fretfully.

"In your pallet. While Bach is still here, there are no searches."

"Bach is under arrest, Bella says." Lieberman frowned. "Tomorrow I have to cross the compound to the watchtower. In the daylight."

This was Lieberman's real worry. It was a distance of some three hundred meters, past the latrines, the carpentry shop, and the coal cellar.

"Wear a coat," Cohen advised. "The gold weighs only about four kilos. Get some cord and let it hang from your belt under the coat. Stuff some rags in with the gold so it won't jingle."

"And how do I bring the rifle back?"

When Cohen knit his brows hardly a wrinkle appeared in the smooth young skin. A Mauser rifle, he explained patiently, could be stripped down into three pieces. He had discussed the matter with Dobrany.

"But I have a better idea, Herr Lieberman. You don't have to take any risks. I'll go in your place."

"Taddeus doesn't know you."

"Then let me come along to help you."

Lieberman patted Cohen affectionately on the cheek. "It will frighten him if there are two of us. He's nervous enough already. You're a good boy, Leo. I used to say bad things about you, but I don't anymore. You can do one favor for me."

"Consider it done, Herr Lieberman."

"If I have to wear a coat tomorrow ... pray for rain." Lieberman groaned a little. It always made him feel better.

When he was troubled, Martin Kirmayr walked the perimeter of the camp inside the barbed wire, trying to stay clear of the Jews. He was as shy as they about looking a man in the eye. Today he planted his boots recklessly into wet cow dung from the farm. The rain had ended; the sky slowly cleared.

Am I a hypocrite? he wondered. It may be so. But what was the alternative? To be like Stein? To enjoy it?

He turned back in the direction of the main gate.

He thought uneasily of Paul Bach. I misjudged the man. I believed he was hard and dedicated, but he's proved to be a weakling, a sentimentalist. A professional, no doubt—but not for this kind of place. And now what? If I convene a court-martial, I'll have to answer to Colonel Dietrich. It will be messy. Unnecessary. I just want to do my job, he thought, and avoid problems.

He knew he was not a disciplinarian, a true commandant. He was a man in the grip of forces over which he had no control. What can *I* do? he asked—just as Paul had asked.

He rapped twice on the door of the guest cottage. Bach opened it. He looks awful, Kirmayr thought. Like one of *them.*

"Captain," he said, "I'm prepared to forget last night's unfortunate little incident. You were upset for good reason—it could happen to anybody. I want to file a report now, and I require your signature."

"For what purpose?" Bach blocked the doorway with his thin body. Kirmayr could smell vodka on his breath.

"This man Wallach was the Angel. There's no doubt of it. The case is closed." Kirmayr essayed a confident smile. "I intend to commend your diligence in the entire matter."

Paul hesitated. He could agree and leave Zin. But that no longer suited him. Before he left, there was at least one thing he wanted to do. He took a deep breath.

"At the time of Margulies's death," he said, "the dental commando was in full operation. Wallach was with them. Wallach was a university graduate from Vienna. He wrote perfect German. The note on Lieutenant Hrubow's body was the letter of a man whose German was flawed."

The commandant shook his head like a bull terrier. "Captain, those are just details."

"Exactly," Paul said.

A stubborn fool. Kirmayr was so upset that he stamped his foot, spattering his trousers with mud.

"Come with me," he ordered.

Almost on cue, from the short distance separating the two bungalows, he heard his telephone ring in a paired series of beeps. Zuckermann would answer it, of course.

But the telephone kept beeping.

With Paul following, the commandant flung open the door. Zuckermann sat slumped at his desk, hair askew, mouth hanging open, gently snoring. A reek of alcohol struck the commandant's nose.

Rushing to his own desk, he snatched the receiver from its cradle. He heard frenzied clicking; then Gestapo HQ Warsaw came on the line, demanding him for Colonel Dietrich.

The timing, Kirmayr thought, couldn't be better. Still puffing, he gasped, "This is he. . . ."

In a moment Dietrich's loud and cheerful voice repeated his name. "And how are you today, Herr Commandant?"

"Fine, Colonel, fine!"

"My friend Paul Bach is still with you?"

"Right at my side . . ."

"Your little problem is solved?"

Kirmayr suddenly felt less sure of his ground. If Bach's doubts were valid, the Angel might strike again. Then it's *I* who'll look the fool. It's Bach's responsibility, he decided. Let him explain his failure.

"Not quite yet. Some interesting developments, however. An excellent man . . . I have complete faith . . . I want him to explain. . . ."

A measure of cheer seemed to vanish from Dietrich's tone. "I have some news for you, Kirmayr. A change of plans."

"What sort of change?" The commandant's voice flattened out.

The disturbances in Warsaw, Dietrich explained, had taken an unfortunate turn. The Jews were resisting the order to liquidate the ghetto. A struggle between a fly and an elephant, but the fly was armed with stolen grenades and heavy machine guns. Military units were being mobilized in central Poland.

"We're most concerned that the uprising shouldn't spread to the Polish section of the city. We have quite enough men to handle the Jews. For the other, we need available troops. How soon can you close Zin?"

Kirmayr's heart jumped out of rhythm and began to thump wildly against his rib cage.

"I beg your pardon, Colonel?"

"We need your people in Warsaw. You'll be in the Lazienki Park district with the 2nd Battalion of the 22nd Polish Police Regiment.

The camp was going to close anyway. Auschwitz can handle everything now. I need to know how soon you can liquidate."

"Colonel, I wasn't aware of this development—"

"Don't waffle, Major," Dietrich snapped. "Give me a date."

Kirmayr tried to stay calm. "What do you mean by liquidate?"

The Gestapo colonel sighed, then took a minute to explain. The
commandant thought it over for a few moments.

"A month," he said dully.

"Ridiculous. In a month we could liquidate Birkenau. A week is
what you've got. Understood? You say Bach is with you? Kindly
put him on."

Standing nearby, Paul had heard only distant metallic snatches
of Willi's voice. But Kirmayr had asked what was meant by *liquidate*. He had seen his deepening pallor. Now the commandant sat
down on the edge of his desk and pressed one hand to his cheek, like
a man with a severe toothache.

"Willi?"

"Paul! How are you? You haven't found your man?"

"I'm on the track," Paul said. "Does it matter now?"

"You heard? I suppose not. But you might feel better if you
march to a successful conclusion. Look here . . . is Kirmayr listening? What kind of man is he? Can you answer discreetly?"

Paul hesitated before he said, "Better than the others."

"I have my doubts. He sounds like an ass. I'm coming down in
two or three days' time. It's up to me whether he goes to Auschwitz
or the Dnieper, and I don't even know the man. Tell him that, will
you? It may spur him to greater efforts."

"All right, Willi."

"You can go back to Berlin or finish up, as it suits you. But if you
hang on until I get there, I'd be grateful. I've missed you."

"Yes, I will," Paul said.

"Excellent! I have to go. Give my message to the commandant,
Paul. You won't forget?"

After Paul hung up, he turned to face Kirmayr, who still
slumped on the edge of the desk. His uniform seemed to have

grown two sizes too large for him. The cuffs of his jacket drooped past the wrists, the trousers billowed at the thighs, the brown shirt slopped over his belt. His coffee-colored eyes regarded Paul dolefully.

"Colonel Dietrich will visit us before the week is up, Herr Commandant."

"Good," Kirmayr said quietly. He looked up, and a tiny spark of hope appeared in his eyes. "Did he say anything else?"

"Yes," Paul said. "He requires that you give me your exact timetable for the liquidation of the camp."

24

To get in, Lieberman thought, is always easier than to get out.

In the middle of the afternoon he slipped into the dampness of Block B. He had waited all day, praying that the skies would cloud over, the thunder rumble, the rain drip and pour as it had done every day that week.

But it was a fine blue day. The kind of Sunday, he thought, that should make for rejoicing. Lovers in Poznań would stroll around Kornik Castle holding hands, children would romp on picnics, sleepy old men in rowboats would glide down the heart of the Warta. If he were there, he would have placed a rocking chair on the sidewalk in front of his bookshop on Wieniawski Street and read some poetry, letting the bald patch in the center of his skull grow pink in the benevolent spring sunlight.

But today he had to wear a winter overcoat. Taddeus was waiting with the rifle. *We must have the rifle.*

Peering through the fly-smeared window, he saw nothing but a speckled blaze of yellow light. The little bag of gold had been squeezed under his pallet. He had already knotted it with tough twine from the carpentry shop. He snatched it free. An end of the twine protruded, and he tied that swiftly to the back of his worn leather belt. The bag hung awkwardly between his legs. He buttoned the only two buttons of the brown woolen coat that had seen him through the long winter. I'll walk like a duck, he thought.

Outside the barracks he steadied himself and breathed deeply, sniffing the sweet aroma of pine wafted by the breeze from the forest. The sky was so blue, so brilliantly clear and lovely. He turned his steps toward the right over the barren field already speckled with green weeds. Don't hurry. First stop, the latrines, to make sure the knot isn't loosening. His equilibrium was poor—the soles of his feet dragged over the stones. Within ten paces he had to wipe away sweat that trickled down his forehead.

Lieutenant Stein skipped jauntily down the steps of the commandant's bungalow. He had just received from the commandant's lips the order for the liquidation of Zin. He had always known it would happen—it was only sooner than expected.

This was Sunday. The last trains would arrive on Tuesday; the last carbon monoxide would be pumped into the shower ducts. On Wednesday all farm animals and excess supplies would be trucked to the Wehrmacht depot at Poseń. The buildings would be dynamited and razed, one by one, beginning with the workshops. The camp Jews would be told that they were being transferred to Auschwitz at the end of the week. Whether they believed it or understood their fate would be of little importance—security would be immediately doubled. On Friday, after the barracks had been demolished, the five hundred last Jews would be shot and then cremated in the lower camp. The last fires would go out.

Later in the spring a unit from Breslau would return to plow the ground and build a peasant cottage and farm. Young pine trees would be planted. Zin would no longer exist, except in memory.

I'll miss it, Stein thought, but I'll find something else. A man has to keep growing. If it's Russia, the fit survive. . . .

As his short strides carried him across the earth, he found himself humming and then, under his breath, singing a phrase from the camp anthem.

"And we will never leave . . . 'til destiny winks an eye."

The commandant had ordered him to give the news to Lieutenant Vogl, on duty today in the lower camp. Stein passed through the busy north quadrangle, swung between the laundry and the hair depot, and veered up the slope toward the sentry post at the end of Freiheitstrasse.

236

A man in a heavy old brown overcoat had just emerged from the latrine about fifty meters farther on and was slowly heading his way. At that distance, with his poor eyesight, Rudy had no idea who it was, other than a Jew.

Why, on a glorious spring day, Rudy wondered, does a Jew wear a heavy overcoat? He must be crazy. He slowed his pace.

So did Lieberman.

Well, they're *all* crazy, Rudy decided. In winter they froze, so in spring and summer they'll want to boil and stoke up heat for next winter. For them there won't be a next winter.

He resumed his march across the broken field of stones toward the sentry gate of the lower camp.

Lieberman did not understand that Stein's shortsightedness prevented him from recognizing anyone at a distance of more than twenty paces. Stein could tell Jew from German, German from Ukrainian, officer from enlisted man, but that was all. The face was a pink blur.

He's seen me, Lieberman thought. He's thinking: why is the leader of the doggie battalion heading for a watchtower? Why is he wearing a heavy coat on a warm day? Why does he walk in such a clumsy manner?

What's he carrying under that coat?

At the same moment as Stein shrugged his shoulders and resumed his march toward the lower camp, Lieberman became infected with panic. He was already sweating violently. Sweat is a sign of guilt. Surely Rudy sees *that*.

Blood pumping, Lieberman turned awkwardly on one rundown heel and began to clamber up the slight hummock of ground back toward the latrine. In the latrine he would be safe. He could dump the bag of gold into one of the stinking vats of shit . . . recover it another day. Tomorrow he would explain to Taddeus.

Another day . . .

Stein had taken only half a dozen short steps when in his peripheral vision he became aware that the brown-garbed figure was simply no longer there. His pace never slowed; out of curiosity he swiveled his head. He saw a Jewish shape moving swiftly away

237

from him . . . a shape that only a moment ago had been heading his way.

Someone's playing games. Contraband food—a stolen loaf of white bread. And we're not supposed to interfere, not as long as the Kripo captain is in the camp.

But they're doomed. What difference does it make, now or later? Now is exactly the time to begin reinforcing discipline. It will make the end that much easier to accomplish. They'll march down Freiheitstrasse like lemmings.

Rudy Stein drew his pistol. Boots reflecting the glare of April sun, black cap at a rakish angle, he moved rapidly up the slope toward the blurred figure.

Lieberman did not look around. The panic had evaporated like a drop of ice water on a hot iron. A visual memory battered through to his mind: Rudy's pace had not altered. He's not following me.

Nevertheless, to be on the safe side, Lieberman acted. A warm foul odor filled his nostrils. In summer, he wondered, how will we stand it? In summer, God willing, we'll be dead or gone. . . .

In the shadows amid buzzing flies he struggled out of his coat and began fumbling at the twine that attached the bag of gold to his belt. His fingers were clumsy; he had tied the knots well, the way his father had taught him when he was a child. There were two other Jews in the latrine, sitting on the wooden planks above the steaming black well of excrement, but they paid scarce attention to him. It was no special thing to see a worried Jew or a Jew in a hurry or a Jew trying to get rid of a bundle.

Lieberman finally wrenched the belt around in the loops of his trousers and picked the knot apart. The bag dropped to the dirt floor with a clink.

The wooden door flung wildly open on its rusted hinges, clattering and banging, admitting a blast of hot light in whose center, framed against a shimmering gold and blue landscape, stood the black thin shape of Prince Rudy. But to Lieberman he loomed like a giant from a children's fairy tale of evil in a midnight forest. One hand held his nose, the other his pistol.

238

Lieberman knew that there was no way out. No route of escape, no explanation. He wanted to shriek with fury. All that stopped him was his fear.

At close quarters, with the bar of sunshine through the open door bathing Lieberman's terrified shrunken visage, Lieutenant Stein recognized his prey.

He was puzzled. This was the camp leader. A responsible man, a model prisoner. Stein had often heard him shouting with genuine impatience at the newcomers alighting from the trains.

"Lieberman . . . it's *you?*"

Lieberman snatched the bag of gold, intending to stuff it into the nearest hole over the pit.

Stein reacted instinctively. With a little cry of rage, he jumped forward, slashing downward with the barrel of his pistol.

Lieberman yelled in pain. The gun had struck his elbow—he felt the brittle bone shatter. A burst of nausea shot from his brain to the tips of his nerves. The bag of gold slipped from his grasp. He huddled groaning on the wet dirt floor, clutching his elbow.

Thrusting a hand into the sack, Stein felt the smooth round surface of coins.

"Get up," he ordered the two other Jews, who sat on the planks, hands between their legs, eyes swollen with terror. "This man needs urgent medical treatment. Carry him to the hospital."

An end to pain, Lieberman thought. From the moment that Rudy had broken through the door, death had never been in doubt. So his promise to the old woman was broken. But not the revolt . . .

Gritting his teeth to stifle any groans, under his breath he began to recite the mourner's Kaddish that glorified God's wisdom.

With the bag of gold tucked under one arm, Stein jumped out of the latrine. As soon as he was clear of its stench, standing in the gently warming sun and sucking deep lungfuls of fresh air, a thought came to him.

There's money in that sack—a lot of it. But how much was a lot?

The two Jews had started to haul the limp figure of Lieberman over the rocky ground. "Hold on a minute," Stein commanded.

Bending to one knee by the stump of a tree, he rested the bag in the dirt. He began stacking the coins on the stump. Twenty-dollar American gold coins with the ridged screaming eagle. He stacked them methodically, making ten piles of twenty coins each. They glittered wonderfully in the sun.

But that's exactly four thousand dollars, he realized.

At first he had assumed the old man meant to escape. There was enough gold here to bribe a man's way clear across Europe, to Lisbon and beyond. But no zlotys for Poland? No jewels? And why a round number?

It nagged irritably at Stein's confused sense of the probable. He swept the gold back into the sack.

"Change of plan," he said to the bearers. "To the coal cellar."

Lieberman had watched the counting procedure with growing fright. He had expected to be shot and dumped into the sulfur pit. It would be quick. Now he knew he would be tortured. He wet his pants. Dobrany was right. I'm not a warrior, not a zealot. I can't bear pain. If I live, the revolt is doomed.

"A moment . . ."

He spoke softly in Yiddish to the men who pulled him. He freed his left arm, reached across his body into the right-hand pocket of his trousers, and pulled out the little bullet-shaped cyanide capsule. He hesitated for the blink of an eye, but it seemed to be forever. Amazing . . . despite all suffering, life was still sweet.

But he was curious. Was he joining his lost children and wife, his parents? Would he see God? Would God explain?

"Sh'ma Yisroel, adonai elohenu, adonai echod . . ." he whispered, then thrust the glass into his mouth. Looking up at the blinding sun, the giver of life, he bit down hard.

His body stiffened. His knees jerked, his eyes grew red with blood. He slumped down. Lieberman was dead.

Stein had seen, but it was too late for him to do anything. The two Jews babbled in terror. They still supported the slack body of the dead man. His head lolled drunkenly. His teeth were stained with blood; flecks of broken glass clung to his lips.

Running toward them, bellowing like a branded calf, Stein leveled his pistol and fired twice at each screeching Jew. One bullet remained—in his venomous rage he shoved the barrel into Lieberman's dead face and pulled the trigger.

The echoes of the shots rolled slowly back from the forest. Soldiers were running out of the barracks.

"Not the rabbi," Dressler said.

"All."

"I still need him. I know the man, Rudy. He wouldn't steal a bent pin."

"Something's going on," Stein said stubbornly. "I don't know what, but I'm going to find out. All right . . . not the rabbi."

Stein ordered that all six men who worked under Rabbi Hurwicz's supervision in the gold commando be escorted to the hospital. He made them kneel at the edge of the sulfur pit in the twilight.

"I have a bullet for each of you. But only one has to die. Tell me which of you gave the gold to Lieberman. I'll spare the others. You have my word as a German officer."

Commandant Kirmayr was in his office, wringing his hands. Stein had sworn it was necessary. They would all die anyway when the camp closed, but this way a question would be answered.

The men pleaded innocence. Stein shot them in turn and kicked them into the smoking ditch. Then, in a fury, he strode back to Roll Call Square where the Jews were assembled.

Stein dispensed with cap drill but made them sing the camp anthem. Then he ordered Lieberman's naked body, shrunken in death like a very old man, its face smashed almost beyond recognition, strung by the ankles from the projecting beam of Block A that was used for hangings. The sun was setting over the western forest. Violet and pink light oozed over the compound.

Stein handed his whip to one of the Ukrainian guards.

"Thirty lashes," he calmly ordered. It was his usual punishment for disobedience—enough to kill a man.

The body was like wax with black stripes. No blood would flow.

Aron Chonszki and Leo Cohen stood together in the ranks of Jews as the whip curled, cracked, and fell. They had all heard the shots coming from outside the latrine. The whispered name of

Lieberman raced through the camp. Chonszki fell to the ground and bit the earth in pain.

At any moment he and Cohen expected to be hauled from their jobs and handed over to Prince Rudy at the coal cellar.

The whip cracked again. "He told them nothing," Chonszki whispered.

Cohen only nodded. He clenched his fists, digging ragged nails into his palms. He wondered if ever in his life he would permit himself to cry, to howl.

In the darkness, later, they found Avram Dobrany. The Czech's shoulders were hunched. Then he wiped his face with the dirty sleeve of his jacket and straightened up. In a hoarse voice he said, "Lieberman once told me that at the right time, the right man always appears. This was true. I see it clearly. But he was the man."

"He didn't know," Cohen said quietly.

"He knew." Dobrany, a soldier, understood something that had escaped even Lieberman. "Because he was the right man, he never said so."

Stein returned to the commandant's bungalow. All the officers, including Bach, had gathered there. Zuckermann busily worked the bellows in front of the iron stove.

"The mystery is not solved," Stein said coldly. "He was carrying four thousand dollars, all in American gold coins. No zlotys. No cash at all. He didn't intend to escape."

Dressler said, "It may have been meant for a bribe."

Stein, pacing the carpet with short, precise steps, halted and raised an eyebrow. "What do you imagine you can buy here at Zin for four thousand dollars in gold?"

"A Mercedes," Lustig said, chuckling. "He was going to drive to Switzerland."

"That's not unlikely." Paul cleared his throat and quickly had their attention. Until then he had said nothing. His eyes were clear and grave. He had made his plans, and Lieberman's death fit them perfectly.

Leaning forward, he placed his hand flat on the oak table. "I spoke to Lieberman the other day. I interrogated him. It was an extraordinary conversation. He told me he believed the world was soon coming to an end. There would be an unparalleled catastrophe—a flood such as only Noah had survived, an eruption of the earth here in Poland even greater than the one that buried Pompeii. Only a chosen few would be spared."

Stein frowned. "I don't follow you."

"He was insane," Paul said.

Rocking on his swivel chair, Kirmayr made a little temple of his fingertips. But he was listening.

Paul went on determinedly. "He said that the doubters must perish. Some already had, he said. I discovered that he could write fluent Hebrew. German and Yiddish, too. He had total freedom of movement in the camp. I concluded that he was the man who strangled Margulies and murdered Lieutenant Hrubow. The Jew Wallach, as well. I lacked only a confession. In a day or so, I'm sure, I would have had it. Instead, he committed suicide. All his actions today were those of a guilty man bent on ending his life."

"Too old," Stein said thoughtfully. "Not quick enough or strong enough."

Dr. Lustig tapped the ash from his cigar. "The criminally insane can achieve remarkable strength." He turned in his chair. "Isn't that so, Bach?"

"There have been many such cases."

"So you killed two birds with one stone, Rudy," the commandant said brightly. He had made up his mind. He had his man now. The case was closed. With Bach's signature he would file a report tomorrow and send it by special courier to Colonel Dietrich in Warsaw.

"Well, I was right," Stein concluded. "They're all crazy."

The discussion concerning Lieberman ended. The officers gathered together more closely about the table in the glow of the oil lamp to discuss the timetable for Zin's liquidation.

When Paul left, he paused a moment in the gray twilight to look up at the first stars. He closed his eyes and murmured, "Forgive me, Herr Lieberman."

25

Lance Corporal Reitlinger knocked on the door of the guest bungalow at nine o'clock the next morning.

"Captain, it took me a while to find where the gravel commando is located today. They're in a quarry just north of the camp. I've sent the rabbi and a guard to fetch the man you want."

"I wouldn't mind a walk," Paul said, glancing out the window at a sky that was the soft blue of spring.

He had been up most of the night making his plans. It was clear what he had to do; the question was *how*. He slept a few hours, woke with gritty eyes and a sour taste in his mouth. After the Jews had gone to work, he spent half an hour alone in Block B, then fifteen minutes in Block A. It was enough to tell him what he needed to know. Then he had given his orders to Reitlinger.

He tucked his briefcase carefully under his arm. They exited through the main gate under the eye of the watchtower, walking in single file on the narrow path between the minefields. They caught up with the rabbi en route. He moved jerkily, arms and legs swinging like the limbs of a wooden puppet. From a distance, when Paul first sighted him, he seemed a homely figure: the scholar out for a stroll in the country on a Sunday afternoon, admiring the flowers, cocking an ear for birdsong. But when they reached him, they saw that his eyes were bloodshot, barely dry.

Blessed be Mordecai. . . .

Paul dismissed the Ukrainian guard. Ahead of them lay the

forest of gray-and-white birches. Thickets were beginning to bud; a patch of hilly earth was purple with violets. The air grew fresher with each step. Paul's head began to clear. From somewhere he smelled the fragrance of lilac. His eyes had stopped itching, and he no longer sneezed.

He slowed his pace to look behind him. A lone puff of white cloud floated leisurely above the railroad depot. Zin lay about a mile distant, bathed by the bright April sunlight. No sound came from it. It might have been a deserted military outpost, except for the red smoke wreathing from the lower camp.

They entered the cool forest. The gravel pit lay in a clearing fifty meters in diameter. Armed guards stood at the four corners. The Jews working in the pit had thrown their shirts in a heap and were sweating in the sun. Only a few had the bodies of men—the skeletal ribs and shoulders of the others pressed against papier-mâché skin.

Some small peasant dogs snapped at their heels. A Jewish kapo named Jozek ran back and forth sweating and shouting, "Tempo! Faster . . . fill up, you lazy swine. . . . You! Tempo!"

The men glanced at Paul without curiosity. Their hands were blistered, their thighs bruised from the pressure of the shovels. Most worked silently, as if they felt nothing.

"Cohen," Paul said.

The young Jew rested a moment on his shovel before he turned his head.

The sweat had dried on his body. He sat shirtless in the shade of a birch tree, legs splayed out, facing Paul. They had walked about three minutes, beyond sight or sound of the gravel pit. Reitlinger had retired into the forest to look for birds. The rabbi was nowhere in sight.

Paul offered Cohen a cigarette. "Do you smoke?"

"I used to. No longer."

Paul lit one for himself, stubbed the match into a patch of wet earth, then looked up.

"You strangled Margulies," he said calmly, "and you cut Lieutenant Hrubow's throat. You stabbed Wallach the other night outside the commandant's bungalow. I need to know why."

Cohen blinked in confusion. But his gray eyes were hard as stones. "If you believe all that," he said, "You should follow Lieutenant Stein's example and shoot me. When I'm dead, you can whip me as proper punishment for my crimes."

"But you don't deny it."

Cohen laughed harshly. "Of course I do."

"You didn't do it, or you don't admit doing it?"

"Is there a difference, Captain?"

Give him play, Paul thought.

"To a police officer, yes."

"To me you are a German officer."

"And so you despise me."

Cohen's eyes glittered. He took the offered opportunity, as Paul had hoped.

"Poor Captain. You're not part of this at all. You're a civilized man. You're sorry that Lieberman had to die. You flung your pillow of hair in the commandant's face. You want to puke at what you see here—" A hand flicked in the direction of the camp. "You've lost an arm, so you think you understand pain. Prince Rudy is an animal. Some of your best friends back in Germany are—shall we say, *were*—Jews. You would do it all differently if you had the power."

Paul waited a moment. He listened to the distant yap of the peasant dogs. "Yes, I would do it differently. Or not at all."

"But you don't have the power, Captain. So you do as you're told."

"Who wrote the notes for you?"

Cohen sighed. "If it were true that I was the commandant's avenging angel, would I answer your question?"

Paul was pleased. The pleasant air of the forest, the isolation, the fact that no point had been pursued, had achieved this purpose. A game of wits in which only Cohen knew the whole truth, in which he was master. The stony glare of his eyes had perceptibly softened. He was relaxed; he was almost enjoying himself.

"What did you do with the gold?" Paul asked.

"What gold?"

"Margulies's gold."

"Did he have gold? Another greedy Jew." Cohen laughed again but more nervously than before.

"He was kapo of the gold commando. Fewer Jews have passed through the camp since Rabbi Hurwicz became kapo, but more gold has been collected each week. The rabbi is an honest man. I made a calculation. Margulies was stealing thirty thousand dollars in gold each month. He could have had several reasons, but they're of no interest. He was kapo for two months. So there's about sixty thousand dollars in gold missing. Margulies hid it under the floorboards of his room—the room that the rabbi now lives in. It's no longer there. Just some loose zlotys that I found behind one of the support beams. He must have traded some gold for cash. You missed those, or you didn't think them worth taking."

"Nonsense," Cohen muttered.

"But I don't believe you killed him for the money alone. Margulies was not an admirable man. Are you sure you don't want a cigarette?"

"I told you I don't smoke."

"But you used to. Don't you miss it? Take one."

"I don't *want* one," Cohen said petulantly.

Paul leaned forward. "There was a suicide after the commandant's edict. The Angel left a note. The dead man was an informer named Guttman. You hanged him. Margulies was an informer, too. The Wijnberg sisters were barely of age. Belgian girls—not your countrywomen but close enough. Margulies may have deserved his fate. I won't argue that with you. Don't you think he deserved it?"

Cohen snorted warily. But it was more agreement than denial. That costs you nothing, Paul thought.

"So you took Margulies's gold. It was there. You could use it to escape."

"But I didn't escape," Cohen pointed out.

"Not in the middle of winter. That would have been foolish.

You decided to wait until the snow thawed and the weather turned warm. You knew you'd survive that long, thanks to Lieutenant Vogl's patronage. So you hid the gold somewhere else. Around now, let's say in late April or May, you thought you'd scoop up your treasure, carry a little bit of it every day here to the forest, use some to bribe one of the Ukrainians on the gravel commando—and off you go."

Cohen had moved his face into a bar of sunlight that streamed between the branches of the birch tree. He tilted his neck a little to catch some of the warmth.

"Amazing," he said.

"No, quite logical. The act of an imaginative man."

Cohen smiled and made a slight gesture with one hand. "Not as imaginative as you, Captain."

He's enjoying himself again. He's young, Paul thought. Young and brave. It's like a game to him. He adds up my many mistakes and feels far ahead—safe.

"You could get through Germany easily posing as a German. You look German. You look, in fact, as if you could be my younger brother—even a son. Have you noticed that?"

Cohen nodded, lowering his eyes. A concession, Paul thought, which couldn't have been easy.

"And then to Holland. Join the Dutch underground. I'm told it makes a great deal of trouble for the Reich. How does that sound to you?"

"Desirable."

"I would think so. May I call you Leo?"

"As you wish, Captain."

Paul, sitting cross-legged as he talked, had extended his hand to let the smoke of his cigarette curl closer to Cohen's nostrils. For the third time he shook out the pack.

"Are you sure you don't want one?"

Cohen accepted. He slid it between his lips and used the red tip of Paul's to light his own. After the first puff he coughed harshly, but then he inhaled and let the smoke drift slowly from his nostrils. He shook his head a moment, dizzied.

"One day," Paul resumed, "Lieutenant Hrubow walked into Block C. You were lucky . . . you saw him. You became alarmed. What was he doing in there? He was a greedy man. He killed Jews with shovels. He raped Jewesses in the snow. Does that describe him?"

"As you say, Captain." But his breathing, Paul noticed, had quickened.

"You entered the barracks. He was there, scraping in the dirt with the bayonet of his carbine. He may have been tempted to shoot you, but then he'd lose his booty. You got close enough to him to cut his throat. You cleaned up and left a note—you didn't want the other men in the block to be blamed for the murder. And you left." Paul sat up straighter on the hummock of dry ground he had selected. "Now don't tell me I've dreamed all this."

"I have to, Captain. You're wrong."

"In what ways?"

"In all ways. I didn't do it. Not Margulies, not the Blackie. Certainly not Wallach." As soon as the last phrase slipped through his lips, Cohen's shoulders twitched. He looked as if he wanted to bite the words back from the air.

But Paul only smiled. "Leo, you make me feel like a fool."

"You're a good storyteller, Captain."

Paul looked up quickly with a hopeful expression. "Will you do me one favor? I'd prefer not to have to order you. Then you could prove to me that you're right and I'm only a teller of tales." He said, "Take off your boots. Show me there's no knife in one of them."

Cohen's ruddiness ebbed. But with hardly any hesitation he reached down to grasp one boot and ease it off.

"No," Paul said. "The other one. And don't take anything out of it. Don't give me the boot, either. I have only one hand. Just turn it upside down."

A shaft of sunlight struck Cohen's bare chest. His stomach looked like bars of hard white leather. His long fingers scratched at the scuffed old leather of the Wehrmacht boot. They toyed with the stitching. He forced a bland smile.

"What would it prove, Captain? Many men carry weapons. We have our reasons."

"I know you do."

Paul lighted another cigarette, keeping his eyes locked on the young Jew. He wanted no surprises. He could feel Cohen's mind thrashing, the tumblers clicking.

Will he bring me to Stein at the coal cellar? Straight to Lustig at the hospital? No, he's made too many mistakes. He's only guessing. He can't know.

Paul could see him beginning to feel strong again.

"If I carry a knife, Captain, it means nothing. You know I couldn't be the Angel. I don't write Hebrew or Yiddish. I wasn't even here in January when the first notes appeared. I told you so the other day. You didn't check it."

"But I did. Rabbi Hurwicz confirmed the date."

"Then you know."

"I wasn't familiar with Hebrew characters," Paul said. "I assumed the first notes were written in the same hand as the ones in German that followed. Then I recalled working on a case where I looked at thousands of printed applications for car licenses. I remembered how basically alike they were. I'd made a stupid assumption. You counted on it. Everyone obliged. You didn't write the first notes in Hebrew. Your friend Pieter did that. He was a young scholar, the son of a rabbi. When you arrived, he confessed to you what he'd been doing. Then Stein killed him." Paul shrugged. "You simply took over where he left off . . . but with another purpose."

"If that's so," Cohen demanded, "why would I—or the man who killed Margulies and Hrubow—need to leave notes *at all?*"

Paul smiled thinly. "So that we would still believe the murderer wrote Hebrew. Which would eliminate *you* as a suspect."

Cohen began to scratch his nose. Paul had seen the gesture before in men who were lying; he couldn't account for it, but it was a common trait.

"I was confused for a while," Paul admitted, "until I realized that

the note on Hrubow's body—which the murderer wrote himself—
had such bad grammar. No elegance. The previous notes were well
phrased. An educated mind was at work. That's when it occurred to
me that the Angel must have a confederate, someone who composed the other notes in advance of their use. So the fact that you
weren't here in January and didn't know Hebrew or Yiddish lost its
significance. The rest, as the rabbi might say, was obvious."

"And after Pieter was killed," Cohen asked, no longer able to
stem the nervousness in his voice, "who do you think composed the
notes?"

"That was not so obvious," Paul said. "But then I received the
Angel's petition. It mentioned my pillow. My pillow wasn't stuffed
with down from the Hungarian goose, it claimed, but with the hair
of dead Jews. That was true," Paul added quietly.

"Which proves what, Captain?" Cohen seemed genuinely at a
loss.

"I asked the commandant to whom else, other than me, he had so
proudly described his pillow factory back in Rosenheim. He told
me."

The sun among the branches created spotty shadows. Cohen's back
was still braced against the birch tree.

"If you believe all this, Captain . . . what do you intend to do?"

"I don't believe all of it," Paul confessed. "I did until yesterday
afternoon. Then Stein shot Lieberman. I was fond of Lieberman."

"A Jew?"

"As you said before, everyone back in Germany, including the
worst antisemites, had his favorite Jew. The rest we thought were
opportunists who were ruining Germany, but there was always one
decent one. I had no Jewish friends, probably because a policeman's friends are almost always other policemen and there were
few Jews in the Berlin Kripo. So I was saved from that hypocrisy.
But if I'd had 'a favorite Jew,' then it might have been Lieberman . . .
or someone like him. I don't know how I would have dealt with that
after Kristallnacht," Paul said darkly. "Probably not well at all."

252

Cohen cocked his head warily. "But Captain, you still haven't said what it is that you don't believe."

Paul said, "I don't believe for a minute that you meant to escape to Holland."

"Why not? If I strangled Margulies, what else would I want with his treasure?"

"It was close to two hundred thousand Reichsmarks in gold and currency. You couldn't carry all that with you. Not even out of the camp. Not alone. It was meant for another purpose."

Cohen let out his breath. "Such as?"

"Lieberman took a cyanide capsule before Stein shot him. Stein had counted the gold. It was an exact amount—four thousand dollars in twenty-dollar coins, what the Americans call double eagles. That raised a question that Lieberman didn't care to answer. What did he need it for? In the end I suggested that Lieberman was simply a madman, and Stein believed me. He lacks your imagination, Leo. But where did Lieberman *get* the gold? And what *did* he need it for? I know the first answer, and I can guess the second. He got the gold from you."

Cohen curled his lip. "That's a guess as well, Captain."

With a snap of the brass catch, Paul unlatched the briefcase, then lifted the flap. He brought out a handful of American double eagles that gleamed in the sunlight, then a bundle of Polish zlotys bound by a dirty rubber band.

"You never asked, Leo, how I knew the gold was in Block C. I dug up the block some time ago. Not the whole block. That wasn't necessary—I had to look only in one place. It was natural instinct on your part to move Hrubow's body as far as possible from where the gold was buried. I counted on it, and I was right. I found almost all double eagles—this is just a fraction of it. Margulies stole them because they're the most negotiable currency in Europe. It's what Lieberman was carrying."

The young Dutch Jew's composure broke apart as the surface of a pond struck by a rock. The splash lasted only a moment, but the ripples spread, and no effort of Cohen's will could restore the calm.

"The rest is still there," Paul assured him. "I told no one. My corporal went with me, but I kept him outside."

Cohen's nervousness flickered on and off like a light bulb. "Why did you do that, Captain? If I'm guilty, why protect me?"

"Because I know the answer to the second question. This morning I searched Lieberman's bunk area. Of course there was nothing. But I have a good nose, like Lieutenant Hrubow. Not for gold . . . for other things. I searched elsewhere in the barracks, which no one has done since I arrived at the camp. Policemen know how things are hidden. I found a Mauser pistol under the trough. Several knives and a sharpened screwdriver elsewhere. A crude gasoline bomb, such as I've seen in Russia among partisans. There may have been more, but I stopped looking. I replaced everything as I found it. I told no one."

Paul continued doggedly. "Forgive me trying to trick you before. I was looking for a reaction, and I got it. I know you didn't kill Wallach. You were in Vogl's bungalow. I saw you there. Vogl was in Breslau. I can guess whom you were waiting for. I have no idea who *did* kill Wallach, but the fact that it wasn't you started me thinking about something I'd said to Lieberman. Other men in the camp were armed. A group? A group that needed gold and weapons? So I searched the blocks."

The Dutch boy shook his head stubbornly. He would give nothing, admit nothing. Neither would I, Paul thought, if I were in his place. He'll never trust me; but I can make him *believe* me.

He stuffed the gold back into the briefcase, snapped the catch, and pushed the bag through the dust. Then he lifted his pistol from its holster. Cohen's muscles tensed—but Paul turned the pistol so that his fingers encircled the barrel.

"The weather is perfect. You have the briefcase. I have only one arm—I'm no match for you. You struck me in the head, left me lying here. I can give you at least an hour's start."

The irises of Cohen's eyes were razor-thin.

"You see the pistol's loaded," Paul said. "If you really want to escape, this is your chance. Money, a weapon, and time. But if you and Lieberman had something else in mind . . ."

He tossed the pistol at Cohen's feet.

Cohen rose on his haunches, then straightened his back until it was flush against the birch. The sun rising through the trees slanted into Paul's eyes. He heard a rustling in the forest, as if an animal moved in panic; but when he glanced there, he saw nothing but streaky light and black shadows. He was sweating. He remembered Lieberman's eyes when he had said, *I would rise up in revolt.*

"Why, Captain?" Cohen's voice was pitched even higher than normal; his face was smoothed, a little dazed. For the first time since Paul had known him, he looked like a nineteen-year-old boy. "I still don't understand why you do this. . . ."

Because in the van at Demyansk they jumped like kangaroos. Because of a woman who offered her wedding ring for water. A flung child. The smell, a bubble at my feet. *Two thousand a day.* The necks . . . they gave bad dreams. The claw marks on the brick walls. *The process is beyond one man's control.* A pillow stuffed with hair. A young woman who lived on Brahmsstrasse with a young woman's dreams. A dead husband in the rain. I couldn't recognize Lieberman's face when he hung dead, upside down, smelling of piss and blood, on Roll Call Square and Stein ordered thirty lashes as punishment. Because once I had pride in my work, love for my country, my wife and children. *At Auschwitz they're building day and night. . . .* The three hundred children who came with you, Leo, in the railway and marched up the Road to Freedom . . .

"Sit down, Leo," Paul said wearily. "You don't need to know why. It would be too difficult and painful to tell you. A long story. You would not be impressed. Let's just say I owe it to Herr Lieberman and myself. And I can't help you more than I've done so far except in one way. So sit down. Listen to me. You haven't got much time."

26

Rabbi Hurwicz made his preparations for the Passover ceremony. If you mourned for too long, even for someone as beloved as Lieberman, there would be no end of it. It was necessary to prepare for tomorrow, not grieve for yesterday.

He had the flour and the clean potato peelings safely stored under the floorboards of his room. Mashlik in the bakery would prepare the matzoh. He had the salt, and Bella had promised to bring him bitter herbs from the commandant's garden. Bravel of the kitchen commando gave him the saccharine for the sweetened tea. Wohlberg, who worked on the farm, made some vague assurances about a roasted shankbone.

He had his guarantee from the commandant that his congregation might worship according to the Law. The commandant thus far had never lied to him. And the rabbi had fulfilled his part of the bargain; every morning he had trudged through the rain and mud to the administrative bungalow to report on Captain Bach's progress. The commandant rarely commented other than with a grunt of disgust, a nod of dismissal.

But on the morning of the fourteenth day of Nisan, after he had returned from the forest with the captain, Rabbi Hurwicz's optimism slowly ebbed. It was replaced by a growing dread.

He went around to the administrative bungalow. The commandant was drinking tea and eating from a tin of French biscuits.

"What is it, Rabbi?"

"My report, Herr Commandant . . ."

Kirmayr blinked his red eyes and looked glumly into the rabbi's disturbed face. "No more reports. Your job is finished. We know who the Angel of Death was, Rabbi."

"Was?"

"The kapo of the welcome commando. Our late camp leader, Lieberman."

"Lieberman?"

"Don't repeat every word I say. It was Lieberman. Captain Bach is positive. Our investigation is at an end."

"Captain Bach is positive?" The rabbi let his mouth hang open at the end of the query.

"Get out, Rabbi," Kirmayr said impatiently. "Go say your prayers and get on with your worship of Moses. I have work to do."

The rabbi walked slowly back through the warm morning in the direction of the gold commando. The dread now positively shouted in his ear. *Lieberman was the Angel of Death. Lieberman had left the notes . . . strangled Margulies . . . cut the throat of the Blackie. . . .*

Faithful Lieberman.

If I wish, Rabbi Hurwicz thought, I can say nothing. The commandant told me the investigation was at an end. He told me to go, to worship Moses. Which I must do. Not Moses. God. Tomorrow evening and for seven more evenings to celebrate the Passover.

He remembered an old proverb. *When a thief has no opportunity to steal, he considers himself an honest man.*

I am become that thief, he thought miserably.

Dobrany stared at Leo Cohen, thunderstruck. *"In a week?* That's not possible. I don't believe it."

It was lunchtime in the block. Some men were praying, others sipping the tepid leek soup or gnawing on scraps of their own food, most lying on their bunks staring with dulled eyes. The sun stood high in the sky and barely a breeze blew through the open windows.

"He had no reason to lie," Cohen said. "But I checked. I looked around. I opened my eyes."

Hunching forward, he placed his hands on Dobrany's shoulders, as Lieberman used to do. They sat with Aron Chonszki in the dirt at one end of the trough, a place that most men avoided. The unseasonable warmth of the day made the smell almost overpowering.

"Listen, Avram! That's why they're crating all those tools in the machine shop. I checked with Mashlik in the bakery. He said they've been ordered to use all their reserve supplies. He was told there's a shortage of food in Poznań. But obviously that's an excuse. There's an uprising in Warsaw, in the ghetto. Jews with guns! They need men. So the camp is going to close."

"But in just a *week*?"

"You haven't been listening," Cohen said, but not with annoyance. "The week began yesterday. After today, we have five days. The captain gave me the exact timetable. The last trains arrive tomorrow. The next day we'll be ordered to knock down the gas chambers. A truckload of dynamite arrives tomorrow from Breslau. Sledgehammers, pickaxes—demolition equipment. On the fifth day we'll be taken to the lower camp. Shot. Burned like garbage."

"Impossible," Dobrany muttered.

"I talked to Bella for a minute. She said the commandant's getting his papers in order. He never did that before."

Dobrany repeated the words he had said to Lieberman on the day of his arrival at the camp. "How is that possible?"

"Why not?" Chonszki asked. "You don't believe it . . . or you don't *want* to believe it?"

"Why did Bach tell you all this?" Dobrany demanded.

Cohen had lived with his knowledge for half of the day; to the others it was like the stroke of an ax.

"He had his reasons. He wouldn't say. It makes no difference to us what they are."

"Suppose it's a trap?"

"Avram, here's a proof. He searched the block and found a Mauser pistol taped to the bottom of the trough. It's yours, isn't it?

You never told me where it was. He found it. He didn't take it. You can look—it should still be there."

Dobrany got up immediately, walked to the end of the trough, and then returned. His green eyes were pinched at the corners. He walked like an old man, with sagging shoulders. Once more he sat with them.

"What's impossible," he said quietly, "is that all our preparations count for nothing. . . ."

He pressed his nails deeply into his temples, so that when he removed them there were white marks graven in his skin. "The revolt is finished. Tell your people. Everyone must do what he thinks best. . . ."

Dobrany sighed, already thinking about how to get to the forest on his own.

Aron Chonszki's mind worked at a slow pace. It absorbed words and facts like the earth absorbed rain; it reacted later. He knew this and had always accepted it.

In his youth he had been known as a thief, in his manhood as a dullard. This had been more difficult to accept. Despite his fidelity he was never sure that men trusted him; despite his great strength he had always thought he was an inept man.

The honor of serving under Mordecai Lieberman in the so-called Jewish Revolutionary Army of Zin, he believed, was the highest ever accorded him. Lieberman had been a father, a mentor. He had always called him Aron—never Shoelace. When the committee voted, he had watched how Lieberman voted and had done the same.

He clung to his memory of Lieberman's words. They had thrilled him into doglike obedience. *"Our submission here wasn't cowardice. The world must know that at the bottom of the abyss, in the pit of hell, we refused to descend farther. Let them say that when the Jews found the spirit to resist, the means to fight back—nothing on earth could stop them."*

Some nights as he lay on his bunk, flexing his thighs to remind himself he was still alive, Chonszki repeated those words softly like a hymn. They gave him knowledge and a feeling of peace. After a while he could sleep.

Not to betray them, Lieberman had taken his cyanide pill. He didn't do that, thought Chonszki, so that we should grovel at a setback.

A setback? Not a setback. *It's a disaster.* Even so . . .

He remembered the Angel's words: *Of two solutions, a Jew always chooses the third.*

Chonszki ran thick fingers through his black hair. He shook his head stubbornly. Everything was quite clear. Amazingly clear. So *quickly* clear.

"No, Avram. Not every man for himself. You heard . . . Jews are rebelling in Warsaw. Fighting back! So will we! We'll still attack them. *All* of us. The only difference is that instead of doing it in two weeks' time, we'll do it in three days. Or two. Better yet, one."

"Don't be a fool," Dobrany said quietly.

Chonszki was wonderfully unruffled. "Why is it impossible? Because we stand no chance? We never did. Because we'll all be killed? That was always so. The difference is that now we know exactly when it will happen. But let's make it our choice, not theirs. Let's take some of them with us."

"Good," said Leo Cohen. He gave Chonszki a silver-toothed smile. "I vote for tomorrow. Bach told me that as soon as we tear down the gas chambers, they're going to tell us we'll all be transferred to Auschwitz. To give us hope. But it's a lie. In case we realize it, Stein will double the security guard. That will be the day after tomorrow. So instead, tomorrow, we'll fight them. Are you with us, Avram?"

"We have no guns!"

"We'll get them tomorrow. You'll be in the armory."

"Lunacy!" Dobrany cried.

"Tomorrow, after the bugle, I'll burn down Vogl's bungalow. Everyone will do what he was supposed to do. Forward march to death."

Dobrany was not afraid, only confused. "It hasn't been *planned*," he said angrily. "Wallach's men were supposed to cut the barbed wire. Who'll take Lieberman's place and get the people through the fence? They'll be trampled to death!"

"Let's go out through the main gate instead," Cohen said eagerly. "My group will take care of the Germans at the sentry box. I'll get up to the main watchtower. If we can control that one machine gun, there's a chance. For a few of us!"

Dobrany raised his voice one more notch. "The forest is in the other direction, Leo!"

"So we'll go the long way around," Cohen said, with a bitter laugh. "The Jewish way."

27

April 12, 1943

Dearest Erich and Ushi,

I'm sitting at my desk in the early afternoon, in the guest bungalow of a little camp called Zin, in central Poland. I had a lovely walk today in the forest. The sun is shining after a week of rain.

Zin is a camp rather like Sachsenhausen in appearance but with a different purpose. It was built to kill human beings—Jews. A thousand a day in winter, as many as two thousand a day in spring and summer. They are gassed to death with carbon monoxide.

In the one year of the camp's existence, 300,000 Jews have been murdered in this manner.

This is what is called "resettlement." You've heard the word. Now you know what it means.

The fifty German men who run this camp, the SS officers and soldiers whom you have been taught to admire, are not acting on their own initiative. They are carrying out our Führer's policy, our German government's policy, and the passive will of the ordinary German people brought to its logical and inevitable fruition.

Do you understand? Are the words too complex for you?

Think, Ushi. *Imagine*, Erich. Suppose that the French, whom we know have always despised us (although we're normal human beings like they are), occupied the city of Berlin. Suppose that all the people on Claudiusstrasse were pulled from their apartments by French soldiers, driven off to a gas chamber—and killed. Old people, mothers, fathers, children like yourselves, babies. *All.*

And on the next day the same thing was done to the people on Flensburgerstrasse. The next day, Handelallee, and so forth—until 300,000 people of Berlin had been ruthlessly murdered. Your friends, your parents, *you.*

What would you say to that, if you had the chance to say anything? What would you do?

This is what happens here at Zin, except that those who are murdered here are not Germans. We Germans kill the Jews. The young and the old, like you and me.

Of course I know what you feel about Jews. I've overheard your conversations, read your book reports. The Jews lived off us like parasites. They tried to undermine all that was noble in Germany. They were ugly, inferior beings—noses shaped like number 6, fat bellies, hands like claws. Hardly human.

You have eyes. You have brains. You must know it's not true.

But you've allowed yourselves to believe it.

I don't blame *you.* You are not alone. The German people stand with you. I never contradicted what you read, what you grew to believe. I feared your disapproval.

I suspected as early as 1933 that Germany had chosen a path of self-destruction and ugliness. I voiced those suspicions timidly. No one listens to a timid man. Knowledge can be like poison.

When people were taken to the concentration camps like Sachsenhausen for no better reason than their dislike of the Führer and their doubts that National Socialism was the answer to our ills, I looked the other way. I didn't even want to *see* Sachsenhausen.

I was a coward. To a coward the easy way always seems best.

I had my life to live. So I said to myself, "It has hardly anything to do with me."

Many Germans felt as I did—and that's why we are at war. If the Führer has his way, we will fight on forever until our country is a wasteland.

Many Germans felt as I did—and that's why we are murdering Jews. Because hardly anyone dared to stand up and cry, "Stop!"

And so, after a time, our leaders believed that the people approved of their policy. War to the death. State-sponsored sadism. And it has come to this—to Zin, a death camp.

In the book you're reading, Ushi—in *Mein Kampf*, which sits on your bedside table where you used to keep your dolls—the Führer advocated this. It was no secret. We should have known *long ago*. Maybe we did know and just didn't care. That was the beginning of our sin.

There are those who pull the triggers or release the gas. There are those who write the orders to do it. And there are those who turn their backs. Some few of the latter say, "Yes, kill them!" Others say, "If you must do it, don't involve *me*." The rest say, "Don't even *tell* me. I don't want to know."

I am so deeply ashamed of myself. I was a policeman. My task was to combat disorder and evil. Now I swim in the muck of orderly evil. It was my job to protect the innocent by bringing murderers to justice. Here, the murderers are my own people.

You always think, "What can *I* do? I'm just one little person." But there must be something that can be done, at least tried, and when I return to Berlin, I will do it.

If it requires a sacrifice, I write to beg that you understand. I might not have had the tenacity to say these things to your faces. You might have turned away in anger before I finished.

But you *will* read this letter.

Dear children, forgive me if I impose upon your life and your certainty. I feel so soiled. Nothing will wash out

Paul's pen halted its scratch across the onionskin paper. A sound had broken through his concentration. Someone was knocking softly, persistently, on the door of his bungalow.

He stubbed out his cigarette, hesitated a moment, then crossed the room to open the door. Rabbi Hurwicz in his dark rags stood in the milky sunlight under gathering clouds. It was the day before Erev Pesach. He had already begun his fast in gratitude for God's having passed over the houses of the children of Israel, their door-posts sprinkled with the blood of the Paschal lamb, when He smote the firstborn in Egypt.

"Captain . . . do I interrupt you?"

"What is it, Rabbi?" Paul inquired.

"Some thoughts . . . it occurred to me . . . if I'm not disturbing you too much . . ."

Clearly the rabbi was plagued by some unspoken ache. The letter can wait, Paul thought. I'll finish it later. Maybe tear it up and start over. Was it more than a moan of self-pity? I'll tell them about the camp, that's all. The rest when I see them, face-to-face.

Fresh air would be good. The edges of the clouds were a glaring white; the sun seemed to battle for room. A humid breeze blew from the south.

"Shall we walk, Rabbi?"

Until they passed beneath the north watchtower and were nearing the farm, the rabbi was silent. A hectic spot of pink appeared on each shrunken cheek. Then, drawing and expelling a harsh lungful of air, he said, "Captain, it was Lieberman who strangled Margulies?"

Paul's step faltered for only a moment. "I believe so," he said uncomfortably.

"That's what you told the commandant?"

"Yes, I did."

"And Lieberman cut the throat of the Blackie? Excuse me . . . the lieutenant?"

Paul had no choice. "Yes," he said.

"You *believe* that, Captain?"

He grunted an acknowledgment.

"So Lieberman wrote all those notes, Captain?"

"It would seem to follow."

"Why would he have done all those things?"

Paul coughed and averted his face. "The general feeling, Rabbi, is that he was mad."

The rabbi once more lapsed into silence, but of a different kind than before. He thought so furiously that his forehead seemed to burn with the effort. His scar turned a deep fiery pink.

Kicking up dust, he stopped short in his tracks just as they turned from the farm in the direction of the barracks.

"Captain!" he said shrilly, very nearly angrily. He raised a bent, pencil-thin index finger. "Lieberman didn't write the notes! I translated the notes before you arrived. They were written by a right-handed person! Did you ever see Lieberman's right hand, with the two fingers missing? Did you see him hold his teacup with it? No! He was left-handed!" The rabbi poked another finger in Paul's face. "Margulies was strangled in the month of Adar, on the Friday before the Sabbath of Purim. Lieberman observed with me the fast of Esther. All through the lunch hour that day, when we didn't eat, we discussed where the evening service would be held. So Lieberman is innocent!" He raised a third, definitely angry, finger. "You asked Lieutenant Vogl if the dead Blackie's head was facing the ceiling. He said no, it was twisted to the left. Surely the murderer didn't want to get blood all over his only clothes and be found out . . . so, God forgive him, he had to get behind the Blackie to cut his throat. If he was right-handed, he would twist the Blackie's head to the left with his own left hand and cut his throat with the knife in his right hand." He grimaced at the ugliness of his vision. "That's why you asked. That's why the head was twisted to the left. The murderer of the Blackie was right-handed! So, again . . . not Lieberman!"

The rabbi had finished his tirade. He lowered his hand, inch by slow inch, and glanced at Paul's stern face. He had come to the crux of the matter. He murmured unhappily, "But you knew that all along, Captain . . ."

"Yes, I knew," Paul said wearily.

"And you also know who is the real murderer."

"Yes."

The rabbi's eyes popped. "Don't tell me! I didn't ask!"

"But you know *everything*, Rabbi," Paul said. "Don't you know that, too?"

The rabbi's face grew gray beneath his yellow pallor. At last, almost inaudibly, he said, "I know."

"Know . . . or think you know?"

"Know," he muttered.

"If I ask, will you tell me?"

He groaned. "If you ask, I can't lie. God is listening."

Paul considered for a moment. But there was too much at risk. "I think you'd better tell me."

The sun slipped from behind a cloud, turning the earth from a dun color to a burning brown with shoots of flaming green. The rabbi blinked at the glare.

"It was Leo Cohen," he said grievously. "May a thunderbolt find his head!" His eyes flashed. "A curse on murderers! *Un a suff zol dos zine—un an ek zol dos ne-men! Yisgaddal v'yiskaddash sh'may raboh!* An end there must be to this—it must all stop! Hallowed and magnified be the name of God!"

Paul had come this far the way a man crawls up a steep mountain in the dark, clutching at roots and rocks and brambles—clambering this way on instinct, that way on knowledge. Looking for chinks of light from an implacable heaven, praying not to slip, halting his progress time and time again to consider where the path might lead—and finally, exhausted and joyless, reaching the bitter goal.

He had divined motive for more than wanton murder. He knew what the Jews planned to do. But destiny, in the form of Willi Dietrich's order, had winked an eye.

I can help them, Paul had realized. I can give them knowledge, and with knowledge they can act.

But now the rabbi had knowledge, too. He must have come to it, Paul thought, in a way beyond my understanding. A ragged arrow from the bow that wavers in flight, vanishes in the sun, then dips as if by a miracle to quiver in the bull.

How much knowledge? And to whom has he revealed it before now?

Cocks crowed from the farm. A dog barked somewhere deep in the forest. "Rabbi," he said, "I have to ask you some questions. I know you'll tell me the truth. How long have you known it was Leo Cohen?"

"Since yesterday," Rabbi Hurwicz said quietly.

268

Paul indicated a patch of greening earth. "Let's sit. I'm sure this will take a while. How did you reach your conclusion?" But the rabbi made no move to sit.

"It won't take so long," he said. His dark eyes wandered nervously. "You took me with you to the forest . . . I was behind a tree. . . ."

Only slowly, Paul grasped his meaning.

"You *heard*?"

The rabbi blushed.

Paul remembered the rustling of leaves; he had thought it was an animal.

"You heard *all*?"

Rabbi Hurwicz's head drooped so that Paul could no longer see his eyes.

"Not all. And not so clearly. Not as if you'd talked right into my ear. Enough. Maybe once I dozed off. Maybe you talked some more after I left. . . ."

"*When* did you leave?"

"When you offered him your pistol." The rabbi raised his eyes, shot through with pink. "I ran away. I was frightened. I prayed for your life and for Cohen's soul. A Jew who murders in cold blood, even a German captain, is cut off from Israel."

"Did you report to the commandant this morning?"

"I went there. I went every morning."

"What did you tell him today?"

"He didn't want to hear me. And he never asked what I knew," the rabbi said, brightening just a shade from the grip of gloom. "If he had done that, I couldn't have lied. But he said to me, 'Whatever you see, whatever the captain tells you, I want to know.' I agreed to that. But I didn't see you and Cohen talking. My back was turned! There was a caterpillar crawling on a branch that had all my attention. And you never told me!" Struggling with his conscience and the dictates of the Law, he let out a yelp of panic. "Isn't that true, Captain?"

"I told you nothing," Paul said gravely, gratefully. "God is listening. It's you who told me, Rabbi. May a thunderbolt find my head if I lie."

28

Erev Pesach dawned warm and gray. Dew sparkled on the barbed wire. A dank mist covered Roll Call Square. None of the leaders of the Jewish Revolutionary Army of Zin had slept more than a few hours. At dusk the previous evening they had gone around to the farm, the bakery, the laundry, the machine shop—all the commandos—and said, "The camp is closing in four days. It's true! *We know*. But tomorrow at seven o'clock, we do everything as planned. The bugle will blow to end the workday. We'll arrange for the guards to be down off the watchtowers. Wait for the fire to start in Vogl's bungalow. That's the signal. Use whatever weapons you have. Attack them! Dobrany will get guns to us. However many are left, we'll go out by the main gate. Head for the forest, for the gravel pit. We'll meet there. . . ."

They distributed the gold and zlotys. Chonszki knew where Lieberman had hidden the pistol he had bought from Taddeus with the rabbi's gold. As soon as it grew fully dark, he walked out to the latrine and then, bent double, scuttled to the long hedge bordering the lower camp. He found not only the pistol but a knotted scarf full of bullets. He slipped the pistol into his belt beneath his jacket.

"Do you want it?" he asked Dobrany. "You'll need it most. You've got to get us more guns."

"Keep it, and don't forget about the safety catch. I have the one under the trough. I gave one to Leo. Listen, Shoelace—can you get hold of a nice big potato?

"You're hungry? I have some bread. . . ."

"No." Dobrany explained: The sooner he could dispatch the SS guards in the armory, the faster he could begin to distribute loaded carbines and grenades. But a loud report would alert the entire German garrison. Engel in the machine shop had been trying to make a crude baffle silencer, a copper tube stuffed with cotton. He was now unable to finish the job.

"I heard somewhere that if you jam a potato into the muzzle of a pistol, it will do the trick. Messy, but who cares? I'm going to try it," Dobrany said.

He had already shown some men how to make Molotov cocktails, filling empty liter bottles with gasoline over oil, then stuffing a gasoline-soaked rag into the mouth as a fuse. Bella had stolen three empty wine bottles and corks from the commandant's bungalow.

"But only three! . . ." Dobrany agonized over how to distribute them. Finally he gave one to Cohen, one to Jozek of the gravel commando, and one to Wohlberg, a man who had served briefly in the Wehrmacht and would know how to use it.

In the morning the insanity of their task had made Dobrany soak his pallet with sweat. Again and again, during the night, he had calculated the odds. The fifty Germans, officers and enlisted men alike, kept their weapons close at hand in the bungalows and barracks. The thirty Ukrainians on duty carried carbines; the rest of their force, off duty, was unarmed.

We outnumber them five hundred to a hundred and thirty, Dobrany thought. In a wrestling and biting match, weak as we are, we might stand a chance. But at the moment we have only three pistols against their eighty rifles and four heavy machine guns. The battle, therefore, will be decided by who controls the armory. Therefore it's up to me.

Chonszki looked up at the lowering yellow-gray sky as he made his way to the train platform. Would it rain? Would rain be good or bad for them? Bad because the Blackies wouldn't be keen to come down from their shelter in the watchtowers. Good because no one except the Germans on duty would be roaming the camp looking for trouble.

It suddenly struck him that the Germans must know what was happening. How could they *not* know? The Jews's faces were flushed. They were jittery, unable to keep still. On their way to work they whispered constantly, jabbing each other in the ribs to punctuate each sentence. A man turned white, clutched his heart, and fell down in Roll Call Square. Stein ordered him taken to the hospital. Another man at the welcome commando began to vomit into the dirt behind the platform.

Chonszki took deep breaths, pressed his diaphragm to calm himself. A train arrived from Milan and Bolzano. This time there was no question of selection. Four hundred stunned and silenced Italian Jews were dispatched to the gas chambers.

Sergeant Grauert said to Chonszki, now kapo of the welcome commando, "No more trains. Take the rest of the day off."

"Don't they see it?" Chonszki asked Dobrany. He passed him outside the armory in the middle of the day. He heard the soft rumble of distant thunder. Quickly he slid a potato from under his jacket into the Czech's pocket. "Can't they *smell* what's going to happen?"

In the administrative bungalow Commandant Kirmayr paced the floor, hands clasped behind his back. He stopped for a moment before each of the Weimar prints on the wall, then in front of the stuffed squirrel, then by the cuckoo clock. It ticked with an enviable calm, its brass pendulum swinging noiselessly. He still had half a dozen bottles of Napoleon brandy, and he had laid down two cases of Mâcon '34. He wondered what to do with the clock and his collection of Meissen. Crate them and take them to Warsaw? And then? You couldn't carry a cuckoo clock on your back to Russia.

Lieutenant Hrubow had once told him that before the battle of Demyansk some of the Ukrainian soldiers ate kilos of butter. When their flesh turned yellow, they pleaded chronic jaundice to be excused from combat. Others froze one arm in a snowbank, then cracked the ulna bone cleanly with a rifle butt.

But there must still be Russian prisoners. Someone's got to take care of them.

He began hauling papers from his desk and the filing cabinets. It was a damp afternoon—a fire crackled noisily in the big-bellied iron stove. He piled all carbon copies on the blaze. He would miss this place, he realized. It had been like a home but more peaceful.

"Find some boxes," he told Zuckermann.

The sergeant was about to go when the commandant had another thought; this was not a night he cared to spend alone. "Stop by the hair depot. Tell Fräulein Bella to be here at five o'clock. And when you get back, put a bottle of French champagne on the ice."

He worked for another ten minutes, then heard the purr of an engine and the grating of tires on gravel. Boots drummed on the steps of the bungalow.

A stubby, ruddy-cheeked SS officer in a black duty overcoat and flaring breeches barged energetically through the door. He had a cigarette holder, without a cigarette, clamped between strong white teeth. It took a moment for Kirmayr to register the fact that the collar patch on his overcoat bore the plaited silver threads of a full colonel.

"Colonel Dietrich?"

Willi nodded. "I'm chilled to the bone, Kirmayr. Get me a big cup of black coffee, one sugar. Then tell me what's going on."

The voice was harsh, but the dark eyes were intelligent and wonderfully merry.

A thorough housecleaning was customary on Erev Pesach, so the rabbi swept his room, mopped the floor, searched carefully for any scraps of leavened substance, then dusted the corners with some old rags. Under the floorboards he had the salt and the shankbone, the flour and the potato peelings that he had wiped with patches of a clean white tablecloth supplied by Lieberman. The sweetened tea was hidden in the Jewish kitchen with his helper, Bravel.

Without Lieberman, nothing was easy to accomplish. And within a few hours the rabbi was feeling very frustrated. Bravel had vanished. Mashlik had baked only a small part of the matzoh. And the rest?

274

"Yes, yes, Rabbi . . . later . . . if there's time."

"*If* there's time? Mashlik, are you crazy!"

Mashlik said, "Please go away, Rabbi. One of the Blackies is watching us through the window. Whatever can be done will be done."

Rabbi Hurwicz grew pale. He left the bakery. Bella had not yet appeared with the bitter herbs from the commandant's garden. Where was Bella?

Lieutenant Stein walked with Lieutenant Vogl across the compound to the armory. In the middle of the morning, the truck full of explosives had been unloaded and its cargo stored. A demolition expert from Breslau, a young Wehrmacht lance corporal named Traub, was in charge of the dynamite. Two other German soldiers, Corporal Munzing and a private named Kreber, were on duty in the armory. Two Jews, including the tall lean one whom Stein liked to think of as the toy soldier, were still dressing the roof beams. Stein glanced up, and for a brief moment he met Dobrany's cold eyes.

The armory had two small barred windows. It was chillier inside than outdoors. Rifle and Schmeisser racks lined the walls, and there were wooden crates of grenades and ammunition. On a planked table the Germans had an electric coffee pot and a pile of dirty cups and saucers.

Stein gestured at the Jews working on stepladders. He spoke quietly to Corporal Munzing. "In a few days we're going to blow this place to smithereens. Dismiss them."

"I already did," Munzing said. "They insisted on finishing the job. They said it's a matter of pride that it be done well."

Stein had to smile. The mentality never ceased to amaze him. Well, he thought, I suppose it keeps them busy and out of mischief. He nodded his approval.

He beckoned to Traub. "Come along with us now. I'm going to show you exactly what needs to be done."

The two lieutenants and the corporal walked under the low gray sky, first to the brick gas chambers, then around Roll Call Square, then down to the train platform, then back up to the north quadrangle. Traub made careful notes in pencil on a little white pad. The tour and their discussion took more than an hour.

By then Stein was uneasy. Something was different. He couldn't put his finger on it, but he knew it was so. Ordinarily the Jews avoided his probing, nearsighted gaze or else greeted him with unctuous smiles. But today those who passed stared boldly. The sunken eyes in the wasted faces glowed like chips of warm wood. Their cheeks were flushed as if a form of low-grade fever had attacked the entire camp.

"Werner," he said, "do you notice anything unusual?"

"Yes," Vogl mused. "They look sick."

"No. They're excited. They're on edge. Do you think they know what we're up to?"

"How could that be?"

"Someone may have tipped them."

"Who would do that?"

"Zuckermann and half our men are drunk the whole time. The other half are drunk part of the time. Maybe they let it slip, and the Jews heard."

"But they don't seem frightened," Vogl said, wrinkling his brow.

Stein blinked in the glare. "When we're done with our little tour, I'm going to ask the commandant to double the guard. We can issue small arms to the Ukrainians who aren't on duty. Get rid of those Jews working in the armory. You know the one up on the ladder? The one I whipped at roll call?"

Vogl nodded. "He was in the French Foreign Legion. Imagine— a Yid! I took a gold medal from him when he got here."

"I don't like the way he looked at me. We don't need his skills anymore, whatever they may be. Have him picked up and brought to the hospital. Tell Lustig to take care of him."

29

At a few minutes before five o'clock, Bella Wallach nodded to Tzippora, the girl who worked with her in the hair depot. Tzippora clutched her forehead, groaned a little, then fainted. As soon as she struck the dirt floor, two other women rushed to her side. The Ukrainian guard put down his bottle of beer and got up from his stool. Bella plucked a pair of scissors from the wooden table. She slid it under her dress, held by the tight elastic of her underwear. The steel felt icy against her thigh.

In a few minutes she excused herself and left for the commandant's bungalow.

In Block B a terrified Aron Chonszki stuffed his pair of wire cutters and the Mauser pistol into his pants pocket beneath his jacket. Dobrany had shown him the little safety catch above the pistol grip. "Don't forget to release it," he warned.

Chonszki lifted his great hands toward the roof of the barracks. He praised the Lord for the ordeals He had visited on His sinful people. He thanked Him for His terrible wrath.

"I above all—an oaf, a knotter of shoelaces—am unworthy of any mercy. But if on this one occasion, Lord, You could just spare the time to give me a sign . . ."

He could not remember if in its current down position the safety catch on the pistol was on or off.

The gravel commando was at work today in the storage huts

helping to crate supplies. Leo Cohen's can of gasoline, to set fire to Lieutenant Vogl's bungalow, was hidden under a grate behind the infirmary. He carried his pistol in a back pocket under his pea jacket. The young men he had recruited—Prager, Wohlberg, Jozek, and Engel—were armed with only kitchen knives. But they had hidden the Molotov cocktails near three of the watchtowers. Their task was to cripple the machine guns. They had volunteered to die. Cohen had chosen them carefully. They were the best and bravest.

"No one dies before his time," Prager said, shrugging. "If ours hasn't come, Leo, we'll see each other next year in Jerusalem."

Jews in the garage and machine shop carried sharpened screwdrivers. The carpenters would use their hammers and saws. Men on the farm had buried axes and shovels.

In the armory Avram Dobrany worked the steel chiseled end of his adze slowly along the timbers. The Mauser pistol was tucked safely into his boot. A potato made a small bulge in his pocket.

"No question but that I'd rather be in Paris. Or Brussels," Willi Dietrich said. "Even Berlin, despite the raids. Still, if you can bear the great horde of the unwashed and the semiliterate, Warsaw's not so bad." He laughed quietly. "It's a policeman's paradise—no matter what they do, they're bound to be breaking one law or another. And some of the women are superb. They're blonde animals."

He lay on the sofa of Paul Bach's bungalow, hands clasped behind his shaggy dark head. His jacket was unbuttoned and Paul could see that his waist had thickened, bulged in a roll over his black breeches. He had not commented, not after Willi had first slammed through the door into the bungalow and said, "Good God, Paul, what's happened to you? Have you been ill? you look like *death*."

A pine fire crackled in the stove. A tray filled with cold cuts, white bread, and empty bottles of Polish beer stood on the desk. The unfinished letter to Erich and Ushi lay face down on the black notebook in which Paul had written his case notes.

278

Paul sat in an easy chair, smoking a cigarette—a blue haze curled toward the oak beams. He tapped the face of his watch.

"It's nearly six o'clock. Don't you have to be on your way?"

Willi yawned, stretching his arms above his head so that the bones in his shoulders made sharp noises as they separated from the ligaments.

"My little Sonja can do without me for one night," he said lazily. "I'll stay right here on your sofa if you can bear my snoring. Like the old days. Kirmayr promised me a bottle of Napoleon brandy. It's good to see you—who knows when it will happen again?" The grin on his square-cut face faded slightly.

Paul flicked the ashes of his cigarette. He leaned forward.

"Willi, there are more rumors than lice in this camp. You have better sources than I do. We've retaken Kharkov, but they say we can't hold it—the Panzerkorps lost half its tanks. I've heard that the Americans have Tunis under siege. Apparently the south of France is next."

"I'll bet on Italy. The rest is true," Willi said.

"Then is the war lost?"

Willi sighed. "That's what everyone wonders these days. Or asks, privately, to the few men he still trusts."

"And what's your answer?"

"I'm not a prophet. And this is between us. Understood?" He hardly waited for Paul to nod. "I think there's a movement afoot, among some rather highly placed military people in Berlin, to make a separate peace with London and Washington. The Russians couldn't hold out for six months without convoys and supplies. It's purely a joke of history that they're all on the same side against us. You know whom we have to thank for that."

Paul's face twisted in confusion. "Do I hear you correctly? The Yanks and the Brits will fight *with* us now—against Ivan?"

"If they have any sense. Bolshevism's the real enemy. Always was. Churchill said that years ago."

"But they're democracies, Willi. Ruled by the great mass of the weak and the unwashed. Marble doesn't make the statue, as Goebbels says. Churchill and Roosevelt are not Führers."

Willi sat upright on the sofa, his bronze Olympic ring flashing in the lamplight. "We know from our own experience, dear boy, that you can move the masses to *anything*. You just have to tell them often enough that they're an elite, that they're fighting for their destiny, for a better world—for their freedom! Freedom's the most stirring word in any language; a man will become a slave in order to get it. Just tell them that the survival of their precious way of life depends on one last, just war. They swallow it like sheep . . . even when a guttersnipe says it."

Paul remembered that last phrase from the old days, before they had joined the party. It's back in fashion, he realized, since Stalingrad.

"So we'll just invite the English, the Americans, and what's left of the French to march across the Reich and join up with us? A celebration! Tea, hot dogs, croissants and sauerkraut. Is that the idea?"

"We're not back to the Bug, not yet. We're still drowning in the Dnieper."

He laughed bitterly. "And what happens when the Americans pass through Poland? They have Jews in their army. Do Private Levy and Colonel Isaacson get a tour of Zin?"

"Zin won't exist," Willi said. "Neither will Birkenau. Auschwitz will be a small city populated by happy, industrious, freshly washed Poles."

Paul regarded him with a seemingly emotionless gaze. "No evidence."

"That's the general idea."

"And no survivors."

"Let's hope not."

"You knew from the beginning, didn't you, Willi." It was not a question.

"I knew, yes. I didn't like it much, but of course I knew. I'll never deny that."

"And now?"

"Hindsight is wonderful. Now I think it was a mistake."

Paul twitched an eyebrow. "You call it *that*?"

"We could have put them in real labor camps. Kicked them out

280

of the banks and the ministries, taken their money. Or thrown them out of the country, the way the Inquisition did back in Spain. In the end we would have achieved the same result. And it would have been a far more intelligent solution. But those louts in Berlin had to have it their way. Once it got started, obviously it couldn't stop. Yes, I think it was definitely a mistake."

"You're a monster, Willi." There was no lightness in Paul's voice, no edge of humor.

Willi snorted, then issued a cold bark. "Everyone knew, and everyone profited, including you. No holier-than-thou, my friend. When I put down the phone after I called you in Berlin, I had a good chuckle. I thought, 'Same old Paul. Can't stand the idea of getting his hands dirty. Wants to keep in his burrow, chuck his kiddies under the chin, do his comfortable job, screw the current lady of his choice, and think to himself, "I'm a good fellow,"' But it won't wash. You're like everyone else, and you know it. Looking out for the fellow you care for more than anyone else in the world." He laughed more warmly now. "Am I right, or do I tell the truth?"

Paul stared out the window. He knew what Willi meant. He was a man who made gestures and no more, to appease his conscience. He had written the letter to General Eicke after the fact; he had stood around at the train in Wolkowysk and done nothing except annoy a Gestapo sergeant; he had dismissed the Jews at roll call instead of laying a whip across Stein's ear. The only thing I've ever done that counts, he thought, is tell Cohen that the camp was closing. And that cost me nothing.

He turned back to Willie Dietrich and said, "What do you mean, 'everyone profited, including me'?"

"Gold—blankets—eyeglasses—baby carriages. All handled by the SS Economic and Administrative Office, distributed by the Main Trusteeship Office East. A public corporation. What do you think happens to that stuff? Do you think it's junked? There isn't a single German alive, from the age of one to one hundred, who hasn't benefited."

"My children don't sleep under Jewish blankets," Paul said angrily.

Willi thumped his bottle of beer on the floor, annoyed.

"The gold goes into the Reich's treasury. It pays for the camps, it helps feed the Wehrmacht. If we didn't have Yid gold, the good citizens of Leipzig and Frankfurt would eat even worse than they do. If we didn't send Yid blankets to SS field hospitals, where would we get them from? From Hamburg! From Berlin! From Erich's bed and Ushi's bed. So you benefit, whether you know it or not, whether you desire it or not, and certainly whether you admit it or not. I'm not sentimental about these things, Paul. I can't afford to be. If that makes me a monster by your definition, I don't care. And now," Willi went on relentlessly, "like it or not, you've seen how it works. And you did your job, as I knew you would. Dug up this loony old Jew, according to Kirmayr—the one who was terrorizing the commandant's warmhearted peaceful existence and giving him nightmares about service on the Eastern Front. Well done, Paul. On balance I think it was good for you. You'll get a commendation from Warsaw HQ. You'll make major now."

Paul thought he would either lash out with his fist or scream. He gripped the side of his chair.

"Kirmayr's lucky, too." Willi seemed oblivious to any reaction. "Ran this place like an old folks' home. He once tried to get Polish ration cards for these people, as if the Yids weren't disposable. He's a pretender, like you. But I'm sending him back to Germany. There's a factory in Munich. They make heavy-duty boots for the Waffen-SS. They need a director—"

Through the open window they heard the report of a pistol shot. Then silence . . . then three more shots. Willi, who had dropped back down on the sofa with his beer, raised himself quickly on one elbow.

"What's going on?"

"Nothing for you to worry about," Paul said grimly. "They came from the camp hospital. The good Dr. Lustig is collecting more eyeglasses."

He leaned forward.

"You think I'm a pretender? I won't pretend anymore. You're a swine, Willi. An educated barbarian. You always were, but I was too fond of you to admit it. I detest you and everything you stand

282

for. I detest the uniform you wear—that I also wear. I'm ashamed to be a German."

Willi, with glacially cold eyes, said, "I see."

"No, you don't see," Paul said. "You don't see at all."

30

Lieutenant Vogl, following the orders issued by Lieutenant Stein, appeared at the armory with no warning. He murmured a few words into the ear of Corporal Munzing, who in turn spoke quietly to Private First Class Kreber.

Kreber was a young man with a sad, horselike face. "I understand," he said quietly.

He beckoned to Avram Dobrany, working on the stepladder.

"Come along," Kreber said.

Dobrany tried to smile. "Where to, sir?"

"Just come along. No talking."

Dobrany glanced quickly at the little white metal alarm clock that ticked placidly on Munzing's desk. It said ten minutes to six. In exactly one hour he would have shot Munzing, Traub, and Kreber. He would then have locked the door, waited the few minutes for the fire to break out in Vogl's bungalow, and then, as the alarm spread, begun handing out rifles and grenades to the Jews who would rush to the armory. He would be able to handle the three Germans; he was positive of it. But now they were taking him away for some unnamed purpose. Whatever happens, he thought, I've got to get back here in under an hour.

Kreber and Munzing were both facing him. Dobrany came down obediently from the stepladder.

He tried to stay calm as he walked through a gap in the hedge, across the neatly raked gravel path of Freiheitstrasse. Behind him, as they walked under a leaden sky, Private Kreber's hand rested lightly on the butt of his holstered pistol.

"What is that in your pocket?" Kreber asked.

"A potato," Dobrany said, over his shoulder.

"You'd better eat it now."

"I'm not hungry. I'd rather wait."

Kreber sighed with a deep, resigned sadness. He was not an enthusiastic soldier and had only joined the SS in the hope that it would save his life by keeping him as far as possible from a battlefield.

"Eat it now," he said, with intended kindness. "That's my advice."

Then Dobrany knew where he was going and that they meant to kill him.

Two Ukrainians sat cross-legged in the dirt by the sulfur ditch in the back of the hospital playing two-handed skat with a deck of bent, begrimed cards. Their carbines lay beside them. Dr. Lustig appeared with an open paperbound copy of Karl May's *The Love of the Uhlan* in one freckled hand.

"A patient for you," Kreber said quietly.

While Dobrany held his breath and measured his chances, Lustig reached into his pocket and brought out a purple swatch of velvet. He inserted it in the book to mark his place.

"You can go, Kreber."

Kreber saluted and vanished rapidly through the hedge. There were no shadows outside the hospital. The sun hid behind packed clouds. The air was very still. The Ukrainians kept playing their game of skat. One threw down a knave and the other seized it, chortling.

"Turn around," Dr. Lustig said. "Get down on your knees facing the ditch." He had made this short speech a thousand times—he never took out his pistol until his patient's back was turned. It's easier for them that way, he realized. The commandant is right. Until the very end, they have a shred of hope.

"May I take off my boots?" Dobrany asked.

They made many odd requests. Most wanted time to pray. Lustig usually shot them in the back of the neck before they were done.

"Why not?" he said.

Dobrany sat down in the dirt, facing the doctor. He reached into the warmth of his right boot and flicked the safety catch on the Mauser. He made sure it was snug in his hand, his finger curved full about the trigger. Tugging the pistol free, he raised it quickly in the two-handed grip taught in the Czech army. Dr. Lustig stared at him dully, uncomprehendingly. There was not a glimmer of fear in his blue eyes, only flat disbelief. Dobrany's bullet ripped through his breastbone into his heart.

The two Ukrainians had been studying their cards, starting to yell their bids on the next contract. The book flew from Lustig's arm into the smoking ditch. His body was already crumpling. The amazed Ukrainians tried to scramble to their feet, drop their cards, and snatch their carbines at the same time.

Dobrany shot one of them in the stomach, the other in the shoulder. He jumped forward through the dust, jammed the pistol into a button of the second man's black coat, and pulled the trigger.

Four shots, he thought. But from the hospital. No one will come.

Breathing hard, he worked the Luger pistol from Lustig's holster and then dragged all three bodies to the edge of the ditch. Both Ukrainians bled all over him. They were both alive, pale eyes rolling, voices softly begging him for mercy.

"Woof, woof," Dobrany said, and with the nailed sole of his boot he shoved them, one at a time, into the warm yellow muck.

They floated a moment, thrashing, then rolled like whales and vanished. A few thick bubbles rose before the surface of the sulfur flattened out.

Sweat dripped down Dobrany's forehead. His old gray military coat was slick with blood. He hefted the two carbines from the dirt, then strode into the hospital. I'm alive, he thought. And armed! I'm a soldier again, not a victim. A cardboard box of .38 caliber cartridges for the Luger stood on Lustig's desk. He had five spare cartridges for the Mauser and two carbines with five rounds each.

But then he cursed in Czech. He struck the desk with a clenched fist.

He couldn't go back to the armory. Munzing or Kreber would be there! The plan had to change.

Be calm, he told himself. You have time. Think like an officer. Think like a legionnaire. If necessary, think like a Jew. Make a new plan.

At ten minutes past six Lieutenant Stein walked into the administrative bungalow. Sergeant Zuckermann sat at his desk, furtively trying to slide shut one of the drawers that concealed his flask of vodka. The wood stove glowed cherry-red. Boxes full of official papers had been piled in one corner of the room.

The commandant stepped out of his bedroom in shirt-sleeves, his man-in-the-moon face even gloomier than usual. Stein knew that a Gestapo colonel had arrived from Warsaw. No more bottles of pear shnapps and Courvoisier. No more chess while Gieseking pounded out the Emperor Concerto.

From the candlelit shadows behind Kirmayr, gliding silently in woolen socks, the Jewess appeared.

And no more free black-haired whores, Stein thought. But he paid no attention to her presence.

"Major, Lieutenant Vogl and I jointly recommend that you double the guard. We also request that arms be issued to the Ukrainian off-duty force. Jewish barracks must be locked after the workday."

With a hand to one breast, Kirmayr thudded like a sack of meat into his swivel chair.

"What in the devil's got into you, Rudy?"

Stein hastily described what he and Vogl had sensed. "We then inspected the Jewish barracks. We found four kitchen knives and a sharpened chisel under mattresses in Blocks B and C."

Kirmayr blew a burst of air from his puffed cheeks. "You're telling me you think they *know*?"

Stein glanced now at Bella, whose eyes were wide with fright.

"Never mind her, Rudy! Do they or don't they?"

"In my opinion," Stein said, "they do. And they're plotting something. If I knew what it was, I would have taken measures. In the interim, I repeat my request. Double the guard. Issue arms to all Ukrainians. Have the bugle blown immediately thereafter. All Jews locked into barracks."

288

Dietrich's going to think I'm running a lunatic asylum, Kirmayr thought. But if Rudy's right and I do nothing, it will be worse. Let Dietrich see that I'm a prudent man.

"Do it, Rudy. But no bugle. Squads of men to take each group individually from their jobs to the barracks—now. Rifles and bayonets but no executions until after Colonel Dietrich leaves the camp."

Then he realized that he was the commandant. "I'm going to take charge of this," he said decisively.

He swung past Bella, avoiding her eyes, into the bedroom where he had hung his dress jacket, dagger, and pistol. If Dietrich came out to watch, he wanted to make the proper impression.

Bella felt numbed. The only pain came from the clenched muscles of her breasts. She gazed into Stein's eyes behind their swollen lenses, and in his stale little smile she saw the confirmation of everything she feared. If she let him and Kirmayr loose now, there would be no warning.

To die, yes. She was ready to die. That was ordained. But to fail?

Leo, help me, she breathed. I always helped you. I told you what to do. Now I need you to tell me.

It flooded her mind in one riptide. She remembered the first day in the snow outside the latrine. He had called her a whore; she had slapped him. He wanted no more than paper to write notes; he wanted her to steal it from Zuckermann's desk. Zuckermann, the drunk, would never miss it. But there was risk, he explained. If she was caught, they would kill her.

I'll do it, but I want more. It was what she had always wanted. The word *always* had a new meaning. There was no life before Zin. She had said to Stephan, hardly knowing then what she meant, "Those who survive can serve."

I'll help you, Blondie. I can write Yiddish, German. I write well. I wanted to be a journalist.

He agreed. After that it happened so swiftly. Time also had a new meaning at Zin. Every day was a life saved. Another day and another life that they didn't get. Another day to breathe and grieve and hate. Leo had found young men who wanted to fight, to rouse the whole camp to escape. The absurdity of it, the ferocity, the hope of revenge, claimed all her allegiance. Hope was no longer an enemy.

But I think someone overheard us, Bella. A man named Gutt-man. An informer.

Hang him, she said coldly. *Make them believe it's a suicide. Write a note. I'll tell you what to say. We'll drive them a little crazy. . . .*

And we need gold, Bella, to bribe the Blackies for guns.

Margulies has gold. Anneke and Leah told me.

Then we'll steal it!

He would blame Anneke and Leah, denounce them to Dressler for some other reason. But there's a way, Leo. Come with me one day at noon when he's there alone. He'll let me into his room. He won't know you're with me. . . .

She had guided him every step down the path, guided him into her body so that both of them felt reprieved from their whoring, at hazard but wonderfully alive . . . convinced him to join his little force with Lieberman and Stephan when she learned that they too were ready to strike back.

Then the captain from Berlin had arrived.

She had seen with a woman's eyes that Paul Bach was not one of them. He was a human being—a prisoner, too. Open your eyes, Captain.

The petition that she slid under his door on her way to the commandant's birthday celebration was her triumph, her finest work. Be moved, Captain. Understand—as Mordecai claims—that this may be only the beginning of man's possibilities. Stop it before it's too late, before we all become beasts. Help us. I don't know how, *but help us.*

And he had listened. She had not been a total fool. He had told Leo the camp was closing, given them a chance before the door clicked shut on all hope.

Now, while the commandant dressed, she thought of those on whom the door had already closed. Stephan, become a stranger before death . . . Mordecai, become another dead father . . . a thousand faces rose in her mind, then faded. Had they ever lived?

The sensuous human world that others took for granted was so dim. As never before, she had touched it in the darkness with Leo. A moment of wonder on the path to death. Did I ever tell him that? I want him to know. He must know before we die.

Help me, Leo. I know you love me. I sucked at your love like a dying sponge. Did I give anything back? I didn't believe I knew how to love anymore. I thought I knew only how to hate and die. But if I was wrong . . .

Tell me what to do. . . .

Breaking into her reverie, Kirmayr suddenly bustled from the bedroom. He was buttoning his white dress jacket, fussing with the angle of his dagger. He fled by. But she had to stop him.

"Martin . . . !" she called breathlessly.

He turned, starting to smile without comprehension. Bella raised her dress and drew the steel scissors from the elastic of her underwear. Falling against him in a last embrace, she thrust the scissors under his arm, deep into the fat. He let out a hurt little cry.

She had meant to wrench the pistol from its holster and shoot Stein. But Kirmayr was too heavy—he lumbered backward from her clutch, falling to one knee. Blood bubbled over the white jacket, slopped to the floor.

Stein froze. He saw only the bizarre motions of Kirmayr, heard only his lament. Zuckermann was spinning in the swivel chair, tugging at the rack above his head for a carbine. Then Stein focused on the bright red scissors in Bella's hand. She dropped them and with a sob fell on the commandant, clawing at his holster.

Snatching his pistol, Stein fired twice. Bella felt a terrible shock. Zuckermann, vodka fogging his brain, pulled the trigger of the carbine, and in the little room the shot boomed and echoed like a thunderclap.

Zuckermann's bullet swerved through Bella's soft flesh and out the other side into the heart of Martin Kirmayr. Her hand pressed on his spine, stiffening. Their bodies quivered together. Kirmayr sighed, then lay still.

The crack of the shots flew cleanly through the camp.

In Paul's bathroom, Willi Dietrich hurriedly buttoned his fly.

Dobrany, hidden in the hospital, began to curse. Chonszki, head bent, hands thrust deep in his coat pockets, came to a halt as he shuffled across Roll Call Square.

Leo Cohen lowered a box of tinned fruit to the floor of the storage shed. Something awful has happened, he realized. *It's gone wrong.*

The other Jews stared at him. He could swear he heard Bella's voice begging him to act. The three Blackies crowded toward the door, jabbering in their own language. Cohen reached under his peajacket for the pistol.

31

Willi Dietrich and Paul Bach ran through the gathering dusk to Kirmayr's bungalow. Corporal Reitlinger sprinted from the German barracks.

Stein met them on the steps, lips drawn back, teeth bared, glasses fogged. Behind the lenses his eyes flared with determination. The acrid smell of gunsmoke drifted from behind him out the door.

"The commandant is dead—" he cried majestically, as if he spoke of Caesar—"by the hand of his whore!"

Before he could begin to explain, there were shouts from the north quadrangle. Men broke from the buildings, awkward thin figures stumbling and shouting, waving their arms, flashing bits of steel. *Jews.* A shot rang out—then a burst of machine-gun fire. More men were running.

"They're rebelling," Stein said instructively.

"They're insane," Willi said, drawing his pistol.

Aron Chonszki crawled gasping through the hedge, past the gas tanks and the water tower, squirming on his belly past the commandant's bungalow to the one part of the compound where the telephone wires ran low enough along the garage wall to be reached without a ladder. He had no way to know that Bella was dead, that Zuckermann had already called the Wehrmacht garrison at Breslau. With his powerful hands he wrenched the wires loose from the wall and then, with his wire cutters, snipped the strands.

Bullets scorched the air, cutting chunks from the concrete basing. He dived around the corner.

He crouched in the shelter of the garage's rear wall. No bullets could reach him there. He offered one last prayer, then nudged the safety catch of his pistol to the up position.

A Blackie skidded around the corner of the building and came to a stumbling halt, staring in dismay. He had not thought to find an armed Jew. Chonszki pulled the trigger, felt the gun buck like a wild thing in his hand, heard a dry angry snap. The Blackie cried out plaintively, fell to all fours, and began to crawl away. Chonszki decided not to waste a second bullet. The fallen carbine lay in the dirt. He reached out quickly and snatched it.

God heard, he thought. He's listening. *He* hasn't give up.

None of Chonszki's men knew where he was. He had none of the grenades promised by Dobrany. But he was in a safe place—no one could get him unless he showed himself or they were fool enough to come around the corner.

All I have to do, he thought grimly, is wait here to die.

Dobrany zigzagged in a crouch from the latrine to the deserted kitchen on the north quadrangle. He went in the back door, unseen. He had been prepared to shoot his way in, but it was unnecessary. A faceless Blackie and four Jews, three of them women, lay dead on the floor in a spreading pool of blood. One of the women still grasped the handle of the cleaver that had killed the Blackie.

Dobrany flung open a window and rested one of his two carbines on the sill. He had a good view of the armory. Yelling orders, Corporal Munzing stood at the door, passing out weapons to a mob of clamoring Ukrainians who had come running from their barracks.

Bringing Munzing's black chest into the notched V of his sights, Dobrany squeezed off a shot.

"For my son!" he cried. "Swine!"

Munzing lurched back into the armory. Dobrany kept firing into the pack of hysterical Blackies until the magazine was empty. He switched to the second carbine with barely a break in his rhythm.

Bullets smashed the glass over his head. Something cut his neck. Behind him, over the big double sink, the other window shattered. A grenade arced through, hit the floor, rolled lazily on the pine boards at his feet—then exploded.

Dobrany's back was turned. He felt only the briefest disorientation. He never knew what happened. He died a soldier, a happy man.

The air reeked of sulfur, charcoal, and blood. There had been no chance to lure the guards down from the watchtowers. The Jews flowed from every door in the north quadrangle and Roll Call Square, then froze, with no idea where to go next. For the machine gunners on the towers it was live target practice.

Mordecai Lieberman had once said, "No earthly power has ever been able to destroy us." But under the heavy sky the earth ran red, as if the massed clouds had opened, pouring a substance thicker and brighter than rain. Men skidded in it, slipped in it, fell in it. Most never rose. The dead became like dark bruises on the earth. Carbines cracked from the windows of the German barracks, and the earth grew darker.

A group of Jews under Jozek, kapo of the gravel commando—whipper and shouter of "Tempo!"—broke through to the watchtower behind the Ukrainian barracks. Jozek threw his Molotov cocktail before the machine gun stitched a path through the mud and toppled him.

The watchtower burned like a funeral pyre. Some of the flaming wooden beams fell on the roof of the Ukrainian barracks. The barracks began to blaze.

Standing on the gravel path outside the administrative bungalow, Paul had also drawn his pistol. Stein ran off through the red dusk. More shots rang out and echoed from the north quadrangle, from Roll Call Square and the lower camp.

Willi's dark eyes were hot with purpose. He was a veteran police officer, a commander of men. He had dealt with insurgents before. These were pitiful examples—they could be brought to their knees in minutes. Peering into the smoke, pistol at his side, he reached a swift decision.

"Kirmayr is dead. I'm taking over the command. The idea is to drive them in a single direction. Paul, what other exits are there beside the main gate?"

Paul's mouth went dry. "I won't help you do this," he said harshly.

Willi, who had already taken a step, planted his boot and spun around. "What the hell are you talking about?"

"You son of a bitch," Paul raged, the blood in his temples throbbing as if it would burst from the veins. "I won't help you to kill them!" He raised his pistol and pointed it at Willi.

Willi stared at him.

"You're quite mad," he said quietly, "but you must be aware that I could shoot you where you stand. These Jews are enemies of the Reich. They're attacking German soldiers. If you don't do as I order you, I give you my word you'll face a firing squad."

Paul pressed the muzzle of his pistol into the black jacket below Willi's heart. "You're in command. Give our people the order to stop firing."

Willi gravely considered a moment, then turned his head slightly toward Reitlinger, who stood to one side with his carbine, sweat popping from his forehead.

"Corporal," he said calmly, "you've heard Captain Bach threaten me. I'm a Gestapo colonel. No matter what he does to me, I'm giving you a direct order. Shoot the captain. *Now.*"

Paul remembered the look in young Reitlinger's eyes when they had toured the gas chambers and the lower camp. Reitlinger had said, "They've done nothing to deserve being killed." A good fellow, with simple human instincts. But now the Jews were fighting back; they were an enemy. Reitlinger was a soldier in uniform. He would obey the command of a Gestapo colonel. He follows orders. It never occurs to him that he has a choice.

I can't shoot Reitlinger, Paul thought. I don't want to kill anyone.

But from the corner of his eye, he saw the carbine begin to swing up slowly in his direction.

A frantic flurry of shots reached their ears from the main gate. The machine gun rattled; there were angry cries in German. Willi snapped his head around just as the German sentry box near the gate almost disintegrated in a slapping hail of bullets. The two German guards crumpled like rags. A Jew in a navy pea jacket manned the tower machine gun. He had worked his way quickly and cleverly along the barbed wire, scaled the tower, and shot the two Ukrainians on the perch.

Bullets began wildly to plow along the gravel to where the two officers and Corporal Reitlinger stood in front of the administrative bungalow.

Willi let out a single ripping curse—he dived up the steps toward the door of Kirmayr's office with Reitlinger at his heels. Paul slammed his body against the wall, ricocheted, then sprinted for the guest bungalow. A squad of Ukrainians appeared from the armory; the machine gun traversed toward them eagerly, seeking them.

The bungalow was warm and dry. The stove hissed and softly crackled. Paul tossed the pistol across the room, so that it struck the sofa cushion and bounced once before it lay still. He walked to the desk and picked up the unfinished letter to Erich and Ushi. Suddenly it seemed his only purpose, his salvation. They must know, he thought fiercely. There was no more he could do.

Black coils of smoke swirled past the window. The sound of small arms and machine-gun fire rattled the pane. Clutching the letter, he stared out at the wrecked twilight. He heard shots, shouts, and screams, the dying cries of men. God won't forgive us this, he thought, not for a thousand years. There were tears in his eyes.

The SS officers, in the Prussian tradition, led the attack. But some of the Jews had discarded their knives and hammers, snatching weapons from dead or wounded Germans and Ukrainians. They rushed the Germans in packs, waiting until they could thrust the pistols or carbines directly into the black jackets and fire. When one Jew fell, another scrambled to pick up the weapon.

Sweating in what was now a hot evening, Werner Vogl led a squad of soldiers at a trot from the German barracks to the north quadrangle. The tower machine guns tapped steadily like a flock of crazed woodpeckers.

"We'll clean out one hut at a time! Follow me!" Vogl yelled.

He kicked open the door of the carpentry shop and rushed in, firing his Schmeisser. A thin, wiry-armed Jew named Pinchas Levy stood trembling behind the door.

Before he was shot, the blade of his whistling hacksaw cut halfway through Vogl's neck.

In the flame-filled evening the Jews left alive in the camp were running, limping, crawling toward the gate. The big machine gun in Leo Cohen's grasp, chattering like a berserk sewing machine, swept the officers' quarters, infirmary, and hedge with enfilading fire.

"He can hold us off until he runs out of bullets!" Willi shouted to Corporal Reitlinger above the din. In a short dash from the administrative bungalow, they had gained the shelter of the water tower in front of the hedge. They crouched there. The rich smoke of the burning Ukrainian barracks flowed southward in the evening wind, obscuring Willi's vision. *Some of these people are going to get loose! Find grenades!"*

Weaving a path among clumps of the dead, Reitlinger raced for the armory.

In the main watchtower, Leo Cohen clenched his teeth, bit the flesh behind his lips, tasted salty blood. He breathed in quick gasps, like a long-distance runner nearing the tape. One shoulder was numb. A bullet had struck the bone as he climbed the tower. The blood rolled smoothly, warmly, down his arm, and he was growing drowsy. The two dead Ukrainians sheltered him from the Germans' fire. Lying flat, he could still peer above their bodies, traverse the heavy gun, jerk the steel trigger.

He fired bursts into the hedges, along the line of timbered bungalows, at anything in uniform that moved. The Angel of Death flapped his dark wings. He swooped to win the victory of the dead.

"Bella!" he cried, knowing he would die up here. "Bella!" he shouted again. *"Remember me!"*

A German soldier dashed from the barracks. The machine gun rattled and shook. The barrel grew red with heat; the trigger burned his finger.

From his perch he saw Rabbi Hurwicz lurching through the smoke in front of the infirmary. His crooked body swayed. His broken shoes were colored red.

Behind the bungalows a handful of stumbling Jews wavered inside the barbed wire, headed toward the gate. He saw Prager, Wohlberg, Engel. Their faces were streaked with dirt and blood; their eyes blazed like dark stars. Aron Chonszki led them. Chonszki the bull. Chonszki the peasant, moving slowly but delicately, surely.

"Shoelace!" he screamed. "Run! Go—go—go! To the gate! Get up and run! Go *now!*"

Stein had taken refuge behind the infirmary. When he beheld the spindle-shanked figure of the rabbi picking his way through the gusting smoke and the sprawled bodies toward the main gate, he almost did not believe what he saw. The rabbi's head on his bony neck bobbed like a cork in water. His eyes were wet and dazed.

Stein fired once and missed. His sight at that distance was poor.

Thick smoke surged, casting a pall. The rattle of the watchtower gun halted. Stein seized his opportunity.

He rushed out into the hot haze toward Rabbi Hurwicz in front of the guest bungalow, pistol cocked, aimed at the back of the narrow white neck.

The hairs on the back of Paul's neck rose like the hackles of a frightened animal. He stood at the open window; his pistol lay on the sofa across the room. Stein closed the distance to Rabbi Hurwicz.

For a moment Stein and the rabbi were lost in the eddies of

smoke. Paul vaulted out the window onto the gravel, stumbled, then gained balance.

With a harsh cry he leaped forward. Drawing the SS dagger from its sheath, he roared, *"Stein!"*

Stein heard him and halted. The rabbi passed into the shielding smoke. Stein saw a man looming . . . a black German uniform. He felt a vexing rip of pain in his stomach. The pistol fell. His eyes behind the glasses filled suddenly with tears. Paul slid the inscribed blade free, laid the red edge against Stein's throat; then his hand moved in a blur.

A gust of wind caught the smoke and pushed it in swathes toward the barbed wire.

Jews were running out the gate. From the windows of the German barracks, rifles cracked.

Falling flat, Paul scooped up Stein's pistol, aimed carefully, and began firing at the barracks.

Behind the water tower, Willi Dietrich cried out his name. "You fool . . . !" Snatching Reitlinger's carbine, he laid the barrel hard on a metal crossbar, sighted with cold eyes on the prone black uniform, and squeezed the trigger twice.

Paul seemed to relax. His head rested on the gravel. The pistol slipped from his fingers.

At the same time, Reitlinger hurled a grenade.

Gripping the trigger of the machine gun, Leo Cohen saw something descend from the high indigo sky. A winged black shape, spinning slowly . . . growing larger.

The Moravian Forest: April 1943

Thirty Jews reached the forest, following Aron Chonszki along the narrow path. The rest lay dead within the compound or among the mines outside the barbed wire. A black night touched with plum and violet color spread across the land. The moon had not yet risen. Chinks of light, like stars that had come too near, glittered in the distance. A shocking pink blush lit the southern sky where the barracks still burned.

Chonszki and the survivors hunched under some birch trees near the old gravel pit.

His chest heaved; his legs felt like iron bars. Amazing, he thought. All through the battle he had stayed calm, firing his pistol and then the carbine only when necessary, taking cover before he decided upon any kind of new move. Passing the dead sentries at the gate, he had had the presence of mind to snatch another weapon. It was a Schmeisser submachine gun, but he had no idea how it worked. You pull the trigger, he thought, and hope for the best. He still carried the pistol and five extra rounds, and stuffed into the pockets of his jacket and trousers were a bag of gold coins, a wad of zlotys, a small loaf of bread, and a can of olives.

Lumbering toward the forest, he realized that the Germans were not following. It was too dark—they knew the Jews were armed. When we have guns, he thought, we become their equals. This elated him one moment, then saddened him the next. And in the end it made no difference. He knew that tomorrow, at first light, they would come.

Rabbi Hurwicz had lost his shoes. The soles of his feet were bloody and swollen, but he sat in silence without complaining. Three of the others—Prager, Wohlberg, and Engel—had carbines slung around their shoulders. They were young Jews, thin but strong, men whom Cohen had recruited. Anneke Wijnberg had a pistol. They all sat dazed, out of breath, stunned that they were alive and in the forest. They could smell the damp earth, pine sap, the southern wind.

Nothing had gone as planned.

But look! Here we are. . . .

Chonszki had seen the tower explode. He knew that Leo Cohen was dead. Dobrany and Bella had never appeared. He wanted to weep. The best of us are gone. Why was I spared?

They all looked bleakly at one another. "Does anyone have food?" Engel asked suddenly. "I'm starving."

Chonszki offered the little loaf of black bread. Engel leaned forward with his knife to slice it.

Appalled, Rabbi Hurwicz opened his mouth to protest. It was

the first night of Passover. The black bread was leavened—forbidden. To possess it was already bad enough—but he who ate it would henceforth be cut off from Israel.

The rabbi bit his tongue until he almost gasped with the pain. The bitter herbs, he tried to reason, mark for us the bitterness of slavery. The eating of unleavened bread reminds us of the haste in which our ancestors fled the house of bondage. We too have fled in haste. We too were slaves in Egypt.

With a trembling hand he took from the pocket of his torn coat the few crumbs of flour, mixed with the clean potato peelings, that he had salvaged from the bakery oven.

"For those who want it," he said softly, nearly choking on the meaning of his words, "I also have matzoh. . . ."

They ate quickly, while half-aloud, half under his breath, the rabbi recited the Kiddush prayer and a very small part of the Haggadah.

"Pan Chonszki," Engel said, "where shall we go? In what direction?"

The others looked to him.

Aron Chonszki gazed into the darkling forest. The wind in the branches whispered no message. An owl hooted mysteriously from afar. God was with them, he now believed, but not as a guide. Where men went, He followed, interested.

Chonszki had no idea where to go. He knew that one direction was as safe, as unsafe, as any other, but he also knew that a leader must know. And if he doesn't know, he must choose.

He clambered to his feet. "That way," he said confidently, thrusting a finger toward the southwest. He hitched the Schmeisser over the pad of muscle in his shoulder and plunged into the forest.

Zin: April 1943

In the early afternoon of the next day, under a chill overcast sky, First Lieutenant Klaus von Hartung of the Wehrmacht Armored Grenadier Battalion Number 5, temporarily billeted in Breslau before returning to the Eastern Front, surveyed the carnage at the camp near Zinoswicz-Zdroj.

Lieutenant von Hartung was a wiry, dark-eyed young man of twenty-five who had never joined the Nazi Party and had even managed to avoid membership in the Hitler Youth. He hated parades. Until he entered the army, he had followed his father's example by saying *"Grüss Gott"* (God greets you)—instead of *"Heil."* He was from Füssen, a small town in the Bavarian Alps, and at the age of four he had owned his first pair of skis. His grandfather had been a *Graf,* a count. The title and revenues were long gone, but the *von* passed on to Hartung's father, the village doctor, and all of his sons. Its use and the respect it brought often made Klaus von Hartung smile.

He wore the Iron Cross Second Class. He had fought at Narvik in Norway against British forces, in the strike at Abbeville against the French, and then against the Russians in the Caucasus. It never occurred to him that he wouldn't survive to tell the tale to his grandchildren. After the war, which he now realized Germany could never win, he hoped to own his own ski lodge near Oberammergau.

Today he was in full Wehrmacht battle dress except for his steel helmet. When they had arrived at Zin last night, no one in the 5th Battalion had known what to expect.

He had counted the bodies of 467 dead Jews both inside and outside the barbed wire of the compound and one dead dog, lying near the infirmary. The dog had been shot twice in the muzzle, once each in the head and chest at point-blank range. It was a huge beast, heavily-muscled and well fed.

The dead Jews, on the other hand, had been half-starved. When they were lying on their backs, the abdominal flesh stretched down so deeply that it seemed to rest against their spines. Whatever flesh was not covered with blood was covered with sores and pustules. The faces were all angles, no curves. Their limbs were as brittle as twigs. Von Hartung had seen dead soldiers often, but at one point he almost vomited.

His platoon, wearing raincoats and winter gloves so they would not have to touch the bodies, loaded the Jews into dump trucks brought over from Poseń, and drove them to the lower camp for cremation under the supervision of Captain Dressler. The camp smelled of blood and burnt gunpowder. The ground was a carpet of soft gray dust mottled by black stains.

Dressler was the only resident commissioned officer to survive. Four German SS officers, nine enlisted men, and ten Ukrainian conscripts were dead. A fifth officer, Captain Dr. Lustig, was listed as missing. Sixteen German and Ukrainian wounded had been trucked to the military hospital at Breslau. It was a high casualty rate for a battle, but von Hartung understood that most of it had been hand to hand.

Another platoon of the 5th Battalion and the sixty-odd Ukrainians left at Zin were currently deployed in the forest hunting the escaped prisoners. So far there had been no report.

Von Hartung had no exact idea of what had happened. He was even less clear as to what kind of prison this had been. He was a combat lieutenant, not an SS functionary. I don't think I care to know too many details, he decided.

A few crows flapped like dark rags in the windy sky. Four bodies—the officers—had been laid out neatly under blankets in front of the infirmary. Von Hartung had their ID tags in his pocket.

Before lunch he met at the main gate with Colonel Dietrich. Dietrich had been here during the battle but so far had made no comment. He wore his SS field cap and slim boots over breeches with oversized wings. His face was gray.

He's exhausted, von Hartung realized.

"Colonel, it's my understanding that the camp is to be destroyed."

Willi nodded abstractly. "Captain Dressler's in charge. A demolition squad will come from Breslau."

Von Hartung produced the ID tags of Major Martin Kirmayr, Captain Paul Bach, and Lieutenants Rudolf Stein and Werner Vogl. He went on.

"Colonel Dietrich, I observed that all these officers died in the line of duty. I noted the positions of their bodies. Major Kirmayr was shot in his office by a woman who must have gained entry for that purpose. He defended himself to the extent that he was able to kill her as well. Captain Bach was shot in the back while trying to prevent the escape. Lieutenant Stein's throat appeared to be cut by one of the prisoners. Lieutenant Vogl was attacked from behind and" . . . Hartung coughed . . . "beheaded."

After a moment he said quietly, "It would seem appropriate that they all receive the posthumous War Merit Cross for bravery other than in the front line. You were here, Colonel. Do you have any comments or objections?"

Willi's eyes tightened into wrinkles at the outside corners. "An excellent idea, von Hartung. No objections."

"Will you help me draw up the citations?"

"I didn't see any of them fall," Willi said. "But I know they all behaved heroically, in the best traditions of the SS. I'll endorse the citations. I leave it in your hands."

He turned away toward the garage, head lowered against the wind, to make his arrangements for the return to Warsaw.

Lieutenant von Hartung made a final tour of the officers' quarters to retrieve anything of value that might be sent to next of kin.

In one of the bungalows, where a few coals still glowed under a bed of ash in the iron stove, he discovered a letter lying on the floor.

305

Shivering from the chill, he kicked open the grate of the stove and stirred the coals with the tip of his boot. He fed in some fresh slivers of pine and oak. The fire hissed . . . white smoke curled upward.

He was glad of this chance to learn something personal about one of the men for whom he would write the citations. The letter was unfinished, therefore unsigned. But von Hartung soon realized that it had been written by the one-armed captain to his children in Berlin.

He read carefully, until he was afflicted by a feeling of vertigo. The next moment it seemed as if the walls of the room were about to crush him. He breathed deeply through his nose to steady himself.

When von Hartung finished reading, he lowered himself slowly into a chair. He looked around to see if there was anything to drink, but there were only two half-finished bottles of flat beer.

"God save us," he whispered.

When the war is over, he thought, we have to build a new Germany.

The wind creaked against the windowpanes, the oak fire sizzled in the stove. Von Hartung sat quite still for five minutes, trying to make up his mind. He forced himself to scan the letter again. Certain phrases caught his eye.

I was a coward. To a coward the easy way always seems best. . . .
Knowledge can be like poison.
Erich and Ushi . . .

These are decent children, he thought. They will need to believe their father was a hero. And they are our future. They are not guilty of what happened here—why should they be forced to bear any burden? He hesitated, troubled by something just beyond his grasp, then crossed the room and fed the pages one by one into the fire.